THE
DEEP

They stood for a long moment, eyes on each other. Luke felt the warmth radiating off Alice's body. There was appreciation in their gazes—the appreciation that prevails among soldiers sharing a bunker under heavy fire . . . but there was a raw hunger, too.

"Right," she said, breaking eye contact. "Back in a jiff."

She darted through the crawl-through in her tank top and fitted shorts, arranged their overalls on the other side, and slid back. They hefted the generator and slid it into the chute; it fit easily, with room to spare.

Alice powered it through, pushing it with her feet; Luke followed shortly behind her. The generator nosed out of the crawl-through and hit the floor with a crunch. They inspected it. It looked okay. They put their overalls back on and continued.

The tunnels seemed to be lengthening with a sly stretch and pull. They were narrowing, too, their ceilings lowering. The station's geometries were shifting subtly. The beat of what sounded like footsteps came irregularly. These were not the mincing footfalls of the waterlogged children—these were plodding, dogged, and they came from somewhere inside.

Maybe it's the thing from the crate, darling, Luke's mother piped up. *You must assume it's got big feet to go along with its big hands . . .*

Shut up, Mom, Luke thought. Who could it possibly be? Clayton was the only one left. Maybe it *was* Clay. Maybe he was stalking them. He really *did* want Luke to be here, and now he didn't want to let him go.

Luke propped open the storage hatch. They shimmied the generator through, Luke doing most of the work on account of Al's hand. A flashlight was clipped to the wall; Al grabbed it, flicked it on. It did very little to illuminate things.

The generator snagged on the grate. Luke hissed, a release of pent-up anger and fear, and gave it a kick, which only sent a spike of pain shooting up to his knee.

He collapsed, breathing heavily, his eyes stinging with sweat. A stone lodged in his chest—panic, but only a dull murmur of it now, mingled with a heavy sense of despair. The station wouldn't let them go. Its overseers would erect roadblocks, allow them to feast on false hopes, then shred their escape plans.

Somehow, something would thwart them; Luke had become convinced of that. A small and silly matter, which would only sharpen the agony. A blown fuse. A stripped wire. A setback that wouldn't daunt them for a moment on the surface—but down here, it would end them.

Or you may decide you want *to stay*, said a coal-dark voice in his head. *Why not? It'll be fun. Ooooh, the things we could show you . . .*

Luke rocked the generator. His arms screamed and his shoulders nearly popped out of joint. The damn thing tore free with a screech of metal. He and Alice rolled it the final ten feet to the *Challenger*. Al unspooled three heavy-gauge cables and flicked a switch on the genny.

"If we're lucky, we'll have enough juice to skeedaddle," she said. "But I want to pump every volt I can into the *Challenger*. That'll take a few hours."

"You're gonna be able to do it with your hand like that?"

She nodded. "Just pushing buttons and flicking switches. I'm fine on my own. Plus it's better if you keep an eye on your brother. I'd rather keep him in plain sight."

Those footsteps thudded again. Closer now—just outside the storage area? The hackles stiffened down LB's back.

The footsteps drew nearer, producing a thudding echo on the grates. Luke imagined someone—*something?*—standing—*hunching?*—in that dissolving edge of light. The outlines of this person or thing shifted restlessly, solidifying momentarily in Luke's mind before adopting a new guise.

The footsteps stopped. In the silence came a low, liquid breathing. Unrushed and calm: the breath of a man on a leisurely hike.

"Clay?" Luke called.

The breathing stopped. Next, the source itself was gone. The presence vanished, evaporating like steam off a hot bath.

"It's just the station," Al said. "Groans and moans."

"The station, sure," Luke said, accepting her reasoning, as it made more sense than the alternative. "How you feeling, Al?"

Al held the flashlight under her chin like a boy telling a scary story around a campfire. "I'm feeling fine as cherry wine, Doc." She chuckled. The walls sponged up her laughter. "We're going to be okay, Luke. Aren't we?"

"I think so. We just have to get a little lucky. And hope someone up there is watching over us."

"Go on. Find your brother. Take the dog, too. And Luke—*stay awake*."

3.

THE MAIN LAB was deserted. The lights burned at quarter power.

Luke flicked the switch to activate the exterior spotlights. They didn't turn on. He flicked them again. Still dark. The viewing window reflected his haunted eyes.

He felt it out there. That sucking, hungering nothingness.

He found a flashlight in a drawer. He turned it on and trained it on the sea floor. The beam illuminated that mounded whiteness, marine snow piled in layers.

There are places on earth where light is unwelcome, Luke thought. *Light has no power down here. Darkness is king. Light flees the dark, or it gets devoured.*

He watched darkness eat into the glow of his flashlight, dissolving its weak radiance like acid. The beam winnowed and broke apart until—

Something snaked into the dregs of that light, lashing fretfully. Thick and reddish, an enormous night crawler flicking against the window. LB yipped in fright. Luke backed away . . . then was hit with another image, so much larger and so terrible that his soul withered at its prospect. And yet he didn't *see* anything—it would've been impossible in that blackness. He only intuited it. Luke caught a sense of something out there. Its presence was enormous, mind-filling. In that moment, he saw how things would look if the seas were drained: the station surrounded by monolithic alabaster cliffs that went up and up until their faces welded with the blackness above. The trench unfurled flat and featureless to the base of those cliffs—and in his mind's eye, he could see this . . . this . . . *thing* on those towering sheets of stone. It clung to the cliffs with many limbs, spanning all around the trench the way a spider fans its limbs across a web. It had no head to speak of. It was all limbs—all *tubes*—and each

THE
DEEP

THE
DEEP

NICK CUTTER

GALLERY BOOKS

NEW YORK   LONDON   TORONTO   SYDNEY   NEW DELHI

G

Gallery Books
A Division of Simon & Schuster, Inc.
1230 Avenue of the Americas
New York, NY 10020

First Gallery Books hardcover edition January 2015

GALLERY BOOKS and colophon are registered trademarks of Simon & Schuster, Inc.

For information about special discounts for bulk purchases, please contact Simon & Schuster Special Sales at 1-866-506-1949 or business@simonandschuster.com.

The Simon & Schuster Speakers Bureau can bring authors to your live event. For more information or to book an event, contact the Simon & Schuster Speakers Bureau at 1-866-248-3049 or visit our website at www.simonspeakers.com.

Interior design by Davina Mock-Maniscalco
Cover design by Black Kat Design
Cover photographs: sky © plainpicture/Naturbild; ocean © plainpicture/goZooma

Manufactured in the United States of America

10 9 8 7 6 5 4 3 2 1

Library of Congress Cataloging-in-Publication Data

Cutter, Nick.
  The deep / Nick Cutter.
    pages cm
  I. Title.
  PS3603.U883D44 2015
  813'.6—dc23
                2014017213

ISBN 978-1-4767-1773-9
ISBN 978-1-4767-1776-0 (ebook)

PART 1

THE 'GETS

1.

THE OLD MAN'S HEAD was covered in mantises.

At first Luke thought it was a wig or some weird toupee—but he was at the southern tip of Guam, a few miles from the Pacific, and the man was wearing tattered clothes and what looked like strips of old radial tires lashed to his feet. Why bother with a toupee?

The driver saw the old man, too. He hissed between his teeth—an uneasy *tssshk!* He said something under his breath: a curse, maybe a prayer? Luke didn't speak the local dialect.

"I'll do it," Luke told the driver. "You wait here."

He elbowed the Jeep's door open. Sweet Jesus, the heat. It'd hit him like a fist when he stepped onto the runway at the Agana airport. It hit him again now—the tropical air, laden with the nectar of heliotropes, caused beads of sweat to pop along his brow.

The old man stood facing the wall of a one-story workshop. The ground was strewn with hubcaps and crankcases snarled in rusted wiring. Wrist-thick vines snaked out of the greenery to twine around the industrial junk; with nobody around to hack it back, the jungle would reclaim this spot in a matter of months.

The old man was walking into the wall—his sandals made a gentle *whush-whush* as they brushed the yellowing adobe. The spotting was pronounced on his bare arms and his throat. The scabs were dime-sized, bigger than what Luke was used to seeing. Some of them had cracked open and were leaking grayish pus.

Luke had no clue what had drawn the mantises. Maybe they'd dropped from the creeping ivy snarled across the shop's roof. Or maybe something on the man's scalp, or leaching out of it, had attracted them.

They were the largest insects Luke had ever seen. Each mantis was the length of his thumb, and muscular-looking. They had swollen, canti-levered abdomens that curved above their sharp, considering faces. A baker's dozen or so carpeted the man's skull.

Luke got the sense of them turning to stare at him, all at once.

Luke retreated to the ditch. His feet sank into the muck. He didn't like the way it sucked at his boots—greedy, a lipless brown mouth.

He found a stick and went back. The insects squirmed quarrel-somely on the man's head, which was covered with wispy white hairs as downy as those on a baby's skull. Their exoskeletons made a brittle chit-ter. What the hell were they doing?

Luke watched their choreographed manner. The stink of burned die-sel mixed with the heliotropes to create a sticky vapor that coated his throat. Distantly, he heard the driver repeat what he'd said before—that breathless curse or prayer—and Luke was worried he'd set the Jeep in gear and take off, leaving him with the old man and the mantises, the heat and the crawling jungle.

What in God's name were those bugs *doing*?

One mantis pinned another in a violent vise grip, then widened its jaws and bit down, cleaving the other's head in half. Their abdomens were wed. What was clearly the female continued to eat the male's head while his antenna whipped about frantically.

Using the stick, Luke brushed the mantises off the man's skull. A de-capitated male skittered wildly across Luke's fingers; he shook it into the mud with the rest of them. The urge arose to step on them. Squash them all to paste.

Instead, Luke set his hands on the old man's shoulders to turn him around. His expression was familiar: *The Big Blank*. His eyes gone milky, the edges of his eyelids pebbled with nodules of acne that gave his skin the look of an orange rind. His mouth wide open, his tongue coated in white film. He may not have drunk water in days. He'd forgotten to, probably.

That's how it went with the 'Gets: you forgot the little things first, then the not-so-little things, then the big ones. Next, the critical ones. In time, your heart forgot how to beat, your lungs how to breathe. You die knowing nothing at all.

As soon as Luke pointed him in a new direction, the old man started to walk. He'd go on until he fell down or stepped off a cliff or stumbled into a leopard's den, if they had those around here. And Luke couldn't do a damn thing about that.

He climbed back into the Jeep. The driver eased past the old man as he tottered down the road, that clingy mud sucking up past his ankles already. Luke watched as they pulled away, the old man's body becoming indistinct through the stinging fumes.

2.

A VISTA OF HEAT-STOOPED PALMS gave way to the town of Inarajan. The buildings were pueblo-rustic and had a worn but functional look, with whitewashed tin roofs.

A fan of red grit rose in the Jeep's wake; it appeared to hover in the intense heat, refusing to settle. The Jeep's vents blasted humid air. The creased skin at the back of Luke's neck was grimy with sweat and dirt.

The Pacific rolled out to the south. The water deepened to an icy blue. Two old women sat on a buckled porch smoking cheroot cigars. None of the villagers looked worried. None of the shops had been looted. That had occurred in other places, but for the most part, humanity had simply carried on. If this was the apocalypse, it was to be an orderly and complacent one.

The village children watched the Jeep rumble past. One of them, a girl of about eight, smiled at Luke. A cluster of dark specks dappled her elbows, like the bruises on a banana as it turns overripe.

The Spots. They would get bigger, cover her body, turn crusty then pustulant . . . then she'd begin to forget. Minor stuff at first. Where she'd left her dolly or how to tell the time of day. Then she wouldn't know how to tie her shoelaces; she might spend hours bent over her feet, trying to lace however she'd been taught—the bunny ears method? Loop, swoop, and pull? She'd laugh at first—*I'm being such a silly-billy!*—but she would soon become frustrated, as children do, and start to cry.

Next, she'd forget her brother's name and the smell of her father's pipe tobacco, and soon enough, her own face in the mirror. She'd forget what hot or cold should feel like, and then even the concepts of heat and cold. That would have to be the worst part, Luke figured: forgetting those elemental assurances everyone is born with. She'd look at the nut tree in her yard and forget the sensation of its leaves brushing her skin; soon she'd forget what leaves were to begin with, and how vital they are to that tree, the same way our veins are vital to our bodies (she'll have forgotten about veins by that point, too). She'd forget how wonderful those nuts taste—after that, she'd forget why eating mattered much at all.

The tree would make no sense to her. Nothing would, actually.

3.

THE YACHT WAS MOORED five hundred yards off the Inarajan wharf.

Its original owner was a Vegas casino magnate. Its home dock was in Okinawa, Japan, but Uncle Sam had recently conscripted it in the service of science. Its owner didn't argue its seizure, Luke had been told, due to the fact that he'd forgotten he'd ever bought a yacht. The 'Gets had a way of loosening prior rights of ownership.

Luke grabbed his duffel and nodded good-bye to the driver. The sun-bleached planks squealed under his boots. Fiddleback crabs skittered around the pilings, raising puffs of sand. An eel—a black, sinuous ribbon—darted out, plucking up a crab before vanishing beneath the wharf.

Animals were unaffected, for whatever reason. No spotting, no 'Gets. All except honeybees, which had been the first and only.

A few skiffs were moored at the end of the wharf, their rusted bottoms spread with mildewed nets. A haze of flies boiled up at Luke's approach. One landed on his forearm. A horsefly, its compound eyes reflecting the sunlight like disco balls.

Luke slapped it. The horsefly buzzed, trapped between his palm and the flesh of his arm, a sensation so off-putting that Luke lifted his hand. The fly escaped with cool indifference.

The yacht wasn't too far off. Luke could swim it—*wanted* to, in fact. It was goddamn hot, he was dirty, and a weird hum had settled into his bones. Shielding his eyes from the sun, he squinted toward the vessel. He could barely make out a figure on it.

He dropped his duffel into a Zodiac boat. He yanked the engine's ripcord and steered away from the village's squat buildings, away from the girl with those terrible specks.

The water was a chilly blue—it reminded Luke of Barbicide, the disinfectant solution the old barbers in Iowa City used to soak their combs in. *That stuff'll kill you dead if you drink it*, one of the barbers told Luke when he was a boy, as if suspecting Luke had harbored that very desire.

His gaze trailed north over the crested hills. He spied a church. It must've been centuries old, perhaps the very first thing the area settlers had built. It was burned. The spire must have gone up first, the roof beams reduced to cinders until what remained of the steeple had come crashing through the narthex.

Nothing else had been torched in the entire village. Only the church.

4.

THE YACHT WAS ANCHORED at the edge of a half-moon bay. A man stood on deck. Tall and thin with articulate limbs that reminded Luke, however unfairly, of the mantises on that old man's skull.

"Dr. Nelson." The man extended his hand. "I'm Leo Bathgate. So glad you made it safely."

Luke inspected Bathgate's outstretched arm—Luke's eyes strayed toward people's hands and arms habitually, a reflex action. Research showed that the 'Gets wasn't spread through physical contact, the transmission of bodily fluids, or as an airborne pathogen. But it had taken a while to discover this, and sadly, several tragedies had occurred before it was fully understood. Men had been shot in cold blood as they had struggled to recall some hard-to-remember fact. The phrase *It's on the tip of my tongue* had become the basis for justifiable homicide for a while there.

The yacht was luxurious, everything gleaming. Luke felt as though he was floating on a pile of cold currency.

Bathgate read his face. "I've never set foot on anything like it, either."

A bottle of champagne sat in a bucket. Bathgate shrugged.

"I found it onboard. Figured it'd just go to waste," he said.

Krug Brut 1988. Pricey suds. Bathgate poured the bubbly into crystal flutes and handed one to him. Luke tipped the glass to his lips, the champagne sending a tickle up his sinuses.

Bathgate said: "How was your trip?"

Endless, Luke wanted to tell him.

Roughly eight thousand miles separated Chicago, where he'd caught the first flight, and Agana, the capital city of Guam. Those eight thousand miles had unfurled like a strange waking nightmare.

On his way out of Iowa City, Luke had stopped at an Exxon off the interstate. The highway wasn't snarled with stalled or abandoned cars, the way it always is in stories about the apocalypse. *Because this wasn't exactly the apocalypse*, Luke had to constantly remind himself. *It was just something awful that was happening.*

For that reason, or maybe just out of old habit, the important things went along as they had. Ideas of ownership prevailed. The dead were still being buried—not always in cemeteries, but the bodies certainly went into the ground. Rituals were still being observed. And that was good.

The gas station had been empty. The pumps were shut off. The door to the convenience store was open. The aisles were shadowy in the late afternoon. Muggy, seeing as the A/C wasn't working. Ants trooped up the glass of a cooler case.

Luke could've done anything. Unwrapped a Twinkie and wolfed it down. Stripped the plastic off a *Penthouse* and flipped out the gatefold. There was something very freeing about that—but scary, too.

He'd pulled back onto the interstate. The gas gauge needle had nudged past *E* when he found a Cenex station . . . which was bustling. People were gassing up, paying for chips and sodas, blissfully unaware or pretending to be. It had been good to see the lights on. Good to *pay* for things. That feeling of normalcy returned. The world was still spinning as it always had, right?

That troublesome kind of stuff happened a lot now. You couldn't find gas, or a new tire if you got a flat. You could set off for a destination and never reach it. A thousand new roadblocks popped up—not always physical or jurisdictional ones, either. Just the system breaking down in little ways.

O'Hare Airport had been surreal. Most of his terminal's kiosks and shops were closed, the shelves picked over, restaurants offering a reduced menu.

Luke had passed through security without incident; he carried a notarized document that eased his passage. The plane was a twin-prop puddle jumper. It was so full that two U.S. Marines had to sit in the aisle. That would've made life tough on the flight attendants, had there been any.

The plane touched down in Denver. After he disembarked, Luke stood before the airport's windows watching the flights taxi in. He could make out a man at the edge of the landing strip, propped against a chain-link fence. Motionless, with his arms outspread.

A plane roared down the runway; as it rose, it flew directly above the man. His clothes fluttered with the terrific force of the jet's engines. His body jerked, his head snapping back and forth. Did the pilots have to look at the man every time they took off?

"Somebody should do something about it."

The woman standing beside Luke was fiftyish, with salt-and-pepper hair and a faint British accent. She tapped the huge window with her knuckles, a fussy *rap-rap-rap,* as if in expectation someone—a butler?—would appear to deal with her complaint.

"They should bloody well *do* something about that poor sod, wouldn't you think?"

She seemed the sort of woman who was used to getting things done. But things didn't always get done nowadays. People just got on with things the way they were.

Luke's connecting flight landed at San Francisco International, where he was met by a pair of unsmiling soldiers. They led him to a private airstrip, where a C-23 Sherpa cargo plane waited. Luke was its sole passenger. Resting against the bulkhead, he let the hum of the engine fill his skull. He fell into a black sucking vacuum of sleep—dreamless, joyless. When he awoke, his plane was circling Agana.

"Long," Luke said, finally answering Bathgate's question. "A long goddamn trip."

Bathgate gave a sympathetic nod. "You must be exhausted."

Luke's watch was still set to Iowa time. His body clock was reading 5:00 a.m. as Guam's midafternoon sun beat down on his skull. The champagne mainlined straight into his veins, making him swoon.

"Your berth is down below," Bathgate said. "Why don't you get settled?"

As Luke made his way to the sleeping quarters, Bathgate called out: "Dr. Nelson?"

Luke turned to see Bathgate wringing his ballcap in his hard-knuckled hands.

"Your brother . . ." he said falteringly. "They say he might have the answer to all this. Whatever he's doing down there in the deep. You think that's possible?"

"I really don't know, Leo. I guess we're gonna see."

"Yeah, but . . ."

"I'm hopeful. We all are."

"Right." Bathgate offered an uncertain smile. "Hopeful, absolutely hopeful."

Wasn't that why Luke had been brought here at great expense, after all? To talk to his brother? To rekindle the tiniest shred of hope?

Luke's brother, who was eight miles deep in the Pacific Ocean.

Luke's bizarre and brilliant brother, whom nobody had heard from in days.

5.

LUKE DREAMED of his mother.

It was a familiar dream that came in times of stress. In it, his mother entered his bedroom. Luke was seven or eight years old. His mother was enormous, as she'd been at that point in his life. Over four hundred pounds.

She slipped into bed with him. Threw back his *Star Wars* bedcovers and slid under them with chilling dexterity. Her body was warm and soft as bread dough, perfumed with the excretions that leaked from her skin. Her breath feathered the hairs inside his ear canal. She began to whisper. Luke could never quite make out what she said. Her voice hit a sub-audible pitch that crawled directly into his brain.

Luke awoke, his breath coming in leaden rasps. The dream drained from his brainpan, thick as syrup. He checked his watch; he'd slept less than two hours. Goddamn. His mother. All these years later she was still there, haunting the corridors of his mind like a hungry ghost. He closed his eyes and she bloomed in his mind's eye again: Bethany Ronnicks—she had forsaken her husband's family name, preferring her maiden one. Battle-ax Beth.

She was a huge presence in every way: her room-filling personality, her booming laugh, and in time, her vast physical bulk. She'd always been a large woman: broad shoulders, wide hips, over six feet tall. *A lady skyscraper*, as Luke had heard her spoken of around town. She held an imposing beauty, or she had before her "bad years," and the two hundred pounds they had packed onto her frame. She walked with a regal bearing, her chest thrust out as if in the expectation that a visiting dignitary would affix a medal to it.

She worked at the Second Chance Ranch, a "home" for mentally troubled male youths—*No Chance Ranch*, as she referred to it in her poisonous moods. She had been hired as the duty nurse but soon transferred to orderly, the first female in the state hired for that position. She preferred the hands-on aspect. Better than doling out pills and sanitizing bedpans.

"It stinks," Luke overheard her say once in conversation with Edie Emmons, one of her few friends. "The piss of those mad boys. There's a chemical they produce—a compound *specific* to crazies. Trans-3-methyl-2-hexenoic acid."

"Oh my," said Edie, sycophantically. "Sounds terrible."

"It *is* terrible. The stink of insanity, Edie, sharp as malt vinegar. It's bad enough when they sweat it out. But their *piss*? The worst."

At first the other orderlies—all male, predominantly black—grumbled. They had a bar bouncer's mentality: yes, Beth had a no-bullshit disposition and could handle the nut jobs well enough with words. But what happened when words failed? Beth was a big woman, but still a woman—did she have the brawn to subdue a foaming-mad boy who cared little for his own body or that of others?

But Beth was a hellion. She was the first to jump on any dog pile, grabbing a boy's wrist or neck and cranking with all her might. The orderlies came around to having her in their ranks. They nicknamed her Battle-ax Beth.

Many years later, working as a veterinarian, Luke had run into one of his mother's old charges. Kurt Honey—whom Luke knew slimly, having gone to the same middle school—had spent time at the ranch for the aggravated assault of his eleventh-grade math teacher, whom he'd stabbed with a compass. Honey was a hired hand at a dairy farm where Luke had been summoned to tend to a sick Guernsey.

"She's your ma, ain't she?" Honey had asked.

Luke looked up from the cow's inflamed udder. "Who?"

"Battle-ax Beth."

Luke had no idea Honey knew she was his mother, but he assumed

Honey would speak ill of her. Luke wouldn't stop him. The days when he would've defended her were long gone.

"She was a viper." Honey gave a spooked laugh. "Smart, you know? But in ways that don't really profit a person, except in special situations."

Luke went back to the udder, hoping that would be the end of it.

"She scared the bejesus outta this one guy, Brewster Galt. Ole Brew was none too smart—that's half the reason he ended up at the ranch. This one time, he caught hell for stealing an apple from the cafeteria. Small things were big things at the ranch. Even a missing apple couldn't go unpunished. Now Brew had this condition, okay? His one eye was all bugged out of its socket. He told me it was too much pressure, pushing the eyeball out. Your ma, she noticed that sort of thing."

Luke had winced, his face turned away. Yes, his mother had always noticed things of that nature.

"After Brew got caught stealing the apple, your ma asked for a minute alone with him. Brew came away white as milk. A big kid, tough kid, but I ain't never seen a boy so shit-scared. I found Brew one afternoon by the picnic tables a few days later. By and by, he gets around to telling me what your ma said . . .

"Brew said your ma told him he had *two* sets of eyes. One set behind the set in his face. That's why his one eye was pushed out so bad, see? It was the other set trying to get out. Your ma said those other eyes were blood red and looked like a cat's. Then she says maybe she'll give that other set of eyes a little push—sneak into the bunks at night when Brew's fast asleep and slit his eyes up with a razor blade. Then that would give those new peepers a chance to push out and see the world. The devil's own eyes staring out of Brew's face. 'Wouldn't that be real nice?' she told him."

Kurt Honey just shook his head. "Brew was *fourteen*. He didn't have a damned clue what kind of black thing he'd run across."

Black thing. Luke's own mother. *Black. Thing.*

"That woman was half devil. Three-quarters, I'd go so far to say."

"I'm sorry she said that," was Luke's only reply.

Honey snorted. "Christ, *I'm* sorry for *you*. You had to share four walls with that monster, didn't you?"

Luke's hands relaxed on the bed's coverlet. The nightmare-sweat had dried on his chest, but his thoughts continued to circle restlessly around his mother. He hadn't thought about her—really, clearly *dwelled* upon her—in years. Yet he couldn't wrench her out of his mind tonight.

A few years into her stint at the ranch, Beth had been attacked by a resident, Chester Higgs. She'd been supervising the yard work assignments. After the incident, a few residents said that they'd seen Custodian Ronnicks talking to Higgs as he'd hoed the weeds . . . sidling up close and whispering to him.

Chester Higgs had been sent to the ranch on seven counts of animal cruelty. He'd snuck into a neighbor's sheep pen and slit the yearlings' bellies with a sickle knife known colloquially as a witch blade. When asked why he'd done so, Higgs said the lambs had been keeping secrets. That day and without warning, Higgs struck at Beth with the hoe. He brought it down on her leg, shattering her kneecap; then, as she'd screamed and grabbed for her riot baton, Higgs set about beating her mercilessly. A vicious and well-aimed swipe broke her left hip in three places.

By the time the custodians arrived to haul Higgs off, Beth lay prostrate, bloodied and broken. According to eyewitness reports, Beth—bleeding through her stark white uniform, her face puffed and dangerously shiny—had screamed: *"Lord love a duck!"* Screaming this inane phrase over and over: *Lord lovva duck! Lord lovva duck!*

Chester Higgs was taken to another facility and, at eighteen, transferred to a state penitentiary. He'd never confess to what set him off. Beth meanwhile was laid up for some time in the hospital. Her hip had to be fused. Her kneecap didn't heal properly. She was placed on long-term disability and would never work at the ranch again.

From the day she returned from the hospital until the end of her life, Luke's mother rarely left the house. She'd sit alone in the TV room, an odious shape in the shadows. When Luke got home from school, she would summon him to her side.

Lucas! Come sit with your mommy.

Luke's feelings for her changed gradually. Before the incident, he'd loved his mother openheartedly in spite of the worrisome signs—the spankings that left welts, the way her gaze could sit upon his skull like a tarantula ready to sink in its fangs.

But during the Bad Years, she became truly cruel. In time, Luke realized that cruelty was an implicit facet of her nature; she'd simply taken a while to express it.

6.

LUKE FINALLY FELL BACK ASLEEP and awoke hours later as the yacht slit the night sea. The feeling was not unlike being in a luxury sedan speeding across a freshly laid strip of asphalt; Luke sensed the velocity in his marrow, but the fine calibration of the machine prevented him from truly experiencing it.

He sat up in bed. If he'd had another dream, he couldn't remember it.

He hadn't dreamed regularly since he was a child, sleeping in the same room as his brother, Clayton, their beds separated two feet apart—Clayton had measured that distance, bedpost to bedpost. He measured a lot of things, space being vital to him.

Clayton had suffered night terrors pretty regularly as a child; he'd thrash, shriek, even make these doglike yelps. Usually their mother would shoulder through the door to shake Clay awake so violently that his head snapped back and forth.

You're fine! she'd say, slapping Clayton's cheeks hard enough to pinken the skin. *You're perfectly fine, for heaven's sake!*

Some nights, when Clayton started to thrash, Luke would slide under the covers with him. Clay's skin was clammy and too hot—it made Luke think, horribly, of slipping into bed with someone who'd been boiled alive. Sometimes he'd wrap his arm around Clayton's chest and whisper softly to him.

Ssshhh, Clay. It's okay, just a nightmare. You're okay, you're home safe in bed.

Luke rose from the bed and padded into the bathroom. The carpet of the yacht's interior was incredibly soft; it felt like walking on cotton batting. He twisted the bathroom spigot, but no water came out. Luke's throat was gluey with thirst.

He made his way topside. His watch read 3:09 p.m. He could reset it, but time wouldn't matter soon. Where he was going, everything was pitch-black all the time.

The ocean stretched out. A low-lying moon was halved by the horizon; they were steering straight at it, giving Luke the impression of heading toward a huge tunnel carved out of the night.

"You're awake."

Leo Bathgate stood on an upper deck. Shirtless, his hipbones jutting above his shorts like jug handles. "You sleep okay?"

"Out like a light before my head hit the pillow."

"Good to hear it. Hungry?"

At the mention of food, Luke's stomach snarled.

"Starving, actually."

"We got grub onboard—but temper your expectations, Doc."

Bathgate led him to a kitchen as well appointed as any restaurant's. The food was stashed in cardboard boxes. Japanese snacks. Cans of wasabi peas, bags of shrimp chips, Choco Baby bars, Pocky, plus bottles of Fanta and Pocari Sweat.

Luke said: "Is that *squid jerky*?"

"Wild, huh?" said Bathgate. "This tub was brought down from the Land of the Rising Sun, right? We're loaded for bear with Japanese delights."

"Anything you'd recommend?"

Bathgate said, "The shrimp chips aren't half bad. Kinda of like Cheetos except, y'know, *fishy*."

Luke tore open a pack of squid jerky.

"Pretty good," he said, chewing thoughtfully.

Bathgate said, "I found this, too." He held up a bottle of Japanese whiskey. "I had a warm beer the other night," he continued, "but there's something about drinking hard liquor alone on a boat. But now you're here, want me to crack it open?"

Luke bit into another rawhide squid, chased it with a handful of wasabi peas, and snorted as the burn hit his nostrils.

"You only live once, Leo."

Leo poured a stiff belt of whiskey into two glasses and cocked his head at Luke.

"Want a splash of Coke? Some'd say it's sacrilege, sugaring up good hooch. But hell, I'm a low-class man with animal tastes."

"Oh, I doubt a low-class man would have a yachting license, would he?" Luke told Leo with a grin.

Leo tipped a wink. "No, but a low-class man *would* have a trawling license. A trawler and a yacht are pretty much the same thing. Just one's a helluva lot nicer than another. Like upgrading to a Ferrari when you're used to driving a Kia. Now you, however, a *doctor* . . ."

"My brother's the brainiac," Luke said. "I'm just a veterinarian."

"*Just?* I'd say that's a damn noble living."

"Sure, and I love what I do," said Luke. "Just, y'know . . . had to get there on my own. My folks couldn't afford to send me or my brother to school. Now for Clay, there were scholarships and grants and bursaries. Me? Shoveling shit out of dog cages at the ASPCA, midnight-to-8-a.m. shift, to pay for school." Luke smiled. "So believe me, I'm no top-shelf liquor drinker."

Leo tipped Coke into Luke's glass. They gave their drinks a quick stir around with their index fingers, thumbing their noses at propriety, and clinked glasses.

"Cheers, Doc."

"Cheers to you, Leo."

Smoky, with a burned aftertaste. Whiskey had never been his tipple. Guilt crashed over Luke. Here he was drinking another man's property—a *dead man's* property in all likelihood—and he had no appreciation for it.

7.

LEO USHERED LUKE to the helm. The instrument panel was lit in ghostly greens and blues. A monitor charted the present depth of the sea: 2,300 feet.

"I've been on the ocean since I was a kid," said Leo. "My pops owned a lobster boat. I was out on it soon as I could walk. By seven, I was holding the wheel while he dragged the pots. Dad had me stand on an old telephone book."

He laughed at the memory, his gaze returning to the water.

"I love the sea, and I understand it—much as you can understand something like this. But I haven't spent time *under* it, y'know? In my line of work, if you find yourself there, well, you've screwed the pooch."

The points of isolated stars reflected off the water. Luke and Clay used to stare at the stars from their bedroom's skylight.

The light we're looking at right now, Clay had told Luke, *took billions of years to reach our eyes. Light travels at 299,792,458 meters per second. And still, it takes a billion years to get here. That's how big the universe is. It's 99.99999999 percent darkness. And did you know that the stars we're looking at right now could be dead already? Burned up, nothing but a black hole. We're just seeing their ghosts. Ghosts that traveled a quintillion miles just to say* Boo!

If they're ghosts, Luke had asked, *then how come we're not scared of them?*

Clay just looked at him as if he'd fallen off the turnip truck—which, apart from an expression of mute dispassion, was the most frequent look he used on Luke in those days.

On the main instrument panel, the ocean floor dropped beneath the yacht: 2,309 feet, 2,316, 2,325, a brief rise to 2,319, followed by a dip to

2,389. A different world existed down there—an inverse of the one human beings existed on. After a hundred feet, it was permanent midnight.

"Didn't mean to put your feet to the flames earlier," Leo said. "Asking about your brother and all."

It didn't really matter to Luke. He hadn't spoken to his brother in years. Clayton had never cared about maintaining their connection, anyway. A day, a week, a year, a decade. Time was immaterial to him—and people were even more forgettable.

"*Hope*," Leo said. "That's the hardest part. Maintaining hope after what happens, happens. Because it already happened to my wife."

Leo's eyes met Luke's—Luke caught that wretched *need* to tell him what had happened. And Luke would let him. That was part of the pact in this new version of the world. Listen to people's stories, tell your own. It was the only way to cope sometimes.

"I met her in middle school," Leo said. "Mona Leftowski. The skinniest, gangliest, most remarkable girl. We lived on the same block, and I made every excuse to spend time with her. That didn't mean I was stuck doing girly things. Mona had a slingshot; we'd peg cans down at the town dump. One time I suggested pegging one of the dump critters—the big rats, maybe a raven—and she slugged me so hard that my shoulder was purple the next day. God, she was so *mad*. She said that ugly creatures got a right to exist same as you or me."

Leo chuckled, the skin at the edges of his eyes crinkling. He gave Luke a knowing shrug that said: *You've heard this story before, haven't you?*

Luke had. Just about everyone left had heard it, or lived it, or both.

"I proposed to her on her nineteenth birthday. Down on one knee in Doyer's Burger Barn, of all places. When she said yes, my heart just about floated out of my chest and bobbed in the rafters like a balloon on a string. I took over my father's business. Mona taught at the local elementary school. We had great years together, twenty-one of them in a row. The last two were harder, sure . . . but hell. That's life, right?"

Leo refilled his glass and drained half at a go, his Adam's apple jogging.

"Happened first was, Mona forgot our anniversary. It wasn't such a big deal, except she had a mind for dates. But what the heck, Mona forgets our anniversary. No big deal."

He finished his drink and poured another belt. He didn't drink it; he just cupped the glass in his hands as if to draw warmth from it.

"It happened so gradually you could half convince yourself it wasn't anything to worry about. You could say: Well, hell, Mona *is* past fifty; a little memory loss is par for the course. But it got worse. She forgot to flick the turn signal when she was driving. No big whoop—our town was small, traffic's light. But then she forgot that a red light means 'stop' and blew right through an intersection; our Toyota got T-boned by a Lincoln. She was okay, thank God, but after that we decided it was best that I hold on to the car keys."

Leo beheld Luke miserably over the rim of the glass.

"Mona brought it up after the accident—was it *Alzheimer's*? Early onset? That made the most sense. Heck, at first that's what all the wonks thought it was, too—a hyper-aggressive strain of Alzheimer's. But as we figured out, the 'Gets is something else entirely. She started writing notes to herself. When it was getting bad, I mean, when she was breaking out in those god-awful scabs. She'd fill notebooks with dates and times and little fragments of info. She had a stack of them, all filled with her neat schoolteacher's handwriting."

Luke set a hand on his shoulder. "Listen, you don't have to—"

Leo waved Luke's suggestion off with impatience. "What, am I dropping your mood, Doc?"

Luke thought: *The story I could tell you, my friend, would sour your mood far worse. So don't you worry about it one bit.*

"Go on, Leo."

"I watched it," Leo continued. "God. I *watched* her forget. Then one day, she's staring at me across the kitchen table. And her mouth falls open and out comes a half-chewed dinner roll. She hadn't spoken for days at that point. I don't even know how much of her was left anymore. We sat that way for a few hours. Mona slumped there, mouth open. I tried to close it for her, but it'd just fall right open again.

"That night, I carried her upstairs and undressed her. I took off her . . . Doc, she was wearing diapers. Those were hard to lay your hands on by then. Pharmacies all sold out. It busted me up to pull those god-awful things on and off my wife—but if you love someone, you love them in all their states, don't you? Sickness and health.

"I put her nightgown on and put her in bed and lay down beside her. I was crying, yeah, but I tried to be real soft about it. I don't imagine it troubled her. Sometime that night, she . . . *stopped*, I guess? It happened quickly, which was a relief. She forgot how to live, or . . . damn it all, I don't know how this disease finishes us. It didn't seem real."

It didn't seem real. Luke understood that. He'd felt the exact same way the day his son had gone missing.

"I'm so sorry, Leo."

Leo sawed his palm across his nose. "It's all percentages, Doc. *Life* is percentages. When Mona came down with it, hardly anyone had *gotten* the 'Gets. Less than 1 percent of the population. But that's the thing about percentages—no matter how small, they've got to affect someone, right? After Mona passed I sold the house, packed up, and caught on as a commercial boat captain. When the 'Gets started spreading, a few guys at my company started ferrying supplies to the *Hesperus.*"

Luke said: "Is that what I am, then? Supplies?"

Leo smiled. "The work keeps my head straight. I like to think I'm doing a bit of good here. When your brother went down . . . I'm not a religious man, but I prayed he'd find answers. Not for me. The one it could've helped is gone from my life. But I harbor that hope all the same."

The marine band radio squawked.

"What's your ETA, Bathgate?" someone asked.

Leo consulted his monitors and then keyed the mike. "This is Bathgate. Thirteen hours, twenty-two minutes. Over."

"Bump it up." A prolonged silence. *"Something has surfaced from the* Trieste. *It's . . . Is Dr. Nelson with you now?"*

"He's right beside me. Over."

"What's surfaced is . . . You better get here as soon as you can manage."

A knot—something as hard and sticky as clay—twisted in Luke's stomach.

"I'll go full bore, then. Bathgate out."

Leo adjusted his controls. The turbines churned. The yacht surged.

"Home again, home again," Leo sang. "Jiggedy jig."

8.

THE *HESPERUS* HOVERED against the horizon, holding its position against the rising sun.

God of the Evening Star—Venus. That's what *Hesperus* meant in Greek, Luke had been told. But it was frequently mistranslated in Latin as *Phosphorus*. Namely, Lucifer. Of all the names in creation, why risk that invocation?

There wasn't anything especially demonic about the *Hesperus*. The research station looked a lot like an offshore oil rig. It sat atop the Mariana Trench, the deepest point in any ocean. The trench went down six miles—the same distance to reach the top of Mount Everest. And Luke's brother was two miles below that, in the heart of a narrower fissure called Challenger Deep.

The *Hesperus* floated on huge nitrogen-filled bladders. *Each one can shoulder ten tons, Leo had told Luke earlier. The* Hesperus *floats on thousands of those things.*

Its sheer enormity was staggering. Though squat—most of its structures were only a single story—the station sprawled across the water like a raucous frontier town. Ten thousand metric tons of low-slung architecture, salt-whitened scaffolding, and waterproof storage canisters. Dozens of ships were moored around it like moons ringing a planet.

Leo said: "Impressive, huh? That's what happens when a bunch of first-world countries toss their moolah in a big pot."

"It is amazing," Luke said.

"Not half as amazing as what's happening down below."

A shiver cat-walked up Luke's spine. They were now floating above the *Trieste*—above Clayton. And Luke would be down with his brother soon enough.

Something has surfaced . . . get here as soon as you can manage.

Leo nosed the yacht alongside the *Hesperus* and docked neat as a pin. By the time Luke had gathered his belongings and returned topside, stationed soldiers in camouflage fatigues had swung a gangplank into position.

Who the hell wears camouflage on the ocean? Luke wondered.

"Should we go?" he asked Leo.

"Not me, Doc. All this"—Leo nodded at the soldiers—"is above my pay grade."

How long had Luke known Leo? No more than a few hours. Seemed much longer. He wanted Leo to come with him, pay grades be damned. But he could only shake his hand. "Pleasure meeting you. Thanks for the lift. And the squid."

"Anytime, Doc. I'm so glad you're here. Like I said, I'm hopeful."

Luke headed down the gangplank and slid into the backseat of a golf cart. An adenoidal soldier drove them down a walkway strung with windowless structures. People passed in and out of doors, some in fatigues and others in lab coats. The *Hesperus* reminded Luke of a MASH unit: the stumpy outbuildings, the hum of generators, the calls going out over a loudspeaker system: *L-Team to SQR, Code Orange . . . L-Team to SQR, Code Orange . . .*

The cart snaked down narrow paths strung between the buildings, jogging left and right. Sparks fanned from a darkened doorway; the soldier drove through the glittering fall, the embers falling painlessly on Luke's exposed arms—they had the dry sulfurous smell of Fourth of July sparklers. The cart shot through a tight corridor between two domed structures tipped with inverted satellite dishes that resembled a pair of perfect conical breasts, veered left, and followed the edge of the *Hesperus* for a hundred yards. The sea shone like a bronze mirror in the sun. Luke was amazed. They must have driven the length of a city block. He couldn't have found his way back to Leo's yacht without a map.

The cart stopped in front of a black-sided building. As Luke was collecting his bags, a guy in a lab coat popped his head out of the door. Short and squat with a bottom-heavy, bowling ball build. His sunburned face was either cheery—*His eyes, how they twinkle*, Luke thought; *His dimples, how merry!*—or faux-cheery, as his eyes shone with cold scrutiny.

"Dr. Nelson, yes?" he said. "Of course—you have Clayton's eyes . . . and nose! I've been waiting on your arrival. Come in, quickly."

9.

LUKE FOLLOWED THE MAN down a hallway that doglegged into a small, dark room. A bank of monitors dominated one wall. Strips of medical tape were affixed beneath each monitor, all labeled in black Sharpie: Lab 1; Lab 2; Mess; Nelson's Chambers; Toy's Chambers; Westlake's Chambers; Water Closet; Kennel/Storage; O_2 Purification; Containment; Quarantine.

Most of the monitors were either black or fuzzed with static. The few still in operation offered stationary black-and-white shots, similar to a surveillance video. One, Toy's Chambers, offered a fish-eye view of modest sleeping quarters: a cot that hinged down from a curved wall, one wafer-thin mattress, a latticework of steel grating that functioned as a walkway.

"The power could be failing," the man—who had yet to identify himself—told Luke. "We don't know. Our communication link isn't working."

"How long?"

"How long what?" The man turned and stuck out his hand. "Dr. Conrad Felz, by the way."

"You're my brother's partner?"

Felz made a sour face. "Have you talked to your brother lately?"

"Not in some time, no."

"Weeks? Months?"

A strained smile from Luke. "A titch longer than that."

It had been over eight years since they had spoken. But why burden Felz with their dour brotherly history?

Felz's chin jutted. "*Partner.* Huh. I don't know if Clayton's ever had a partner—more subordinates. Subservients. Not that I'm complaining."

It sure sounds like you're complaining, Luke thought but didn't say.

"Clayton doesn't exactly play nicely with others," Felz went on. "I'm sure you were jabbed by the pointy end of that particular stick, being the younger brother."

"Not so much as you'd think. Unless you count being ignored as abusive."

Felz's eyebrow cocked, as if to say: *You don't consider that abuse?* "Clayton does what he does," he said, "and because he's supremely talented, his ways are tolerated. It's the way it is with savants. Or geniuses, if you'd prefer. That line is so thin sometimes.

"We were competitors at first," Felz went on, "though I'm certain Clayton never saw it that way. Your brother competes against DNA helixes, against scientific absolutes, against the universe. The notion of competing with another person is, I'm convinced, totally foreign to him."

Felz's fleshy lower lip protruded sullenly, a foamy dab of spit collecting in its vermilion zone.

"Your brother and I met at MIT," Felz said. "He didn't have to apply, of course; his reputation allowed him to waltz on in. I soon discovered that Clayton wasn't so much driven as pathological. The man doesn't *sleep.*"

It was true that as Clayton hit adolescence, sleep had become nonessential. He'd been up at all hours, squirreled down in his basement lab at twelve years old. He'd stopped going to school by then; he'd been granted an exemption when it became clear that his knowledge outstripped that of his teachers—the equivalent of forcing a piano prodigy to take lessons from a dotty church organist.

"What your brother was doing even before he arrived at MIT was astounding," Felz said. "Were you on hand to see what he did with that mouse?"

Of course Luke remembered the mouse . . .

Ernie. The mouse's name was Ernie. Clay named all of his mice—a grisly fixation, considering their fates. Clayton had heard about this anesthesiologist, a Dr. Charles Vacanti, who'd grafted a human ear onto a mouse's back; the "ear" was cartilage grown by seeding cow cartilage cells into a biodegradable ear-shaped mold, which was then implanted under the mouse's skin.

Clayton made it his mission to outdo Vacanti. How he'd managed to do it baffled Luke to this day. As a veterinarian, Luke understood the vagaries of flesh and trauma and disease, but Clayton occupied a different stratum of intellect. He could see doors set in the ordinary fabric of things that were invisible to everyone else—and if he lacked a key to those doors, he goddamn well *made* one.

Luke had helped Clayton shave the test mice. Clayton was a teenager by then; Luke a few years younger. He was rarely allowed into Clayton's lab, which was set up in their father's old workshop. Clayton kept it scrupulously clean, as even a speck of dust could ruin his projects. When he was deep into an "objective," as he called them, Clayton could go days without food or sleep.

But Clayton had allowed Luke in to prep the mice. Luke used the old Wahl clippers his father used on his wiry neck hairs. For the "Vacanti Objective," there were thirteen mice, all named: Doug and Pepper and Dot and Beanie and Clyde and Percival, et cetera. They squealed and pissed and shit perfect little chocolate-sprinkle-shaped turds as Luke worked the clippers over their squirming bodies.

"Okay, you can go now," Clay said brusquely after Luke had finished. Not even a thank-you.

That was the last Luke had seen of his brother for days.

At night, the squeaks of those mice traveled through the vents. One morning Luke found one of them in the garbage can, atop the old coffee grounds and eggshells. A weird lump projected from the mouse's back: it looked like a horn, or a shark's fin. Luke plucked it from the trash and dug a hole in the garden and buried it.

A few weeks later, Luke was downstairs tossing his soccer uniform into the dryer when the door to Clayton's lab opened.

"Come see," Clayton said.

The mouse, which Clayton had named Doug, trundled awkwardly around a plastic bin. Luke was stunned.

"Is that a . . ."

"Nose?" Clayton smiled. "Yes, it is."

A nose—a human-sized *nose*—spread across Doug's entire back, from his tail to the tip of his spine. The nostrils fanned around Doug's rump. The mouse staggered around like a donkey lugging an overloaded saddlebag.

"How did you . . . ?"

"It's not so hard," Clayton said. "You wouldn't understand."

It was typical for Clayton to be dismissive of his own accomplishments—and he was right, Luke wouldn't have understood.

Incredibly, the nose twitched. The nostrils *dilated*.

"Is it—?"

"Breathing?" Clayton said. "No. Doug's muscles have grown through the new tissue. When its body twitches, so does the nose."

"What . . . what are you going to *do* with him?"

Clayton shrugged, as if he hadn't thought about it. He'd accomplished his goal—outdoing Dr. Vacanti. Now Doug existed. But what did the world want with a mouse with a nose on its back?

Squeals came from under the lab bench. Luke noticed another tub.

"What's in there?" he asked.

"Oh, that's just Ernie."

Luke reached down and pulled the tub out. Clayton made no move to stop him. For a long moment, Luke's eyes couldn't register what they were seeing.

"Oh no . . . oh . . ."

The single mouse—could it really be called that anymore?—in the tub was hairless, its body as pink as the skin under a scab. Ernie's legs . . . it *had* no legs. Three nubs projected from the bloat of its body—it was as if its legs had melted into scarified bulbs of flesh. One of its ears was normal, but the other tapered into a whip of flesh: its misplaced tail, the one that should've rightly been growing at the back of its body.

"Clay . . . oh God what . . ."

A pink, misshapen sac hung off Ernie's side. It was sheer as a bat's wing; tiny capillaries braided over its surface. Under this greasy stretching of skin, Luke could see the torpid movements of Ernie's guts: its stomach quivering, its intestines shuddering. The foreign structure was vaguely peaked, and there were two shallow divots on one side.

"The nose didn't hold its integrity," Clayton explained clinically. "The cellular walls broke down, its insides migrating into the new structure. And . . . other structural collapses. You wouldn't understand."

Ernie pulled itself in a lopsided circle using a smooth hook of skin that projected from its sternum. It dragged itself to a pile of food pellets and dipped its tubelike mouth to eat. The squeals became slurps, which switched back to squeals when it couldn't get the pellets into its toothless mouth.

"I've been crushing the pellets up," Clayton said. "So Ernie can eat."

"Why? Why is it still alive?"

"I don't know," Clayton said honestly. "Organisms are tough. They do not want to expire. But don't worry. I was able to harvest tissue from Ernie and used it on Doug. And Doug *worked*."

Luke noticed the plugs of flesh that Clay had carved from the deformed mouse's flanks. Seedlings from which Doug could grow. That was how Clayton saw things: as workable premises, or simply one of many faltering steps toward that workable premise. And Ernie belonged on Clayton's blooper reel.

Luke cupped Ernie in his hands. The mouse-thing mewled and shuddered.

"I'm taking it," said Luke.

Clayton shrugged. "I don't need it anymore."

Luke filled a bucket with water from the hose and drowned Ernie on the porch. It seemed the quickest, most painless way. He buried Ernie in the garden. While he was digging the hole, still backhanding tears from his eyes, he'd seen Clay staring at him from the basement window, his face set in a bemused and slightly scornful expression.

"Yes, of course," Luke told Felz after a long pause. "I remember what Clayton did with that mouse."

Clayton's miracle mouse had set off a furor in the scientific community and soon, the media. Clayton was feted in some circles, demonized in others. Over the next year the press coined a number of monikers, from "Kid Frankenstein" to "Cute Clay" on account of his striking good looks (he remains the only scientist to grace the pages of *Tiger Beat* and *Bop* magazines, which dispatched photographers to snap him coming and going from his house) to "Jonas Sulk," for his moodiness with reporters. Clayton was approached by the heads of several major medical institutions; they pursued him with the ardor of a blue-chip athletic recruit, offering full run of their facilities. He also entertained overtures from Big Pharma and more than a few genetic research firms. He turned them all down. When asked why, he said, "I'd miss my mother's meatballs too much"—this was a lie, and Luke knew it. Clayton *hated* his mom's meatballs.

Felz directed Luke's attention to the bank of monitors. Luke's gaze was drawn to one marked O_2 Purification. White objects resembling oil filters were screwed into the room's walls. Luke figured the oxygen inside the undersea station must pass through those cylinders, which siphoned off the carbon monoxide to make it breathable again.

The monitor's image adjusted. A fragmentary darkening in the lower left hemisphere. It was so brief, so inconsequential, that Luke wondered if he'd seen anything at all. Could it be a technical malfunction? The signal had to travel up through eight miles of water after all.

"So who's down there?"

"Other than your brother?" Felz said. "There are two others, both Americans. I'm sorry, Jesus—there's *one*. There were three at first, but . . ."

"But?"

Felz held up a hand. "We'll get to that. Right now there's only your brother and Dr. Hugo Toy, the molecular biologist."

"That's it? Two people?"

Felz nodded. "Their vital signs monitors indicate they're both alive and . . . functional? Sorry, I don't know a better word. So them, plus the test subjects. Two Labrador retrievers, various reptile species, guinea pigs, and of course, the bees."

Luke nodded. "Okay, so here's the billion-dollar question: *why* are they down there at all?"

Felz's face held the look of a boy with a secret so monumental that holding it in caused him physical pain.

"What we've discovered appears to exist beyond all explication."

10.

FELZ OPENED A DOOR, which led into a small lab dominated by a steel bench. A hum filled the air. It held an uneven cadence, the odd chirp or hiccup, the way a computer sounds when it's processing huge amounts of data.

Felz walked to an upright black box. It had the dimensions of a hotel fridge, with a keypad on its front.

"It still amazes me that access could be so simple," he said. "Five years ago, we'd have had to pass through an armed checkpoint, a titanium door, a retinal scan, a blood serum scan, and a body-cavity search just to fill out the *requisition forms* to look at what I'm about to show you. The *Hesperus* exists because of this . . . but we don't know what *this* is. So in that way, it's like leaving the Hope Diamond in a bus station locker: as long as nobody really understands its value, it's perfectly safe where it is."

Felz entered a pass code. The lock on the black box disengaged. He cracked the lid. A stream of supercooled air escaped.

Luke leaned forward, dimly aware of the throbbing tension in his chest.

"I really don't think security matters much, anyway," Felz said, more to himself than to Luke. "I'm not sure anyone could move it, even if they wanted to."

"Why?" Luke asked.

"Because," Felz said softly, "it's exactly where it wants to be."

The cooler contained a single sealed petri dish. Felz reached for it with great reverence, fear, or some combination of both.

"You need to keep it that cold?" Luke asked.

Felz gave a tepid smile. "We don't know. It seems unwise to place it in an environment conducive to growth. I mean, we don't want it growing. Not yet."

He set the petri dish on the lab bench. The lid was fogged. The condensation evaporated, the glass clearing by degrees.

"Isn't it magnificent?" said Felz.

11.

MAGNIFICENT was one word for it.

But *mundane* also came to mind.

A gelatinous blob the size of a robin's egg. It looked like a glob of partially set Jell-O. Not one of the colorful flavors, either. A drab *nothing* color—the color you'd get if you scraped a billion thumbprints off a million windowpanes and collected them into a ball.

"What is it?"

"It's resistant to categorization," said Felz. "Every standard test—DNA cataloguing, cellular identity, chemical pattern bonding . . . all inconclusive. No matches to any known flora, fauna, DNA structures, or chemical compounds. It's . . . well, like I said, uncategorizable."

"Is there a name for it?"

"Formally? Scientifically? Nothing yet," Felz said. "It's known internally as Specimen 1-G. We've had a few other specimens in hand, but they vanished."

Vanished. Luke hated that particular word.

"What do you mean?" he said. "They died or . . . ?"

Felz shook his head. "No. They just disappeared and . . . *evanesced.* Vaporized. Gone away. Informally, your brother and I have a name for it. *Ambrosia,* after the Greek word for nectar of the gods. Initially it was lying on a bed of agar gel—the standard petri dish base. Microbial growth does not destroy the gel structure, as microorganisms are unable to digest agar. But this specimen did something to the agar. It, well . . . *harmonized* it, I guess you could say."

"You mean *ate* it?"

"No, no, it *added* the agar to itself. Transmuted the agar to make *more* of itself. The sample used to be much smaller. There's nothing left of the agar, and its mass has been added to the ambrosia. It would be the equivalent of, oh, I don't know—say instead of eating a loaf of bread, you somehow *added* the loaf to your body. Changed its cell structure to mimic your own, retained its shape and size, and ended up with a new appendage exactly resembling that loaf." Felz pointed. Luke followed his finger—which he noticed was trembling. "If you look carefully, you can see it's started to do the same to the dish."

Luke noted a slight depression in the petri dish, as if it'd been eaten away by acid. He imagined the ambrosia eating through the glass, then the cooler and the floor until it plopped into one of the nitrogen-filled bladders, assimilating the gas somehow, making itself bigger, spreading across the bottom of the *Hesperus* like a tenacious weed.

"Is it some kind of parasite? Or something from the fossil age?"

"It's something much more than that," said Felz. "If it's primitive, I suppose it would be in the way sharks are: they were perfectly built from the start, so they never needed to evolve. But sharks are common. They're of this world. This thing is infinitely more complex."

"What do you mean—it's *alien*?"

Felz didn't answer. Luke realized that the specimen wasn't quite as lusterless as it'd seemed at first. It *sparkled*. The shimmer reminded Luke of marbles. Marbles in a mesh sack, each one glossed by the sun. The marbles he'd played with as a child.

Luke leaned in to get a better look. Veins of light streaked through the ambrosia's interior. Coin-bright shafts of light, like zaps of lightning but more colorful: reds and violets and emeralds and incandescent whites.

So transfixing. Luke could watch it all day and night . . .

Felz squeezed Luke's elbow. "Hey. You shouldn't look at it for too long. It's got a strange way about it."

Dull anger hived in Luke's stomach. He wanted to look some more, but Felz—the killjoy bastard—was intent on stopping him.

"I'm okay," Luke said. "I'm fine, damn it." Luke snapped back to himself. He smiled sheepishly at Felz. "I'm sorry."

Felz returned the dish to the cooler. "It'll pass. It's one of the effects the ambrosia possesses."

"So where the hell did it come from?" Luke asked, half knowing already.

Felz pointed downward. "The deep."

"How did you—?"

"Four years ago a pollack ship, the *Olympiad*, was bottom-trawling twenty miles north of here," Felz said. "Their winch broke, so to avoid damaging the net the captain charted a course for the Mariana Trench. It's so deep that the ship could circle safely until the winch was fixed. When the net was dragged up, it was full of by-catch—that is, marine life they hadn't set out to capture. They found a lantern fish, a species that commonly dwells several miles beneath the surface. It was still alive, which was the first shock. Lantern fish live in darkness, under tremendous pressure. If they swim toward the surface, the lessened pressure pulls their body apart. Not only that, but the sunlight attacks their flesh like acid. The only way to study lantern fish, or anything that dwells at those depths, is to do so in their habitat. Which is why so little is known about them."

"The lantern fish they found was intact?"

"Not just that, Dr. Nelson. It was *alive*. It may've been thrown over the side if not for the intervention of Dr. Eva Parks, a marine biologist who was onboard to study pollack migratory patterns. She spied the fish and recognized its inconceivability. She was scrupulous: she pegged the ship's longitude and latitude, fixing its position. Otherwise your brother and I wouldn't have known where to begin our search. Dr. Parks took a few measurements—length, girth, weight—before the fish started to show signs of incipient mortality. She began to hastily count the annuli on its scales. Perhaps you know of these?"

"They're what, age rings?" Luke said. "The same as when you cut down a tree; count the number of rings, you get its age."

Felz nodded. "Exactly so. But Parks couldn't count the rings. There were simply *too many*. They were lapped over and over, ring upon ring *over* ring, making an accurate enumeration impossible."

"What do you mean?"

"I mean, Dr. Nelson," Felz said, "the fish was functionally ageless. So old that the common method of analysis was useless."

"How long do lantern fish live?"

"Twenty or thirty years, likely. This one could've been several hundred years old, a thousand years old, or even older. As in, immeasurably old."

"How is that possible?"

Felz showed Luke his open palms as if to say: *It shouldn't* be *possible.* "During Dr. Parks' examination, the fish expired. As she related it, it didn't just die—it *decomposed.* Almost instantaneously, it surrendered cellular integrity. It rotted in real time. Imagine the trauma it would've sustained while rising to the surface, the attacks by pressure and sunlight. Now imagine it all happening at once. Dr. Parks took a video of the aftermath. A black pool of gunk. And shortly after that came another shock."

Felz gestured to the cooler.

"Dr. Parks discovered a tiny particle of ambrosia beside the carcass. No bigger than a few stuck-together grains of sand; it's a miracle she was able to distinguish it from the rotted matter. She put it in a petri dish, as scientists do."

"So you're saying . . ."

"That the ambrosia kept the lantern fish alive for a minor eternity? That the ambrosia kept that same fish alive, protecting it somehow, as it rose through the oceanic zones? That the ambrosia didn't *allow* that fish to die until it deserted its body, either voluntarily or through some other organic process?" Felz showed Luke his palms again. "Many signs point to yes."

"So this stuff is floating around down there, attaching itself to aquatic life?"

Felz shook his head. "The lantern fish was an anomaly. We've found no further presence of ambrosia at that depth. Our speculation is that the fish hunted near a thermal vent; a tiny shred of ambrosia could have floated up from below and moored to the fish. The only place we've found any concentration of ambrosia—or what we *believe to be* ambrosia—is much deeper. The deepest part of the Mariana Trench, in fact. Right in the area of Challenger Deep."

"Which is where the *Trieste* is."

Felz nodded. "We sent down observation cameras first, when the idea of constructing a station at that depth was still in its infancy. We had to know if the effort was worthwhile. The camera lenses kept shattering under pressure, but the footage was promising. Globules of matter drifting over the trench floor. Strange movements—the sort commonly associated with sentient life. Which goes against all prior understandings of those depths. For decades, nobody thought *anything* could exist down there. The monolithic pressure, a total absence of nourishing light. How could anything survive?"

"And that was enough to kick-start all of this?" Luke said. "A few blobs fluttering around at the bottom of the ocean?"

"Desperate times, Dr. Nelson."

Luke lapsed into silence.

"You seem underwhelmed," said Felz. "Or is it dubious? I felt the same way at first. *Nothing should live down there. What good could it do us, anyway?* But then I saw for myself. Your brother showed me."

"How did Clayton get involved with all this?"

Felz said: "When you discover something like ambrosia—the equivalent of an intricate organic riddle—who would you summon, if not the world's foremost riddle solver?"

He waved Luke toward the back of the room.

"Come here. Let me show you something else."

12.

FELZ'S LAPTOP sat on the lab bench.

"Hang on. It's here somewhere." He scrolled the mouse across the files littering the computer's desktop. "You've followed your brother's work, I take it? Surely you know about his cancer mouse?"

How could Luke not? It was his brother's best-known contribution to science, far more impressive than Doug, his nose-mouse. Clayton hadn't discovered a cure for cancer, far from it. But he had found a way to *give* cancer to a mouse. And he gave it with pinpoint precision—he could isolate the location, the organ or tissue, and control the complexity of its spread: malignant or benign, dormant or devouring.

Clayton's very special mice were *born* with cancer. They were engineered to be sick—specifically and perfectly, from a scientific point of view. A researcher could order fifty mice with Stage 2 lung cancer. Or a hundred mice with advanced liver cancer, or ten with benign stomach tumors. Clayton's mice were a boon to science. They were born carrying the pathogen that would kill them—and they were never truly healthy, not for one moment of their lives. Animal rights activists were none too thrilled, to put it mildly, but that didn't stop researchers everywhere from hoisting Clayton on their collective shoulders.

"Your brother heard about Dr. Parks and the foreign matter she'd isolated," said Felz. "Shortly thereafter, the sample was delivered to our lab for study."

"And Dr. Parks had no problem with that?"

"Dr. Parks was given an opportunity to stay with the project. She opted not to take that opportunity."

"Clayton muscled her out?"

Felz looked up sharply. "Nothing like that, I assure you."

Luke saw no use in pursuing the issue. "So when the sample arrived . . . ?"

"Your brother absented himself for several days. He'd emerge from the lab weary but excited. As the days ground on, confusion wore through that excitement. *I don't know,* he told me. *I really can't tell you anything about this substance. It's like nothing we've seen before on this earth.*"

Felz located the .mov file he'd been searching for.

CANCER MOUSE AMBROSIA, TEST 1-B.

"For this test, Clayton created a special mouse," Felz said. "It didn't have *one* cancer; it had virtually all of them. It was sick in every way it was possible to *be* sick. Liver, pancreatic, spinal, skin, bowel. It was on death's door by the time the first experiment took place."

"Why 1-B?" Luke asked. "What happened to 1-A?"

"The ambrosia didn't interact with the first test subject. It . . . refused to, is I suppose the only explanation. As such, the subject expired. Now watch, Dr. Nelson. I think you'll find it quite extraordinary."

Felz clicked the *play* arrow on the file.

A tight shot: a mouse in a lab tray. It squeaked in obvious pain and tottered a few inches across the tray before toppling over, breathing heavily.

A hand entered the frame—Clayton's hand, his fingers gripping a pair of tweezers. Clayton's other hand appeared, and in it, a petri dish. He tweezed out a speck of ambrosia and laid it beside the mouse.

The mouse lay still. Luke was aware of the passage of time only in the tension that built up in his arms and fingers, and the sheen of sweat slicking his forehead.

The mouse dragged itself to the ambrosia. Its squeaks sounded different: almost *pleading,* though that was surely only Luke's interpretation. It drew nearer to the speck until—

"Whoa, what the hell happened there?" Luke said.

Felz moved the cursor, backtracking the file. He played it again. Luke concentrated this time—he *knew* it was coming. And still . . .

"I can't make it out."

"Yes, none of us can," Felz said. "I've replayed that section hundreds of times. We gave it to an audiovisual wizard, had her blow up the image and slow it down—it clarifies nothing. It simply happens too fast."

"It looks like—"

"Like the ambrosia goes *into* the mouse, yes. Penetrates its skin. But the ambrosia is gelatinous. How could it solidify itself to pierce flesh, and not leave a wound? We inspected the mouse afterward. No hole. No blood. No scar. We thought since the entry point is near the mouse's mouth, perhaps it entered there. We slowed the footage down, looked at it frame by frame. One frame, the ambrosia's there. The next, it's gone."

"And it's inside the mouse."

"It simply must be," said Felz.

The video resumed. The mouse lay still a few seconds, then hopped up and began racing around the tray, faster and faster until it flung itself out onto the bench.

Someone said, *"Damn!"* as the mouse skittered across the table with gleeful abandon. Clayton entered the frame, chasing it. Another man dashed behind him. Next came Clayton's voice. "I've got it."

The video ended.

Felz said: "Likely you already know what I'm going to tell you. You've realized that the *Hesperus*, the *Trieste*, and the trillion-odd dollars funding this project wouldn't have materialized were it not for what happened to that mouse."

Luke said: "It was cured."

"The cancer was eradicated. There was not one discoverable cancerous cell in its body. It was *riddled* with the stuff and then, all gone."

"What about the ambrosia?" Luke said. "Was it isolated inside the mouse?"

Felz shook his head. "The mouse was totally unchanged, other than the eradication of its cancer. Its amino profile and bone density and factors x, y, and z—all unchanged, except for changes that would naturally occur with the cancer gone."

"But it's just a mouse," said Luke. "And it's cancer. How can we know this stuff will address the 'Gets in humans?"

"Dr. Nelson, we would have searched for this *stuff*, as you call it, if all it did was cure cancer in mice. It's a remarkable discovery any way you slice it. If your brother could have infected a mouse with the 'Gets, well, we would know to a certainty. But the disease doesn't interact with animals, as you well know. We did, however, perform tests on cancerous human cells. Lab tests only, but the results were promising."

"And that was enough to spur all this?"

"My God, man, what else were we waiting for? If not now, when?"

"So," Luke said, "what you've found is some kind of—"

"Universal healer?" Felz shook his head wonderingly, a stunned smile on his face. "It would seem so. Imagine a drug that cures everything and anything. Whitewashes all the sickness in your body, fixing you completely. It seems crazy, but—"

"But this isn't a drug. This is an organism. How do you know the effects aren't temporary? Or that that *stuff* isn't doing something to make it run around like that, to subtly injure the mouse?"

"Like what?"

I mean, controlling it in some way, Luke thought but didn't say, remembering the weird prickle he'd gotten when he'd stared at the ambrosia.

Felz said: "Are you a religious man, Dr. Nelson? Your brother isn't. Men like us rarely are. But you?"

Luke shook his head. "My mom used to say she prayed at the church of State and Main, which was the intersection where the local bank sat."

Felz nodded and said, "I only ask because of something your brother said. It was the one time when he sounded truly helpless—casting his lot with the fates, you could say. He'd been researching the 'Gets before this business with ambrosia. He couldn't crack it for the life of him. Totally stymied. Then he encountered the ambrosia and couldn't make heads or tails of it, either.

"One night after another fruitless session with the ambrosia, he said: *What if the devil unleashed a perfectly unexplainable plague on humanity? If so, isn't it equally possible that God created the perfect, if inexplicable cure?*" Felz shrugged. "Clayton believes in keys and locks. For every lock, there exists a key. You just have to find those keys. Find them, and trust in the will of a higher power."

"Locks and keys."

"Exactly, Dr. Nelson. Locks and keys."

"And this particular key—you think it's eight miles down?"

Felz closed the laptop. "That's the hope. Perhaps there's an abundance of it. Perhaps—and this is an admittedly out-there hypothesis—what we've found so far are shreds off a far larger organism. A mother-organism, if you will."

A quaver passed down Luke's spine. A *mother-organism*. Huge and amorphous and ageless, lying in darkness at the bottom of the sea. Jesus.

"Why wouldn't Dr. Parks want to be part of this?"

Felz started. "I beg pardon?"

"Dr. Eva Parks. She discovered it. Why wouldn't she want to be part of perhaps the greatest discovery in human history?"

Of course, Luke knew it had to be Clayton. His bullying ways. He was thinking about their childhood sandbox: how Clay had commandeered the toys for no other purpose than to deprive Luke of the satisfaction of playing with them.

"Dr. Nelson . . ." Felz licked his lips, smearing that ever-present dab of spit across them. "Dr. Parks committed suicide shortly after the sample arrived in our custody. She hanged herself in her apartment in Maine. In her closet, with a length of nautical rope."

"Good God. Why would she do such a thing?"

"That I do not know. From all outward appearances she was happy. A good career. Engaged to another doctor she'd met at graduate school." Felz glanced at the cooler and licked his lips again. "There is no sensible cause, but suicide is not a sensible act."

A door banged open. Luke and Felz craned their necks toward the sound.

"The very man I'm looking for," a new voice said.

13.

THE VOICE BELONGED to a woman in combat fatigues. Tall and incredibly broad across the shoulders, that broadness tapering toward her waist, which was cinched in a thick belt. She wore no insignia of rank. Those things didn't mean as much now, the same way a policeman's badge carried less heft. Ever since the 'Gets, people were measured by their abilities rather than by the pieces of tin pinned to their chests.

Her hair was clipped short and her jaw had a long angularity that gave her face a sharpness, an intensity that was of a piece with her piercing green eyes. She carried herself with a controlled bearing that seemed almost robotic, each movement calibrated to deliver maximum function with minimal exertion. A scar roped up the side of her neck and trailed behind her left ear—thick and ribbed and pink, the color of bubblegum.

"Dr. Nelson?"

"Yes."

She offered her hand. "Alice Sykes. Lieutenant Commander, U.S. Navy. But feel free to call me Al. Paul Simon may come sniffing around for royalties, but I can deal with that hassle personally."

Luke liked her immediately—yet he got a sense of forced jocularity off of her, too: her smile was screwed on too tight.

She turned to Felz. "I take it you've filled Dr. Nelson in on the magical goo in deep freeze?"

Dr. Felz stood up straight. "Yes, we've covered just about everything."

"Fine. We gotta get this show on the road." Alice's expression darkened. "Have you spoken to him about what's surfaced?"

Felz said, "No. I thought . . ."

"That's okay. It's not an easy matter. Let's hop to it."

A four-seat golf cart waited on the deck. Al sat up front, Felz and Luke behind.

"A hell of a thing, isn't it?" Al said to Luke as they careened through the floating minicity. Each building was painted a reflective black; the sun knifed off every angle, painfully bright. Luke caught sight of the sea through a gap between the buildings—the horizon shimmered, the sky a searing blue against the plate-glass water. Everything looked new and modern, but so many of the structures seemed to be half built or unused. It reminded Luke of those model communities on the outskirts of Las Vegas, built in anticipation of a boom that never came. The *Hesperus* had that same ghost town feel—it was a place built for great things that had not quite come to pass.

Al craned her head around to see if Luke was taking it all in—Luke diverted his gaze. He'd been focused on the scar that went all the way around the back of Al's neck, a pink band that petered out at her right ear-lobe. It looked as though someone had tried to slit her neck, starting at the back. If she noticed him looking, she was tactful enough not to mention it.

"Who paid for all this?" Luke said.

"Everyone who earns a paycheck," Al said. "You, me, the butcher, the baker. Not just American greenbacks, either: Japanese yen, British pounds, Chinese yuan, German deutsche marks."

"That would be euros," said Felz, fussily. "They replaced the deutsche mark in 2002."

"Thank you, Dr. Felz, for your scrupulous attention in regards to matters of international currency."

"You're welcome."

"Anyway," Alice went on, "what you see here is the whole world, holding hands. We got a lot of support from private enterprise, too. CEOs, CFOs, magnates, philanthropists. Everyone's smashing their piggy banks. Everybody's lost something to this by now, y'know? And what's money worth if there's no future to spend it in?"

"Why is it all Americans, then? I mean, down on the *Trieste*? Dr. Felz said the researchers are all from the U.S."

"I guess because America always rides point," Al said.

They stopped beside a compact submarine. Fifteen feet long with a porthole window at one end. It lay in a massive canvas hammock. It looked like a huge lozenge—a vitamin pill for Neptune.

"*Challenger* 5," Al told Luke. "It's being prepped for your descent."

Luke said, "You've got to be kidding me. I have no idea how to operate this."

"Yeah, that would take some serious training. Thankfully, you'll be in the company of a skilled pilot." Al thumped her chest. "Like I said, tight squeeze."

She leaned over the seat, jammed her face close to Luke's own.

"Breathe on me."

"*What?*"

"I said, breathe on me. Come on, don't be shy."

Luke did as she asked, too startled to refuse. Al sniffed.

"Okay, good. Nothing worse than being cooped up for hours with a guy with bad breath."

Luke exhaled, chuckling now. "I've got Tic Tacs in my bag."

She winked. "Even better."

If I have to journey eight miles beneath the water's surface, Luke thought, *this Alice Sykes seems as fine a companion as any.*

"Dr. Westlake came up in *Challenger* 4," Al said. "It's still under quarantine."

Luke said, "Dr. Westlake?"

"Dr. Felz hasn't mentioned him yet?" Al darted a glance at Felz, a darkness settling into her eyes. "He was the third member of the team. Dr. Cooper Westlake. He was a—remind me what was his job again, Doctor?"

"Computational biologist," Felz said as the cart got rolling again.

"I got to know Dr. Westlake pretty well," Al said. The forced jocularity was gone. In its place was somber concern. "I liked him a hell of a lot. He seemed put together. But it's incredibly hard down there. Not just the physical pressure; there's the added pressure of what they're trying to achieve. Dr. Westlake surfaced nine and a half hours ago, while you were in transit. Let me ask—has your brother ever mentioned him?"

Luke said: "I've never met Dr. Westlake. Never even heard his name."

"I believe that's the truth as you know it," said Al.

The cart stopped before a building with a red cross on its exterior. Al rested her gaze gently upon Luke's.

"What's behind that door," she said, "is Dr. Westlake. What surfaced of him. You don't have to look . . . but maybe you'll want to, seeing as you've agreed to go down."

"What happened to him?" said Luke.

Alice showed him her palms, same as Felz had done. A helpless gesture.

"It's still our world down there, Dr. Nelson," she said, "but that's like saying that the ice ten thousand feet beneath the arctic icepack is, too. Yeah, it *is*, but not anything we know. Our government has spent thirty trillion dollars on space exploration, and less than 1 percent of that to explore the world underneath us right now. But it's just as unknown. You'll be entering another world, really and truly."

"It's Luke," he told her. "Call me Luke. And I'll go. I'll see."

Al's clipped nod made Luke think she wished he'd chosen otherwise.

14.

THE AIR WAS MEAT-LOCKER COLD on the other side of the door with the red cross. Luke's arms instantly broke out in gooseflesh.

The room was uncluttered. Halogen lights buzzed down on a bank of steel vaults. Luke had visited morgues as a veterinarian, most recently to perform an autopsy on a police drug dog that'd died after ingesting a perforated balloon of heroin.

"Every vault is empty save one," Al said. "We've been lucky lately with the 'Gets. A few in quarantine, but none dead and no new cases reported in a week. Must be the sea air." A gravedigger's smile. "Sorry. Poor taste."

They walked with aching slowness toward the vaults.

"Dr. Westlake and the others had settled into their roles inside the *Trieste*. The station was holding up. Electrical function, oxygen purification, waste disposal—all systems operational, which on the technical side of things was the main concern.

"Mentally, the crew seemed sound. Your brother was the point man—he gave the majority of the updates, so our perceptions up here were filtered through him. But we watched the other two on the monitors. They were eating, sleeping, engaged in productive labor. You'd see them talking and laughing with one another.

"There was the odd sign of strain, but that could be chalked up to their situation. Add to that the sensory deprivation. No sun, no fresh air. But our psychs are versed in signs of trauma fatigue; they assured us the trio was holding up well. Then . . . well, Westlake went off the grid."

Al gripped the handle of the centermost vault and cracked it open a few inches. A chemical tang puffed out, sliming Luke's tongue and making him slightly nauseous.

"Westlake may've been getting squirrelly," Al said. "He'd been isolated inside his lab for quite some time. No updates, no contact. The
video camera in his lab was busted. We couldn't see what he was
doing . . . or what was being done to him."

Done to him? Luke thought.

"We thought about going down. Maybe he'd cracked, right? But de-
scents have been tricky the past few weeks. A lot of subsurface disturbances,
the most serious being a current ring situated directly above the trench."

"Current ring?"

"An underwater tornado, basically. An eddy sucking a billion-odd tons
of water into itself, creating a funnel. We sent a supply drone down last
week; the eddy caught it, spun it, and smashed it into the trench wall."

"And you expect *me* to go down into that?"

"The ring cleared two days ago. The sea's gone sleepy again. Anyway,
we didn't go down for two reasons." She held up a finger. "*One,* because
of the current ring"—she held up a second finger—"and *two,* because
your brother, whose contact had become sporadic, assured us things
were fine. Then today, in the early hours of morning, *Challenger* 4, which
had been docked to the *Trieste,* began to rise. Westlake was inside. How
he'd managed to get the sub working—he hadn't been trained in its operation—is unknown.

"A few things happened during Westlake's ascent, all of them bad.
First, we lost contact with the *Trieste* altogether. The comm link went
kerflooey, or else someone shut it off. Second, we lost most of the monitors. We'd already lost a few, but this was a whole whack of them, all at
once. Could be a technical issue. A major circuit blowout. Or else someone down there wanted them off."

*Someone or some*thing, Luke thought irrationally.

"Something else happened as Westlake came up. Happened *to* him.
He could only have done it to himself."

Al's fingers were steady on the vault's handle, but a fragile muscle
fluttered next to her eye.

"You go ahead and open it," Luke said.

Without another word, she did so.

15.

AT FIRST LUKE COULDN'T TELL what he was looking at. His eyes rejected it, as it didn't fit any prior conceptions of the human form.

Dr. Westlake's naked body was a swollen mass of scar tissue. His body was *all* scars. A ballooned, inflated parody of the human form.

It appeared as if Westlake had been wrapped in pink elastic bands. Some were thick as garter snakes, others thin as copper wires. Some fibrous as canvas rigging, others frail as onionskin. They lapped over in gruesome profusion, each one nurtured to a sickening, sensuous bulbousity. It seemed as if at any moment they might burst open and thin ribbons of flesh would spool forth, covering the old scars in layers that further obscured the body trapped inside.

Westlake's frame was bent, each limb wrenched at an unnatural angle. The bends. Nitrogen bubbles had built up in the blood, snapping Westlake's bones as they expanded.

Luke wanted to look away. Couldn't.

Sweet Christ, his *face*. The scars were the worst there. Elsewhere they seemed to have been laid down haphazardly, but the ones on his face had a more considered appearance. They had been delivered with special care. His eyes were trapped inside swollen bulbs of flesh—if Luke were to touch them, he imagined they would feel like India rubber balls—each so huge that they projected from the wrecked tapestry of his face like plums. His lips had been sliced and had healed until the flesh knit together, upper lip wedded to bottom, fused into a thick band that curved upward in a grisly rictus. His nostrils had a feathered look, the flesh slit back in fragile petals that revealed candle-white sinus cavities.

"Shut it." Luke's voice was a frail whisper. "Please."

Al did so. Luke jackknifed at the waist, hands braced on his knees.

"How . . . ?"

"I wish I had any idea," Al said softly. "We found a scalpel in the sub. Its blade was gouged up, dull as a butter knife. We figure it'd been used to cut through flesh, tendon, cartilage. Eventually it went dull on the bone."

"It's not possible, Al. I mean, that kind of trauma . . . how long does it take to surface?"

"Eight or nine hours usually. Westlake came faster, which is why he got the bends. He decompressed too fast. Truth is, we were fully expecting that it wouldn't be pretty. But no way could we have imagined this."

"He did this to himself?"

"Who else? The submarine was empty."

Totally empty? Luke wondered. *What if Westlake had been carrying that goo?*

"We didn't find any ambrosia," Al said before Luke could ask. "We tore the sub apart and found not a trace of the stuff. Just the scalpel, Westlake's body, and one more thing."

"What was that?"

"Luke," Al said carefully, "Felz showed you the mouse video, right? You see what that stuff can do. A godsend? I can see that. But I can see other things, too."

She didn't need to finish. Luke had the same vision. Westlake rising up from Challenger Deep, hacking into himself—and every time he cut himself, he healed so fast that it was almost immediate. Luke pictured an endless zipper: Westlake's flesh opening, only to close a few moments after the scalpel slit it, leaving very little blood and a ragged scar. Westlake could have sliced himself for hours, reducing himself in some exquisite way, laughing or shrieking or crying or who-knows-what, mindlessly—or *mindfully?*—layering scar over scar until . . . what? How did he die? Had the ambrosia deserted him? *Evanesced,* as Felz said?

Luke closed his eyes. The absolute worst of all was the expression frozen on Westlake's face. Luke was quite certain he died smiling.

"What else, Al? What was inside the submersible?"

She set a hand on Luke's shoulder. Luke didn't realize how badly he'd been shaking. It had nothing to do with how cold the room felt.

16.

DR. FELZ WASN'T THERE when they returned to the deck of the *Hesperus*. They got into the cart, both of them sitting on the rear seat.

"Go," Al told the driver.

Luke couldn't inhale enough air to inflate his lungs. He couldn't unsee Dr. Westlake's horrible, twisted body. For the first time, doubt seeped into Luke's mind. Why did he have to go down, anyway? He wasn't saying he *wouldn't*, but why him? He hadn't asked this most elementary question when the phone had woken him two days ago. He'd flown to Guam unquestioningly, as many people might when their government made the request. He paid his taxes and renewed his license and never caught more fish than his limit, too. He wanted to help, to do something good, just as Leo Bathgate did. Governments approved of citizens like Luke Nelson.

Plus there was no one on the other side of his bed to tell Luke *not* to go. And the room down the hall that his son had once slept in was empty, too.

"Why me?" he said. "Clayton's my brother, but we aren't close. I don't have any specific skills that might help you out down there."

"We'll make a motley pair then, won't we?" said Al. "What you're asking, I take it, is why don't we send down a crew of Special Forces badasses and put things right? We considered it. Dismissed it. First, that current ring made it dangerous to get down until recently. Second, the two men still down there—your brother and Dr. Toy—wield the whip hand now. They're inside, we're outside. I'll give you a full debriefing later, but suffice it to say, the *Trieste* is fragile. All it takes is one screwdriver—pierce any wall just a fraction and it's pancake city. So if we head down cocked and locked, well, what do we stand to lose if things go sideways? Everything. Absolutely everything."

"That's a cheerful thought. Jesus."

They passed down a row of low, black, flat-sided buildings connected by linked walkways; they made Luke feel like he was touring a medium-security prison.

"But why *you*?" Al said. "Good question. You're as green at deep dives as I am at neutering spaniels, right? The main reason, Luke, is that your brother asked for you."

"Get out of here."

She pulled an iPhone from her pocket and thumb-shuffled until she found what she was looking for. "This came through fifty hours ago. You received a call in Iowa City shortly thereafter. Sound file, no video. It stands as our last contact with your brother. We were debating whether to act on it, but the Westlake situation forced our hand."

She pressed *play*. Clayton's voice floated out of the speaker.

"Come home, Lucas. Come down, Lucas. We need you, Lucas. Come home."

Clayton's flat, monotone cadence was rendered tinny by the recording. Clayton sounded as if he was asleep; his voice was syrupy and water-warped, like a 45 rpm record playing at a relaxed 33 rpm. That could be a problem with the transmission itself, which had to carry through eight miles of water. Clayton repeated himself again before the message cut out abruptly.

"We need you, Lucas. Come ho—"

"It took a while to figure out who *Lucas* was," said Al. "Your brother doesn't speak about his family. We figured it could've been a research associate, a friend, a lover even. Our intel people dug around a bit and figured he must've been talking about you."

"But Clayton doesn't need me. He doesn't need anyone. He never has."

Except for those nights when the sleep terrors descended on him, he thought. *The nights when you'd climb into bed with him until he settled down.* But that was years ago, when they were only boys.

Yet Clayton had been saying *We need you*. We. WE. We who?

"Think of him as our pampered rock star whose rider calls for a big bowl of M&M's, only the red ones," said Al. "In this case, he's asking for his brother. We give him what he wants—making every effort to preserve your safety, of course."

"Why would he want me down there?"

Al cocked her head. "You put people's minds and bodies under that kind of pressure . . . Things snap, right? We want to do everything possible to avoid that snap."

"So that's what I am, then? A bandage?"

"Think of yourself more as a key."

Luke couldn't imagine his brother needing a bandage, anyway. He was armor plated, titanium coated. But that voice . . . it hadn't sounded entirely like Clayton. Granted, it had been years since they'd last spoken, but still, something was *off* about it. The difference wasn't in the words themselves or the pitch of his voice—it lurked somewhere behind the obvious, sly and scuttling like rats in the walls.

Come home, Lucas. Come home come home come home . . .

"That's not my home down there," he said.

Al said: "It's nobody's home. Trust me."

Two rights, a left, and they came to another dry dock. Three subs were cradled in hammocks. The numbers 2, 3, and 1 lay on their flanks. A workman was filling a seam in one of them with foam that pumped from a sophisticated caulking gun.

"That's the secret ingredient," Al told Luke. "Some kind of superfoam that expands or compresses depending on pressure. It can withstand fifty tons per square inch. The *Trieste* is held together with the stuff. Cost a billion-plus to develop, but it's worth every dime."

Luke followed Al across the tarmac. It was like being on the deck of an aircraft carrier—the sky was wide and trackless, the sun beating down from a cloudless sky. It was so hot that the patching tar had softened; it clung to the treads of their boots like Black Jack chewing gum.

Another sub was partially obscured by a pile of pallets; all Luke saw was its back end canted over the water. It sat in moody isolation, its stocky shape banded by yellow tape—the kind that ringed a crime scene.

"The MPs are still investigating," Al said. "It seems worthless." She laughed without mirth. "Like investigating a haunting or something."

The *Challenger* 4 rounded into view. Luke's lips curled in an instinctive expression of distaste.

It looked no different than the sub he'd seen earlier, and yet it repelled his gaze. There was something profoundly awful about it. He sensed that Al felt the same way about it—and he imagined it unnerved her just as it did him, because rational minds objected to unreasoned fear.

Perhaps it was because it had traveled so far below the sun's reach. The pressure had warped it, giving its shape a madman's hint of those depths. Or perhaps it was what happened within it—in Luke's head, the sight of it melded with that of Westlake's tortured corpse. The vessel was hateful in some way he could not accurately distill.

Al approached it, and Luke reluctantly followed. An awful coldness wept off the sub's metal. Had it carried up that icy chill from the Challenger Deep itself?

Al wrenched the hatch wheel. The muscles trembled up her arms, as if a subconscious part of her rebelled at the act.

The hatch was circular, slightly smaller than a manhole cover, a solid foot of steel. Al let it *clunk* against the hull.

A smell wafted out. Luke had never inhaled its equal. Raw, adrenal, and profoundly human.

The stink of insanity, Edie, sharp as malt vinegar, as his mother once said.

Luke bent to peer inside. Several deflated bladders dangled down inside the cabin; he could only suppose that they were the equivalent of nautical air bags.

What he didn't see yet was blood, which was incredible considering what had occurred inside. Maybe the MPs had swabbed it out already?

"You're gonna need to crane your neck," he heard Al say. "Look higher."

He crouched, neck twisted at an uncomfortable angle. Something was written on the far wall. Rust-colored scratches. Messy, frantic.

He dipped lower, aware of the blood-beat in his ears. The scratches resolved themselves into . . . letters?

And that rusty discoloration.

Blood. There it was. Dried blood.

Letters, but he could make out only their undersides. The bulbous lower swoop of a *C*; the jagged horizontal slash of an *E*.

Luke knelt until his knees hit the deck. It was the only way to contort his head enough to see what had been written inside.

Five words. All written in a crazed, spiky scrawl—written in the blood that had momentarily gushed from Westlake's innumerable wounds. Five words in one string, seven in the other.

THE AG MEY ARE HERE
COME HOME WE NEED YOU COME HOME

Crystals of ice gathered up Luke's spine. The words were grotesque in the same way Westlake's body had been: the letters were swollen and lewd, the blood dried thickly on their outer curves like paint slopped heavily on a fence slat. More unsettlingly, those words recalled Clayton's voice, calling out to Luke from the icy depths of the sea.

We need you, Lucas. Come home.

PART 2

DESCENT

1.

THE EVENING DARK hung against a paling sky. Alice had left Luke to his own devices while she made the final preparations for their descent.

It seemed absurd: less than an hour from now, Luke would be inside a cramped sub, free-falling eight miles down through the Pacific. But then, was it absurd? The circumstances of his life made him the perfect candidate, if you looked closely.

Luke was a divorced veterinarian. He spayed calicos and repaired budgies' split beaks. He still lived in the modest home he and his wife once shared with their son, not far from the university campus. On quiet Saturdays in September he could hear the roar from Kinnick Stadium.

His son, Zachary Henry Nelson, had vanished seven years ago. He had never been found. His bedroom was unchanged: the baseball motif wallpaper, dusty toys shoved underneath the bed. All waiting for him when he got back.

Luke's life had stopped, fundamentally *stopped*, on a cool autumn evening seven years ago. As pitiful as it may be, he had no reason *not* to be here, accepting the task set before him. It gave his life a small but vital sense of purpose.

He sat on the edge of the *Hesperus*, his feet dipped in the sea. The water held cascading shades: a pure aquamarine deepening to more enveloping blues. A school of orange-and-pearl fish made lively darts at an algae-slick chain. The fish had curved, sickle-shaped jaws. They looked predatory, like midget piranhas.

Those fish would've scared Zach. There was a time in the boy's life when he'd been scared of *everything*. Luke recalled how, at five, Zach (like many five-year-olds) had become convinced that a monster lurked in his closet. Luke reacted by flinging Zach's closet door open and rattling the coat hangers.

"See, Zachy? No monster. You're perfectly safe, I promise. Monsters aren't real. They're just figments of your imagination."

Zach looked even more petrified. "Fig Men?"

Luke nearly burst out laughing. He pictured these bloated, misshapen, fruitlike creatures, the Fig Men, massing in his son's closet.

"Not Fig Men, Zach, fig*ments*. Figments aren't real. Your mind is making them up, that's all. No Fig Men. No monsters."

But that night, Zach crept into their room and curled up on the floor.

"What are you doing here, buddy?"

"The Fig Men are in my closet," Zach whispered.

Luke got up and marched his son back to his bedroom.

"There is *no* monster, Zach. No Fig Men. Didn't I show you that?"

"That was in the daytime," Zach said with bone-deep worry. "Monsters hide from grown-ups in the day. It's night now."

But Luke was adamant. "I'll leave the hall light burning, buddy. That's the best I can do. You've got to sleep in your own bed, okay?"

Zach pulled the covers up to his throat and nodded wretchedly.

Back in bed, Abby said: "You're not being fair, Luke. Zach's allowed to be scared. He's a kid. There shouldn't be a penalty in this house for being scared."

Luke knew she was right. Your child doesn't owe you loyalty or obedience. You owe your child love and understanding, owe it unconditionally, and if you love them strongly enough, eventually that love may be returned. Luke's own mother had never seen it that way. She thought Luke and Clay owed her love regardless of how she treated them.

Luke got out of bed and grabbed his toolbox. He returned to Zach's room and pointed at the closet.

"So this is where the Fig Men are lurking?"

Zach nodded forlornly. Luke cracked the toolbox and pulled out a stud finder. He ran it over the closet walls and made a few exploratory taps with his knuckles.

"There are traces of ectoplasm," he said in the tone of a veteran con-tractor. "That's monster slime, in layman's terms. What do these suckers look like?"

Zach said: "*Old*, all wrinkly, like they've lived a million years."

The short hairs stood up on the back of Luke's neck. Something about the way his son said that one word, *old*, was chilling. Luke didn't feel like laughing this time. The Fig Men—these twisted, ancient, cal-culating little devils hunched in the dark closet, peering at his son through the slats with cruel avidity—had taken on a sinister shape in his mind.

Luke gripped his chin, putting on a good show. "The Fig Men. I've never heard of them specifically, but harmless monsters do infest closets and crawl spaces. They usually like sweet stuff—you haven't been keep-ing anything tasty in your closet, have you?"

"That's where I put my Halloween candy."

"Well, that'll give you a Fig Man problem. Now, I'm sure they're not dangerous—just gross. But if you let a few hang around they'll call their buddies and before long you've got an infestation on your hands."

"I don't want that, Daddy."

"I've got good news and bad news," said Luke. "What do you want first?"

Zach said: "Good."

"Good news is I can get rid of the Fig Men."

Luke rooted through his toolbox for a pouch of fine red powder.

"This is cardamom; it's made from the crushed shells of stag beetles. It's used in monster containment spells."

Luke laid down a line of powder in the shape of a keyhole.

"Now this," he said, "is the trap. The Fig Men will wander up this path, which gets narrower and narrower until—*bang-o!*—they get stuck. The circle closes and the Fig Men will starve overnight. They'll turn black and hard as a rock. Now the bad news, Zach. You have to pull one hair out of your head, and that'll hurt a bit."

"Why?"

"Fig Man bait."

Zach plucked a strand of hair. Luke laid it in the middle of the trap.

"You know what'd help? Something sweet. Why don't you and Mom go downstairs and grab a few chocolate chips."

While they were downstairs, Luke hustled into his bedroom and grabbed two small chunks of obsidian he'd picked up during a trip to Hawaii years ago. He set them in the middle of the ring and shut the closet.

When Zach returned, Luke strung the chocolate chips along the edge of the closet door.

"The sweetness will draw those Fig Men out of hiding. Now Zach, the trap is set. But if you open the closet the spell will be broken. So you *must* not open it until tomorrow morning. Promise?"

"I promise."

"Cross your heart and hope to die?"

"Stick a needle in my eye," Zach said solemnly.

"Do you want to sleep in our bed tonight?"

Zach shook his head. "I'm okay now."

Back in the bedroom, Abby kissed him with uncommon ardor. Luke enjoyed a deep dreamless sleep, feeling very much like a minor superhero. The next morning, Zach flung the closet open.

"The trap worked!" he cried.

He raced into their bedroom clutching the blackened, calcified Fig Men.

"It's a cocoon," Luke said. "Except these ones are hard—a prison. The Fig Men will never be able to escape. Put them on display as a warning to any other monster that might wander along. It's not every day that you can hold a monster in your palm."

Zach set them on his nightstand. They were still there, in the room Luke had left untouched since the day his son had gone missing—

A shadow fell over Luke's shoulder, snapping him back to reality. The minipiranhas scattered, zipping under the *Hesperus* in a silvery flashing of scales.

"You about ready?" Al asked.

Spider legs scuttled up the lining of Luke's stomach.

2.

CHALLENGER 5 WAS SUSPENDED from a miniature sky crane. Its hatch hung open like a hungry mouth.

Luke carried only a duffel bag with a change of clothes and a cable knit sweater. Plus a toiletry kit with a toothbrush, toothpaste, a stick of deodorant.

Where will I spit my toothpaste? he wondered. There couldn't be a drainage system. No conventional toilets, either—one flush and the pressure would probably cave in the *Trieste*.

I'll swallow my toothpaste, he thought. *And pee in a bottle.*

"I'll get in first and take the cockpit. You'll sit a little lower." Al smiled. "It's a good news, bad news scenario. Good news is, you get the better view. Bad news is, your head's going to be parallel with my behind."

Luke grinned despite the quivers that kept rippling through his belly. Al ducked through the hatch. Luke realized for the first time that the vessel was designed to dive vertically: they'd be arrowing straight down into the black.

Luke ducked and stuck his head inside the sub. The sight reminded him of the cockpit of a commercial jetliner, only much more cramped.

"Hop in," Al said from inside, already flicking switches. "You'll have to tuck your knees, and be careful not to touch anything unless I ask you to."

The webbing of Luke's seat sagged like a hammock; Luke sank into it so deeply that his chin nearly touched his knees. Instrumentation panels sat a few inches off each shoulder, their uncomfortable electrical warmth bathing his face. His body tightened instinctually, his muscles and posture contracting; it felt a little like being trapped at the bottom of a village well, except there wasn't even a view of the sky. Al sat a few feet above with her back to Luke. She craned her head down.

"Comfy, uh? Wish I could let you pop an Ambien and sleep through the descent, but that shit does a number on your blood—added pressure, yeah?"

Luke had never considered how it might feel to be buried alive in a buzzing, blinking, high-tech coffin, but he had a good sense of it now.

The hatch closed with a satisfying *thunk*—the sound of a luxury car door slamming shut. A gassy hiss was followed by a volley of pressurized *tinks!*

Al said: "It's a high-pressure vacuum, drawing out every bit of excess air. Then the seal will engage."

A workman appeared in the porthole window. Luke couldn't hear anything outside now. The sub must be noise-proof. The man's hands clutched one of those high-tech caulking guns; a puffy crust of foam began to encircle the window.

"They're foaming the seals," said Al. "The entire vessel will get a coating, except for the bank of high-intensity spotlights running down each side. You okay?"

"Yeah," Luke said. "Just . . . this is really happening."

"Try to relax. I'm kicking on the air recycler."

Cool air pumped around Luke's feet from pinhole vents. It had the same chemical tang that puffed from the vault containing Westlake. Luke was worried that his lungs would lock up, refusing to inhale the foul stuff.

The crane lifted the sub and pinioned it over the water.

"Buckle up," Al said. "The crane operator's got a heavy hand."

As soon as Luke's belt clicked, they dropped. His stomach leapt as it would on a roller coaster. They hammered the sea's surface. Water climbed the porthole. Luke's breath came in shallow gulps.

Breathe, he chided himself. *You're safe, totally safe.*

His final surface sight was of a new moon hovering in its eastern orbit: a waxen ball whose light plated the slack darkness of the sea.

Then they slipped under and were gone.

3.

AL FLICKED SWITCHES and twisted knobs. Her hand entered Luke's peripheral vision, toggling a joystick near his ear.

"This tub's got three motors, but they're strictly for stabilization and maneuvering," she said. "We're carrying three thousand pounds of lead weights. We just *drop*. When we want to surface, we'll start shedding those lead plates bit by bit."

"How fast are we falling?"

"About thirteen hundred meters per hour. I'll increase that as the currents subside. Once we enter the Mariana Trench, three miles down, there's no current at all. Then we'll go faster—the proverbial hot knife through butter."

Some part of the vessel whined. Al made a minute adjustment, and the unpleasant noise stopped. Air bubbles scrolled around the window, delicate as those in a glass of champagne. The darkness was as absolute as the bottom of a mine shaft.

Luke said, "Christ, that's desolate."

"That's the sea at night," Al said, laughing a little uneasily. "Don't you worry, it'll get even darker. You've never seen the kind of dark we're gonna encounter."

They were already beyond the point of the deepest free-dive; Luke figured it wouldn't be long before they passed the point of the deepest scuba dive. After that they'd reach the depth where oxygen toxicity set in: the nitrogen levels change and the air in a scuba diver's tank turns poisonous. Finally, they'd enter the lung-splintering depths where humans simply didn't belong.

A fizzy pop shot through Luke's veins. He felt a subtle expansion between his joints. It wasn't painful—more like being tickled inside his bones.

Al modified their trajectory. The submarine stabilized.

"Nitrogen buildup. You feel it? We'll hang out here a minute," she said. "We're in the 'Midnight Zone,' by the way. Complete darkness. We'll stop again at twenty-five hundred meters—the 'Abyssal Zone.'"

The tickle subsided. The sea was a solid wall of black through the porthole. There was nothing out there. The bleakness crawled inside Luke's skull.

"Check it out," Al said. "Light show coming off your starboard side in five, four, three, two—"

It started as tiny, vibrantly glowing specks. They accumulated slowly, drifting on the current. A hundred became a thousand became a numberless quantity. A swarm of neon creatures a hundred feet wide, giving a sense of depth to the ocean in the same way the sweep of a flashlight will reveal a huge cave.

Some were small as grains of sand; others were the size of no-see-ums; a precious few were the size of summer fireflies. They glowed warmest amber. Their bodies brightened and dimmed like embers in a fire.

"Phytoplankton," Al said. "They're bioluminescent. You'll see more of this kind of thing the deeper we go. Until we get too deep . . . then you won't see a damn thing."

The plankton flurried like flakes of snow. Just like the night Luke met Abby.

In that moment, Luke was back in Iowa City with his ex-wife—except she wasn't even his wife then. She was twenty-two-year-old Abigail Jeffries of Chicago, Illinois. He met her at an intra-faculty mixer for seniors at the U of I. It happened that very night. Luke fell madly in love with Abby Jeffries. All parts of her, even the parts that remained unknown to him then.

In time he'd come to love her chipped canine tooth, her snaggletooth as she called it, which she never bothered to get capped under the belief that a face without flaws was a face lacking character. He loved her habit of squeaking after she sneezed. He loved the way her skin sparkled after sex. He loved everything about her, indiscriminately.

That first night they left the mixer and hit a bar. When everyone got kicked out at last call, they'd staggered happily down East Jefferson hand in hand. Snow had been falling, big fat flakes swarming out of the sky like the plankton was doing right now . . .

The glowing flakes scattered as a monolithic shape passed by the *Challenger*. Luke glimpsed a pitted wall of blue-gray flesh. For a heart-stopping instant, he saw an eye the size of a dinner plate, a ring of shocking white banding a black pupil.

The *Challenger* rocked; the displacement of water felt roughly akin to a tractor-trailer flying past his car on the highway.

"Sperm whale," Al said. "It's the only creature that big that could exist down here. I've never spotted one this low."

Al cut the motors. The descent continued.

Luke's back was beginning to ache.

"Can I stand up?"

"Go right ahead."

Luke managed to stretch a bit, taking the pressure off his hips.

He watched Al work. She piloted the *Challenger* with easy authority—it reminded Luke of observing an experienced veterinarian perform routine surgery. There was an air of practiced boredom to the way Al's hands moved over the controls.

"You don't seem too concerned about all this," Luke said.

"If you're talking about the dive, I'm okay," she said. "I brought your brother and the others down. Supplies and food and scientific doodads after that, before the drones were operational. Hell, on my last descent I brought a poster of Albert Einstein. I'm a glorified delivery girl.

"The thing is—and I'm sorry if this doesn't make you feel any better— at a certain depth, it doesn't matter. Where we're going, the pressure per square foot is the equivalent of twenty-seven jumbo jets. If we spring a pinhole leak, the water will come through with enough force to cut through three feet of solid steel. It'd slice us apart like flying Ginsu knives. This sub will crumple. It'll happen in a fraction of a heartbeat. Imagine being crushed between panes of extrathick glass traveling toward impact at the speed of sound." She *thwapped* her hands. "We're talking flesh pâté. Say good night, Gracie."

"Comforting image, that."

Al exhaled, jiggling a joystick using a few deft strokes.

"Listen, Luke—dying that way, crushed in the blink of an eye . . . there are worse ways to go down here. We've only lost two men so far. But we've lost a bunch of drones and . . ." She bit down, her teeth making an audible *click*. "You ever hear the term *short*, Doc?"

"You mean of stature?"

"No, there's another meaning. It's a military term: *short-timer*. It's when you're at the end of a long hitch, just before you hit furlough. In a combat zone, that's the most superstitious time. When the fates are gonna take a swipe at you. People get hinky. *I'm so short I could parachute off a dime, man.* That's kinda how I feel. The more dives I make, the more I test this big black motherfucker, the Mariana, the more I'm sure it's going to . . . Jesus. I'm sorry. I'm rambling. We're fine and we're going to *be* fine."

"I trust you," Luke said simply.

A stiff bark of laughter from Al. "Try to catch a nap if you can. Sleep might be tough to come by the deeper we go; the pressure can mess with your REM patterns."

The sea swept against the *Challenger*'s hull with a lush suctioning. Luke felt as though he was in an elevator plummeting to the bottom of the world—closing his eyes, he envisioned red numerals flashing past:

10, 9, 8, 7, 6, 5, 4, 3, 2, G, P1, P2, P3, B, SB, SSB . . .

Sub-subbasement—did floors go any lower?

"The Ag Mey."

"Hmm?" said Al.

"*The Ag Mey Are Here.* The words written inside the *Challenger*. They have any meaning to you?"

Al sounded curious. "Is that how you read it?"

"What, you saw it differently?"

"Yeah. *Man*," she said. "The Something-Man."

"The Ag Man are here?"

Al shrugged. "Nonsense words, Doc. The grammar doesn't even jibe. I don't presume they'd have meant much to Dr. Westlake by the time he wrote them."

4.

LUKE SHUT HIS EYES. He was hungry but he didn't feel like eating; the sea seemed to reach through the submarine's walls, pressing uncomfortably on his stomach. His thoughts circled back to his mother. He was anxious, and during such times his mind would stalk the walled-off corners of his memory relentlessly, chasing a handful of dire recollections like a terrier down a rat-hole.

After she was put on disability from the Second Chance Ranch, Luke's mother began to eat. It became an obsession. Though she'd always been sturdy, she'd never been much of an eater—only enough to sustain her frame. She took no apparent joy in eating, and that never changed—only the *quantity* changed.

Porridge. She'd cook it in a huge steel pot—three, four pounds of edible sludge—and gorge herself in front of the television, eating it with the same sterling silver baby spoon she'd used to feed pabulum to her infant boys.

After a while the smell of cooking porridge was enough to make Luke feel ill. He'd come home and find his mother in the dark, eating congealed porridge with a wet-mouthed vacancy, her lips moving like a horse eating sugar cubes.

At first she simply got thick . . . a solidity over her arms and legs and bosom that gave her a matronly look. But she kept shoveling in that gray gruel and soon thickness gave way to bloated girth. Her arms projected from the sleeves of her shapeless shifts like the booms on a sailboat, larded with folds of quaking flesh that resembled hunks of wet wool. Her thighs widened to the point that when sitting, her legs appeared to be welded together: a vast blanket of quivering skin. When she limped from her spot on the chair, her thighs rubbed together with a raw whispery note. Her features receded into the shapeless bloat of her face. Her eyes stared out of that netted flesh like two raisins thumbed into proofing dough.

"We are all but flesh," she would say to Luke's father when he dared mention that she might think about cutting a few carbs, "and we will all go the way of all flesh."

As her size increased, so did her cruelty. Especially to her husband. It was a sport to her. She'd belittle the man in front of his boys and torture him far worse in private moments.

One night, unable to sleep, Luke had crept downstairs for a glass of milk. On the way back to his room, he passed his parents' open door. He caught the rustling of sheets, the movements of bodies.

Next: a breathless exhale. It sounded like the moan of a man who'd been stabbed and wanted to deal with the injury as quietly as possible.

"You dirty boy."

His mother's voice.

You dirty boy.

It wasn't an endearment or a sly encouragement. No, this was more as if Luke's father really *was* a boy, a depraved and softheaded one, who'd been found under the porch steps smeared with his own excrement. Yet his father moaned in that soft, gut-stabbed way and whispered: "*Yes, yes, so fucking bad.*"

She ruined Luke's father, decimated him until he sickened her. Her bulk would have cooled the ardor of some other men, but it only intensified his father's servility. Like a whipped dog, he mooned around her petticoats, begging for scraps of affection, which only deepened his mother's loathing.

All day she had nothing to do but sit in the dark, dreaming up ways to dominate the household. She'd squashed her husband already. Clayton was either down in his lab or, in later years, pursuing his projects at sponsoring labs. Beth's immediate project was Luke, who by then had discovered the vast well of malice that lurked inside his mother.

Luke had once returned from his fifth-grade classes to find her in the tub. She was in the bathroom Luke and Clay used, even though she had her own. She didn't sound a warning as Luke climbed the staircase and stared at him silently when he opened the door. Her body was ghostly and pale. Bubbles clung to the edges of the tub, gray and scummy, darkened from the dirt off her body. Her belly was ribbed with fat, her breasts huge and sallow.

Luke's eyes dipped. She'd said nothing, *willing* them to rise again. He slammed the door.

"Don't you ever *knock*?" her voice boomed from behind it.

Despite this, Luke continued to bring her a glass of Ovaltine after school, sitting at her feet like a lapdog. She'd slurp it and gawp at the TV—it played soaps or infomercials, although Luke figured she'd be just as happy with a test pattern. Sometimes she would say the nicest things. *Lucas, you're my angel. How would I live without you?* But she could turn sadistic without warning. One time she'd stared at him dolorously and spoke in a dry monotone. *I had such high hopes for you. Such high, high hopes.*

In time, Luke believed his mother only said the nice things so that the barbs would sting even more.

Not long after the bathtub incident, he'd come home to find his comic book collection on the front lawn with a sign reading: FREE.

"You're too old for comics," she'd told him, sunk down in her easy chair with a dollop of porridge on her chin. "We must all let go of childish things."

"But—"

Her head swiveled, eyes peering out from pits of buttery flesh.

"But nothing. Let some younger boys in the neighborhood have your funny books. You've read the damn things how many times already."

Funny books. These weren't Archies or Casper the Friendly Ghosts. These were Daredevils and Wolverines. They weren't *funny*.

"But . . . they're mine. I'm collecting them."

"All they're collecting is dust. They're gone, Lucas. The matter is settled."

He'd turned his back on her, tears scalding his cheeks. Those comics weren't just ink on paper—they represented freedom from the increasing hostility of his home life. He could dive into those pages and spend time with characters who were larger than life, fearless, and did right by others. He'd even created a superhero alter ego, joining the cast of caped crusaders and crime fighters in his favorite comics. The *Human Shield*. As Luke envisioned it, his alter ego had touched a glowing asteroid that bestowed a singular trait upon him: his flesh was impenetrable. Nothing could hurt him: not bullets, not blades, not even a heat-seeking missile. The Human Shield's role was to stand in front of children and single mothers while his superhero pals battled their archenemies; any stray laser beams or pumpkin bombs would strike his body, which safely absorbed the blast. He wasn't one of the top-tier superheroes, but he was allowed to hang out at the Hall of Justice and X-Mansion, rubbing elbows with Aquaman and Marvel Girl. What Luke liked best about being the Human Shield was his ability to protect the innocent without fear—because his home life was by then characterized by a marrow-deep, ever-present dread.

Looking back, Luke was sure this was why his mother had chosen the comic books. It could have been his action figures or his bike, but he could've parted with those easily. The comics opened up a new world to him, a place where he was safe. And his mother wanted to rip that haven away from him.

Luke hadn't dared retrieve the comics from the lawn. By that evening, the grass was picked clean. From that time forward, Luke made a point out of secrecy: if his mother was unaware of the things that gave him joy, she couldn't take them away. But she had other ways to maintain her dominance.

One night she'd climbed the staircase, each step whining under her bulk, and opened his bedroom door. Luke had been sleeping alone; Clayton was in the basement most nights. She crossed the room with thudding footfalls, threw back the covers, and slid into his bed. The springs squealed and the mattress took a sickening downward lurch. Luke felt as if he were being sucked down into greedy quicksand.

She nestled her body up with his, spooning him. There was nothing motherly in the embrace. He caught the acrid whiff of her armpits and the dense, peaty scent wafting from her mouth.

She curled an arm around him; his pajama top had rucked up, and she spread her hand across his bare belly. Her flesh was sickeningly warm, a hot water bottle packed with boiled lard.

Her index finger tapped his stomach in time with the beat of his heart. As its rate accelerated, so did her tapping. Her mouth was close to his neck, her breath moistening the downy hairs. He was certain she'd sink her teeth into him, holding tight as she ate him the way she ate her porridge: in tiny, tiny bites.

Part of Luke realized she was trying to break him, as she'd already done to his father. Fear equaled control in the mind of Bethany Ronnicks. It was an effective tool. But only if you stood for it.

She wasn't really clever. Luke had been coming to that realization for a while by then. Not smart, just cunning. Animals were cunning. Animals also ate their own shit and chewed live electrical wires.

The only way to deal with monsters—real or imagined—was to show no fear. You had to become the Human Shield.

Luke opened his eyes and gripped her wrist. Her muscles tensed under their encasement of flab. Shifting his weight, he slung himself out from under her and landed on the floor with a graceless thump. He stood and retreated to the door.

"Where are you going?" A mocking coo.

"This isn't your bedroom, Mom. You don't sleep here."

"This is my house." All mockery gone. "I sleep where I goddamn like."

"Then I'll sleep somewhere else."

"Get. Back. *Here.*"

Luke hesitated . . . then left. He got halfway down the hallway and collapsed. What had he done? He was only thirteen. He couldn't leave the house. He was trapped. What would his mother do to him now? What would she—

Luke awoke with a start. The dim ticking of instruments, the rush of water against the hull. He was in the *Challenger*. The heat of the instruments pulled sweat out of his pores. Alice stared down at him with concern.

"You're okay, Doc. You were dreaming."

Luke wiped at the drool on his chin, mortified. "How long was I out?"

"Couldn't have been more than a few minutes. You were grinding your teeth; sounded like rocks in a blender. Mumbling, too."

Alice was leaning over, her hand on his shoulder. He felt the warmth of her flesh and caught the scent of her body—the softest note of vanilla. It wasn't perfume; Al didn't seem the sort to wear it. Probably just a dab of hand cream—it was dry as a desert inside the sub, which was weird seeing as they were surrounded by water. She'd unzipped her overalls a little—the heat was intense—and Luke couldn't help his eyes from orienting on that slice of bare flesh trailing down to the dampened hem of her tank top . . .

He wrenched his eyes up to her face. She was watching him impassively, her head slightly cocked.

Enjoying the view? her expression seemed to say. There was no recrimination in it, just a vague sense of mirth.

"What did I say?" Luke asked. "When I was sleeping, I mean."

"*Get behind me.*" She smiled as if to say it wasn't anything he ought to be embarrassed about. "*Get behind me where it's safe* or something like that."

5.

THE *CHALLENGER* LEVELED OFF. They were presently over twenty thousand feet undersea. Luke heard sly pops and crackles, the sound of Rice Krispies doused in milk.

"Relax, that's just the foam," Al said. "It's compressing to bear the strain."

The view was disorienting. Profound, terrible darkness. What could possibly live down here? Luke pictured the water rolling away for miles in every direction, empty and pitiless. This stratum was cleansed of nearly all the fundamental assets that foster life—sunlight, warmth, air, food—so the only creatures that lived in it should be, by definition, less than whole. Their skin would be jellylike; Luke imagined bodies draped in a thin stretching of greased latex, like condom skin. He almost laughed at the idea of schools of condom fish flitting through the deeps—

Tink!

Something struck the porthole's glass, then pelted away.

Tink! Tink!

"Do you hear that?" he whispered.

Al's voice was tight. "Viperfish, I'm thinking."

The water exploded with frenzied movement.

Tink! Tink! Ti-tin-ti-ti-tink! Tink! TINK!

Luke recoiled as quicksilver flashes smashed into the glass.

Ti-tin-t-t-t-ti-TI-ti-TIN-TINK!

It sounded as if they were being shelled with machine-gun fire.

"Al, hey, is this normal?"

"Yeah, it's pretty unnerving," she said. "We'll be okay. Viperfish are the undersea version of wolverines. They'll attack anything, even if it's a hundred times their size."

Just then, a viperfish got snagged before the glass. Its jaws—huge, sickle shaped, fearsomely toothy—were enmeshed in the foam. The creature was long and eelish, with fluted gills and oily black eyes socked in a polished-steel face. It was the most predatory thing Luke had ever seen.

"They're mean as catshit," Al said. "And I'd say we've hit a swarm of them."

TINK! Ti-ti-ti-TINK!

"I've never seen so many of them. They're fixing to tear that foam to shreds. We gotta boogie, Luke. Hold on."

The *Challenger* plummeted. Luke caught a flash of the massing school of viperfish: a glowing sheet of bodies staggered into the water, tens of thousands of whiplike fish darting furiously about.

The sounds ceased as Al stabilized the vessel.

Tink!

"Fucking things," said Al. "We must be in a cone of them—there's no *way* they could drop that fast."

Again, the *Challenger* plunged. The pressure built in Luke's ears. That tickle returned to his bones, becoming quite painful now.

"Hold on," Al said. "I'm feeling it, too."

Luke's gums tightened around his teeth until he was sure they'd shatter. The plates of his skull ground together.

Al stabilized the sub again. She shot a look down at Luke. A rill of blood, as thin as a pencil line, was trickling out of her nose.

"You're bleeding," Luke said.

She wiped it away. "Yeah, you, too."

Luke wiped his nose. His fingers came away clean.

"Higher," said Al.

Luke felt wetness leaking from his eye. He wiped away a single, bloody tear. "Am I bleeding from my *eye*?"

Al nodded. "You'll be fine. Happens a lot down here. The blood comes out of you in funny, nontraditional places."

Luke wiped the bloody tear on his overalls. "That will take some getting used to."

They waited for those dreadful *tinks!* to resume. When they didn't,

Luke's heartbeat settled into its normal rhythm. Al jimmied the controls and got the *Challenger* dropping again at a more leisurely rate. Water *shushed* against the hull, causing the foam to issue splintery popping sounds. Luke blinked and swiped a finger under his eye. A watery rill of blood tracked across his fingertip, warm and—

SWACK!

Luke jolted in his seat. Something entirely different was stuck to the glass now. A band of albino tissue, shockingly thick.

"What the—" Al said as the *Challenger* juddered. "Oh, are you shitting me?"

The band thinned out as it flexed across the glass. Eight inches across, with a vein running under its skin that was so black it could've been filled with ink. Studded all along it were disks—they reminded Luke of the plastic suction cups you'd use to stick sun-catchers to your kitchen windows.

"It's a giant squid," Al said, although Luke somehow knew that already. "I didn't think we'd encounter one this far down."

The *Challenger* rattled. An alarm shrilled.

"For the love of fuck!" said Al, the words exiting her mouth with a brittle snip. She flicked a switch and the vessel went dark.

Luke's lungs locked up as an icy ball of terror crystallized in his chest. It was as if the sea itself had slid inside the *Challenger*, filling his eyes and throat and brain.

The squid's tentacle *sluuurp*ed across the glass. A shape shot out—*THACK!*—snapping violently. It was the squid's beak, which resembled that of an enormous parrot.

THACK!—harder this time.

Luke waited for the glass to crack and his life to end.

The lights flicked on.

"I thought it might leave us alone if we went dark," Al said in a low voice. "Let's try the opposite."

She hit the spotlights. They didn't illuminate much, despite their incredible intensity—a pall of sickly light picked up a patina of deep-sea sediment that swirled like dust in an enormous room.

The squid immediately detached and vanished with one convulsive flex. Luke got a split-second sense of its size: stunningly long, torsional and many limbed, whipping into the darkness like a bullet train speeding into a tunnel.

"Hold on," Al said, and again they dropped.

They seemed to be falling even faster—the depth gauge near Luke's head spun wildly, around and around like a cartoon clock. Al was busy with the readouts; thankfully, it appeared neither the squid nor viperfish had dealt the *Challenger* a terminal blow.

Shock-sweat had broken out all over Luke's body. Tiny beads of moisture clung to the hull, too.

"The sub's sweating," he said.

"That's normal," Al said tersely. "Condensation. Our breath. Cold as a witch's tit down here. Minus thirty or so."

"Doesn't the water freeze?"

"Never with saltwater. Not this deep."

Al shut the spotlights off, plunging the sea into darkness again.

"Wow. That was the weirdest thing," she said, exhaling heavily. "You have to understand—this is like the desert down here. It's barren. Picture it this way: we're a pin dropped into an Olympic swimming pool almost totally devoid of life. So why and how we've run across all these critters . . . it's just *weird*. And that they'd *attack* us . . . The viperfish I get, but the squid? And back-to-back like that? No. Just no."

"Not outside of a Jules Verne book, anyway." Luke's laughter held a glass-snap edge.

"Right, and then we've had that current ring the last week or so. Every possible disturbance you could encounter, we've been facing it lately," Al said. "If I didn't know any better I'd almost think . . ."

She trailed off, not saying the words. But Luke was thinking the same thing.

It's as if something is trying to stop us from reaching the Trieste.

6.

"THEY SHOULD'VE INSTALLED A RADIO in this thing," said Al, "or a CD player or something." She blew a raspberry. "They sunk a trillion bucks into this operation. A radio's gonna bankrupt 'em?

"They spent hand over fist," she went on. "Nobody had ever tried building anything like the *Trieste* before. Space shuttles, sure, but in space you're dealing with an absence of pressure. You can put on a suit, step out, float around. Try and do that down here and . . ."

"Flesh pâté."

"Bingo. They had to bring the station down in sections. Lots of trial and error, lots of problems. Dropped them with heavy weights, collected them with robotic dive craft. Every section came down encased in a protective shell, with a seam of foam sandwiched between. They got slotted together, riveted by the pressure-resistant robo-divers, foamed, then the shell was cracked away. The station was designed in the principles of orb physics; the egg was the designer's blueprint. Push on the sides of an egg, right, and it'll break. But if you press on the top and bottom, it's nearly unbreakable. A miracle of nature, or so they tell me.

"Plus the material the station's made out of . . . it's metal but *not* metal. Some kind of high-tech, ultra-state-of-the-art polymer core—it allows the tunnels to flex and bend and . . . *bubble,* I guess you could say? Instead of cracking under pressure, the material will expand the way rubber does. The water can warp it, but it won't burst through.

"Anyway, once the pieces of the station were all slotted together, someone had to go in and open it all up from the inside. There was this membrane linking each section that had to be cut and foamed simultaneously; if it sprung even one leak, the whole structure would flatten. Otto Railsback—that was the name of the guy. Wee scrap of a thing. A single man did the whole job. You want to talk about a real hero? I brought Otto down. He was the first man inside. I attached to the entry port, cracked the hatch, then he went inside."

"So what happened?" asked Luke, now fascinated.

"Well . . . I remember the smell that came out at first," Al said. "My family ran a ranch in Colorado. There was this cave system where I lived, Cave of the Winds. The main part was a tourist trap—drunk dudes wandering around with miner's helmets, calling themselves spelunkers. But the whole thing sprawled twenty miles underground. You could enter it through a vent in the forest floor about a mile from my home. Just a dark cut into the rocks, right? I went down there one day, alone. I was thirteen, fourteen. Thought I was a badass. I had a flashlight and a sack lunch.

"Predictably, I got lost. Thought I knew where I was going. Didn't. It got so deep and twisty that if it weren't for gravity, I wouldn't have known up from down. My flashlight went on the fritz. I sat in the dark with the rocks dripping around me." She paused, wrapped in the memory. "That darkness had *weight*, Doc. As a kid, it seemed *hostile*—like it wanted to keep me right where I was. And I was scared for practical reasons, too. I could've missed a step, slid down a shaft, and busted a leg. I'd have died down there. But I'd gotten into it, right? I had to get out. So I just listened. The dripping water helped. I figured it had to be trickling *down*, so I just had to follow it up. It was way past my curfew when I reached the cut. My dad skinned my ass raw."

She sipped water from a silver pouch that reminded Luke of a Capri Sun drink.

"Anyway . . . the smell in that cave was the same as what came out of the *Trieste*. This overwhelming *reek* of darkness. A raw mineral smell; it had presence, an aliveness, like in Cave of the Winds. It freaked me out—no good reason; just that old childish worry—but Otto went right in. He sealed the compartments, made the *Trieste* truly safe for habitation. After that, others came down to set up the gennies, the air purifiers. But Otto was the guy who got it all rolling. He was the only one who died in the *Trieste*, too."

"Jesus. How?"

"He just never came back out," said Al. "I waited and waited, but when he didn't show up they told me to resurface. I couldn't get inside, anyway. But surface diagnostics indicated the station was safe to enter, meaning Otto had completed his task. When the electrical team came down, they found him curled up in the animal quarantine. Dead. Embolism. He just finished his job, then laid down in the dark and died."

The only one who died, Luke thought, *except for Westlake.*

"It's all self-contained," Al said. "Electricity, air, waste removal. Food and water are brought down as needed. A perfect little microsystem that thumbs its nose at the laws of physics."

Luke barely heard her. He was still dwelling on Otto Railsback, who'd crawled diligently through the tunnels with his foam gun until he reached his own end.

7.

THERE IS A SPECIFIC DEPTH you'll hit where the soul finds it impossible to harmonize with its surroundings.

It's not the darkness. A man is acquainted with it by then—as acquainted as he can ever be. It's not the vast silence or the emptiness or the absence of any life-forms he can draw warmth or certainty from.

It's not the pressure. It's not even the fear of death that constantly nibbles at the edge of his mind.

It's the sense of unreality. This out-of-body feeling that you've stepped away from the path your species has always tread. Things become dreamlike, inessential. Your mind, seeking solace in the familiar, retreats to those things you understand, but those things become so much harder to grasp.

Memories degrade. You remember parts of people, but you surrender their wholes. Abby could crack an egg with one hand. It was a quirky skill Luke remembered wishing he had. He could still recall the sight of her doing it and the yearning that he could do it, too. But the more essential parts of her were already failing him.

The water wasn't the same down here.

Water is what runs out of our kitchen taps or a playground drinking fountain. It fills bathtubs and pools and yes, of course, the ocean—but at a certain depth, water becomes a barrier from all you remember, all you think you know.

You're trapped within it, a plaything of it.

Focus erodes. Your thoughts mutate. The pressure.

The *pressure*.

The soul can't cope with that. It shouldn't be expected to.

Humans weren't built for this. There's a reason nothing lives down here.

Or nothing should.

8.

LUKE WAS UNAWARE of the exact point when it began to snow.

Marine snow, according to Al. The detritus of animal and plant life that had died miles above. It fell steadily through each zone of the ocean, down and down, shredding into flakes, leached of pigment until it became bone white. A snow of death.

It fell without cease, each "flake" composed of lace-edged rags of flesh and bone and gut. Looking at it, Luke thought back to that first night with Abby—the snow falling from a coal-dark Iowa sky. He tried to isolate the details of Abby's face but they slithered through his mind, eel-ish and ungrippable.

Al toggled the joystick, angling the *Challenger* slightly downward.

"We're here," she said quietly.

Luke squinted through the porthole. Darkness thick as grave dirt. Then, permeating that darkness, the tiniest speck of light.

This speck attached to another speck, and another. From these specks, a rough shape resolved and the *Trieste* came into view. Luke sat by the window, jaw open, staring.

It was repulsive.

The blood backflowed in his veins, the strangest sensation—like a clock running backward against its mechanics, stripping gears and snapping springs.

We need to ascend now, he thought wildly. *Seek the sunlight, fast, and never come back.*

PART 3
THE TRIESTE

1.

LUKE COULD ONLY GLIMPSE the *Trieste* in sections. Whenever Al swung the *Challenger* around, illuminating a section he'd already seen, it looked different to Luke—as if it had shifted subtly, somehow reconfiguring its arrangement.

Luke's mind continued to fight the reaction of his initial horror. It was nothing but steel and foam and space-age polymers. A marvel of engineering. It of course had no mind, no will. And still . . .

It was awful. He couldn't isolate what repelled the eye, the revulsion that squatted so leadenly in the lizard brain. It was snakelike, for one—of course it was: the *Trieste* was all tubes. They spooled along the ocean floor, which was clad in a powdery drift of marine snow. The tubes were oddly segmented, branching off at unnatural angles, as to appear vaguely arachnid: long dark legs extending from a central hub.

There was a manic union between its various parts; it shouldn't cohere as a structure. Its angles were bizarre and somehow despairing. Some tubes appeared to end abruptly . . . that, or they burrowed into the sea floor like an enormous worm.

Maybe the pressure exerted the same warping effect it had on *Challenger* 4, bending each angle slightly out-of-true—which, cumulatively, made the *Trieste* look disgustingly alien. Or maybe it was the fact that the bulk of it hadn't been assembled by human hands: robots had no sense of beauty or symmetry; they simply slotted link A to coupler B. The structure throbbed with a numbing hunger—but for *what*? Luke was overcome with a sinister shrinking sensation, as if his soul had dwindled to a pinprick and the *Trieste* had swarmed in to fill that space, reducing him under its brooding, inanimate power. Luke couldn't shake the ludicrous sense that the *Trieste* had built itself to serve a purpose known only within itself. It seemed sentient, watching like a snake coiled in placid contentment under warm desert rocks. Knowing, in the seething core of itself, that it need only to wait.

"It's got a certain look to it," Al said.

"You've been inside?"

"A few times. Not for long, and only to drop off supplies. To speak the truth, none of us like spending all that much time down here. Docking's the trickiest part."

She edged them toward the *Trieste*. The *Challenger* swayed under the enormous pressure of water, which no longer *shushed* and gurgled against its hull but instead pushed back with leaden insistence as if they were moving through hardening concrete.

As they approached, Luke saw what had made those initial pinpricks of light: windows, same as the porthole on the submarine, dotted the length of one tube. Weak fingers of light spilled from each.

One of Al's navigational tools *pinged* as she zeroed in.

Five feet, four, three, two . . .

Al guided the sub to the porthole and cut the engines. The *Challenger* met the *Trieste* with the sound of a locket snapping shut.

Other sounds: whirrings, clickings. A pneumatic whine—the noise you'd hear in a mechanic's shop when they're tightening the lug nuts on your all-seasons.

"It should be sealed now."

Luke said, "And if it's not?"

Al gave him a grim smile. "We won't feel a thing." She unsnapped her belt. "You're going to have to step through first."

"Me? Why?"

The flesh tightened around Al's eyes. For the first time, she got that mildly irritated look a person gets when they're dealing with a newbie.

"I've got to keep an eye on things from this end, Doc."

There isn't anything on the other side of that hatch, said an unsteady voice in Luke's head. *Nothing but your brother and another wonk and a few dogs and bees.*

Luke wondered: had Dr. Westlake told himself the very same thing the first time he stepped inside?

"Once you're through and I've shut things down, I'll follow," said Al.

Luke laid his hands on the hatch. The metal thrummed with an odd tension, as if a heavy motor was running behind it. His biceps tensed in expectation—but after the slightest strain, the wheel turned easily.

"That's good." There was relief in Al's voice. "The seal's tight."

The hatch swung open. The thinnest trickle of saltwater beaded along the upper curve of the hatch, a single drop falling—*plip!*—to splash the metal. The light inside the *Challenger* wept into that hole of darkness. A smell perfumed the air. Cavelike and slightly alkaline, as Al had mentioned. The foreign odor of the deep sea mixed with something else, something unnameable.

A high note of dread sang through Luke's veins—a mocking aria that sent a shiver through his bones.

What are you so afraid of? said that same voice inside Luke's head.

Everything, another voice answered.

There was no reason for his fear, other than the obvious ones: they were eight miles underwater, about to enter a station built on the structural principles of an egg.

"Go on," Al said. "I'm right behind you."

Luke could make out the insides of the *Trieste*: the dim slope of a wall, the dull wink of metal.

He reached out to anchor his hands on the hatch. Then he saw something. His breath caught.

What the hell *was* that?

2.

WHEN THEY WERE BOYS, their father used to take Luke and Clayton for a haircut at the Hawkeye barbershop. *Give 'em a high and tight*, he'd tell Vince, the old Italian barber. That, or *These boys are getting shaggy. Give 'em the ole whitewall*. It was the only place in town Luke had ever seen his father get even a hint of respect, and even then it seemed grudging.

Luke remembered the ancient magazines with names like *Men's Adventure* and *Rage: For Men*, their lurid covers featuring men wrestling bears or coldcocking alligators, their cover lines reading: "Swastika Slave Girls in Guatemala's No-Escape Brothel Camp!" and "Rabid Weasels Ripped My Flesh!" He remembered how the barber's scissors would snip around his ears with the speed of hummingbird wings.

After every haircut, the barber would show Luke the back of his neck in a mirror that telescoped from the wall on metal armatures. When he angled the mirror, sometimes Luke would see Clayton sitting silently, or catch his father with his nose stuck in a magazine. That mirror offered a hidden view, Luke used to think. The face of the world when it wasn't aware you were looking at it.

His mind fled back to that childlike sensibility—a mirror that showed the world's hidden face—when his gaze focused on the insides of the *Trieste*. It was as if his view had shifted, *tilted*, the way that barber's mirror had, like a solid pane of glass. His body was suddenly awash in warmth. He stared closer, transfixed by that pitchlike black . . .

His breath gritted in his chest like steel wool. Were *things* moving in there?

Sly liquid shiftings, mincing suggestions of activity, all attended by a silky sound that made him think of sightless crabs shucking over one another in a shallow tide pool . . .

"What's wrong, Doc?"

Luke tore his eyes from the hatch.

"Some trick of the light," he croaked.

"That happens down here," Al said. "The light reflects differently, gets absorbed in weird ways."

Don't go in there, shrilled the voice in Luke's head.

What choice did he have? What could he say: *Sorry, I couldn't do my part to save humanity because I'm a teensy bit scared of the dark?*

Anchoring his hands on the hatch, Luke bit back his fears and propelled himself into that funneling blackness.

3.

HE TOPPLED THROUGH AWKWARDLY, having shoved himself hard enough to silence that inner voice that kept shrieking:

Don't-don't-don'tdon'tDON'T!

He'd expected some kind of crash pad, but there was nothing but steel gone frosty as the insides of a meat locker. He hit the floor; pain lanced down his collarbone and needled up his throat.

The *Challenger*'s hatch swung shut.

Luke rolled up, knees tucked to his chest. A goose egg was already swelling on his forehead. Lights winked on the floor, much like those of an airport runway. They didn't help much—he could barely see six feet in either direction.

Cold. God, it was bracingly cold. This couldn't possibly be the temperature throughout the station—everyone would freeze to death.

Who's to say they're still alive? a new, maddening voice asked, joining the chorus in his head—this one sounded a lot like his mother's voice. *Who's to say they didn't die days ago, Lucas my dear?*

Noise from directly overhead: *dap-dap-dap-dap*, a sound that could be mistaken for the footsteps of eager children. This image now entombed itself in Luke's head: a pack of waterlogged youths with their eyes vacuumed from their skulls scampering clumsily above him.

Where the hell was Al?

Luke stood, his adrenaline spiking. His head slammed into the tunnel. He couldn't stand at his full height; the ceiling was too low. Claustrophobia assaulted him; for a moment he was suffocating inside his own skin.

This is a tomb, he thought. *Nothing but a vast undersea crypt, and I'm alone inside of it.*

Laughter.

Luke's blood seized. Dry, nerveless dust caked his veins, as if he'd been pumped full of fast-dry cement.

There it was again, unmistakable. This wasn't that *dap-dap-dap* noise from above. Unmistakably, it had been laughter. And it was coming from deeper down the tunnel.

A boy's laughter.

No way could it—

". . . Zach?"

Luke clapped a hand over his mouth. He couldn't believe he'd spoken the name, even now, disoriented at the bottom of the world. His lips burned with the shame of it.

Of course his lost son wasn't down here. He wasn't *anywhere* on earth—he was in heaven. He was safe from harm now.

You don't know that.

His mother invading his head again, her voice honeyed and lacerating at once.

They never found him, did they? He could be anywhere, Lucas. Anywhere at all.

Sound from behind him. Luke spun on his heel. It came again. A tentative, staccato skittering. The urge struck to scurry back through the hatchway—a hatchway he feared was locked in any case—but instead Luke leaned into that sound, his eyes hunting desperately.

A rhythmic panting traveled through the dark. A shape carved itself out of the gloom twenty yards away, squatting motionlessly. Luke could just make out the wet jewels of its eyes and the whitened plume of its breath.

Come on, he thought, his hands balling into fists. *Come on if you're coming.*

Which it did. Eagerly in fact, attended by a rapid *clickety-click-click*.

Luke swung at its mad approach, wondering in some fear-shrunk chamber of his mind if this was something you could fight in the conventional ways—with fists and feet and teeth. How did you fight a monster?

His fist passed harmlessly over the creature's head, then it was on him—

Panting and whimpering and wagging its tail.

4.

A CHOCOLATE LABRADOR RETRIEVER. It twined around Luke's legs, nuzzled its snout into his crotch, and whined companionably.

"Oh, Jesus. Hey. It's okay, boy," Luke said, running his hands over the dog's head. "Oh, wait—girl."

The dog looked healthy, though a little too thin and clearly quite cold. Her hind legs were shaking. She rucked her snout under Luke's armpit and rooted until her head popped out under his arm, giving his chin a slobbery lick.

One of Clayton's lab animals? Did that mean the other specimens (Luke hated to think of them in his brother's clinical terms) were out of their cages, too?

The porthole opened. Al's boots appeared, her body gracefully following. She scanned the tunnel in both directions. Only then did her eyes settle on Luke.

"Your hands," she said. "You're cut."

Luke nodded. "I didn't exactly nail the dismount. I'll live. What took you so long?"

"The porthole shut after you went out. It shouldn't have. I had to disengage the pressure locks all over again."

Al had a flashlight. When she flicked it on, Luke noted that they were situated in a gooseneck: the tunnel curved ninety degrees to the left and right, roughly thirty yards ahead on either side.

The tunnel was ovoid: narrower at the top, wider at the bottom. Pipes and tubes ran along the walls, each labeled with their use. Many appeared to be wrapped with . . . Christ, was that friction tape? It *was*— the stuff the army called "hundred-mile-an-hour tape," as its manufacturers claimed it could hold a Jeep together at that speed.

My God, Luke thought with a dizzy species of dread. *Is this fucking place held together with* tape?

Black foam had been applied around the entire tunnel in twenty-yard increments, in buckled seams running from floor to ceiling—Otto Railsback's handiwork, had to be. Elsewhere Luke spotted signs of low-tech, on-the-fly fixes: baling wire and putty and soldering lead—the station had that shopworn, fix-me-up quality he remembered from the spaceships in the *Alien* movies.

Al gestured to the dog. "I see you've met Little Bee."

"Little Bee?" Luke said. "Did my brother name her?"

"He named all of them."

Luke should have known. Pchyolka and Mushka. "Little Bee" and "Little Fly," in English. They were the dogs, in 1960, that were shot into space aboard *Sputnik 3.* But the Russians miscalculated the satellite's return trajectory; the poor dogs had been incinerated during reentry. It was just like Clayton to name his specimens after those doomed pooches.

"So where are we right now?" Luke asked. "What part of the station?"

"Docking and storage," said Al. "Your standard dumping depot. You can see the start of the storage zone down thataway."

She aimed the flashlight. Luke could make out a pile of discarded air canisters. The beam threw wavering shadows on the wall beyond. Long thin tendrils seemed to lick and lash just out of sight, only their serrate tips visible.

"Is it usually this dark? This cold?" he asked.

Al shook her head. "It's running on phantom power. That's not un-usual—saving power is always key. But . . . the heat's been cut, too."

"What's she doing in here?" Luke said, petting Little Bee.

"Dunno, Doc. That's why we've been sent—to find out what's the rhubarb. It's why I've been sent, anyway. You're more the PR guy."

That chilling noise kicked up again: children's feet dashing above them, through the coal-dark sea.

"You'll hear it a lot," Al said. "It's just the pressure from outside. The *Trieste* is built to disperse it, in kind of a parabolic wave. Sounds freaky, huh? Like scuttling rats."

Luke petted LB (as he'd decided to name her) until she quit shaking. She peered at him with a grateful gaze. The edges of her eyes were a tallowy white. She was probably suffering from hypothermia.

"We have to get this dog someplace warm, Al."

"Right," she agreed. "Let's get at—"

The scream came from somewhere to the left, although in truth it was so piercing that it seemed to radiate out of the tube itself. Al broke into a run, moving in the sound's direction. Luke dashed after her. LB remained pinned where she was.

Luke said: "Come on, girl. Let's go. Move your ass."

The Lab whined, her eyes rolling as the glow of Al's flashlight vanished around the gooseneck.

Luke crouched down and cradled the dog to his chest. She whined again, mournfully this time—*please don't leave me*—but began to stiffen when Luke set off after Al with her in his arms.

"Shhhh, girl. You're okay."

The dog softened into his chest. She kept her chin tucked tight to Luke's shoulder, looking backward, studiously avoiding whatever lay ahead.

5.

TUBES. SOME KIND of laboratory setup. A snarl of copper tubes spiraling at weird angles, like an octopus frozen in a huge lump of amber.

This is what I saw before, Luke told himself. *Not the tentacles of some monster or mutant. Just a mess of lab equipment.*

He avoided its spiky metal fingers while cradling the dog, which was already growing heavy.

More clutter: MRE packets and empty jugs whose mouths were ringed with crusted pinkness.

Shish-shish-shishshish-shish-shish . . .

That eerie pattering overhead again. Luke craned his head up; his skull rung off the ceiling. He cursed, his body set in an uncomfortable stoop. Never in his life had he been so bummed to be six foot two.

Portholes were strung along the ceiling. Luke saw nothing except the black water pressing down. If anything, the holes made the interior darker.

You may as well install a porthole in a coffin.

They reached a dead end. The tunnel had narrowed considerably; Luke's elbows nearly scraped the walls. He and Al couldn't stand side by side; Al stood slightly ahead, Luke hunched off her shoulder. The dog was squashed between them, though she didn't seem to mind.

"Some of the tunnels bottleneck as they reach a junction," Al said. "It fattens out on the other side."

"Was that a *scream* we heard?" said Luke.

Al shook her head. "Steam, I'd say. Another release valve."

Luke didn't spot anything that looked like a release valve. They stood before a metal hatch with a single porthole. Al swung the flashlight. The ground was littered with junk—mostly busted glass, but also a gelatin-like lump that was dripping through the diamond grating. Its smell was spoiled and somehow malarial: the odor that might perfume an African village racked with disease.

Luke peered through the porthole. After ten feet, the tunnel widened into what appeared to be a chamber. Luke could just make out its scalloped roof and the edge of a cot. It looked cramped, but still much warmer and more hospitable than his present situation.

Luke set the dog down; his arms had grown weary. She bit his sleeve and held fast. Luke had seen this behavior with shelter dogs. Abandonment issues.

Al shone the flashlight through the porthole. "If anyone's in there, they're being coy about it."

She tapped on the glass.

"We can't get in here," she said. "It only opens from the other side."

"Why?"

"It's designed that way. There are two exits, this one and another exactly like it on the other side. This area . . . primarily it's storage, but the thinking was that in certain cases, it could be used as containment, too."

"You mean a jail, Al. Right?"

"Or if one of the scientists got sick with the 'Gets. We needed a spot where a person in that state could be put."

"Who's to say that person doesn't lock the healthy ones in here?"

Al said, "An imperfect system, I'll grant you that. Like a few other systems down here. Most of them we never expected to use."

"So where does that leave us? How do we get out of here?"

"Short answer? We don't, for now. Unless your brother's waiting down at the other hatch."

"Wait a second. You're saying it never occurred to anybody that we'd be locked in?"

"It did, absolutely. But we had to get down here all the same. They might be able to work a manual override up on the *Hesperus*, pop one of the locks electronically."

"*Might?* Are you kidding?"

"Well, there could be technical issues."

Luke couldn't believe it. He'd been sent to a trillion-dollar deathtrap at the bottom of the sea without any surety he'd even be able to reach his brother. He and Al could roam this storage tunnel until they froze to death.

"So, are we just going to wait until Clayton opens the door?" he said. "What if he refuses to?"

"That's what you're here for. To sweet-talk him."

"Oh my God. You obviously don't know my brother."

Al's nose was running from the cold. "We'll be okay. Look, we've got emergency blankets in the *Challenger* and a few days' worth of MREs. This isn't the best-case scenario, but it's not the worst."

"And what the hell was your worst-case scenario?"

"Well, look around you. The station's still here. It's all uphill from there."

Luke managed to return Al's cockeyed smile.

"Let's check the other hatch," said Al. "Maybe your brother—"

Just then, a face filled the porthole glass, flexing and seething and threatening to shatter right through.

The coppery, festering face of madness.

6.

ITS FEATURES WERE WRENCHED into an expression of tortured hostility. Its eyes, threaded with broken capillaries, bulged from their sockets.

Luke flinched as he would from a vicious dog snapping at the end of a chain.

The man behind the glass screamed; flecks of spittle hit the glass.

He's slipped a gear, Luke thought. A familiar phrase back home, used to describe someone who'd become addle-brained. But Luke figured this guy had done more than slip a gear—he'd fried his entire damn gearbox.

"It's Dr. Toy," Al said. "Hugo the Horrible."

This then was Dr. Hugo Toy, the molecular biologist Felz had mentioned. The only one still down here other than Clayton.

"He doesn't look so hot," Al deadpanned.

Dr. Toy's expression reconstituted itself into a mask of chilly observation. His hands drifted in front of his face, his fingers tapping and fidgeting. One hand stretched toward the porthole, two fingers knocking on the glass as a child might tap on a terrarium to rouse a pair of sluggish lizards.

His lips moved, repeating a simple phrase. His fingers tapped along in time.

You are not who you are . . . you are not who you are . . . you are not, you are not, you are NOT who you are . . .

One of his hands disappeared, then reappeared with a scalpel. Toy held the tip to his own throat and pulled it slowly across, not breaking the skin.

Is he threatening us, Luke wondered, *or threatening to do it to himself?*

Toy retreated down the tunnel with a scuttling crablike gait. He vanished around a bend and out of sight.

"Well," Al said finally, "I don't figure he's letting us in, do you?"

7.

THEY TREKKED BACK toward the *Challenger*. The cold crept into their bones. Luke was getting used to the patter of footsteps overhead—they had a rhythm he found oddly comforting.

"Do you have any clue what that was all about?" he asked Al.

It didn't look like the 'Gets. Toy wasn't spotting.

"Down here, people . . . they go nuts," Al said. "You see it a lot on subs. An extremely concentrated form of cabin fever. Even if you're cooped up in a cabin in the woods in the middle of winter, you can still open the door and breathe fresh air. Inside a sub it's the same gray walls, same cold lights, same smells of bearing grease and dust burning in control consoles.

"On a sub, if a bubblehead looked to be coming down with a case of the sea-sillies we'd give him a color wheel, same as you'd do with a grade-schooler. Or let him run his fingers through a book of carpet samples. I remember one guy carrying around a book of carpet rags, petting his favorite ones the way you pet a dog. But if you're prone to the sillies, you'll catch them eventually. The sea whittles at you like a sharp knife taking curls off a log until you just . . ."

Al mimed snapping a twig between her hands.

"So Dr. Toy's gone batshit?" Luke said. "Didn't you say everyone down here was under psychiatric examination?"

Al shrugged. "We had to go on what we could see through the monitors—were these guys eating properly and sleeping on a regular schedule, that kind of thing. Westlake, Toy, and your brother were supposed to report for a counseling session every few days; lately they've all been AWOL."

Luke said: "Why did you call him that, anyway? Hugo the Horrible."

"That's everyone's name for him. He embraces it. He's not just a biologist—he's a chaos theory wonk. You know much about that?"

When Luke shook his head, Al said: "Basically it's a mathematical field based on trying to make sense out of random events—which seems in hindsight like a solid prescription for psychosis, wouldn't you say? Apparently Toy was given to forecasting worst-case scenarios. Every silver cloud had a dark lining. And hey," she asked, "did you make out what he was saying?"

"I'm pretty sure it was, *You're not who you are.* Over and over."

"Yeah. That's what I was seeing, too."

She made that stick-breaking gesture again.

You are not who you are.

They forged down the tunnel like parasites trapped in the guts of an organism so huge it was oblivious to their presence. The darkness closed in, running swiftly on their heels.

Luke wanted to tell Al about the laughter he'd heard. The singing laughter of a child . . .

. . . his son's laughter?

He couldn't. She'd think he'd gone nuts himself. He pictured the look of tolerant concern that would grace Alice's face when she heard.

First Toy, and now this poor fuck's gone around the bend already, she'd think.

More crucially, Luke didn't want to associate the memory of his lost son with this unfriendly, unfeeling place. But that laughter continued to ring out in a recessed quadrant of his mind . . . maddening, so maddening.

8.

LUKE'S SON HAD GONE MISSING on a crisp fall day. He was six years old.

Missing . . . the word didn't quite fit. *Vanished* was better.

And like a tight-lipped magician, the world would never tell Luke how it had performed this horrible trick.

It happened seven years ago, at a public park not far from home. They often stopped by after Zach's first-grade class finished to let some steam off before meeting Abby. The park faced the road, the grass rolling out fifty feet in every direction until it hit a dense forested area to the west.

The afternoon was like any other. Luke took a late lunch, left the veterinary clinic, and picked Zach up. They walked home through the fallen leaves, holding hands; Zach made a point of stepping on the crinkliest leaves, loving the sound they made under his boots.

At the park, Zach swung on the monkey bars and slid down the slide into a drift of leaves Luke had heaped at the bottom. Luke relished this time, knowing that before long Zach wouldn't be caught dead in public with his goonybird father. Too soon, the sun began to set over the firs.

"Five more minutes, sport."

How many times had Luke imagined that they'd left that very instant? How many times had Luke wished that he'd taken his son's hand and ushered him home? He'd lost count. The thought never fully left his mind.

"Let's play hide-and-seek, Daddy!"

"Okay. One game. Then we hit the road."

Zach smiled. It was the last clean look Luke would ever have of his boy. Zach's left canine had come out days before; his smile was lopsided with that fresh gap. Luke remembered that. He remembered every little thing.

"I'll hide, Daddy."

"Okay, but don't hide too far off. It's getting dark."

Zach nodded obediently. "Count!"

"I'll count to twenty, then I'm coming to get you!" Luke said. "One . . . two . . . three . . ."

"Count slower!" Zach's voice was fading toward the trees. "You have to give me time to hide!"

Those were the last words his son would ever speak—the last ones to touch Luke's ears, in any case. Whenever Luke closed his eyes he could hear them, breathless and manic, as Zach hunted for a hiding spot. A spot he'd found and never left.

". . . eleven . . . tweeeeelve . . . thirteeeeeen . . ."

Zach's giddy laughter carried back to Luke.

". . . fourteen . . . fifteeeeeeen . . ."

Luke heard another noise, impossible to identify. A ragged *zippering* sound, was the closest he could get to explaining it. Nestled within that wet ripping note was another one: a resonant *sucking*. *Suck-suck-suck*, a pair of enormous lips pulling on a straw.

". . . sixteenseventeeneighteenninteteentwenty!"

Luke rattled off the last five numbers rapidly, adrenaline spiking in his chest. He couldn't say why he was so suddenly petrified; he could only accept that feeling inside of him and act on it.

He rounded the corkscrew slide and scanned for a sign of his son. Nothing. Just this horrible emptiness, the wind screaming over every blade of grass.

"Zach?"

The wind snatched the name from his lips. Panic filched into Luke's chest. Diffuse and dreamlike, wormed with self-consciousness . . . it was silly, so silly, to be worried. He'd spy the top of Zach's head peeking around that boulder over there, or ducked behind that trash can. And when that happened, Luke would chuckle at his foolishness and chase

his son down and heft him, squealing with delight, into his arms. They'd
go home, where supper was waiting, and after dinner Zach would sit in
his room contentedly, assembling a jigsaw puzzle he'd bought with the
money the tooth fairy had left under his pillow.

That's exactly how it would happen, Luke figured. That's how it *had*
to happen, because until that very moment Luke had believed the world
was essentially reasonable. If you followed the rules, the world played
fair with you.

Kids didn't just disappear off the face of the earth. Not in empty
public parks. Not in the time it took to count to twenty. Things like that
never happened.

"You can come out now, buddy. Olly olly oxen free!"

The swings creaked in the wind. The streetlights were popping on.
Why had he stayed out so late? Daylight saving time had just kicked in
and he hadn't made the mental adjustment yet. But that could happen to
anyone, couldn't it?

A possibility came to him: that his son had burrowed *under* a drift of
leaves, covering himself so that Luke couldn't spot him.

Next he remembered the sounds: that meaty zippering, that sucking
inhale . . .

"Come on, sport, you win! I'm sure Mom's got dinner ready. Spa-
ghetti with macaroni noodles, your favorite!"

He'd reached the edge of the forest. Luke had lived in the city his
whole life, treading every inch of it. He'd explored this very place for
hours on end. He'd never gotten a sense of danger from it. But now,
squinting into its dark tangle of branches, trees standing like gloomy sen-
tinels . . . yes, it seemed very threatening indeed.

Abby had lost Zachary a year or so before at a discount store: uneven
floors, bins of irregular clothing. It was only for a minute, but she said
that minute had stretched into an eternity. She was certain he'd been
taken. *Snatched*, she said. Someone had lured him away while her back
was briefly turned. That was all it would take. Next Zachary was in a van.
Next, a remote warehouse or a soundproof basement. When she found
him several aisles over, tickling his chin with a feather duster, she nearly

wept with relief before furiously scolding him to never leave her sight again.

And the same thing would happen now—Luke was still sure of it.

"Zach?" His voice rose several octaves. "Buddy, please, enough!"

A thread of pure unadulterated terror now braided into his heart. Fear mixed with a love more profound than any he'd ever felt, and mingled with dizzying guilt for letting that most precious thing slip from his view at a crucial moment.

He's gone.

The voice in his head was *black*—discolored and malevolent, the voice of something conjured at a Black Mass. It spoke with calm certainty.

Your boy is gone.

Swallowed.

The possibility jolted Luke into action. He stumbled into the woods. "Zach! Zach! Christ, *Zaaaaaach!*"

How long had he wandered through the trees, screaming for his son? Far too long. He should have called the police. They would have arrived in minutes. But even as he'd hunted more and more desperately, the fear and mania mounting, he remained certain that it was all some ridiculous accident—a misunderstanding that, once rectified, would be something they'd laugh about when Zach was an adult.

Remember that time Dad thought he'd lost me in the woods, only what happened is that I'd tripped and conked my head on a tree trunk and knocked myself cold for a few minutes? Har-har-har!

Something just like that, yes, goofy and commonplace and nothing to call the police about because it was fine, really, everything was okayokayOKAY—

Luke staggered out of the woods, wild-eyed and bleeding from the brambles. His mind was a jumble of horrific images: windowless vans and fillet knives and his son's fear-struck eyes. Only then had he dialed 911.

The police arrived within minutes; Abby arrived a short time later. Luke couldn't bear to look his wife in the eyes.

The first twenty-four hours were the real killers. That's what everyone will tell you. In any missing persons case, the chances of success drop drastically after a full day. The search area gets too wide; the potential locations of that person (or, it must be said, their body) become overwhelming.

At first, Luke had been confident. The police cruisers with their cherries alit, the team of tracking dogs, just about every plainclothes officer in the city tromping through that half-mile stretch of forest . . . How could they not find his son? His son, who'd only been out of his sight for twenty seconds—no, *less*.

A search-and-rescue helicopter strafed the forest with its spotlight. Luke had been in the woods by then, searching with everyone else. The helicopter roved toward the creek; maybe Zach had fallen in, borne along in the current that flowed west toward Coralville. Maybe he was lying on its banks, shivering but unhurt.

As midnight passed into the witching hours, a sense of disbelief settled over Luke. A feeling of unreality washed over him. This *couldn't* be happening. It was like waking up to find out your arm was missing—you went to bed, slept well, and when you woke up, it was gone. There was no pain, no scar. Only a smooth expanse of skin over the nub and an empty space where the limb once lay. It was that kind of nightmarish inconceivability he was facing. He couldn't cope with it. Luke could live without his arm. Both arms. Both legs. His tongue and ears and nose. He'd forfeit them all gladly just to have Zach back.

But the world has always been resistant to bargains of that nature.

When dawn paled over the treetops, Luke stumbled out of the woods into a ring of emergency vehicles. His brain was pinned in a merciless vise, on the verge of tearing in half. He overheard some policemen debating the conceivability that someone had been in the woods, watching and waiting until Zach had drawn near before grabbing him and stuffing an ether-soaked rag over his face, then dragging him through the trees and hucking (Luke remembered that clearly; the policeman had actually used the verb *huck*) Zach's body into the trunk of a car. After that, he could have been driven to where the access road met a main thoroughfare. If so, the abductor could be four hundred miles away . . . or only a few blocks distant, in a nearby house.

Luke sat beside Abby, who was wrapped in a blanket and sitting on an ambulance bumper. He slipped an arm around her shoulders and pulled her into him. She resisted, her eyes bruised and reproachful.

"Did he run away?" Her voice had this terrible faraway quality. "No. Why would he run away? What did we do, that he would do that? Oh my God."

There was something else in her eyes, too. Fuming in the green of her irises. Fury. She was so, so angry at Luke. Over time, that fury might've even shaded into hatred.

There were moments over the coming years when Luke wished that Zachary was dead. The fervency of his wish was sickening. But yes, dead. Of cancer or brain parasites or even drowning in the creek. If he'd died of cancer, Luke and Abby could have been at his bedside, making his final days as comfortable as possible. It would have broken them in some ineffable way, yes, but it would have allowed them to love their son through his final days on earth.

Even if he'd drowned in the creek . . . it was awful to envision, but at least it would be done. They would have a body to dress. Rituals to observe. A coffin, a funeral. There would be a sense of knowing where their boy was—even if that meant under six feet of dirt at the Muscatine Avenue cemetery.

But Zachary wasn't dead. His case was classed as missing/unsolved. There was no closure. It was the equivalent of a movie missing its final reel.

Death was final. It meant Zach had passed beyond pain or fear. Missing was so much worse. Missing was a cavalcade of possibilities, none of them good.

NEITHER ZACHARY nor his abductors were ever found. His disappearance made the rounds in the press, locally and eventually nationally, but the media's ardor cooled. There were other missing kids and a million other tragedies besides.

Luke drove.

For a solid year after Zachary vanished, he spent every night on the road. Driving around the city and farther afield, down the streetlit corridors of night searching for his lost boy.

He found him, too. Found him everywhere. It was a phenomenon other parents talked about; Luke and Abby had attended a support group at the urging of their grief counselor. A dozen empty-eyed parents (ex-parents?) sitting in a circle in a chilly community center. They kept seeing their missing children, too. Seeing them in busy malls or whenever they drove past a schoolyard. They saw them in crowds: an arm, a foot, or maybe something in a child's posture that mimicked that of their own lost son or daughter. They had all rushed heedlessly into a throng, scooped up a child whose back was turned—so sure; so *goddamn* sure—only to see the frightened face of a stranger staring up at them.

Luke could understand. He'd see the crook of Zachary's leg folding into a strange car and would follow that car until it stopped and a boy who wasn't Zach got out. He'd seen his son's tousled hair bobbing amid the crowd at the Iowa State Fair. In his more desperate moods he'd considered snatching someone else's boy while his parents' backs were turned—*serves you right! You've got to pay attention every . . . single . . . second!*

He'd drive all night, come home at dawn, and fall into an exhausted sleep. His dreams were horrific. Dreams where Zach called to him from the bottom of a deep well. Or where Zach screamed that he'd run away and never wanted to see Luke again. But the most insidious night terrors were the ones where Zach lay beside him in bed, his breath feathering Luke's neck . . . and when Luke awoke, his son just wasn't there.

One evening, he woke up and Abby wasn't there, either. She'd packed and left while he was sleeping. This came as only a small surprise to Luke. They hadn't spoken, *really* spoken, in months. They were two shells emptied out by grief.

The Human Shield. His old childhood persona, the one he'd cooked up to insulate himself from the predations of his mother. He'd always seen himself as that to Abby and Zach. A shield against the awfulness of the world—an awfulness his son would have to grapple with, yes, but hopefully not for many years. As a boy, he could simply stand behind his father and let Luke absorb the cruelest blows. Except somehow Luke's defenses had been penetrated. The forces of evil had found a blind spot, their tentacles creeping behind his back to snatch Zach away.

Twenty seconds. Lives can collapse in that time span. Abby accepted the fact that it wasn't all Luke's fault—it could have happened to anyone, sure—and yet she came to hate him regardless. She walked out because she wanted to stop hating the man she'd once loved . . . and because she must have realized that her hatred, though powerful, was a pale reflection of the loathing Luke felt for himself.

Luke couldn't blame her. He was even mildly relieved to discover she'd gone. When the divorce papers arrived a few weeks later, he'd signed them without rancor.

In time, he returned to his veterinary practice. Tending to animals gave his life a glimmer of value. And if he occasionally broke down in tears, or screamed or shook, well, animals were eminently forgiving of such behavior.

So Luke did his job, and at night, to avoid sleeping, he'd drive. Consciousness couldn't stave off the memories, though. In time, his memories became waking dreams. It got so that he could actually dream with his eyes wide open.

Luke remembered feeding Zach this one time when he had a fever. Zach, then just a toddler, hadn't wanted to eat. But if he didn't, he'd get sicker. This worried Luke tremendously. He'd wished Abby was there—he needed her calm composure—but she had been working late. In frustration, Luke shoved a spoonful of applesauce into his son's mouth. "Just *eat it*, please!"

Zach went silent, the dismay and bewilderment building as his face turned pink. Then he'd begun to bawl, the applesauce still pooled in his mouth.

Sick with guilt, Luke carried him upstairs to the bath. Zach sat in the tub, withdrawn and motionless. When Luke dried him, Zach started shivering. He wouldn't make eye contact with Luke. This scared Luke so badly. Had he wrecked that beautiful bond of trust between them? Some things you can never get back. Even if Zachary couldn't remember it consciously, the act—his dad shoving a spoon into his mouth and shouting at him to eat—would stick in his developing mind like a barb.

That's why I ran away, Daddy. I ran because you were mean to me.

Luke had been afraid that Zach wouldn't trust him anymore, because he had let him down.

And years later, Luke would let his son down again at the worst possible moment.

As a father, Luke couldn't cope with that.

He still breathed, still functioned, but he was ruined inside. Guilt and despair crushed him into something unrecognizable.

So he drove and grieved, and in time the 'Gets took its hold on the world.

He dearly wished he would catch it. Forgetting was the best remedy, wasn't it? Forget Abby. Forget Zach. Forget the wonderful life they'd had together.

Just let me forget. Please, for the love of God.

But the world was resistant to bargains of that nature, too.

9.

"YOU OKAY, DOC?"

Alice's voice snapped Luke out of these unhealthy ruminations. First his mother, now his son—the sharp blades of a tiller churned through his gray matter, dredging up blackened pulp and old bits of bone. Luke felt them there in the *Trieste*, both Bethany and Zachary. Not in any material way, but their shapes and voices clung tightly to him now—it had started the moment that the *Challenger* slipped under the sea. He was trapped with them now, under the hammering intensity of a trillion tons of water.

"I'm fine," he said. "Just . . . having some trouble concentrating."

Luke was flanking Al. The dog, LB, padded behind them. They'd already stopped to collect their bags at the *Challenger* hatch. Then they'd rounded the gooseneck on the other side of the tunnel, heading toward the remaining hatch.

"Your brother will let us in," Al said. To Luke's ears, her voice held the mad certainty specific to leaders of doomed polar expeditions.

"Oh, yeah, most certainly."

Luke glanced at the portholes along the ceiling. He caught movement across one of them. A pale shred drifting languorously along. "Al—?"

"That's it—the ambrosia," she said, her eyes following his pointing finger. "That's why the portholes were built: to see where it's concentrated."

The ambrosia wafted to the porthole's rim and hung there a moment before vanishing. Luke continued to stare at the ring of blackness where the foot-thick glass and polymer held back the crushing sea—he half expected something to flare across it. A disembodied face, perhaps; a suety pockmarked face glowing a sick maggot-white except for the eyelids, which were red as flayed beef. The pressure had vacuumed the eyes into their sockets—they stared from deep within those cold pits . . .

. . . but of course nothing appeared. Just the bleak emptiness of the deep. Luke wondered if this was how an astronaut felt staring through the porthole of his lunar module to catch a glimpse of space where not a single star shone: an infinite blackness, bleak and dehumanizing.

The tunnel was less cluttered on the other end. Light burned behind the hatch's porthole. Al knocked on it. It sounded as if she was rapping her knuckles on a cast-iron cannon at a Civil War memorial. Nobody answered.

"Thick door," she said as if this were a new fact.

"Not to sound desperate here, Al, but what are our options?"

Al stuck her tongue between her teeth, biting down. "Well, we can wait. Chances are your brother will pass down this way."

"Tip-top plan. And how do we know Toy doesn't have control of the whole station?" Luke said. "How can we be sure he hasn't tied Clayton up, or worse?"

"The thought crossed my mind ever since we lost contact," Al admitted. "Most of the areas can be self-sealed and contained—the lab, the purifiers—so my hope is that it's Toy who's been isolated, or he's isolated himself. But you're right. He may have the run of the entire joint. We have to get in there somehow."

"You said something about triggering the lock remotely?"

"Yeah, that may be our best bet." A shiver racked Al's frame. "I'll head back and see what I can do. You stay here. If I pop the lock, you hold the door."

She squeezed past Luke—the tunnel was so cramped that Luke had to suck in his stomach to let her pass. Her footsteps receded down the tunnel, and with them went the reassuring glow of the flashlight.

Luke dropped his duffel bag and sat on the floor. The dog rested her head on his lap. He felt foolish. Ineffective. God in heaven, sitting beside a locked door in the hope it would open. A glorified bellhop.

"Goddamn it," he said softly. "Christly Jesus goddamn hell."

It felt good to blaspheme—goddamn fucking *good*. Could God even hear him down here?

You go ahead, son, he figured God might say, good sport that He was. *Take my name in vain if it keeps your powder dry. People take it in vain when they stub their toe or get cut off on the freeway. I'm used to it.*

"I'm closer to hell than heaven down here, anyway," Luke said, and laughed. It freaked him out a little how hollow it sounded.

"Hello-oh-oh-oh," he said. His words soaked into the darkness only to come back in a mocking lilt.

Oh-ho-ho-o-o-o . . .

He glanced down and spotted a spiral-bound notebook that had either fallen or been wedged under the grate. Curious, he lifted the grate a few inches and fished the notebook out—and nearly dropped it just as fast. The cover was slick with a dark sticky substance.

Psych Report, the cover read.

He riffled the pages. The first few were filled with neat, clinical handwriting. The overhead lights dimmed, a fluttering brownout. He slid the notebook into an empty pocket in his bag, not wanting that black gunk to touch his clothes.

The lights went out.

All of them, this time, and all at once. The light beyond the porthole glass, the dim runway lights winking in the floor.

Darkness clogged in Luke's sockets and invaded his throat. His brain fused shut in utter panic—he couldn't think, could barely breathe. LB sat bolt upright, her breath feathering the nape of his neck. Her hackles rose against his arm, stiff as porcupine quills.

A new noise slipped out of the darkness. Back where Al had gone.

Not footsteps. No, this was a deliberate, smooth slithering.

LB whined next to Luke's ear. Her breath held a shaved-iron tang. The scent of pure animal fear.

What could possibly make a noise like that? Had Clay brought a snake down for his tests? Oh God, what if he'd brought a python? Could it have gotten loose?

Whush-whush-whush. Soft, silky, advancing steadily through the dark.

No, Luke remembered. *Felz said there were dogs, lizards, guinea pigs, bees. No snakes.*

Those footsteps raced overhead again, but this time the darkness gave them a new, knowing cadence. Luke pictured a group of stunted youths in the water outside the station. Their bodies white as candle wax, sun-starved flesh flaking from their skeletons. Their heads, projecting from their collared shirts, were flat as flounders; their mouths were enormous and studded with the same needlelike teeth he'd glimpsed on the viperfish. They would be staring through the porthole with sightless silvery eyes, not really seeing but *sensing* him . . .

Now the *whush-whush* was joined by another sound: a dry chittering, almost mechanical. The sound of a million tiny limbs dancing lightly along the metal floor.

It's the old man, Luke thought wildly. *The old man with the mantises on his head.* Luke pictured him trudging down the tunnel, his radial-tire sandals *whushing* on the floor while mantises spilled off of his skull.

Then another image darkened his mind—an older memory this time, a recollection drawn down from the surface world.

Yes, said a cold voice inside his head. *Oh yessss, that's it exactly. And it's coming for you, Lucas. Coming for you this very moment . . .*

YEARS AGO, when his life was much better, Luke had been invited to a veterinary conference in Arizona. They had gone as a family, staying at a motel edging the desert. The first night, they settled their infant son into the Pack 'n Play, then once Zach was asleep, Luke and Abby made love stealthily. Luke slipped inside Abby and rocked gently. Afterward they slept, only to be awakened by Zach's horrific screams.

Abby jackknifed up in bed. "Zach?" she said. "What is it, baby?"

Luke could just make out the shape of his son in the finger of moonlight falling through the motel window. He was curled inside the Pack 'n Play. His face was pressed to the breathable mesh, which distorted his features.

Luke snapped on the bedside lamp. Zachary was *shrieking,* these lung-shredding sounds Luke had never heard before. He leapt out of bed. Zachary's face was beet red and alarmingly puffed. Luke picked his son up and pressed the boy to his chest, a calming gesture.

Luke's heartbeat skyrocketed when he felt something squirming against his own chest. Something *inside* Zachary's sleeper, trapped against his son's skin.

Zach's piercing screams unlocked this dreadful hysteria in Luke; each one shot a jolt of scalding acid through his veins. The boy thrashed and squealed as Luke gripped him under the armpits, his little face a balloon ready to burst.

Jesus oh Jesus fuck what IS that?

Something was moving under Zach's sleeper. Luke saw these terrifying whiplike motions in the left leg of Zach's sleeper. It looked like a big fish caught in a net, trying to fling itself free. Luke made a dry gagging sound, the panic swelling in his throat like a sponge.

He tore the sleeper open. There, curling around his son's ankle and all the way up his thigh, was the largest insect Luke had ever seen.

A long torsional tube. Its black body was segmented, sinuous, reflecting the room's meager light. It looked the same at both ends, so Luke couldn't tell where its head was. Luke saw inflamed divots all over Zach's chest where the fucking thing must've bitten his boy.

It moved—*was* moving, even as Luke stared slack-jawed—with subtle undulations, powered by a dizzying multitude of legs. It released itself from Zach's ankle, slipping up the back of his leg and around the frilled, absorbent ridge of his diaper. It was enormous, at least eight inches long; it kept coming and coming like a freight train steaming out of a tunnel, kinking and unwinding and flexing its revolting body.

Luke caught the final half inch of it—disgustingly warm, with a greasy sheen; it reminded him of grabbing the fireman's pole at his old playground, the metal hot and slick from the hands of a hundred children.

He pinched his fingers with the desperate hope of snaring the bug, ripping the fucker in half, but it shimmied free and slithered under his son's back.

Abby tore madly at Zach's sleeve, trying to yank the sleeper off. The fear chewed into the sensitive wires in Luke's brain, paralyzing his nerve centers. He pushed Abby away forcefully, too panicked to notice, flipped Zach onto his back, and pressed down on his sleeper, finding the bug—a millipede, he knew by then—and trapping it in the fabric. He freed Zachary's arms, then leapt off the bed with the balled-up sleeper. The millipede whipped in his grip; Luke absorbed a series of bites as painful as the stings of a wasp.

Luke's only thought: *This fucker's been doing that to my son.*

He threw the sleeper down and stamped on it with his bare heel. A satisfying metallic crunch, like stepping on a beer can. He stomped again and again, fueled by a rage as primordial as any he'd ever experienced.

Die, you fucking brainless monster! Die, you awful thing!

He stepped away, panting. Abby cradled Zach; he was still bawling, but his cries had lost their death-struck pitch.

Luke's gaze returned to the sleeper. Amazingly, it was moving.

The millipede crawled out of one sleeve. Skittering hesitantly, leaking viscid pus-yellow fluid, it curled into a cochlear coil on the carpet.

"Oh no," Luke breathed. "Oh no-no-*no*."

He retrieved his heavy-soled dress shoe and slammed it down. The bug actually *leapt* up, bouncing off the thick, nappy pile. With the same shoe, Luke flicked it through the open bathroom door and onto the tiles, muttering "*Fucking thing oh you fucking* thing," and knelt on the tiles, slamming the shoe down furiously until the insect was nothing but a jamlike smear . . .

. . . AND RIGHT THEN, alone in the *Trieste*'s tunnel, this was the memory Luke's mind conjured:

That slippery *whush-whush* in the cavernous dark was the *whush* of a millipede stalking toward him, chitter-clattering on its million-skillion legs.

This wasn't your garden-variety one, either. Oh, no. The darkness nursed it into something new entirely. A millipede the size of a fourth-generation Aleppo pine, thick around as a trash can. Something primeval, hailing from the Permian age, where the scale of life was all out of whack. Its mandibles, sharp as hedge shears, clashed silkily: the sound of a razor drawn down a leather strop.

Whush-whush . . . pause . . . whush-whush.

Chitta-chit-skriiitch-chizzt-chit-chit.

It advanced slowly, in no rush. Where was there to go? It had all the time in the world.

Impossible, the rational center of Luke's mind insisted. *Even if it did exist anywhere on earth, which it absolutely fucking does not, how would something like that get down here? It's nothing. Nothing at all, for fuck's sake, nothing at ALL.*

His mind took a sickening lurch. That reasonable (if increasingly shrill) voice in his head held no sway down here. Maybe his brain had conjured this nightmare bug out of nothingness. But it was still *here*—if only in this moment.

Either he'd created it . . .

—*or the* Trieste *had*—

. . . or he was coming down with a case of the sea-sillies already.

Your seabag's leaky, sailor. Isn't that what they said in the Navy when a guy went batshit? *Your seabag's leaking its guts all over the friggin' place, swabbie. You've gone Section 8, ya fookin' loonybird*—

Whush-whush . . . WHUSH-whush . . .

You think that's *nothing, Luke?* his mother said mockingly, with that throaty chuckle of hers. *Ohh, I think we both know it's something. After all, the dog can feel it, too, wouldn't you say? Can't you feel her shivering against you? Oh yes, it's something all right, and whatever it is, Luke, it's coming for you.*

Luke pushed the dog behind him and butt-bumped toward the

locked hatch. The tunnel narrowed. His breath came in hot, nauseous gusts.

Whush-WHUSH . . .

Luke swore he could see the segmented shape of the millipede's gargantuan and somehow gothic body, the plating of its exoskeleton exuding its own sick glow. It was approaching with a mincing sidewinder movement.

Jesus, no, this is not happening . . . there's nothing—NOTHING—!

He flattened his back against the hatch. The dog was tucked and trembling behind his knees. Luke leaned forward slightly, terror buzzing in his skull like angry yellow jackets . . .

Whush-whush-WHUSH-WHU—

The airlock hissed behind him. The hatch fell open. Luke's heels stuttered back and hit the metal lip. He squawked, toppling backward as he scrambled away from the chattering noises in the hallway.

Light flooded his eyes. A familiar face stared impassively down at him.

"Hello, brother."

10.

CLAYTON NELSON'S FACE wore a particular expression a good deal of the time. It had begun to grace his features as a child, and although his face had changed over the years, the expression had not. There was a noticeable thinning of the lips and a flaring of the nostrils; the flesh drew tight at the top of his nose where it met the edges of his eyes, while his eyebrows tented in an inverted V. It was the look of a man who'd sniffed something foul, but could not determine the source of the odor.

Clayton Nelson's face could hold this expression for hours. It was the very expression it held now, in fact, as he looked at Luke sprawled on the tunnel floor.

"Thanks for rolling out the welcome wagon," said Luke, feeling stupid, which is how he frequently felt in his older brother's presence.

Clayton was narrow-shouldered and thin-hipped, dressed in gray coveralls. A custodian's uniform. His face was austerely handsome in a way particular to polar icecaps—flinty and remote. As he'd aged, Clayton had come to look more and more like a member of some fallen Eastern European aristocracy.

The only feature working against that perception was his hair, which hung down his neck in a ragged fringe—the beginnings of a mullet. It gave him the look of a Double-A middle-relief pitcher; an aging player who'd had a cup of coffee in the majors and was now playing out the string with the Tuscaloosa Mud Hens or Richmond Flying Squirrels.

The fingertips of his left hand were bandaged.

"Let me help you up," Clayton said mechanically, offering Luke his unbandaged hand.

Luke glanced down the storage tunnel. Empty. No giant millipede.

Of course not. He rubbed his head. A fresh goose egg parted the short hairs on the back of his skull. LB hunched behind him, her tail tucked between her hind legs.

"Ah. You located the specimen," Clayton said.

Anger flared in Luke. It was partly the adrenaline burn-off, and the shame at his crazed imaginings, but primarily the familiar rage he'd too often felt toward his brilliant, careless brother.

"Why was she in there?" he said. "It's freezing. It's dark. She was alone."

"I wasn't aware. Hugo took it."

Luke bristled at the pronoun. *It.* As if Dr. Toy had stolen office supplies instead of a living creature.

"He must've abandoned it in there," Clayton said.

"Why would he do that?"

Clayton's eyebrow arched. "Have you seen Hugo?"

When Luke nodded, Clayton said, "Then I don't need to tell you why he might act irrationally. I don't know why he locked the specimen—"

"*She*, Clay. *She's* not a specimen," Luke said.

"Technically, yes, it is," Clayton placidly replied.

"You named her Little Bee."

"And? It's just a name."

"A stupid one."

"Well, I'm sure the specimen appreciates your concern."

Luke willed himself to calm down. What profit was there in arguing as they had as children? He wished Al would get her ass back. He needed a buffer.

"Clay . . . what the hell is happening down here?" he asked. "The monitors are out, you haven't communicated for days. I get a phone call at three o'clock in the morning telling me to hightail my ass to Guam. They play me a recording where you're telling me to come down—come *home*. After that, they took me into a chilly room, rolled out a slab, and showed me Dr. Westlake."

"Hold on." Clayton held up his unbandaged hand. "What's this about a recording?"

Luke nodded. "The last transmission they received from you. You were saying *come home, Lucas; we need you, Lucas.* Stuff like that."

Clayton scoffed. "Asking for *you*? Why in God's name would I do that?"

"Clay, I *heard* you. Clear as day. *Come home, Lucas.*"

Clayton's features were fixed in that *just-sniffed-shit* expression, and again, Luke was left feeling that *he* was the dog shit on Clayton's shoe, the foul muck that his brother was just now realizing he'd stepped in.

"Whatever you heard, it wasn't me. I have no need of you here." He gave Luke an *are-you-serious?* look. "What would you possibly add?"

Clayton was telling the truth; Luke knew him well enough to see that. Who the hell could have sent that transmission, then, and how? Had someone taped Clayton covertly and spliced a sound file together? Why would Westlake or Toy—the only possible culprits—do that?

"You said something about Westlake," Clayton prodded.

Luke eyed his brother evenly. "Are you saying you don't know what happened to him?"

"We've had no recent contact with the surface. Disturbances in the water have muddied our transmissions. I know Westlake took the sub. I have no idea how he managed it. None of us were taught how to . . ." He exhaled through his nostrils. "I hadn't seen him in some time. He locked himself in his lab. He left in . . . I was about to say the dead of night, but it always feels like that down here. He certainly left without telling me."

"He's dead, Clay." Luke paused to let it sink in. "I mean . . . not *just* dead." The word failed to express what Luke had seen. "I've never seen anything like it. I never want to again."

Clayton accepted the news stoically. Perhaps his upper lip twitched, but if so, it was barely noticeable.

"What the hell is going on down here?" Luke resisted the urge to punctuate each word with a poke to his brother's chest—anything to pierce that Teflon exterior. "You've got Dr. Felz and everyone else in a flap, and that was before Westlake surfaced."

"Our research. The tests are ongoing," Clayton said. He had already accepted both Westlake's death and Luke's untimely arrival; his mind had processed both phenomena, catalogued and dismissed them with typical Claytonian swiftness. "It's remarkable. What we've discovered beggars description. There have been setbacks. Some expected, others less so. Dr. Toy isolated himself . . ." He glanced at his watch with a hint of perplexity. "I can't say how long ago. Time has a funny way of behaving down here."

"*Aaaand* we're in," Al said, abruptly stepping in from the storage tunnel. "Nice work, guys."

She offered her hand to Clayton, who shook it dryly.

"Sight for sore eyes, Doc. I was trying to get the door unlocked remotely, but I can't pass a clear signal to the surface."

"We've been having the same trouble," said Clayton.

"Is that why the monitors are on the fritz, too?"

Clayton shrugged. "I don't know why that might be. I assumed it was a breakdown on your end."

Luke told Alice what Clay had said, about not sending the transmission.

"That seems unlikely," said Al, turning to Clayton. "I've listened to that transmission two dozen times. It's you, Dr. Nelson. It's the reason Luke's here."

Clayton bristled. "It *wasn't* me. Why on earth would I need a veterinarian?"

He spoke the word *veterinarian* with the same dismissive inflection others might accord the word *moron*.

"Well, isn't this a touching family reunion," Al said.

"Maybe you were sleeping, Clay," Luke said. LB barked energetically, as if in support. "When you recorded it, I mean. You didn't sound like yourself."

Clayton wouldn't dignify this possibility with an answer, but Al coaxed Luke to go on.

"You sounded . . . you sounded *gone*," Luke said. "Just, I don't know, somewhere outside your own skin. Your voice had a floaty quality. Maybe you were sleepwalking. Maybe you sent the transmission without know-ing it."

"I've never sleepwalked in my life," Clay said.

But Al was nodding. "Yeah, yeah, I've seen that. Happens a lot on submarines. Sailors getting out of bed, walking around and waking up in funny places. Guys who never had the habit before. Lots of lucid dream-ing, too—talking in your sleep. Your brainwaves go a bit buggy down here. Why didn't I think of that?"

"Well," Clayton said with a stagy eye-roll, "now that's been sorted, perhaps you'd like to leave?"

Alice laughed without mirth. "You crack me up, Doc. I figure since we've come all this way—and factoring in what happened to Dr. West-lake—we best stay awhile, take a proper accounting of things."

Clayton nodded impassively. "As long as you don't disturb my lab or intrude on my work." A hard look at Luke. "Either of you."

"Wouldn't dream of it," said Al.

Clayton's face reminded Luke of a blanket pulled over a nest of scor-pions: seemingly tranquil, but with all manner of thoughts and instincts twisting beneath it.

"Well then, come along."

Clayton turned and walked away with every expectation they'd fol-low, treating them with the indifference you might accord to a pair of slack-jawed yokels who'd just fallen off the hay truck—which, Luke noted with an absence of bitterness, was how Clayton treated pretty much everybody he met. He'd always been an equal-opportunity disdainer.

11.

DESPITE THE LOW CEILING, Clayton moved down the tunnel with the grace of a man who did not so much walk as he did *float* a millimeter or two above the ground, hovercrafting on a ribbon of air.

The tunnel was well lit. Warmth emanated from gilled vents. They walked in silence and squeezed single file through a gap where the tunnel winnowed to a bottleneck. Separated by a flimsy barrier of polymers and foam, Luke could feel the sea pressing against his skull. His eardrums throbbed from the pressure of that static silence.

Luke had never been particularly prone to claustrophobia; as a child, he'd navigated drainage tunnels and dusty attics, happy as a hamster in a Habitrail. But these tunnels truly resembled a kind of digestive tract, with their ridged walls and scalloped ceilings. No wonder Toy's and Westlake's mental states had eroded—on top of the pressure and isolation, they'd spent too much time pacing these sinister tubes.

They rounded a tight bend. Luke stopped so suddenly that LB butted into the backs of his legs, leaving a streak of drool on his overalls.

"Oh, you've got to be kidding me."

The tunnel hit an abrupt stop. It was as if they'd reached a dead end . . . except for the circular hole in the wall at the end of the tunnel, about the size of a manhole. The mouth of the hole was dark, but Luke could see that it stretched off to meet some unknown terminus within the station.

"Relax," said Al. "They're called crawl-throughs. It's a structural necessity. You'll see the same thing at space stations: chutes connecting one area to the other, which the astronauts float through. We, unfortunately, are tethered by gravity. But at least it's got rungs, just like a ladder. It's a twenty-second trip, Luke. Piece of cake."

Luke approached the chute. God, it was tiny—a choking ring. He could see straight through it, at least, to the lit tunnel on the other end. Rungs ran along its ceiling. But why had he thought it was the diameter of a manhole? It looked about as big around as the door on his clothes dryer, if that.

Clayton slid in on his stomach. He wriggled until his ass was past the chute's mouth, transitioned onto his back, and gripped the rungs. He pulled himself through, grunting slightly in exertion; shortly afterward he slid out the other end.

"You go," Al said to Luke. "Then the dog. Then me."

Luke slid himself in. He tried to move as he'd seen his brother do, but it was difficult. He turned over awkwardly. A black tongue of foam ran around the chute, top to bottom. When he exhaled, his shoulders touched its edges: an uncomfortable feeling, one that made his knees rise to his chest instinctively—his kneecaps hit the top of the chute and made no sound at all. There was a terrible solidity to everything down here, put there by the water: he could have been crawling through an underground cave with a billion tons of rock pushing down.

It doesn't matter, he told himself. *If this chute collapses, you'll be dead before your mind even registers the threat.*

Gripping the rungs, he pulled himself through. The chute was coated with a helpful silicon agent: he slid as effortlessly as a plastic puck over an air-hockey table. He reached the other end, turned onto his stomach, and fell gracelessly onto the floor.

Clayton made no effort to help him up. "You really know how to make a guy feel welcome," Luke said.

With some gentle coaxing, LB came next. She whined and whimpered, but Al gave her a push and the dog shot through the chute as if she'd been greased.

Once Al herself was through, they continued. The tunnel followed a gentle curve until it hit another hatch, which opened into a lab area. It was much larger than any room Luke had seen so far. His head nearly touched the overhead lights, which buzzed with an insectile hum. The lab was spartanly appointed: a few chairs, cardboard filing cabinets.

Everything was collapsible, foldable, compressible—as it would have to be to have gotten down here. It's not as if they could back up a moving truck to the *Trieste*'s front door and let burly men in weight-lifting belts off-load supplies. It all would've been ferried down in the *Challenger*s, and been small enough to fit through their hatches.

Luke noted five hatches: the one they'd come through—marked Access 1—plus four more marked LN, LW, LT, and Access 2.

The second hatch, LW, was locked. Luke saw a keypad beside it. LW's porthole was slicked from the inside with coagulated dark matter. A buzz emitted from behind the hatch, which quivered the delicate hairs of Luke's inner ear.

A foldable lab bench was scattered with papers, most of them scrawled with his brother's spiky handwriting. Petri dishes were stacked in a small cooler; empty MREs were heaped in a trash bin.

Luke said: "Is that a viewing window?"

"Yes," Clayton said. "The only one of any size in the station."

It stretched nearly floor-to-ceiling, perhaps eight feet across. Luke's eyes charted the curve of the glass . . . *was* it glass? Probably not. Glass would shatter. Beyond lay a blackness so profound that it unrooted something in his chest.

Clayton flicked a switch. The interior lights dimmed. He flicked another. A bank of high-intensity spotlights flooded the ocean bottom.

12.

THE SEA FLOOR was as flat as a ballroom. It unfurled to the farthest edge of the light's reach—perhaps twenty feet—before rolling under a solid wall of darkness that no man-made light could penetrate. The marine snow drifted in seismic combers, gentle waves of motion . . . or as though something was moving cunningly under the surface.

Luke's heartbeat thudded dully at his temples. He put a hand on the window. The mammoth density of the sea throbbed against his fingertips. He pictured spider-legged cracks forming in his reflection, then water needling through to slice his fingers off painlessly; next the window would shatter inward as the ceiling crumpled down, crushing him before he could make peace with God.

"We watch it out there," Clayton said. "Perhaps it watches us, too."

Luke saw it then, as though it had arrived on cue. Ambrosia. A solid sheet of the stuff. It drifted across the ocean floor, reminding Luke of a manta ray. It shaped itself into a playful O and rolled along like a hula hoop.

Luke got the oddest sense of being teased—it was like watching a lure jigged past his sightline, some canny angler making it dance and shimmy oh-so-invitingly in hopes Luke would lunge and take an incautious bite . . . then what?

Clayton said, "Magnificent, isn't it?"

Luke caught a sense of shapes cavorting where the light turned granular. At the precise point where the spotlights faded and died, he swore he could see . . . *things*. They coalesced, solidifying into something swirling with angry movement, so large that the darkness could scarcely contain it, rushing at him swiftly—

He flinched.

But there was nothing. The drifting snow. That impenetrable wall of black.

"Are you catching much of it?" Luke asked his brother. "Will it . . ."

Will it let itself be caught? was the question he thought but did not say.

"We don't have to catch it anymore," Clayton said.

"You have enough?"

"Oh, you can never have enough, Lucas."

"Then why don't you have to catch it?"

"Because it's coming to us."

He snapped the lights back on. Luke saw that Al had gravitated toward the door marked LW. Her face had a disconnected, swimmy quality—the look of a person suspended in a wonderful, all-consuming dream.

"Al . . . ?" said Luke.

Her expression didn't change. She trailed one finger over the hatch of LW sensuously, as she might over a lover's sensitive flesh.

LB gave a short bark. The fog over Al's eyes lifted.

"Sorry. Off in my own world there," she said sheepishly. "This is Westlake's lab, right?"

"Of course it is." Clayton waved his hand edgily. "Come away from there."

Obediently, Al did so. She was grinning and rubbing the back of her neck, as if she'd been caught doing something embarrassing. Luke watched her circumspectly, a little weirded out by her detached expression: too much like the zoned-out look that would enter an animal's eyes once the Euthasol took hold. LB padded over and sniffed at Al's pocket. She produced a half-eaten energy bar, snapped off a piece and tossed it to LB, who snatched it out of the air and wolfed it down.

From another part of the station arose a dull, monotonous knocking.

"Is that Dr. Toy?" Al asked.

Clayton's shrug said: *Who else?*

"You figure he's dangerous, Doc?" said Al. "We can't have him running around trying to punch holes in the damn walls."

"He's staked out his fiefdom, Lieutenant," Clayton said. "He's squatting in the animal quarantine. He's not bothering me. I'm not bothering him."

Luke said: "What is he doing?"

"Pursuing scientific inquiry, I assume," Clayton said. "What else?"

Luke's gaze tracked from Clay to the hatch marked LW . . . suddenly it hit him. LW: Westlake. LT: Toy. LN: Nelson. These must be their private labs. Luke could see into Dr. Toy's through the porthole—orderly and empty. He could even see into Clayton's.

But Westlake's porthole was obscured by that slick black coating. And there was that odd hum from behind the hatch.

"Has anyone been in Westlake's lab since . . . ?" said Luke.

Clayton shook his head. "It's locked. Only Westlake knew the keypad code to gain entry."

"*Should* we take a look inside?" Luke said, eyeing that black stuff critically.

"That is unwise," Clayton said. "Westlake was working with . . . certain toxic compounds, I believe. There may be a contamination risk, but we're perfectly safe if it remains shut. That hatch is hermetically sealed."

Clayton folded his hands complacently, smiling at them both. Smiles always sat badly on his face: too often he appeared to be snarling. Luke thought his brother looked haggard. Exhaustion was etched into the flesh around his eye sockets.

Something's happened to everyone down here. And it's still happening.

But what? It refused to be pinpointed, no more than a dark speck in Luke's brain, growing steadily and gathering weight.

"Why are you here again, anyway?" Clayton asked Luke icily. "Why *you*, precisely? I mean, of all people."

"Like I said, they called me. The *government*. They thought you might . . ."

. . . Lucas come home we need you come home . . .

". . . need me here. Need something from me."

"I can tell you that you're not needed here," Clayton said simply.

A sheet of anger draped over Luke as he was ripped back through time, a younger brother knocking on the door of his big brother's basement lab. He was holding a small gift—a glass of chocolate milk—and in return only hoped for a glimpse of Clayton's sorcery or, far better, an invitation to help out. But inevitably the door would open a crack, his offering hurriedly snatched away and the door slammed shut in his face.

You're not needed.

Luke was furious that his brother would still treat him so shabbily. That fury crystallized into anger at himself—why did Clayton's predictable scorn still wound him? He wasn't here for his rat-shit brother. He was here for the people up in the real world, the ones who had human feelings and needed the help Clayton might be able to provide.

"You don't know *what* you need anymore, Clay," Luke said. "You ever consider that—that you might be in over your head? Oh, no, not the legendary Clayton Nelson. Not Cute Clay, onetime pinup boy of bubblegum magazines from coast to coast—"

Luke swooned. The lab tilted under his feet, the lights streaking across his vision.

"You're dead on your feet, Luke," Al told him. "You need to get some sleep."

When had Luke last slept? An eternity ago. He'd powered through on fear and adrenaline. But now the fatigue hit him like a hammer blow. The Nelson Brothers' Death Match—the same battle they'd been engaged in off and on for their entire lives—could wait.

"Yeah. Maybe just an hour or two," he said. "Recharge the batteries."

Al took his hand—her grip was strong and calming. "I'll take you somewhere you can rest."

Luke grabbed his bag. Clayton watched in stony silence as Al led Luke down the tunnel marked Access 2. LB padded behind Luke, her head darting side to side alertly.

"How are *you* feeling?" Luke asked Alice. They'd been inside the station only a few hours, but oh God it felt much longer.

"I'll manage." But Luke could hear the fatigue in her voice.

Flee, Luke thought. *Jet. Blow this Popsicle stand. Use your feet to beat the street . . .*

Don't be a worm, Lucas, his mother spoke up. *You could as soon out-run your own skin. What are you, scared? A little fraidy-cat?*

They came to a hatch that opened into a cramped bunk room. A cot, a stack of journals, a heap of dirty clothes. LB sniffed around the cot, chuffed dubiously, and curled up on the floor.

"It was Dr. Westlake's," Alice said. "Will it do?"

Luke thought: *Whyever not? The last body to lie on this cot now lies in a vault.*

"Yes," he said, tamping down his revulsion. "Thank you."

"Sleep. Then we'll put our heads together and figure things out."

Luke stowed his bag and sat on the bunk. LB leapt up, prodding Luke with her snout and eventually settling over his thighs. He shooed her off; she went reluctantly, her eyes shining wetly up at him.

The floor under the bunk was scattered with Westlake's research. A laptop lay atop one pile. The silver casing was sticky with dark matter. He scraped at it with his fingernail; it peeled away in a long ebony curl. It reminded him of the half-set coating on a toffee apple, so sticky it could rip the fillings out of molars.

He sniffed it. Ugh. A sweet decay, like the pool of mystery juice at the bottom of an amusement park trash bin.

Clayton's voice drifted through his mind: *Westlake was working with certain toxic compounds . . .*

Luke opened Westlake's laptop. Files were clustered at the bottom-most left-hand corner of the desktop. Luke used the trackpad to spread them out.

Three audio files. Contact 1, Contact 2, Contact 3.

Curiosity overruled exhaustion. He clicked on the first file.

13.

THE BUZZING.

That was the first thing he heard. Low and ragged, the burr of a malfunctioning servo motor—hundreds of them on the fritz at once.

Next: a voice, close to the microphone.

"Test one. Wednesday, the thirteenth of August, 5:13 p.m."

Westlake's voice. Keening, slightly nasal. The voice of a dead man.

"I noticed it just last night. Last night? I think so, yes, yes—time has a way of slipping through one's fingers down here. In the wall . . . eating through it, you might say. Behind a box of equipment. This was why I missed it at first."

The buzz settled. Westlake breathed heavily into the microphone.

"A . . . hole. This is the best means of description, though that does not adequately describe the phenomenon. A hole, after all, is a . . . an emptiness, yes? This, on the other hand . . . the phenomenon is roughly two inches in diameter. I'd measure to get its exact size but it may be unwise to draw too near. It exudes a certain disturbance."

A hole? Luke thought. *In the station?* Couldn't be. Insanity.

"Its surface is black, shimmery. I cannot discern whether it is simply lying atop the wall, or whether an exterior influence—something outside the station, in the water—has managed to eat its way through. Either way, it appears to be growing incrementally. Amazingly, it has not breached the structural integrity of the Trieste. I wouldn't be here to transcribe this if so."

Ambient noises: clickings, snappings.

"The bees do not seem troubled by it. In fact, they display great interest. They cluster at the edge of their containment unit facing the phenomenon, occasionally bashing their bodies against the glass. The other specimens, my

lizards, display the opposite reaction: they huddle as far away from it as possible.

"I covered it with several long strips of duct tape. I have not alerted Drs. Nelson or Toy. They are occupied with their own labors and . . . this will sound foolish, and doubtlessly unprofessional, but I don't want them interfering. Clayton most especially—if he knew about this, he would swing his hammer of divine authority." Westlake's voice changed. It became flinty, obsessive. "This? This is . . . mine. My discovery."

A gulf of silence punctuated by Westlake's breathing. Then:

"Hah, listen to me! A covetous schoolboy hoarding my packet of candy! Good God, if the ethics committee could see me now! I imagine they would . . ."

Westlake's voice trailed off. His breathing grew heavier.

"Can you hear that? Is the microphone picking it up?"

Luke strained his ears. Nothing but that buzz and Westlake's ragged breaths.

"Sounds emanating from the phenomenon. I hear them . . . feel them. There's a prickling sensation over my skin. How very bizarre."

Silence.

"Can you hear them? Can you?"

Click.

The file ended abruptly.

Dreamily, his blood racing, Luke opened the next one.

"Test two."

The buzz again. Quite a bit louder now.

"The hole has doubled in size. Ceaselessly, the phenomenon chews into the wall. The bees—surely you can hear them?—they are compelled by it. I let one out yesterday and it flew straight toward the hole. But it banked sharply away and settled on the wall a foot above. It made a few creeping attempts to approach the phenomenon, its antennae flicking, but never drummed up the gumption. When it settled back on the lab equipment, I cupped it in my palms in order to return it to its hivemates.

"The little brute stung me! These are the most docile creatures I've ever *dealt with. They were so tame I could almost sing them to sleep. Never once have I been stung without cause. I . . . I killed it. Ground it to paste between my palms. I was in a rare rage."*

The buzz rose and fell rhythmically.

"The other specimens have expired. Every lizard, dead. They made it down here without issue, adjusting well to their new habitat. Then yesterday I awoke—I've been sleeping in the lab the last few nights—to discover them all unmoving. Their bodies stiff, strangely white. It was as if they'd been injected with liquefied chalk. I've never seen anything like this. I wondered for a moment: could they have died of fright? Surely they cannot feel emotions. The bees, however, are thriving. Their numbers seem to be increasing."

Luke could hear Westlake fumbling around. A sharp *click!* Suddenly his voice was amplified, the sound of it much richer.

"I've hooked up a microphone. Hello? Hello? Good. It runs on a long cord. I'll attempt to feed the mic into—through—the hole. This sounds absurd. How could I push a microphone through a hole eaten into the wall of an undersea station? Were I even able to do so, where would it go? That I am unable to answer as yet."

A series of staticky raps. The mic scratching against the weave of Westlake's clothes, Luke figured.

"I've hooked the microphone to a metal rod. I'll feed it through the hole from a safe distance. In all objectivity, the hole . . . alarms me. It exerts a pull. Not on one's body so much as the mind. I can only compare it to the sensation of some kind of, of claw I suppose, sunk into the tissues of the brain."

More noises as the microphone, clipped to the metal rod, bumped along the laboratory floor.

"Careful now . . . careful."

A series of harsh *baps!* as the mic bumped up the wall. Luke could discern the exact moment it slipped through the hole: the resonance became watery, as if the mic had slid into a deep pool. But Westlake's voice remained clear.

"It's in! I've run a secondary audio channel to record my own com-

mentary. Both my voice and whatever the microphone picks up should be clear."

For a very long while, nothing. Only the liquid shifting as the microphone drifted in whatever lay beyond the hole.

Then: a powerful knock. Distant, yet resonant.

"Hello?"

Westlake made a noise of his own: a chiding *tsk*, as if sickened at himself for thinking someone—*something*—might answer him.

The noise came again. That faraway knock. And again. An even, careful cadence. There was something *knowing* in it. Luke couldn't say why he felt that, yet he did.

He broke out in a sweat. The clammy kind he associated with on-rushing sickness—the maiden signs of the flu.

The knock. Watery but insistent. Again. Again.

"Is someone there?"

Knock.

"Who is it?"

Luke almost laughed at the inanity of Westlake's question—but the fearful quail of the man's voice stilled that impulse.

The silence ran thick as a current. Then: *knock.*

"All right. Let's try this. When I ask a question now, you may answer by knocking. One knock for yes, two knocks for no. Will that be acceptable?"

Knock.

"You understand?"

Knock.

"Well. Good. Very good."

The excitement in Westlake's voice was palpable.

"Are you extraterrestrial?"

Knock . . . knock.

"So you are of this planet?"

Knock . . . knock.

"Are you friendly?"

No reply.

"Do you know what that means? Friendly?"

Knock.

"How many of you are there? Knock once for only one. Knock twice for more than one."

Knock . . . knock.

"Do you come in peace?"

No reply.

"Do you come to share information with us? To help?"

Knock.

"Do you know what is happening to us? Of the disease we've come down in search of a cure for?"

Knock.

"Can you help us?"

A gulf of silence.

"Do you know what that is—the substance we're here to study?"

Again, silence. The feathery sound of water swirling around the microphone.

When next he spoke, Westlake's voice was tight.

"Do you wish us no harm?"

Sounds from the liquid. Rustling and shucking.

Knock . . . knock.

What the hell does that mean? Luke asked himself. *No, we wish you no harm? Or no, we do wish you harm?*

"I'll ask again," came Westlake's voice, *"can you help us? We are . . . we may be dying. Our species. Do you understand? Can you—"*

A gnashing grind. The squeal of feedback.

"Jesus Chr—!"

Click.

Fear crawled over the dome of Luke's skull. He was filled with a sense that he was hovering on the cusp of something as terrible as he'd ever known—new knowledge, facts he could live a thousand lifetimes without knowing. He could feel it pulsing against his skull, tapping at the plates of bone with an icy fingertip. He ached with the desire to hurl the laptop at the wall and smash it to pieces. But there was no way he could allow himself to do that.

Heart thudding, he opened the third and final file.

"Test number . . . immaterial. The day is . . . immaterial. Time, also immaterial."

The buzz was incredibly loud now. Westlake's voice drifted hazily, sounding somehow untethered from his body.

"The phenomenon ate the microphone. Ate? Is there a better word than that? Something certainly yanked it through the hole. So yes, ate. *It happened so fast. I was lucky to salvage the laptop."*

A sucking sound, very close. A rapid *suck-uck-uck.* A wet *pop.*

Was Westlake . . . was he sucking his thumb? Like an infant?

"There has been no further contact. Not in the prior-established manner, I should say. But the hole has grown. A great deal, I must say. The bees are now constantly agitated.

"And I . . . I hear things. *Sometimes it's things being ripped. Other times they're noises like nothing I've ever heard. The buzzing of flies—this sounds quite different from the drone of the bees, somehow lower, and not only in register: it is the hum of a baser order of life. Of stupid, witless, shit-colonizing flies. Occasionally, there is also the hammer and clash of machinery. How the hell is that possible? And . . . and laughter? Yes, I do believe I heard that, too. A child's laughter. If it were not absurd to say so, I'd tell you it was that of my own daughter, Hannah."*

Westlake loosed a tortured laugh of his own.

"This is madness, of course. It's difficult to hear anything above the drone of the bees. I haven't stepped outside the lab in some time. Nelson and Toy would only interfere. They wouldn't understand. Their minds are too dense, too literal."

Westlake's voice turned brittle. Luke could imagine him hunched in his lab, his body grown gnomish, his posture covetous as he hoarded his dark secret.

"And I . . . I don't want them to have it. This is all mine."

More sucking. Luke pictured Westlake's thumb, pink from the suction.

"I have to say this. Not long ago, when I was staring at the hole—it commands my attention, I'll tell you that—it changed. Went opaque, is perhaps the word. Like watery milk. Behind it, or through it, I saw shapes. Indistinct but wonderful. Like dark wings fluttering. An enormous space filled with this antic fluttering."

The tone of Westlake's voice was off-putting—there was an uncomfortable echo of Alice's voice in it, the way she'd sounded after she'd been caught staring at Westlake's hatch.

"Whatever this is that I've discovered . . . it, they, can be communicated with, I am sure of it. Reasoned with. They are here to help. I sense no hatred. Only curiosity."

Curiosity. The word stuck in Luke's brain like a quill. Somehow it seemed even more frightening than pure hatred.

"This is my final recording. I will continue to chart my progress in my journals. I am confident that what lies on the other side is beneficial. Are they the bringers of the ambrosia? If so, perhaps they will tell us how to harness its awesome power. I believe in this possibility, and I will endeavor to make it so."

Click.

14.

LUKE'S ARMS WERE TENSED hard as marble; a concerted effort was needed to force his muscles to relax.

He had to consider the possibility that none of this had happened. That Westlake had caught a malignant case of the sea-sillies—that, or a particularly baffling indicator of the 'Gets. These files were no more than a manifestation of his creeping insanity—he'd imagined the whole god-damn thing. He'd isolated himself in his lab the same way a dying bear will crawl into the shadows of its cave; in his own sickness and delusion, Westlake had played make-believe, slave to the apparitions in his head.

What had Luke heard, really? The buzz of bees. Some scraping and scratching. A few knocks—knocks Westlake could have made himself, playing a game of call-and-answer with himself. What about the watery echo? Luke figured immersing the microphone in a glass of water would have the same effect.

Disconcerted, Luke lay down. He was so damn tired. His body was physically shutting down, a power grid starved of electricity. He'd rest briefly, and upon waking, he'd take Westlake's laptop to Al and Clayton. They could listen to the files and decide what to make of them.

He shut his eyes and tried to conjure Abby's face. Instead, a different scene: Abby and Luke in the bedroom of their shoebox apartment, back when they were graduate students. The heat lay thick inside the walls; that late-summer warmth did something to Abby. Set her afire. She'd sat on the bed with that beguiling smile. She pulled his sweats down, then his Fruit of the Looms with one finger, leaving them strung clumsily around his knees.

Get closer, silly, she'd whispered. *This isn't going to work unless we're pretty much touching, is it?*

Luke remembered being overtaken by the friendliness of it. Just a chummy blow job, followed by some aw-shucks sex. Y'know, the kind of thing pals do. Friendly, and practiced—Luke felt the tiniest ripple of concern about that: just how had she gotten so damn practiced? But Luke had felt so overjoyed at the fact that your ideal lover could be your best friend, too . . .

Then Abby's face changed. Her features went viscid, reshaping themselves into something dark and fearsome.

Luke's eyes snapped open. He swore he could see a face at the port-hole now, peering in at him.

Clay . . .

No, Al . . .

. . . then Westlake's tortured face from the vault . . .

All three faces blurred together and became something else.

They became Zachary's face. Luke's son as a tot.

His boy was laughing.

Was there anything more wonderful than a baby's laughter?

Not now, though. This was menacing—too adult, full of cruel mocking.

Luke couldn't look away as Zachary laughed with unhinged gasps, his face shading redder and redder . . . the same color it'd been as he'd screamed with the millipede inside his sleeper.

Laughing at his father. Laughing fit to bust a gut.

Ha-ha! They won't let you go, Daddy! They won't never ever let you go!

PART 4

AMBROSIA

1.

LUKE DREAMED that he was sitting at his kitchen table back home in Iowa City. The sunlight prickled his arms as it streamed through the window above the sink. Distantly, through the open door, came the giddy shrieks of children at play.

Zachary sat in his high chair. The sunlight glossed the downy hairs of his infant head.

"How's it going, buddy?" Luke said, smiling. "How you doin', Zach Attack?"

Zach smiled. His milk teeth had punched through his gums, these rounded slivers that looked like soft, pale cheese. He still had that new baby smell, too; Luke would press his nose to his son's scalp to inhale that fantastic scent.

"Ahhh . . . Mama," Zach said, his chin tilted proudly.

"Close, bud. Dada. Try that. I'm *daa-daa*."

"Ahhh . . . Mama!"

His son had been saying *Mama* for a month now—*Mama* and *ball* and even *kitty*. He'd never once said *Dada*. *Gaga* and *tata* and *baba*, oh yes, those syllables rolled merrily off his tongue. But not *Dada*. Not *once*.

He gripped his son's hands. "Dada, Zach. Say Dada."

"Tata."

Luke's hands tightened.

"Dada."

"Ahhh . . . *yaya!*"

"*Dada*." Say it, boy; you fucking *say it*. "Daa-daa."

Luke squeezed tighter, his son's bones pulsing in his grip.

"Ehhhhh! Wawa!"

Tears leapt into Zach's eyes. Luke had been gripping his fingers so tightly that they'd turned white, the blood crushed out of them.

Luke whistled tunelessly as he walked over to the fridge.

"He's a hungwy boy, issa? Zachy want his wunch?"

He took a bowl from the cupboard. There was a picture of a puppy on the bottom—Zach's favorite bowl.

Luke opened the fridge. Zach continued to cry; tears rolled down his face and splattered his bib. Luke rooted amid the tubs and bottles, still whistling. The jar his hand closed upon was warm—why would it be warm in a fridge?

He had to lever his fingernails under the jar's lid and dig them in; it felt like peeling off a massive scab. He slopped the container's contents into the puppy bowl, not really looking, smothering the puppy's grinning face with . . . whatever it was.

The bowl gave off a strange heat, as if he'd just taken it from the microwave. He grabbed a spoon and sat next to his son. Zachary's tears had dried up; he stared at the bowl with mingled hunger and revulsion.

"Whoo da hungwy baby? Here's some lunchy-wunchy for da fussy Zach."

Luke dipped the spoon into the bowl—it made a gross, squishy sound, like a shovel sunk into a pile of rotten seaweed. He brought the spoon to Zach's mouth. His son's eyes reflected whatever was in the spoon . . . its shifting scintilla reminded Luke of embers glittering in a campfire.

Zach began to scream, a high, hopeless sound. Luke prodded the spoon into his mouth harshly—*Just eat, please!*—shutting those god-damned screams up.

Zach's eyes widened, so huge they seemed to consume all the sunlight in the kitchen. His mouth worked against whatever Luke had shoved into it, lips quivering in a futile effort to spit it out. But his gorge flexed automatically, he swallowed, and when his mouth opened again it was to scream.

But not with pain. With *hunger*.

"Issa good, Zachy? Issa tasty in the belly? Open wide, here comes the aiwwwwooowww-plane!"

The spoon dipped and loop-de-looped, delivering its payload into Zach's screaming mouth. His lips were coated in a glutinous gloss.

"Issa hungry boy, issa? Mmmm, nom-nom-nom."

His son swallowed and opened his mouth again, screaming even louder now.

A fine wire of unease corkscrewed into Luke's chest. The ambient sounds and scents, previously comforting, had changed. The sweet smell of the backyard lilac had become a rancid foulness you might catch downwind of an open sewer. The sounds of children at play had become fear-struck shrieks, as if those children were being pursued by monsters intent on ripping them limb from limb.

He continued to feed Zach. Strangely, the bowl never seemed to empty.

His son's stomach strained against his bright blue onesie. Zach's cries intensified, louder and more demanding. His mouth stretched, the flesh loosening as it puckered into a sucker-fish orifice.

A carp, Luke thought with distant horror. *He's growing a carp's mouth.*

The force of Zachary's shrieks caused the papery flesh of his new mouth to flutter like a flag in a high breeze.

Luke tried to wrench his gaze downward to see what he'd been feeding his precious son, whose every morsel had always been carefully scrutinized. Abby would spend hours at the supermarket, reading labels on the baby food jars and buying organic produce to mulch in the Baby Bullet.

With aching slowness, Luke's neck finally gave out, his skull wrenching painfully down. His breath caught with an agonized hitch.

Oh oh oh oh, was all he could think, his mind skipping like a stone on the still surface of a lake. *Ohohohohohohooooooh—*

The bowl was full of ambrosia. Almost gone now: just a few pulpy balls stuck to the sides.

The puppy's face was gone, too. It had been erased. All that remained was a brownish smear, as if the ambrosia had eaten its face away.

Don't feed him another bite. Throw the bowl away, now. Stick your fin-ger down his throat and make him vomit up all that he can. Take him to the hospital and get the doctors to pump his stomach. Get it out of him, Luke—for Christ's sake, get it out!

But in that awful way nightmares have, he scraped the sides of the bowl, collecting the remaining ambrosia into a tidy dollop. It sat on the spoon, tumorlike, heaving slightly as if breathing.

Zachary issued a string of gibbering hiccups. He bucked in his high chair, his engorged stomach rattling the feeding tray.

"*Dada!*" he screeched, the sound of a nail pulled from a sun-bleached plank of wood. "*Dada! Daaaaaaadaaaaaaa!*"

"Shhhh," Luke said. "Eat all you like. You can never have enough."

Luke stabbed the spoon into his son's mouth; Zach's lips closed over it triumphantly, sucking every last speck off of it. He stared at his father with a feral, too-old expression. Ancient hate radiated from his dead, gray eyes.

He opened his mouth again, screaming, screaming.

"There's nothing left," Luke said, holding up the bowl—which had melted entirely now, a gummy mess running down his fingers, burning slightly as something worked under his flesh.

Zach vented maddening, lung-rupturing shrieks in response. His strange new mouth stretched wider, wider . . .

Luke saw something in there.

Oh God. Oh good God, no . . .

A dozen or more eyeballs stared at Luke from inside Zachary's mouth. They nested in the soft pink flesh of his palate and throat, staring unblinkingly, appraising Luke with cold scrutiny.

We all have different sets of eyes, my son.

His mother's voice.

Very different, yes, but very lovely, Lucas. You only have to let them out, like I said I'd gladly do for stupid Brewster Galt. Let them out to see the world . . .

The eyes in Zach's mouth blinked in unison—a dozen lewd winks. They made an awful *pipping* noise as the inflamed flesh inside Zach's mouth clipped shut for an instant, like the edges of a fresh wound making contact.

Luke scooped his son out of the high chair and into his arms. Zach's body had a sick, pendulous weight. His cheeks showed deep dents as they sucked greedily at the air. He kept screaming through his sucker-fish mouth, bathing Luke's face with noxious breath. The mouth-eyes stared at him balefully.

Luke rocked him, as he'd done every night since Zach was born.

"Husha baby. Husha, husha, sleep now."

Sometimes when Zach was overtired, Luke would hold his eyelids shut. Very gently, rolling Zach's eyelids down and keeping them shut with gentle pressure from his fingertips; he did so now. Zach's eyelids strained as the muscles trembled under Luke's fingertips, much like flies buzzing under Saran Wrap.

Luke pushed a little harder. *Keep those eyes closed, my beautiful boy. Please.*

Zach's screams only intensified. The eyes inside his mouth rotated madly in their cups of flesh. The skin of Zach's chin and cheeks and forehead was developing red throbbing cysts and Luke knew eyes would soon be sprouting there, too.

Luke felt around in Zach's eyes just a little. Gray fluid the consistency of model glue squished between the eyelids.

"Shhhh, now. Sleep. What's there to see? Nothing good."

His son's face was cracking open in a dozen places. Luke peered at these new eyes, each one offering a hateful, shriveling stare.

Luke's fingers sunk into Zach's eye sockets to the second knuckle. They punched into a pocket of curdled sludge that reminded him of the congealed porridge his mother used to eat. There came a hissing sound, but from where, Luke couldn't tell. Stinking fluid the color of molten lead bubbled up from Zachary's sockets.

Luke pushed until the webbing between his fingers touched the bridge of his son's nose. Zach's flesh offered no resistance. Luke's fingertips passed through the grooved tangerine of Zach's brain to touch the inner swell of his skull.

"It'll be over soon," he whispered, hoping his son could hear. "I'm so sorry . . ."

The fontanel on the top of Zach's head pulsed ominously, as if something underneath was struggling to free itself.

Luke stared, trapped in the calm eye of his dread, as his son's scalp split in a bloodless trench. Something pushed through the squandered flesh, horrid and spiky and flecked with white curds . . .

. . . and turned in Luke's direction, staring not with eyes but with a sense of merciless curiosity mingled with furious intent.

2.

LUKE STRUGGLED OUT OF SLEEP like a man crawling out of a mine shaft. Gummy strings of the nightmare clung to his brain. He heard Zachary screaming somewhere as the dream continued to unravel; Luke reached for his lost son—but his fingers closed on empty air.

Luke's brain felt unattached to his senses, the way it often felt following a bad dream. He blinked and stared around Westlake's quarters.

The hatch was open. Just a hair.

Four small appendages were wrapped around the edge of the hatchway.

A child's fingers.

Luke saw them . . . then he didn't. They had slipped away.

Next came a series of excitable, clumsy footsteps trailing down the tunnel.

His son's name passed over his lips before he could choke it down. "Zach?"

Laughter bubbled up the tunnel. The sound grew fainter, threatening to vanish. Luke rolled off the cot and shoved the hatch open.

"Zach?"

That champagne-bubble laughter flooded the dim tunnel in reply— the kind of laughter Zach used to make when Luke hefted him under the arms and lobbed him into the air, catching him deftly as he came down.

This is not happening, chirped a voice in Luke's head. *Your son isn't down here. You know that, Luke. In your heart, in your head.*

But he didn't, really. That was the thing—Zach was everywhere. *Any-where.* That's what tore you apart.

Unthinkingly, Luke followed the laughter.

The tunnel seemed to heave like an enormous pair of lungs, the walls constricting before expanding again . . . just a trick of the light. He stumbled forward heedlessly, borne on a bubbly foam of anxiety. Luke felt his boots sinking into the floor as if into some sort of weird metallic mud. He felt it sucking at his feet, a disturbing sensation, and told himself it wasn't actually happening. His mind was playing a funny trick, was all. *Ha, ha, real funny. Thanks, brain. You have a great sense of comedic timing.* He glanced around in an attempt to moor himself. He noticed a string of pipes jutting upward along the wall like the flutes on a church organ, their curves winking dull bronze in the dim. A rhythmic churn emanated from behind the walls, the sound of motors pounding without cease in the center of the earth.

Ahead of him in the darkness, something moved.

"Who's there?" Luke said, the tendons cabled down his neck.

No answer, only the watery echo of his voice.

. . . there . . . ere . . . ere . . .

When it faded Luke heard, or was certain he'd heard, the low rustle of breathing. He stood in the tunnel dark, the hairs quilling on his forearms. That rustling did not come again. He was set to reject it as a figment (Fig Men) of his imagination, conjured by the terrible pressure of this place . . .

A shape coalesced where his eyes were trained. He saw a pair of pajamas. Oh-so-familiar. They were Zachary's favorites—his *peejays,* Abby used to call them; *Zach it's bedtime get into your peejays!*—with a pattern of fire trucks and police cars, signifiers of law, order, and safety from harm. Small hands and feet jutted from the sleeves and leg holes, shining whitely in the gloom.

He could not see a face. The air above the neckline was dark and empty.

The headless pajamas turned—a coy movement that seemed to say *follow me! follow me!*—and scampered down the tunnel.

Luke obeyed the directive. The floor sucked greedily at his boots; the metal flowed over his ankles as his feet sunk into the chilly muck at the bottom of the sea.

Darkness closed in behind him, deeper and deeper shades. Zachary's laughter pealed off the walls and rebounded all around Luke.

"Zach! Hold on—please, *stop!*"

Zach slipped around a bend in the tunnel up ahead. Luke let out a strangled cry.

Nonononono, not again please not again . . .

He tried to run but his boots were mired, making every step an ordeal. He finally rounded the turn only to see he'd reached a dead end. The blackness was absolute; it was no different than staring down a mine shaft.

Three words were written on the wall in wet letters. Instinctively, Luke knew they were written in blood.

DADDY COME HOME

Something tugged on his sleeve. A small hand, four small fingers gripping his overalls. He didn't want to look. He didn't want to see his headless son . . . or something far more horrible.

He tried to jerk his arm away. But the tugging was insistent.

Look at me Daddy—LOOK!

No, Luke thought. *I don't want to. You're not my son.*

Oh, but I am. I'm your little Zach Attack. Right here in the flesh!

The voice was not that of his son. It belonged to something ineffably older, more calculating, and worse beyond anything Luke could imagine.

A terrific jerk at his arm now.

YOU FUCKING LOOK AT ME NOW.

Luke snatched his arm back. He overbalanced and fell, hammering his skull on the wall—

. . . and came to slumped against the tunnel. The overhead lights burned. LB stood a few feet away, eyeing him with a canine version of concern. His sleeve was wet with her slobber.

His son was gone. He'd never been here, of course. There was no dead end, no bloody words on the wall. He'd dreamed it all. Of course he had. He thought he'd woken from a nightmare only to now discover that the nightmare hadn't yet finished.

And yet he'd left Westlake's room. He'd opened the hatch, never waking, and walked down the tunnel. He'd . . . *sleepwalked?* Bullshit. He'd never done that in his life. LB must've followed him, then tugged on his sleeve to wake him.

Sleepwalked . . . just like Clayton might have been sleepwalking when he sent that transmission to the surface.

Happens a lot on submarines, Al's voice chimed in his head. *Guys who never had the habit before. Your brainwaves go a bit buggy . . .*

"Thanks, girl," Luke said. "You beat an alarm clock all to hell."

LB chuffed as though to say: *No problem, boss. Just doing my job.*

Luke returned to Westlake's quarters . . . then caught noise from the main lab. He followed it, craving any kind of companionship. LB tagged along at his heels.

It was Clayton. He was leaning against the lab bench, his head lowered. He seemed disoriented—*discombobulated*, as their mother might've said. He had the look of a man who'd been kicked awake with a pointy-toed shoe.

"You okay?" Luke asked.

"What?" Clayton's face swiftly recomposed into its regular withering expression. "Yes . . . why wouldn't I be?"

"Clay, I just had the strangest dream."

His brother said, "Yes, they can be incredibly vivid down here."

Luke decided to speak no further about it—the dream about Zachary eating ambrosia. After all, Clayton, wonderful sibling that he was, hadn't even contacted Luke when Zach had gone missing. Not a phone call, not an e-mail, nothing. Complete radio silence. Maybe he hadn't known what to say . . . or perhaps he hadn't even known Zach had gone missing—or worse and probably more accurately, he hadn't cared. He'd never even *met* Zach. Or Abby, for that matter. Clayton hadn't responded to the RSVP for their wedding or Zach's first birthday party. No cards, no gifts. What else should Luke have expected, anyway? It was fine, as far as Luke had been concerned. Better that Clayton exist distantly—his brother, the brilliant scientist. On a primal level, Luke hadn't wanted Clayton's presence wafting through the lives of the people he loved.

"Clayton, do you think it might be a good idea to get out of here for a while? Take a powder, head up to the surface to clear your head?"

Luke wasn't about to mention his sleepwalking incident, either. Or Westlake's audio files. Not yet. He couldn't face Clayton's sneering scorn, not without Al here to back him up at least.

"You can do whatever you want, Lucas," his brother said. "You shouldn't even be here. But I can't leave."

"Why not?"

But Luke already knew the answer. The *Trieste* was the seat of the unknown, and his obsessive brother wasn't about to abandon his attempt unlock its secrets.

"Fine," he said, setting it aside for now. "Where's Alice?"

"She's getting some sleep." Clayton cocked his head. "In the meantime, would you like to see what I've discovered? Now that you're here?"

Clayton clearly *wanted* to show Luke. Childishly, part of Luke wanted to give his older brother what Abby used to call the RFU: the Royal Fuck You.

Nah, not interested, Clay. It sounds pretty boring, to be honest. Hey, you got a TV in this joint? You get decent reception down here?

More crucially, did Luke really *want* to see?

He'd witnessed Clayton's blooper reel before—a mouse with a collapsed nose on its back, for one. Luke's skin crawled at the thought of what his brother had been up to down here where the light never shone.

But of course, Luke *did* want to see. If anyone could figure out how to harness the ambrosia, his brother was that man.

Alice's voice floated to them from another part of the station. She sounded vaguely fearful.

"Luke?" she called out. "Hey, Luke?"

"Hurry up," Clayton said, shepherding Luke into his lab.

"Wait. What about Al?"

Clayton shook his head. Luke hesitated as Clay punched a code on the keypad.

"Family only. You have eight seconds to get inside, Lucas. Then it locks automatically."

Luke didn't move.

eight . . . seven . . .

Clay's jaw tensed.

six . . .

Luke said: "The dog comes with me."

"It does not. No dogs allowed," said Clayton.

It was Luke's turn to cock his head at his brother. He *knew* Clayton wanted to show him. Otherwise he'd never have offered.

Alice's voice drew nearer. "Luke?"

three . . . two . . .

"Fine. Get in, both of you," Clayton snapped, relenting. "Quickly."

Luke gripped LB's collar. She backpedaled, fighting him.

"What's the matter, girl? It's okay."

Really? Was it?

Luke picked her up. LB tucked her head to his throat the way Zach used to do before falling asleep.

one . . .

3.

THE LOCK ENGAGED with a hiss. Clayton draped a blanket over a hook above the porthole, shielding them from the main lab.

Clay's lab was a cube, yet its walls didn't meet at right angles; instead they bellied outward to maintain the *Trieste*'s egg-based physics. A cot in one corner. Clayton must also sleep in here, Luke figured.

Westlake took to sleeping in his lab, too, he recalled. *He wanted to be close to the hole. His hole.*

Luke set the dog down but she remained zippered to his side. Her eyes rolled in their sockets; she was clearly afraid but Luke couldn't pinpoint any immediate cause. A terrarium and a cage housing a pair of guinea pigs sat against one wall. Beside those rested a pair of larger cages—dog crates, one of which had surely held LB.

Where's the other one? Luke wondered. *Where's Little Fly?*

A stainless-steel lab bench occupied the middle of the room; Luke could see where it had been riveted together, as a bench that size would have been brought down here in sections. A large poster of Albert Einstein—that famous shot with his tongue sticking out—was hung on the wall directly behind the bench. The quote read: "If you can't explain it simply, you don't understand it well enough."

"I didn't know you were a fan," Luke said.

"It's good to visualize your competition." Clay smiled. "You will laugh at this, Lucas, but sometimes I talk to Albert. If I've been working long enough, sometimes he'll talk back."

A squat white box sat along the near wall. Clayton opened its lid; plumes of vapor billowed out. He reached inside, whistling absentmindedly. Clayton used to whistle or even sing in his basement lab all the time; the notes would drift up the staircase into the kitchen. The most inane melodies. The theme to *Gilligan's Island*, or even "Whistle While You Work"—except Clayton used to screw with the lyrics:

Whistle while you work, Hitler was a jerk; Mussolini bit his weenie and now it doesn't work . . .

Clayton shut the cooler—but not before Luke noticed a squared-off shape wrapped in black plastic. It looked a bit like a butchered hog loin, though Luke knew it wouldn't be that.

"Don't be alarmed," Clayton said, placing a guinea pig on the lab bench.

The animal was frozen stiff, glittering with frost. Luke wasn't alarmed at all—as a veterinarian in the Midwest, he'd seen plenty of frozen animals.

"How did it die?" Luke asked. "Or is that important to your scientific query?"

The guinea pig tipped onto its side, its legs jutting up at the ceiling. LB edged to the lip of the table, snuffling with keen interest. Clayton swatted at her; the dog flinched away in fear.

Luke reached out and snatched his brother's wrist. He felt the live-wire twitch of Clayton's tendons—he also noticed that Clay's fingers were now bandaged to the second joint, swaddled under thick gauze.

"Not very nice." Luke tsked. "Do you treat all your guests that way?"

Clayton offered a gravedigger's smile. The guinea pig was melting out of its icy encasement; a small pool of water had already formed around it.

Thhhwiiiilppppppippit!

Luke craned his head around. Where had that noise come from? A dripping tap? They wouldn't have running water down here, would they?

The sound stirred a memory, yet Luke couldn't lay his finger on it.

Wait a second. The guinea pig's leg. Had it . . . twitched?

LB spun in an agitated circle, whining pitifully.

The guinea pig's leg twitched again, obviously this time.

"Clay," Luke said. "What's it doing? What's that dead thing doing?"

"Who said it was dead, brother dear?"

It *had* to be dead. The laws of nature dictated as much. Some creatures could be frozen for a short period and be reanimated. Flies, crickets. Not warm-blooded animals of an elevated biological genus.

And yet . . .

The guinea pig's sides began to heave as it took the smallest breaths.

This is not happening, Luke thought. *It's not possible.*

The coating of ice over the guinea pig's face melted. Its eyeballs were vibrantly red—the color of blood leaping from a torn vein. It flipped to its feet and trundled awkwardly over the lab bench.

Clayton picked it up and offered it to his brother. Luke was beset with a profound revulsion.

Why? There was nothing obviously the matter with it, other than the fact it had just come back from the dead. A perfectly ordinary guinea pig, shivering in his brother's cupped palms.

Don't you touch it, Luke, said the voice of caution. *It's . . . diseased. It'll infect you—it doesn't even have to bite you. Touching it will be enough.*

"It's a little-bitty, fluffy-wuffy guinea pig," Clay said. "I take it you're afraid?"

Luke's jaw tightened. He held his hands out and Clay gave it to him. God, it felt awful: like holding a throbbing bezoar—a tumorous hairball, one of which he'd once removed from the stomach of a narcotized leopard at the Des Moines Zoo.

The creature just sat there in his palms, its pert nose twitching. An odd notion came into Luke's mind: it was *trying* to look cute, the same way a calculating child could become doe-eyed and saccharine when there was something to gain from it. Its teeth—*old man teeth; the nicotine-stained teeth of a three-pack-a-day smoker*—clashed like tusks in the wet hole of its mouth.

Clayton opened the cage. "Put it inside."

Luke did so with great relief. The other two guinea pigs, both quite small, avoided the unfrozen one, burrowing into the cedar shavings and squeaking in consternation.

"How . . . ?"

"Oh, come now," said Clayton. "You've spoken to Felz, haven't you?

So you know perfectly well how." He retrieved a kit from beneath the table. Luke had used the same kit thousands of times. Inside you'd find two syringes and a vial of Euthasol.

An EK—Extinction Kit, as it was known in the veterinarian biz.

Clayton unwrapped a hypo and affixed the needle. He extracted 2.5 ccs of Euthasol, enough to flatline a Great Dane.

Agitated squeals broke out inside the cage. The unfrozen guinea pig was now attacking the other two. It lunged at the sensitive webbing of the much smaller guinea pig's legs, hamstringing it. The third guinea pig clambered up the cage to hang in screeching, stupid shock from the upper bars.

The unfrozen one flipped the small one over; its head darted between the small pig's legs, teeth gnashing at the poor thing's exposed privates. Its victim shrieked in terror and pain.

LB advanced on the cage with a growl building in her throat.

"Keep that damn thing away," Clayton said, pulling on a pair of vulcanized rubber gloves.

Luke gripped LB by the scruff. Clayton reached into the cage and vised his fingers around the zombified (except that wasn't really the case, was it?) guinea pig. It squealed as he pulled it off the smaller one. Luke caught a glimpse of the victim's shredded sex organs and blanched.

Clayton pinned the guinea pig to the table. Its face was a mask of blood, its head whipping in crazed paroxysms.

"The needle," he grunted.

Luke handed it over. He wasn't about to question his brother—he'd just as soon protest Clayton driving a stake through a vampire's black heart.

An ungodly shriek bubbled out of the guinea pig's throat. It bit Clayton's glove and tore a groove out of the rubber.

It shouldn't be capable of that. Luke was gobsmacked. *A pit bull would have a hard time biting through those gloves.*

Clayton sank the needle into the guinea pig's flank.

The needle bent.

Jesus Christ. It actually *bent,* as though Clayton stabbed it into a car door.

Clay jabbed it again and the needle snapped with a singing *tink*, the spike of metal spinning through the air.

Luke's mind was reeling but his brother remained calm—calm*ish*. Greasy balls of sweat dotted his brow, but whether that was from dread or exertion Luke couldn't tell. Luke's own body was bathed in sticky heat that radiated up from the balls of his feet, panic ghosting through the ventricles of his heart.

"Screw on the other needle-tip for me, would you?" Clayton said.

Luke did so—an action he'd completed thousands of times, thank God, his fingers working instinctively. Clayton flipped the bleating creature onto its back, located its rectum and stabbed with the needle. It sank in deeply, the guinea pig hissing like a cockroach as Clayton depressed the plunger.

Clayton injected the full 2.5 ccs. Luke thought of telling him to save some for the guinea pig with the bloodied privates . . . but right now, he just wanted this big bastard dead.

The guinea pig's body relaxed. Clayton quickly ducked underneath the lab bench and came up with what looked like a pair of sterling silver bolt cutters. They were Bethune surgical rib shears—an instrument used for splitting the cartilage between human ribs during open-heart surgery.

Clayton was singing now. A familiar children's song, sung in a toneless, dial-tone voice.

"The itsy-bitsy spider went up the water spout; down came the rain and washed the spider out . . ."

He brought the shears down. The blades formed an inverted V around the guinea pig's neck.

"What the hell are you doing, Clay?"

"Look closely." Clayton's eyes glittered. "Part its hair so you can see the flesh."

Luke didn't want to touch the thing again, but curiosity overrode his squeamishness. The guinea pig's fur was stiff like the bristles of a dirty broom, the flesh under it pink and oily. Its body pumped off the noxious warmth of a compost heap.

"Do you see it?" said Clayton. "That shine?"

Its skin held the barest scintilla, as though dusted with powdered diamonds.

"It's the ambrosia," said Clayton.

"Is it leaking out of its body?"

"I don't think it was ever *inside* its body. I think it *covers* bodies in the thinnest skein, so thin it would take electron magnification to spot it. Think of a spider's web. It doesn't take much pure matter at all; an ounce of ambrosia, stretched into skeins, could cover the entire population of our home city."

Luke couldn't help but picture it. The citizens of Iowa City covered in downy threads of ambrosia, finer than baby hair, unnoticeable to the naked eye but coiling deep into their bodies, fastening around their organs and bones. Everybody shimmered in the sunlight, their bodies aglitter . . .

"It *might* send roots inside." Clayton wiped the feverish sweat collecting above his lip. "Roots so slender that they can slip between molecules of flesh and blood; so small they can even twine around *atoms*. Think about it."

Phlooooopppp . . .

That dripping sound again, coming from somewhere inside the lab—

That old childhood memory Luke's mind had been chasing entombed itself in his skull with a concussive thump . . .

4.

THE STANDING PIPE on Old Langtree Road in Iowa City. A concrete tunnel with a grate over its mouth to prevent idiot kids from clambering into its damp, moss-crusted darkness. An overflow pipe—when the river rose, excess water jetted out of it to saturate the floodplain. But the river could go months at low ebb, meaning that the area ringing the pipe was most often a stagnant swamp that on high August days smelled like a pile of mildewed gym trunks.

Clayton visited the swamp often, as its microclimate hosted prize specimens. Unsurprisingly, he favored the most disgusting life-forms. If its body had the texture of a snot-filled bath bead, chances were that Clayton wanted it. Sometimes he'd let Luke tag along, needing an extra pair of hands.

One long-ago summer day, the young brothers had arrived at dusk, when the coolness brought the best specimens out of their hidey-holes. Luke never visited the standing pipe alone. Its wide, cavernous mouth jutting out of the gray caliche—which reminded him, disconcertingly, of elephant skin—sent an unpleasant shiver down his arms. The pipe's interior was hung with rotting strands of moss that dangled down in stiff stalactites. Sunlight couldn't penetrate it more than a few feet; after that it turned grainy, the shadows swimming with clever movements.

It was stupid to think. It was just a tunnel. Sure, it *was* dangerous; you wouldn't want to squeeze past the grate and walk down it—not because there was something waiting for you in its gloomy guts, but because you could trip and fall and bust your fool skull wide open, as Luke's mother was apt to say.

By the time the boys reached the pipe that day, the surrounding swampland was hovering with shadows. The inverted bells of the carnivorous pitcher plants lay bronzed in the dying sun. The creatures that had lain dormant during the day were slithering and spidering from their resting places.

Clayton forged into the swamp in a pair of hip waders, sending up swarms of no-see-ums. Luke's sweatpants—he couldn't bear wading through that bug-infested swamp barelegged—were soaked to his crotch. The fluffy tops of cotton grass poking out of the swamp reminded Luke of Peter Cottontail, the bunny, which led him to envision the grass-wads hiding a thousand drowned rabbits submerged in the brown muck with their tails sticking out of the water.

The brothers reached the mouth of the pipe. A new moon glossed its concrete lips, a silver O enclosing a solid pool of darkness.

Clustered along the pipe were translucent vein-strung sacs, each roughly the size of an oxblood marble. They were arranged in gooey clusters—bunches of albino grapes, or mutant fly eggs.

"They're hatching," Clayton said. "Perfect."

The sacs were breaking open to disgorge tallowy creatures with flagellate tails. They squiggled to the edge of the pipe and—

Thhhwhooolloop . . .

Dropped into the water.

"Pollywogs are interesting creatures," Clayton remarked. "No other amphibian undergoes such a massive change as it becomes an adult. Humans have a few more bones as babies, which fuse together as we grow, but we don't grow new arms or legs or *lose* any part of our bodies as we mature. Humans," he said with something approaching sadness, "are boring."

Luke always felt unbelievably grateful for these moments when his brother treated him like a human being. In such moments Clayton seemed most like a human being himself, full of childlike wonder.

The mama bullfrogs croaked in protest as Clayton dragged a net and deposited pollywogs into the bucket Luke had brought. Luke heard something from inside the pipe—a sound that vibrated the sensitive hairs of his ear canal.

It came again. A gelatinous *sliding* like something coughed up from a kitchen drain . . . and what was the pipe, anyway, if not a drain? A huge, long drain. It stood to reason that the things coughed out of a pipe that size would be massive, as well.

Ghostly spiders scuttled up the back of Luke's neck. His mouth filled with a dry wash of horror—the taste of mothballs covered in a choking film of dust.

The swamp stilled. The bullfrogs stopped croaking, even the insects seemed to stop buzzing. Only the sucking, *slurping* sound coming from the pipe.

The sound, or its maker, was drawing nearer in a stealthy kind of way . . . but not too stealthily. Maybe it *wanted* to be heard. The sucking sound was joined by an icy *clickety-click* reminiscent of cockroaches scuttling behind water-fattened drywall . . . or ragged claws dragged along mossy concrete.

The pipe's mouth was covered with a checkerboard rebar grate to keep stupid kids out. Because kids *were* stupid sometimes. Even the smart ones, like Clayton. They would come to an isolated swamp past dark, say, to collect pollywogs. Far from the reliable streetlit world—hell, they may as well be on another planet. They could disappear and nobody would even know until morning. It was tragic, but it happened all the time . . .

Even a smart kid had to be stupid only that one time.

Clayton's jaw was clenched tight, his eyes fixed above the tunnel's mouth as if he couldn't quite bear to stare directly into it.

The sound came again, closer now: a choked and mocking gurgle, an enormous mouth laughing around a wad of rotting meat.

Pollywogs fluttered against Luke's sweatpants as they flicked past, racing away. He wished he could shrink somehow, become as small and insignificant as they were, and flee with them. He wished he had a minuscule and idiotic pollywog brain, because his own was an inferno of fearful images and possibilities.

The grate will stop it. It stopped dumb kids from getting in, and it will stop anything else from getting out.

But Luke knew this wasn't true. Whatever it was—and he understood, in his lizard-brain cortex, that it was something real bad—it could snap the grate like matchsticks . . . or else ooze through the metal lattice-work like cancerous black taffy.

The brothers backed away slowly, the way you might from a slumbering bear. Clayton's breath came in a flighty whistle like the whinny of a horse. Luke averted his eyes, didn't dare look at the pipe. If he only heard it but didn't see it, it wasn't real. The sounds could be anything. The gurgle of sludgy water over ancient bottles and cans, or even over the water-bleached skeletons of drowned animals.

But if you *saw* it, made eye contact with it . . .

Their heels hit the dry wash. Once that happened, the boys turned and clawed up the pebbly incline, abandoning the bucket and net, hitting the moon-glossed road, and running as fast as their legs could carry them.

Some reckless urge made Luke glance back over his shoulder. Only once, and only for a second.

He saw something. He would swear to it. Something moving. A hand? No, not exactly. It was too elongated to be human. The fingers were twice as long as any he'd ever seen, the digits thin and witchy. Each finger was tipped with a cruel sickle that trapped the moonlight along its curve.

This enormous hand ticked delicately along the rusted rebar, back and forth, back and forth, as if plucking notes on an instrument. A soft and beckoning gesture.

Come baaaack, Lucas. Come baaaack. Bring your brother, too. Three is never a crowd. We'll have . . . all the time in the world.

God help him, Luke felt himself turn around.

His hip, gripped by a compulsion he couldn't fight, wrenched back—his feet would follow shortly, surely as two follows one . . . then Clayton jerked Luke's arm so hard that it almost tore out of its socket. Come morning, the flesh of his collarbone would be a sullen mottle of bruises.

"*No. Don't,*" was all Clay said. His neck was flexed taut, as if he were fighting an insistent pair of hands that were trying to wrench his gaze back to the pipe. "Don't look."

They turned and ran until their lungs burned, until the standing pipe and its noises were well behind them.

The next morning, Luke wouldn't believe what he'd seen. It had been a trick of the moonlight, nothing more.

But he never did return to the pipe. Neither did Clayton, who struck up a deal with the local pet shop owner to buy mice at a bulk discount, which he claimed were better specimens anyway.

5.

SSSSSCHLLLIPPPPPTTZZ . . .

The sound broke Luke out of his reverie—except they had begun to feel less like reveries than waking dreams.

Lacuna was the term that leapt out at him: an old Latin word that meant an empty space, a missing part . . . a *gap*. His mind seemed to slip into those gaps much easier down here. Since he boarded the *Challenger*, he'd been tumbling into and out of these old memories—his past, trapped within these dream-pools, kept reaching out and pulling him into their murky depths.

Now he was back in his brother's lab, where Clayton still held a pair of shears to that awful guinea pig's throat. The sound coming from somewhere inside the lab—*thwwwilliiiippp!*—was almost the same sound those pollywogs had made falling into the swamp when they were boys.

Before Luke could figure out what was making that noise, the guinea pig's leg twitched.

Impossible.

Clayton had injected it with enough Euthasol to stop a full-grown man's heart. There's no way it could come back from . . .

Its front legs stiffened. Its lungs inhaled reflexively. It unleashed a hellish squeal that sounded shockingly like the shriek of an infant. Its eyes burned, twin embers socked into the white fur of its face. It lunged—

Clayton brought the shears together.

SCCCHRIIK!

The sound was that of a bolt cutter snapping a brass Master Lock off a school locker. Luke's eyes widened as the guinea pig's head was snipped neatly off its neck.

No blood at first. Not a drop. The flesh and tendon and bone were clearly visible down the face of each wound, both head-stump and neck-stump—it was like sawing a tree in half.

None of this makes any sense, Luke thought stupidly. *None of this can actually be happening . . .*

Clayton pulled the guinea pig's body and head apart, separating them by a foot. Belatedly, blood began to leak from its neck in thick strings that spread across the bench like fingers.

Blood-tentacles, was Luke's thought.

These tentacles crept toward the guinea pig's body, which was releasing tentacles of its own. They merged in the middle of the bench.

LB whined and buried her head against Luke's thigh.

The tentacles began to constrict. With aching slowness, the split halves of the guinea pig began to inch back toward each other.

They're trying to reattach. They want to make the guinea pig whole again.

Watching this, a small but essential part of Luke's mind untethered itself from the whole. Luke actually heard it—a cartilaginous *thok* like a drumstick wrenched off a Thanksgiving turkey; he felt it go, too: a physical sensation that he could liken only to a lifeboat setting off from a sinking ship, taking some vital cargo with it.

The guinea pig's sundered halves drew closer. The blood-tentacles sucked and squirmed. What would happen once the halves had linked up?

"Stop it, Clay. Please, just stop it."

Clayton retrieved a plastic container with a snap-top lid. He put the gloves back on, grabbed a scalpel, and slit the bloody webbings. Luke heard a snakelike hiss as the blade severed the crimson tentacles.

Clayton picked up the guinea pig's head gingerly, still trailing ribbons of blood, and set it inside the container. He snapped on the lid and left the box on the bench.

The tentacles from the guinea pig's body crept over the container. Investigating, it would seem—sniffing it like a lonely hound at a porch door. They actually climbed the plastic and poked along the seal.

Their progress stymied, the tentacles sagged. A few moments later they surrendered their shape and collected into a pool of plasma. The guinea pig's headless body relaxed, evacuating its contents in a stinking gout.

A tiny speck of ambrosia gathered on the guinea pig's foot. Clayton lifted the ambrosia on the scalpel's edge and crossed to the cage. The guinea pig with the torn privates lay in a pile of bloodied cedar shavings. Clayton set the scalpel near its head.

The ambrosia rolled off onto the wounded creature's ear, then vanished.

The guinea pig bleated and went rigid . . . then it rolled over and scampered to the running wheel. It began to race as fast as its stubby legs would carry it, tearing around and around and around like a mad dervish.

Clayton reached in and withdrew it from the cage. He showed Luke its sex organs. They were whole and, for all Luke knew, functional.

"This is madness. Utter madness."

"No," Clayton said. "It only *looks* like madness. You don't know what you're seeing."

Clayton carried the guinea pig to the cooler. Lifting the lid, he set the creature inside. Luke didn't protest this treatment, putting a live animal in deep freeze. Was that thing really *alive* anymore?

"What use is it?" Luke had to ask. "This ambrosia? Look at what it does, Clay. It . . . *perverted* that animal. Am I wrong? That guinea pig was savage. There was . . ."

Something demonic about it, was the thought his mind spat out. He'd felt the creature's awfulness in his hands, the clammy grossness of its body.

"There could be any number of reasons why it acted that way," Clayton said. "Firstly, it likely had no conception of what was being done to it."

"'Being done to it.' Interesting choice of words, brother of mine. So let me ask you—do *you* know what was being done to it?"

"I'm beginning to understand, yes. There may be pain or trauma associated with the assimilation. The ambrosia may trigger certain psychotropic side effects, leading to heightened aggression."

"My God, Clay—do you realize what you're saying? This substance you're studying won't allow a creature to *die*. Not by freezing it, not by pumping it with a lethal dose, not by *hacking its fucking head off*. There has to be some other intelligence at work here. I don't mean some *take me to your leader* shit; just something we can't possibly understand. The way that blood moved . . . it was *smart*. It had a purpose."

Clayton's expression didn't indicate that he felt the same horror Luke did—rather, it seemed that the prospect of a purposeful intellect excited him immensely.

"How can you know it won't function the same way when used on a human being?" said Luke. "That it won't turn people into raving maniacs?"

"There's only one answer to that, Lucas—we don't know *how* it will work, because we haven't tried it on a human subject yet."

YET. Dear God.

"Clay. *Think*. What about Westlake?"

"What about him?" Clayton said, eyebrows innocently raised.

"You've calculated this angle already," said Luke. "You realize Westlake must have come in contact with the ambrosia."

"I think . . ." A grudging nod. "Yes. That's likely accurate. He must've abandoned the necessary precautions. He forgot the risks."

Or the fucking stuff crawled inside his head, Luke thought wildly. *Or else . . .*

"Clay, what if he *purposefully* brought it into contact with himself? Not an accident or a goof-up," said Luke. "What if he smeared it on himself or swallowed it or some other goddamn thing? What if he let himself be *assimilated*, as you put it."

Luke suddenly and dearly wanted to tell his brother about the dream he'd had. He wanted to spill his guts about the giant millipede that, for a span of pulseless seconds, he'd been absolutely sure was stalking him down that darkened storage tunnel. He wanted to let Clayton know that these depths exerted a breed of pressure that lay entirely apart from the eight hundred fluid tons of water that pressed down on every square inch of the *Trieste* right this moment . . .

. . . but he had a terrible feeling Clayton knew all that already—he'd know it deep under his skin by now.

"Why don't we leave?" Luke asked again. "A little sunlight on your face. You remember the sun, don't you? Hey. Just a few days. Then you come right back down."

And maybe—if we're lucky—this whole place will cave in on itself in your absence. Would that be so bad?

Clayton shook his head, lips pursed in a playful *tsk*.

"It must be hard on you. It must really *sting*, Lucas. Acting as their errand boy."

Luke frowned. "What the hell are you talking about?"

"Think about why you're even *here*, brother dear. They flew you half-way around the world and jettisoned you to the bottom of the sea. Could you be any more a pawn? Did they tell you how to frame it—did they *coach* you? You never were a good liar. You're too earnest. Dr. Felz and the others—and I'm sure there *were* others—what did they promise you in return for retrieving me?"

Luke's jaw hung open in disbelief.

"Holy fuck, what *could* they possibly offer? A new car? An all-expenses-paid trip to Cabo? I came because I wanted to. No, Jesus—I came because I *had* to. There was no choice. Everything's gone to hell. I came for Abby and for—for—"

"Oh please!" Clayton said. "You don't think I *know*? Felz, that incompetent nitwit, would like nothing more than to take over. Why do you think I stopped attending those shrink's sessions? He was orchestrating it! Trying to get them to declare me insane so that he could have me deposed. Do I look crazy to you, Lucas? A mad scientist from a late-night creature feature? Do I *really*?"

Luke noted the itchy squint to his brother's eyes, and the fatigued bags under them. His skin seemed too tight—it was as if a big metal key, same as on a wind-up toy soldier, was screwed into the back of his neck, twisting and twisting, pulling the flesh of his face to a sickening tautness.

Insane? Luke thought. *Maybe not yet, but I'd say you're within spitting distance.*

"I'm not going anywhere," Clayton said. "You go on and toddle up to the surface and tell Felz that. But don't think that I blame you, Luke. Understand this: I *pity* you. This is far too immense for you to comprehend. Go now. *Go.* Let Alice take you, and don't argue with me. We're done here."

"I don't give a shit about Felz," Luke said, a flash point of anger exploding in his chest. "I came here . . . Christ, Clay, you want the truth? I didn't come here for you. *You?* You're just a shitty, careless person whose last name I happen to share."

Did Clayton's expression change just a bit? A wounded wince?

"I'm here for what you might *accomplish*. For the people it could benefit. But now that I see all this . . . I'm not so sure. Hell, maybe you'll figure out how to harness this stuff. But right now I'm getting a seriously fucked-up vibe here, okay? That's all I was suggesting. We head topside and recalibrate. Then, if you want to come back down, I say fuck it. Fill your boots, asshole."

Clayton smiled thinly. "You're a better liar than you used to be. I'll give you that."

The men considered each other, neither talking. The guinea pig scratched at the cooler.

Luke thought: *Westlake's computer.*

"Westlake said there was a hole in the station. In his lab."

Clayton's voice was laced with disdain. "Westlake said this? What a shock. Now, *he* did go crazy—nutty as squirrel turds, as our darling mother would have said."

After listening to Westlake's files, Luke wasn't about to argue that the man hadn't gone insane. But, having spent only a little time aboard the *Trieste*, Luke wasn't about to blame him either. Luke told his brother about the sound files. The tests. Westlake and the hole.

"About these files, Lucas," said Clayton, his scorn undisguised. "Tell me, did you hear anything besides Westlake's voice?"

"There were . . . knocks."

"Knocks. Uh-*huh*."

Luke bit back a jeering rejoinder. Hadn't he dismissed Westlake's claims himself, just hours ago? Mocked them as Clayton was mocking them now?

"Why don't we give them a listen? You tell me what you hear."

Luke was convinced Clayton would dismiss the offer out of hand; instead, he surprised Luke by nodding curtly and saying: "Fine, show me."

6.

THE MAIN LAB was unoccupied.

"Al?" Luke called out. "Hey, *Al!*"

Silence from the tunnels leading into the lab. How long had he been in Clay's lab? Less than a half hour? Luke now felt treacherous for leaving Alice out here all alone, but he wouldn't have gained entry into Clayton's lab any other way.

His ears caught the buzz emanating from behind Westlake's door. The sound crested and ebbed, the sonic equivalent of waves crashing on a beach.

"You're sure that hatch isn't going to open?" Luke asked.

Clayton shook his head. "Password protected. Our labs are meant to be bastions of privacy. If we wanted to share research, we did so out here."

Luke turned from Westlake's lab; it continued to exert an uncomfortable pull on his thoughts—insistent fingers tickling his forehead, seeking entrance.

He faced the viewing window. The sea was endless and hungering. It stirred a childlike fear in Luke: the dread of getting lost in the dark only to find yourself prey to whatever creatures made a home of that inhospitable element.

"Turn the lights on, will you?" Luke said.

Clayton switched on the spots. Twenty yards of sea floor was washed in a skeletal pall.

Something moved at the edge of the light . . . or had it flinched? Skittishly fled? No, it hadn't really done that, had it? When you prod a snail with a stick, it will retreat inside its shell. Things react that way when they're scared.

But the things occupying the mammoth sea beyond the window weren't startled; Luke was sure of that much. If they were there at all, if they weren't just fabrications of his overheated brain, then they had merely withdrawn—the shadowy fluttering of black scarves wavering through the water—because for the moment, they preferred to remain hidden.

"It's not dangerous," he heard Clayton say. "Not if you respect it."

Luke turned to find Clay's cold mineral eyes trapping his own.

LUKE LED CLAYTON to Westlake's chambers. He opened the laptop on the cot. The screen was black. He pushed a few letter keys. It remained stolidly black.

Did the battery die? It still had plenty of juice when he'd shut it down last.

Stupid goddamn thing. He pressed the *start* button with increasing irritation. The computer screen remained obstinately black.

"I'm telling you, Clay. This was working a few hours ago."

"*Oooookay.* Well, it's not working now. And whatever's on it isn't the proof you believe it to be anyway."

Luke wanted to put his fist through the fucking screen. It would feel so damn good—a release of the poisonous tension pulsing behind the bones of his face. Put his fist through it, and then plant that same fist square in his brother's smug mouth. He wouldn't be expecting that, would he? Fuckin-a right. It'd be so easy. His fist pistoning until Clay's skull was nothing but a bowl of red mush, Luke laughing and laughing, his lips flecked with blood.

Luke recoiled, snorting like a man who'd been given smelling salts.

Where had those thoughts come from?

He'd never perpetrated premeditated violence on another person in his life. Yet he'd seen himself doing it. His fist slamming down again and again. His eyes alight with mad glee. An insectile buzz invading his mind as he nursed crude animalistic impulses. . . .

Clayton was scrutinizing him now. "You all right, brother?"

"Yeah." Luke laughed coldly. "Just pissed this thing won't work."

"Down here, it's unwise to let your emotions get out of hand."

Are you coming down with a case of the sea-sillies, El Capitán? His mother's mocking voice. *You weren't built for rough water, sailor.*

Luke shut his eyes and squeezed her out of his head.

7.

THEY FOUND ALICE in the main lab. She was once again staring at Westlake's hatch.

Her skin had a sickly pallor—*cadaverous* was the word that sprang into Luke's mind—her eyes peering out of her cored sockets with bovine confusion. Her lips moved, reciting words or phrases Luke could not make out.

She ran a hand over the hatch . . . intimately, somehow searchingly. Luke could hear snatches of her speech now.

"I want to . . . yes, oh yes, I'd *love* to . . ."

Luke said: "Al?"

Her hand circled the hatch, tracing odd patterns. Her fingers fell to the keypad.

Clayton flicked a switch, bathing the lab in a harsh wash of halogen light. Al blinked, disoriented. In that moment her face held a wrathful, almost murderous look—the look of a person awoken from a dream she wished would never end.

Luke said: "You okay, Al?"

Al swiped her palm across her nose, a childlike gesture.

"Never better, Doc. Feelin' fine like cherry wine."

Luke peered out the window. Those inky scarves unfurled beyond the spotlights. A wave of panic rose in him. He tasted it: the tang of pure dread, acrid as the juice in a springtime leaf.

Get out of here, he thought wildly. *You have to convince Al to leave.*

"Alice, listen . . . Do things feel a bit hinky down here? I'm asking be-cause you've spent years underwater. Maybe it's just me."

Al pulled her gaze away from Westlake's lab with what seemed like a great, almost Herculean effort. Somewhat reluctantly, she nodded. "It's not just you."

Luke pointed to Westlake's lab. "Something happened in there, I'm pretty sure. Something . . . not good. For all I know, it's still happening."

Clayton grunted dismissively. Luke ignored him.

"And oh yeah—Clayton showed me something very interesting."

"Don't you say a word," Clayton snapped.

"Oh, screw off, Clay," Luke said casually. "Al, you should give Clay a round of applause. Why? Well, my brilliant, brainy brother was able to cure a guinea pig of what is commonly viewed as a terminal condition. A condition known in the veterinary biz as *getting its fucking head cut off*."

He told Al everything. The ambrosia, the shears, the blood-tentacles. About Westlake's files, too. The *hole*.

"Is this true?" Al asked Clayton.

Clayton said: "The ambrosia, you mean? Yes. It's a remarkable substance. But regarding this hole my brother keeps babbling about?" Clayton rotated his finger around his ear, the universal gesture for *loony*.

"That does sound a little nuts," Al said to Luke with a charitable smile. "And Westlake . . . well."

"I never claimed it was *sane*," Luke said defensively. "I think it's . . . symptomatic, maybe. Of what's happening down here—how this place tears at your head. Westlake went nuts, fine. A hole in the wall *is* impossible. I thought so, too. But maybe the *Trieste* or whatever, it caved in his mind."

Al nodded sympathetically—but to Luke it seemed too much like the pinched, dismissive nod someone would offer a raving bag lady.

"Some people aren't built for this," she said. "Doesn't matter how smart they are or how rugged in every other way. This is a specific kind of pressure, and you can't toughen yourself against it."

"How do *you* feel, Luke?" Clayton asked with mock concern.

"This from the guy who's walking around in his sleep, sending up pleading transmissions." Luke's voice rose to a reedy falsetto. "*Oh brother, oh brother, where art thou my brother—I neeeeeeeds you!*"

Clayton's jaw tightened. "I did no such thing. I'd as soon have called for a janitor."

Luke turned to Al, refusing to be baited into a fight. "I told Clay we should head up. Just until we can get a grip on what's happening down here."

"I can understand how this may come as a shock," said Clayton, recovering his poise. "The things I've discovered are daunting. Frightening, even. But imagine living in the shadow of a dormant volcano. It's scary at first . . . but you get used to it. People do it all the time. They exist under perpetual threat. And there's so much work to be done here. Up there"—he pointed toward the surface—"people are suffering. *Dying.* They need us to stay here. To be strong and persevere. Surely you understand that?"

Oh please, you sententious bastard, Luke thought. *You only care about yourself and your research, same as it ever was.*

"What about the animals?" Clay continued. It was the first time he'd referred to them as anything but specimens. "If we go, we'll have to leave them. And Dr. Toy, as well, who could destroy the station in our absence. Can we really take that risk?"

"What's to stop him from destroying it right now?" Luke shot back.

"Maybe us just being here?" Al said reasonably. "There's nothing in Toy's quarters that he could use to wreck this place—but if we leave, giving him full run . . ."

Luke was dismayed to see that Al was taking his brother's side on this.

"So we lock the hatches," Luke said. "Can't we do that? Can't we—"

"Look, I told you I'm not leaving," Clay said simply. "There's too much to do, and too little time left. As I keep telling you—do whatever you want."

A sense of despair had settled under Luke's skin, itching like pink fiberglass insulation. Al held the deciding vote.

"Fuck it," Al said after a spell. "Dr. Nelson, no disrespect, but Luke's got a point. I think things may be on the verge of a catastrophic fuckup."

Clayton impassively regarded Al. "I've spoken my piece."

"Fuck it," Al said again. "Luke, let's go talk to topside operations. Dr. Nelson, I want you to stay where I can find you."

"I'll be in my lab," Clayton said.

He turned his back to them. He was singing another nursery rhyme as he retreated into his lab.

"Ladybug, ladybug, fly away home; your house is on fire, your children all gone . . ."

8.

LUKE AND LB FOLLOWED AL to the storage area. They shimmied through the crawl-through chute. It was easier this time. Al caught LB as she rocketed awkwardly out of the chute; she licked her face appreciatively. Luke came last. They continued on to reach the storage tunnel hatch. Al spun the wheel; there was a steady hiss as the pressure abated.

"Hold the door for a sec, Luke. I don't want us getting locked in again."

She hunted around until she found a used air-purification canister. "Okay, come on through."

LB hesitated—she'd been locked in the tunnel for Lord knows how long—before resignedly slipping through the doorway. Al wedged the canister in and let the hatch close under its own weight; it crimped the canister slightly but left the door propped open a few inches.

"That'll hold," she said. "Unless someone kicks it loose."

"Who would do that?"

Al tilted her head—an analytical insurance adjuster's gaze.

"I spent a lot of time with Westlake," she said. "We trained together. Eight, ten hours a day. Most eggheads have got their head in the clouds or up their own clueless asses. Westlake was different. On the level. Even keel."

Al headed down the storage tunnel. Luke followed. The cold locked around his limbs almost immediately, as if it had been waiting to embrace him again.

"Point being," she continued, "Westlake and I got on. Your brother and Dr. Toy were all business. Westlake was different—*normal*. And he was still pretty normal down here, at least at first. In fact he seemed *better* than normal."

"Better how?"

Al shrugged as if to say it was hard to explain. But she tried.

"Training was intense, right? It ground us all down—all but your brother, who seems sorta cyborgish. I'd expected Westlake's furlough down here to wear on him. Doctor Toy *really* struggled in training; he almost didn't make it down, in fact. We nearly replaced him. And like I said before, you can't do mental push-ups to prepare yourself—you've either got that tolerance or you don't. So we were surprised to see that when Westlake first got down, he actually seemed brighter, stronger, healthier. I couldn't pinpoint it, but it was a change. Maybe not a good one, either."

"What do you mean?"

They'd made it around the gooseneck, forging down the tunnel toward the *Challenger*'s entry hatch.

"I mean, just *different*. Something off in his eyes. His movements were weird, jerky, on the monitors. That is to say, before all the screens went blank. When we were topside, Westlake had a sense of what the ambrosia might be able to do . . . but he was skeptical. Once he got down, that changed. At his psych appointments—which were delivered remotely from a special room down here, every two days at the outset—it was all he'd talk about. *The miracle agent*, he called it. A kind of mania invaded him. And then he went AWOL. Stopped attending his psych appointments. Stopped being visible on the monitors. He just . . . poof. Vanished."

Al shook her head. "And then you tell me Westlake was raving about holes in the station and other assorted bat-shittery. I'm not judging—I think I get it now. Luke, I need to ask: when you fell asleep down here, did you dream?"

Luke's footsteps faltered. The phantom children raced overhead, their own footsteps keeping pace with the rapid beat of his heart.

"Did you?" she repeated.

"Yes," he said finally. "A nightmare. The worst I can ever recall."

Al nodded with a grim look of commiseration and of understanding. In the gloom, her teeth were gray: a row of tiny tombstones.

Luke told her about his dream. He trusted Al, and was emboldened by her forthrightness. He told her about Zach, the ambrosia, the eyes. He didn't tell her what happened to his son that day in the park (which had been the reason the dream hadn't just scared him—it *hurt* him, too), but it felt good, *necessary*, to disburden himself.

He kept the sleepwalking episode to himself. He needed her to trust him. She needed to trust that he had things on lockdown . . . because he *did* have things on lockdown, pretty much at least, and was going to keep it that way.

"I managed to catch a few minutes of shut-eye," said Al. "I had a nightmare, same as you."

She leaned against the tunnel. The wall seemed to belly inward around her body—opening up like a toothless mouth.

Stand up, quickly, Luke wanted to say. *Get away from it.*

But that would sound crazy. Like he didn't have things on lockdown.

"I spent three years aboard the USS *Kingfisher,*" Al said. "A nuclear attack sub. We were on tactical maneuvers. Routine stuff. I was junior lieutenant, tactical armaments. We suffered an electrical malfunction. We lost power. Total blackness at three hundred feet underwater. Then we were hit with a power surge. One of the two main engines blew out. Exploded, more or less."

Luke said, "God, I can barely imagine."

"So when the engine blew, our team evacuated into the maneuvering room and locked the hatch. But there was this kid, Eldred Henke. Nineteen years old. He got trapped in the hallway. I tried to open the hatch, but the locks had engaged. The kid hammered his fists on the porthole until his knuckles broke. Another explosion rocked us as the turbine blew. The wall beside Eldred tore apart like a tin can. Bits of the superheated turbine, screws and rivets and what all, blew through the ripped steel and buried into him. He slammed into the far wall and reeled like a drunk. This thin metal rod was stuck through his throat. Bolts and whatever else had ripped his cheeks open. I could see inside his face, places nobody ought to see. Next the hull caved and the sea rushed in. I saw it all. I was safe. The current carried him out lickety-split. The kid disappeared like he'd been sucked out of an airplane cruising at twenty-five thousand feet."

Luke digested this, then said: "Al, there's nothing you could have done. Surely you understand that."

"No, I get that."

"I mean, if I nailed myself to the wall every time I couldn't save someone's dog or cat—"

"I think this is a little different, Doc."

"I'm just saying that guilt carves you up, right? Things happen sometimes and there's no way to fix it—in the moment, or any time after. But no creature is more adept at putting themselves up on that cross than human beings."

She nodded, accepting Luke's logic. "The thing is, I used to dream about that kid. But those dreams weren't so bad, because in them I wrenched the hatch open and yanked him through just before the sea poured in. Those dreams were bittersweet, sure, because some part of my subconscious knew there was a cream-colored headstone in a cemetery in Eldred's hometown with his name etched on it."

"But the dream you had down here wasn't like that, was it?" Luke said. "The dream you had here was worse."

She nodded reluctantly—her face looked softer and almost girlish in the queer light of the tunnel.

"*Much* worse," she said.

The dream had the same setup, she told Luke. Eldred was trapped behind the hatch. Al was torqueing the hatch-wheel—and same as in real life, it wasn't budging. Then the turbine blew and that shower of superheated rubble hit the kid. Except in the dream, Alice noticed something else. There was . . . *stuff* . . . mixed in with the rubble. A glittering patina in the air.

"The ambrosia," Luke said softly. "That's it, isn't it?"

"Ding ding ding. Give the man a prize," Al said.

Alice dreamed it in down to the tiniest detail—every pore on the kid's face. He started to shriek. Why? Because of the bits of metal spiked in his flesh or the ambrosia? She could hear him screaming through the hatch. Fluttery, boyish screams.

"Which is impossible, right?" she said. "Those hatches are sound-proof."

"You don't have to tell me any more," Luke said.

"Don't I?" Alice said wretchedly.

Next, the dream got real funny. Not ha-ha funny. Funny-awful. El-dred's skin . . . it *healed.* Or only sort of. The metal was pushed out of it, the wounds shrinking, then disappearing altogether. He stayed that way for a heartbeat, his skin flawless, then the wounds opened up again, even though there was no cause for it. It was like watching his face get torn open by invisible surgeons with terrible intentions.

"Or like watching the most awful movie," Alice said, "rewinding it and playing it again."

Next the sea rushed in and carried Eldred down. And Alice *knew* the kid would keep suffering . . . but he'd never quite die. He'd keep falling into the dark but he'd live on—and in an agony like no human has ever known.

"The worst part is this," she said. "Before Eldred's sucked out, as his body's swirling out that rip in the sub, he catches my eye. And he says— and I hear this clearly: *You did this to me. This is your fault, Alice Sykes. Goddamn you to hell.*"

She leaned forward miserably, cradling her skull in her palms. LB padded over and settled her head on Al's knee.

"This station," Luke said. "I don't know what's going on. It's in the air, in the metal. Alice, it's the most awful place I've ever set foot inside."

"Clearly you've never felt the need to take a piss at a dog-racing track," Al said with forced levity.

Luke smiled, appreciating her efforts. "There's two possibilities," he said. "One, something unexplainable is happening down here. Or two, and by far and away the more reasonable possibility—"

"Is that we're going a bit batty," said Al. "Jesus, Luke, we just showed up. This is a cup of coffee compared to the hitches I've pulled."

"This isn't a sub. It's a different animal entirely, isn't it?"

Alice ran her hand over her stubbled skull. "I'm inclined to agree with you. Bad enough to make Dr. Toy flip his lid. And Dr. Westlake, God rest his soul."

With strange serenity, the two of them sat with the fact that they could be sunk neck deep into a case of the sea-sillies—or were perhaps even coming down with the preliminary manifestations of the 'Gets. It made more sense to believe they were going crazy or falling prey to the 'Gets than to believe that . . . well, any other logic was not logic at all. It was total insanity.

"Your brother could be suffering, too," said Al. "He may just wear it differently."

Dr. Toy's words floated through Luke's mind: *You are not who you are.*

9.

THEY REACHED THE *CHALLENGER*.

Al said: "Stay here. Keep an eye out for Dr. Toy or your brother. Although I don't think you'll see them. I'll try to get a signal up to the *Hesperus*. I'm not ready to pack up shop down here yet—too much on the line for that."

Luke grudgingly nodded. He'd already come 8,008 miles—the last eight miles straight down—and he didn't want to leave quite yet, either. He could withstand the pressure a bit longer, couldn't he?

Al opened the hatch and slipped through. The hatch closed and locked.

Luke crouched beside LB. She chuffed, a doggy hack, and gave him a look that said: *What are we doing here, boss?*

"Stuck in a holding pattern, girl."

Somewhat stunningly, Luke didn't find it at all weird that he'd be talking to a dog. LB could well be the sanest creature down here. She set a foreleg on Luke's knee and rested her head on his thigh.

"It's okay," he said. The reassurance felt cold.

A faint humming filled his ears. The feverish drone of flies hovering over a heap of shit was the revolting mental image that hum kindled. He didn't hear it so much as feel it—the hum radiated from his bones.

The crushing pressure of the station sucked to him like a second skin. It entered his clothes, stabbing through the material; he felt as if he were wrapped in bands of sinew while a huge muscle contracted, splitting his every vein—

LB licked his cheek. The tang of her breath was bracing.

The hatch opened and Al reappeared.

"There's no power."

A storm of busted glass blew through Luke's chest. *"What?"*

"No power, Luke. Nada. The *Challenger's* out of juice."

"How the hell did that happen?"

"No idea. I didn't leave the fucking headlights on, if that's what you're asking."

Luke flinched at the tone of her voice.

"There was plenty of juice when I left her. Now I can't even get a charge off the glow plugs. I couldn't stay inside too long—it's pitch-dark and freezing cold. But that's not all. I found something on the Edison."

"What's that?"

"A stock ticker. Last-ditch communication method. It runs off a pair of nine-volt batteries. If the power goes, it'll still feed communiqués through."

She handed him a ribbon of paper, same as the stuff that used to fall during a ticker-tape parade. Luke read the words on it in a gathering swell of dread:

CURRENT RING REAPPEARED 8:51 A.M. SEVERE/DEADLY ASCENSION RISK

"It hardly matters," said Alice. "The *Challenger's* kaput. I sent a message back through the Edison, but they won't be able to do anything until the ring clears. It's as powerful as a tornado, and it'll make mincemeat out of any vessel they send down."

"How long will that take?"

"How long will the rain fall? How long will the wind blow? It's nature, Doc. It doesn't operate on a clock."

"You said the last current ring was in place for . . . ?"

"About two weeks."

Two . . . *weeks.* The thought of spending that much time inside the guts of the *Trieste* . . . No. It was unthinkable.

Luke opened his mouth to ask the question—*Are you saying there's no way to get off this station?*—but Al's expression answered it well enough.

"Can we route electricity from someplace else to power up the *Challenger?* I mean, in case the ring clears? Do we have a portable generator?"

Al considered it. "We do have a genny, yeah, and it could work. Draw off the main power source, but we couldn't overdo it—a blowout could black out the whole station, and then we're royally screwed."

The *Trieste* in total darkness. Christ. Luke couldn't even contemplate it.

"If we fed enough juice into the *Challenger*, we could make a low-power ascent," she said. "Providing the current ring clears, or even slackens a little. We'd need enough juice to run the oxygen pumps, a few key utilities. We could surface fifty miles from the *Hesperus*, we could run into the trench wall, or steer right into the ring. Or . . ."

"Or what?"

"Well, I could steer us through the heart of the ring. The water is calmest there, but it's an eye-of-the-needle maneuver."

"But you could do it?"

Al actually smiled. "Believe it or not, I've done crazier things."

"I believe it, Al. So let's find that fucking generator."

"Okay. But we need to head to the communications room first. Maybe I can get in proper contact with the *Hesperus* from there."

They backtracked toward the wedged-open door. Luke glanced over his shoulder, certain he'd heard something—a rustling like a giant moth flapping its wings.

But there was nothing. Was there . . . ?

A gelatinous shimmer along the ceiling—a glittery snail trail that, even as Luke watched, dimmed to nothingness.

We're trapped, he thought. *Bugs in a kill jar.*

"Come on, girl," he said to the dog. LB needed no prodding—she was already at his side.

10.

THE HATCH WAS CLOSING as they rounded the gooseneck.

Luke heard the canister pop from where it'd been wedged with a chilling *tink*. Al had already broken into a run. Luke could see the lip of light beyond the hatch thinning by heart-stopping degrees.

Alice dove like an outfielder laying out to catch a long fly ball. She struck the hatch with a muffled thump and let out a strangled squawk. When Luke reached her, he saw that she'd managed to jam her left hand between the frame and the hatch door.

"Push it open." Al's voice was calm but her face was white. "*Quick*."

Luke rocked the hatch open a few inches; its weight was immense, as though something was pushing from the other side. Al snatched her hand out and cradled it to her chest. Luke assessed the damage. There were twenty-seven bones in the human hand. It looked as if Al had broken more than a few of them.

"Let me see what you've done," Luke said.

Her pinkie was bent at an unnatural angle, her middle finger snapped amidships. The dent in the back of her hand was a clear indication that some of the bones of her palm had been crushed. Her hand looked as if it had been compacted—as if something had set its considerable weight against the hatch and shoved with merciless pressure.

"There goes my juggling career," Al said, her face greasy with shock.

Luke saw the dislodged air canister. He'd watched Al wedge it in. Its metal was dimpled where she'd rocked the hatch shut against it, pinning the canister firmly in place. Still, it had popped out. Had the tunnel heaved slightly—a sensation unfelt by Luke—to knock it loose?

Or had somebody jarred it free?

"Where's a first-aid kit?" he asked.

"Should . . . should be one in the communications room."

Luke helped her up. Al was running on shock and adrenaline at the moment; before long the pain would set in.

"Come on," she grunted.

She stumbled from the storage area and stopped at another hatch set in the tunnel wall, about fifty yards shy of the crawl-through chute.

"You're gonna have to open it, Doc. Can't manage right this second."

Luke cranked the wheel. The hatch opened into a tight passage-way. He followed Al in, LB following them. The tunnel was strung with hatchways—four, by Luke's count. He figured this was a central hub, branching out to other sections of the *Trieste*.

A red X had been slashed across the porthole window of one hatch. Luke remembered reading about when the Black Plague swept across Europe, red X's had appeared on doors of houses—*this place is infected, steer clear*.

After a dogleg, they reached the communications room.

Al said: "What in fucking blue hell happened here?"

The room was tiny. The overhead lights were smashed, but enough light leaked through from the tunnel to see by. A bank of monitors occu-pied one wall, labeled Lab N, Lab W, Pure, Sleep, and so on.

"Looks like someone didn't want to be watched," said Luke.

Nine of the ten monitors had been shattered. It looked like an act committed in a violent frenzy. Glass was scattered on the floor. Luke shooed LB away, fearing she'd get a shard in her paw.

The final monitor—marked Pure—was unbroken, but dead and gray; Luke walked over to it; his swollen reflection played over the screen's convex surface.

"The comm link's busted," Al said. "Fuck me, Freddy."

She pointed to the snapped and skinned remains of the sea-to-surface radio. The receiver was broken neatly in half, the wires stripped out.

Luke said, "You think this was done recently?"

"I can't tell. Whoever did it . . . I mean, they were fucking *anal* about it. Dr. Toy's the strongest candidate for this shit. Or maybe Westlake, before he surfaced? Your brother, even?"

Luke pictured Clayton wielding a bone mallet, destroying the monitors in a state of controlled wrath. The steely calm in his eyes as he methodically stripped the wires from the receiver, stranding everybody down here so that he could study in peace.

"Yes," Luke whispered. "It's conceivable."

Conceivable, if insane. If Clayton or Toy didn't want to be in contact with topside operations, okay, don't answer their calls—there was no need to destroy their only link to the surface. What if an emergency arose?

Lucas, nobody is coming to get you.

Shut up, Mom, Luke thought, bristling at the sound of her voice in his head. *Shut the hell up. Who asked you, anyway? If I wanted your opinion, I'd visit your grave site.*

Al winced, cradling her mangled hand to her chest.

"Hey, let's get your hand looked at," Luke said, figuring it was best to keep busy.

Good idea, Lucas, said Bethany Ronnicks. *As they say, idle hands are the devil's workshop.*

The first-aid kit was clipped to the wall. Luke opened it and snapped on a pair of surgical gloves.

"Lay your hand on the console," he said. "I'm going to splint your fingers, then tape them together. Fair warning, though: this'll hurt like hell."

Al nodded wryly. "Vicodin, Vicodin, my kingdom for a Vicodin."

Al yelped when Luke set her pinkie bones. He did it as quickly as he could, but still, he could feel the broken edges of bone grinding.

"Sorry. I've done this before, but to cats or dogs."

"You're . . . *eeeyyyash!*" Al hissed through gritted teeth. "Yup, yup, you're doing a bang-up job. Keep going."

Luke cut a length of splint tape and wrapped it around her pinkie. The ring finger was only badly swollen; Luke taped those two fingers together.

"Your middle finger got it the worst. It's broken down near the knuckle."

"Does that mean I won't be able to flip the bird anymore?"

"Depending on how it heals, you may not be able to bend it at all. So you might *always* be flipping the bird. Hold on—this is gonna hurt like a fuckofabitch."

Al picked up the broken receiver and jammed it between her teeth.

Luke had to pop the finger up to set the bone. It took three hard tugs. On the third, Al's jaw clenched so hard that the black plastic cracked between her canines.

Luke tore open a roll of gauze to wrap Al's hand, in hopes of keeping all the little nicks free from infection.

"You're good to go."

The lone monitor fired to life. Their heads jerked in unison.

The monitor was labeled *Pure*. The O_2 purification chamber.

"Do you see that?" Al whispered.

The camera angle offered a long view of the chamber: light pulsed at the entrance, but trailed to shadows at the far end. Luke squinted.

Nothing definite. Slow, insistent, rhythmical—movement that reminded Luke of kelp strands drifting in a night tide.

A red warning light began to flash on the console.

Two words were stamped below the warning light.

The first was Oxy.

The second, Low.

"Oh, good Christ," Al said as she sprinted out of the room.

11.

LUKE CAUGHT UP WITH HER in the passageway. She stood before one of the four hatches leading to unknown areas of the *Trieste*.

"This is the one. Can you open it?" she said.

"What's happening?"

"You saw the light, right? We're losing oxygen. The system monitors the amount of CO_2; when the concentrations get too high, it gives a warning."

"That's it? A little light flashing in some room?"

"Usually there'd be an alarm. But the system could be screwy. The *door*, Doc. Hurry."

Luke threw his weight against the wheel. The hatch cracked open with a tortured squeal. The tunnel beyond was narrower than anything Luke had seen so far. A weak welter of light spread across the ceiling, as if sickly fireflies were trapped inside it.

"Leave the dog, Doc. It's safer right here."

Luke agreed. "Stay, girl."

LB regarded Luke worriedly—afraid he'd leave, the way everyone else had.

"I'll be back. I promise."

The dog didn't seem very reassured, but obediently stood her ground.

THEY STEPPED into the tight passageway.

Luke shut the hatch behind him, and his ears popped. He immediately became aware of the oxygen quality: stale and cool, not unlike the ancient air in a subterranean cave.

They inched through the diseased trickle of light. The walls hugged their bodies lovingly; the metal seemed to breathe as they moved forward.

"How far do we go?" he asked.

Al grunted. "I dunno. I've never been in here."

Luke could barely see his fingers in front of his face. The walls brushed his hips; the passage was tapering ahead of them but also, as he sensed it, behind them. He could almost hear the tunnel issuing sly snaps and crunches as it crimped, the steel folding like onionskin.

The air tasted horrible. Not just stale—infused with the taste of dead things. They could've been in the mouth of some enormous monster, picking their way along teeth hung with rotted meat. Adrenaline twined up from Luke's feet; it crawled into his chest and forced his breath out in harsh, plosive pops.

"Fuckin'—what the . . . ?" Al said.

"What is it?" said Luke.

"Dead end."

Spiders crawled over the dome of his skull as a skittish panic rushed over him—an unaccountable fear that reminded him of being a child in Iowa, walking down a lonely country road at night as headlights bloomed over the curve of the earth behind him, conjuring an uneasiness that would linger until the car had passed, the red embers of its taillights dimming around a curve.

"It's not a cave-in," Al said. "The wall is sheer." Her feet shuffled. "There's space at the bottom. Back up, will you?"

The walls pushed at Luke's spine—an adoring suction like the mouth of a hungry lover. He managed to clear enough space for Al to get down on all fours.

"There's something down here," Al said, knocking her fist around. "Same as a crawl-through, really, but it feels even smaller . . . an access chute, I'd say. Could be that the air passes through a series of filters or what-the-fuck above the chute. I don't remember the schematics."

"Can we get through it?"

"We'll have to wriggle—and pray there's no grate at the other end—but yeah . . . it's doable. It's the only way into the purification room."

"You're sure?"

"Yeah. That I do remember from the schematics."

"And there's absolutely no other . . . ?"

"Doc, hey. Not trying to be an asshole here, but this is it. No alter-native."

"Okay." Luke vented a shaky breath. "Fine. *Fine.*"

"I'd let you stay here, but I may need help," she said. "My hand's fucked."

Luke exhaled heavily. "Go on. I'll follow."

Al's body bumped into the tube. Her elbows and knees made no noise at all—it was as if she were crawling through a hole carved into a mountainside.

"You coming, Luke?"

He knelt. His knees and feet were pressed tightly together, the knobs of his anklebones touching. It felt as though the tunnel behind him was no longer an O, but had been crimped into a V: a pair of jaws closing by degrees, forcing him forward if he didn't want to be crushed.

The air changed once again as he entered the chute: heavier, sicken-ingly moist. He worked his way forward on his belly, bucking his hips in a clumsy humping motion.

"Dig those moves," he said, hoping the sound of his voice might drive away the onrushing panic. "Liquid hips, baby, liquid hips."

The tube reduced his voice to a hysterical warble. After a few feet, his arms were pinned to his sides. He could barely move them, other than to spider-crawl his fingers along the inside of the chute. How the hell was Al managing to do the same with her broken mitt? She was smaller than Luke, more nimble. The tube was coated in a thin layer of oil, but instead of making it easier to move—as it did in the crawl-through chute—it had the opposite effect: Luke felt like an insect gummed on a strip of flypaper.

"Al? Hey, Al?"

When the reply finally arrived, it held a funny echo:

"Luke . . . uke . . . uke . . ."

He wriggled forward, his breath coming in hot gasps. He adopted a peristaltic wave, the way a maggot gets around: toes, then calves, then thighs, then ass, then hips; this movement netted a few inches at a go. Al grunted in exertion somewhere ahead. The chute tightened as Luke forged deeper into it. His nose raked the metal, which was pebbled with rough bumps—Luke envisioned a huge greasy tongue covered with diseased nodules.

It's okay, okayokayokay. Even the voice in his head sounded hysterical now. *Al's made it through; you can bet she's already waiting in the purification room. You just need to get a few more feet and you'll be there, too.*

And then? Well damn, he'd just have to turn around and do it all over again.

Don't think about that. Just take it inch by inch.

His shoulders jammed.

Pushing with his heels did nothing—he was stuck, his body pinned. He couldn't budge; his heels drummed a helpless *tat-a-tat.* His lungs constricted as darkness poured into them.

Was the chute shrinking? It pressed on the back of his skull with an insistent, menacing weight—it would keep pressing, slowly and remorselessly, until the bones of his face collapsed.

It's a bend, Luke. Just a little bend in the tube, for God's sake.

Suddenly he felt it: the chute was pressing into his right-hand side, but there was a little space on the left. Luke torqued his elbows and bucked his hips, squirming onto his side. His spine followed the bend of the tube now. He could breathe shallowly again.

He pushed against the chute with his feet, which slipped on its greasy coating. Incrementally, fighting for inches, he propelled his torso around the bend.

The air before his eyes burst with puffs of cottony light. Those puffs were a manifestation of exertion, panic, and a lack of breathable air—he was gasping now, the onset of a claustrophobic attack.

He'd never been prone to that. Crowded elevators and windowless rooms had never bothered him. But now he was eight miles underwater—*Eight miles! Eight miles!* his mind parroted idiotically—in a chute that felt like it was being compressed in a vise. The sea was held back by nothing more than a fragile shell. He heard, or believed he could hear, the subtlest creaks as the water exerted its bone-smashing force . . . except it wouldn't smash his bones, would it? No, it would do something else entirely. He'd be crushed into a cube, like a car at a wrecking yard. It was highly unlikely that his body would be compressed into anything so neatly geometric, but that was the image his mind settled around.

Dap-dap-dap-dap-dap—those nightmare children dashing overhead, the bloated pads of their feet only an inch from his face now.

He wriggled his shoulders, clenched his fists, and inched onward. He was bathed in sick sweat; his thighs chafed. He couldn't hinge his knees more than a few inches. His lungs burned, packed with hot rivets.

Why had he done this? How could he have been such a fool?

It was torturous to breathe—were his sinuses constricting? What if the chute narrowed until he couldn't move another millimeter—what if he caught up to Al, who'd gotten stuck herself, his head butting her heels? What if she told him the exit was grated? Could they get out? Luke didn't think so. Moving forward was hard enough; moving backward would be impossible. They would die in the chute like rats trapped in a heating duct.

. . . whush, whush, whush . . .

The sound floated out of the darkness, dancing delicately up his calves, slipping around his skull and into his ears.

. . . whush, whush . . .

That insistent, unpleasantly familiar sound.

NononononononoNO—

He was nearly around the bend in the chute; he'd been progressing in centimeters, in millimeters, in

—millipedes—

the smallest increments, but he was making headway. His hips were clear; in a minute or so he'd be able to work around the bend and really boogie.

But something was inside the chute with him now.

Whush-tikatikatikatikatikatika-whush, whush . . .

He could picture it behind him . . . twenty feet long, thick and sinuous, its feelers dancing lightly along the mouth of the tube. Its exoskeleton throbbing with moody colors; under that armor its guts were as soft and featureless as mashed bananas. Its compound eyes pulsing with alien hunger.

The millipede was inside the chute with him, its million-skillion legs tapping as it advanced gradually but with complete ease—tubes were its natural habitat, weren't they?

Luke tensed, every muscle quivering. His heart hammered at his rib cage. The fear paralyzed him—his body, his mind. Finally he began to move. Hips bucking, feet shoving. But his body just uselessly accordioned. He felt like a worm stuck in the barrel of a clear, cheap ballpoint pen. Panic chewed his brain into pulp, rendering him stupid with fear.

Bug! yelped a giddy voice from his lizard brain, obliterating every last vestige of calm. *Bug! Bug! Bug! BUG! BUUUG!*

Whusha-whusha-tikatikatikatika . . .

He felt it now. At his feet. Its antennae—long and thick as extension cords—picked along the exposed skin of his ankles. Its mandibles gnashed like scissors. Its proboscis (they had those, didn't they?) was a thick needle dripping venom.

Would it punch through the soles of his shoes, injecting poison into the pads of his feet while he thrashed helplessly? Would that poison kill him, or only paralyze him—would he feel it chewing through his boots, snipping off his toes like Jujubes and funneling them into the clotted hole of its mouth?

The sound switched direction—it was coming from *ahead* of him now.
Whush-whush-WHUSH . . .

Oh Jesus. Oh God no.

His feet would be bad enough, but for it to devour his head—its legs twitching through his hair as it scuttled over his forehead, his face, carrying the insectile stink of a roach nest, noxious nectars drooling out of its mouth as its mandibles fastened around the fragile nut of his skull, its proboscis injected through one twitching eyeball—

Bug! Bug! BugbugbugbugBUG!

Luke shook all over, screeching now, gripped by out-of-body terror. A vein of white-hot fire ripped up his spine as his overtaxed synapses detonated in his brainpan—

Fingers. *Feelers.*

Something was gripping his shoulders and was hauling him into—

12.

"IT'S OKAY, DOC! DOC! You're out! You're out."

Luke lay on the floor of what must be the purification room. Grainy light trickled down the walls, illuminating the canisters screwed into them.

He tried to sit up. His body wouldn't comply, his muscles limp as wrung dishrags. A tidal wave of embarrassment crashed over him. Mindless terror had cracked him right open inside the chute. And over what? There wasn't a goddamn thing inside it except for the cloying stench of his fear.

"I'm sorry, Al. I . . . I lost my head for a second there."

Al touched Luke's shoulder. "I was jumpy by the time I made it out, too. Enclosed spaces, right?" She displayed her broken hand; the fingernail of her index finger was peeled back, hanging on a tenacious strip of skin. "I wrecked my hand some more, too. Thank God for adrenaline, huh?"

Luke swallowed the burnt-chalk taste in his mouth. "That stuff's a godsend."

Al walked to a control panel on the near wall and flipped it open with her good hand. "Sonofabitch . . . goddamnit, the relay chip's missing."

"What does that do?"

"Regulates the warning system, for one."

Luke stood. "Did somebody take it?"

"I don't see it laying around here anywhere, and I can't see how it'd just pop out. I *was* thinking Dr. Toy might've taken it. Some nutty sabotage attempt. But would that bastard, no matter how rat-shit crazy he's gone, go through what we just did to cut off his own air supply?"

"So . . . maybe we're *not* losing air then?"

"Impossible to tell without that chip. Thankfully . . ."

Al forded deeper into the room. Luke trailed her. It was perhaps fifty steps long—the longest room Luke had been inside down here. Thousands of canisters were screwed into the walls. They glowed faintly, like enormous eggs.

At the very back of the room lay a lone crate. The size of an old army footlocker, fashioned from molded black plastic. Its latch shone silver in the dim.

Seeing it, Luke's feet churned to a dead stop.

"Something the matter, Doc?"

"No," Luke said. *Jesus. Jesus Christ.* "Nothing."

He felt it then—his mind opening up, an inky blackness flowing into it. The room spun and swum as he slipped suddenly into a memory hole, his psyche funneling deep down a dream pool.

"You okay, Doc?"

Al's voice was far off, swimmy. *It's fine*, Luke tried to tell her. *It's nothing at all. It's just . . . it's just . . .*

. . . just my old Tickle Trunk.

13.

HIS MOTHER HAD FOUND IT at Treasure Village, a flea market on the outskirts of Lake Okoboji.

It called out to me, she'd told Luke with a self-satisfied smile. *It said: Pick me, Ms. Ronnicks. Pick me for Lucas. His very own Tickle Trunk. He'll just adooore me.*

Tickle Trunk. His friends had the same type of thing—except theirs were called toy boxes. But his mother insisted on the name, as she insisted on a great many things. *A Tickle Trunk for my special boy*, she'd said. *A special place for all his ticklish things.* She'd seen it at the flea market amid the ninja stars and chipped knickknacks—seen it and *known*. It must've shone like a beacon to her.

Oh, she would have thought, *Luke will just* die *when he sees this.*

The trunk was a nasty trick. Luke knew that right away. Exactly the sort of trick his mother liked to play from time to time to show who was boss. But of course she presented it as a gift, a token of love and affection.

Tickle Trunk. That *name*. Luke pictured a trunk lined with disembodied fingers—hundreds of them, callused and bony with nicotine-stained fingernails—and if he wasn't careful those fingers would snatch him, drag him inside, and tickle and pinch him until he screamed . . .

The trunk *appeared* joyful. It was big enough that Luke's seven-year-old body could fit inside, and was decorated with smiling clown faces. His mother urged him to name them, the same way Clayton would name his poor mice.

Look, there's Chuckles, she'd say, pointing them out. *And this one can be Koko. And there's Mr. Tatters and Floppsy and Punkin Pie.*

The trunk's lid was rounded like that of a treasure chest. The clowns' faces stretched over its top, as warped as reflections in a funhouse mirror.

If you looked closer, you'd notice most of the clowns weren't smiling so much as *leering*. Their lips were swollen and too red, as if they'd been painted with blood. And if you looked very closely, the lips of a few of those clowns—the ones his mother had named Bingo and Pit-Pat, specifically— were parted just slightly to disclose what looked like a row of discolored, daggery teeth.

The trunk had a huge silver latch. If you got trapped inside the trunk— if that were to happen somehow, accidentally or not—that latch would keep you locked in. Its interior smelled like the white balls Luke's neighbor Mr. Rosewell scattered under his crabapple tree to keep mice away . . . that, plus another smell, impossible to name. The trunk was lined with cracked brown skin; Luke imagined it'd been stripped off an alligator, or a Komodo dragon. The skin was tacked inside the box with dull brass rivets.

Luke didn't like the box. No, his feelings were stronger than that— he hated it on sight. He wondered if whoever had sold it to his mother had given her a steep discount just to get it off his hands.

Luke hadn't wanted it in his room, which was of course where it ended up. His mother insisted.

Now you've got a spot for all your stuff, she said mock-brightly. *A place for everything, and everything in its place.*

He grudgingly threw his toys into it—all but his most precious ones, which he couldn't imagine leaving inside. His foolish prepubescent self had been scared that when he closed the lid, the trunk would release an acid that would melt them into runny goo like beaten eggs; its lid would open and close, a pair of greedy lips, gummy strings of what had been his Matchbox cars and army men stretched between them.

Feed us, Lucas, he'd imagine it whispering in a guttural voice after all the houselights had been switched off. *We're so hungry. So hungry. Feed us any old thing; we don't mind. It's all meat. Come closer, why don't you, so we can tell you what we really want . . .*

He hated sleeping with it in his room. Clayton had been spending most nights down in his lab by then, so it was just Luke and the trunk and the shadows cast by the backyard maple bending over the walls.

Sometimes he'd awaken with a shudder and swear he'd heard the trunk moving on its casters: the sound of marbles rolling across a pane of glass.

He decided one night to mark the trunk's edge with a piece of sidewalk chalk; the next morning, Luke discovered with fright that it had moved an inch over the line. Slowly but surely it was advancing toward his bed.

When he told Clayton, his brother smirked.

The floor is warped. The trunk is on wheels. Of course it rolls a little, dummy.

The next day, he dragged the Tickle Trunk down to the basement. His parents were both out. Clayton was supposed to watch Luke, but he'd left the house on a specimen hunt. It was Luke's best chance to rid himself of it once and for all.

He hated touching the wormy grain of its wood, festooned with those capering clowns. As he'd backed down the staircase with it, the trunk sat heavily against his chest; its weight was dreadful, a slab of pulsating stone.

He dragged it across the kitchen linoleum and bumped it down the basement stairs. He dropped it, breathing heavily, and opened the crawl space door. A three-foot-tall storage room sprawled over half the basement. Inside were old boxes cowled in spider's webs, full of stuff Luke's parents had no use for but were loath to throw away.

He snapped on the lightbulb, which swayed on a knotted cord, and pushed the trunk past the crawl space door. He got on his hands and knees and pushed it farther inside. Dust motes swam in the air. His heart thumped; his mouth could've been packed with sawdust. He wanted to abandon the trunk at the very back of the crawl space. It seemed to have gained fifty pounds since he'd lugged it out of his bedroom.

Suddenly he pictured the crawl space lightbulb burning out, the door slamming shut, and the trunk lid popping open.

Alone at last. That guttural whisper—but real this time, not just in Luke's mind. *Come here, Lucas, and let us whisper in your ear. No? Okay, we'll come to you . . .*

Anxiety coated Luke's brain in a suffocating glaze as he pushed it to the very back of the crawl space. It was early afternoon; sunlight streaked through a dirty casement window. If it weren't for that fragile link to the outside world, Luke might not have gotten it that far.

He let go of its handle—for an instant his hands wouldn't come un-glued—and started back toward the door. The trunk sat in the fall of weak sunlight, bloated and sullen.

"There," Luke said with a triumphant little smile. "You stay where you belong."

That night, his mother forced him to go fetch it again. In the dark.

She'd immediately noticed it was missing. Luke was positive she had been waiting for Luke to try something sneaky. She crossed her enor-mous fat-girdled arms at the dinner table, eyeing him down.

"The trunk, Lucas. You've moved it."

Luke didn't look up from his plate. He pushed peas around with his fork. "I put it downstairs. It's just, there's not enough room. The trunk's big and our bedroom, with me and Clay both in it, it's really too—"

"What do you suggest? Move into a mansion?" Harsh, barking laugh-ter. "Do you think your father could afford *that*?"

Luke swallowed, forced his head up.

"I don't like it, Mom. I'm sorry. Thank you for buying it, but . . ."

Her mouth set in a hard line—it was the only part of her body that hadn't gone permanently soft.

"You've hardly given it a chance. You will go downstairs, Lucas Ade-laide Nelson. You will bring it up."

The dread etched on his son's face forced Luke's father, Lonnie, to intervene.

"Beth, honey, do we really have to—?"

Lonnie's objection died with a glance from his wife. He gathered his menthols and his cup of tea and slipped into the family room.

"What are you waiting for?" His mother's arms remained crossed. "An engraved invitation?"

Luke sat rooted to his chair. It wasn't a matter of wanting to move—he physically *couldn't*. His mother gripped his wrist fiercely and marched him to the basement door.

"Go," his mother said. "*Now.*"

Luke didn't argue. He had a vague but dire notion that given reason, his mother could conjure torments worse than whatever the trunk held in store.

He trooped down the squeaky, swaybacked stairs. He waved his hand around until his fingers brushed the light cord. The bulb illuminated his father's workbench, the water heater, and the door to Clayton's unoccupied lab.

His mother shut the door. Luke's heart made a donkey kick in his chest.

It's just a stupid trunk, he told himself. *It's ugly and gross but it's not alive, okay? It can't hurt you.*

Then why did you try to get rid of it? asked a second, traitorous voice. *And why did it inch across your bedroom floor?*

The crawl space's cheap plywood door swung open to reveal a darkness that raised the downy hairs on his arms. The trunk lay inside, waiting.

You're back, Lucas! So soon, so soon. Lovely. Do come in.

The crawl space's light cord dangled to the left of the door, a flimsy string with a bell-shaped bob of plastic on the end. It took a few adrenaline-pinching seconds to find it—had it been moved? He overbalanced, nearly toppling face-first onto the floor.

His fingers brushed the cord. He'd reached too far at first.

The trunk sat where he'd left it, at the very back of the crawl space. Boxes were stacked on either side, forming a rough corridor. He hadn't noticed the alignment that afternoon. Had someone—some*thing*—moved the boxes?

He crawled toward it. Silky rustling noises emanated from behind the boxes. Mice? But they didn't have a mouse problem. Clayton had trapped them all. Every last squeaker.

Luke's nose filled with the smells of wood rot and mildew. *Our house is diseased*, Luke thought weirdly. *But only right here, in the crawl space.* And Luke was in the heart of the disease now, crawling toward its decaying tumor.

He craned his neck back to the door—he'd seen something in his periphery, or sort of thought so. Fleeting movement behind the stacked boxes, a skittering of little legs as something moved behind him.

To do what? Close the door? Switch off the light?

Luuuucas. You're such a precious boy. So soft, so pretty. Come closer.

Fuck you, Luke thought. He'd never uttered this word aloud (God only knew what his mother would do to him), but it felt good to say it in his head. *FUCK you, box. I can burn you and say it was an accident. I can flood you until your wood bloats and rots. I can leave you on the stoop on garbage day when Mom's gone and the garbagemen will take you to the dump, where seagulls will drop gooey turds all over you.*

The trunk waited for him, unmoving, unblinking.

Luke's head jerked. He saw it again—something moving behind the boxes. They were in rows like big brown teeth, and he saw or *thought* he'd seen something scuttling between the gaps.

A pair of pants . . . were those pants? They were wadded up like the skin of an enormous serpent on top of one box. And something else that might have been a lampshade. And something that looked like—

The trunk's latch snapped open. It made a silvery snipping sound.

Luke turned in time to see it happen. The metal hasp fell forward lazily like the tongue lolling from a tired dog's mouth.

Luke couldn't believe it—that is to say, his mind couldn't process it. There wasn't a puff of wind. No earthquake had shaken the house's foundation. The latch had simply . . . opened.

The clowns on the trunk suddenly seemed different. Their eyes were tracking him now. Pinning him in their fleshless, jeering gaze.

Luke spun wildly on his knees. As he did, he heard a sound that chilled the ventricles of his heart.

Eeeee . . . the trunk's hinges levering up.

He didn't want to look back. Not one bit. But his skull was gripped by an immense force, which twisted it slowly around.

The trunk was open. Not much. It couldn't open fully, as the lid would hit the crawl space's ceiling.

No, it was open only a bit. Just a hair.

When he faced back the other way, an odd thing happened. The crawl space elongated, its dimensions stretching like taffy. The door was thirty feet away, when it should only be twenty . . . and it was moving farther away by the second.

Lucas, don't go. Staaaaaaay.

Luke began to scrabble toward the door, his fingers scraping madly at the cement. A spider web broke across his face, strangling the cry building in his throat. He wanted to call out for Clayton, his mother, *anyone*, but his voice had fled into his stomach—all that came out of his mouth was a breathless whisper.

He looked back again. He couldn't help it.

A hand was coming out of the trunk.

Gray and waxen—the hand of a long-dead thing. It was thin, the fingers terribly long, the bones projecting under that drab stretching of skin. If it were to grab him, Luke figured each finger could wrap around his ankle at least twice. Every finger was tipped with a sharp black nail.

It was, he realized with dawning horror, the same hand he'd seen inside the standing pipe—the hand belonging to the creature they'd fled in the swamp.

That thing that was here, now, in the basement.

He'd been wrong to fear his mother. His mother could be cruel, yes, but at least she was human.

Is this actually happening?

This was the most adult question Luke had ever asked himself. There was no place in the normal world, the world his mother and father and brother lived in, the world of baseball and snow cones and sunshine, for this thing to exist.

This is not *really happening,* he thought, more definitively now. And quite suddenly, the crawl space turned insubstantial, gauzy—a dreamscape. He felt a strange inner buoyancy, as though his stomach were full of soap bubbles. He drifted on a sudsy wash of horror, but it was dream-horror, unattached to real-life concerns. A giant hand in his Tickle Trunk, how silly! It was nothing to be afraid of, really . . .

He realized, with a thickness of mind he felt only when waking from a very deep sleep, that the voice he was hearing in his head was actually coming out of the trunk. An insidious, narcotizing mimicry of his own voice—it slipped out of the trunk and slid into his ears like some effort-less oil. It matched his own voice exactly . . . or almost exactly: it held a coppery undernote that rasped over the vowels and consonants like a straight razor over a barber's strop.

Nothing to be afraid of . . . not really happening . . .

Luke turned to face the door again and started to crawl desperately. His fingernails and kneecaps scraped the cement, opening the skin up. The door galloped away in heart-clutching increments—he chased it the way a car pursues a heat shimmer on the highway: always tantalizingly close, but you never quite catch it.

The hand spider-walked down the trunk. The attached arm was long and sinewy and seemed both boneless and jointless: a ropy appendage like a fire hose.

I don't exist, Lukey-loo. You said so yourself, didn't you? You're just a big dummy, like your brother says . . .

But it *did* exist—at least right then it did. And that could be all the time a creature like this ever needed.

He crawled, blood welling on his knees, throwing a glance over his shoulder at the trunk. The crawl space light went out.

Luke didn't know if something had switched it off or if the bulb had chosen that exact moment to go out. It didn't matter. The darkness galva-nized his blood. Maybe the darkness was better, in a weird way.

He raised his back, pumped his legs, and scurried across the crawl space. The wooden beams raked his spine but he didn't feel any pain. His adrenaline was redlined, the fear sharpening the edge on his every sense. He could hear the thing's arm slithering and shucking across the grimy cement—a *huthump! huthump!* noise, as if it were flapping in a wavelike motion, those long nail-tipped fingers digging into the cement for purchase and then *huthump!* as it flicked forward another foot.

The door was closer—he could see the light of the basement now, the edge of the water heater. Mercifully, the crawl space was shrinking back to its old dimensions. Or maybe they'd never changed: it was just another nasty trick the thing in the trunk had been playing on him.

HuTHUMP!

Right behind him now.

Luke swore he felt a hard cold finger touch his ankle, a sharp nail leaving a sizzling line of pain.

With a final convulsive heave, Luke propelled himself through the door frame and into the forgiving light of the basement. As he skittered away on his heels, his eyes were drawn to the square of blackness housing the crawl space.

All was silent, only the drumming of blood in his ears.

But he may've seen something. Maybe not.

Eyes? Black, ageless, regarding him from the dark.

Some other time, Lucas. We have all the time in the world.

The adrenaline curdled in his veins. Luke hurtled upstairs, bawling. His mother was too shocked to insist he go back down.

But she got her hangdog husband to bring the trunk up. Luke sat on the front porch, chewing his fingernails to the quick as his father had hauled it up two flights of stairs, quiet as a church mouse. Afterward, he'd given Luke a sheepish grin, his shoulders sunk forward and his hands deep in his pockets. *What are you gonna do?* his expression said. Luke had never known his father any other way. He was broken by the time Luke had been born, and was beyond hope by the time he could've been of any use to either of his sons.

Luke stayed away from his room until bedtime. He begged to stay up a half hour later to read his comics quietly in the family room, but his mother refused. Of course she refused.

The Tickle Trunk sat in the corner of his room. He forced himself to open it. Empty. By then, the events in the crawl space had taken on the taint of absurdity. Nightmares get blown apart in the sane light of day, even in a boy's mind. And Luke was a rational boy; everyone said so. His knees were skinned and his palms scraped, but there was no cut on his ankle from the creature's nails.

No, it had been a silly episode. Luke was embarrassed to think about it.

But . . .

One corner of the trunk had been pried up. A triangle of that strange brown skin was peeled back from its interior, as if something had come out through there.

A tiny rip, no more than an inch. Would that have been enough?

A different boy, one more flighty than Luke, might've viewed it as a sign. Something wanting him to know it'd been inside the trunk. Not a figment of his imagination—no way, nohow. It wanted to show how it'd gotten in, and leave the hint that it could easily do it again. Any old time it wished.

The next day Luke "accidentally" spilled fish oil over the trunk. *God, that smell could gag a maggot*, his father said when he got home. Why he'd been in the proximity of the trunk with a full bottle of fish oil was a fact Luke could never fully explain. But the deed had been done. The room had to be aired out; Luke slept on the sofa for two nights. The trunk was thrown away. His mother had her methods of making Luke pay for that, but at least it was gone. He never saw it again . . .

. . . except for once, years later, in a dream.

He dreamed that the Tickle Trunk sat at the city dump. The moon cast its pallid light over the windblown piles of trash. The trunk's lid hung open like a cavernous, toothless mouth.

A raccoon trundled through the stinking wasteland. It scrambled up a softening heap to the trunk. Nose twitching, it clawed up the bloated wood to squat on top of it. Next it screeched, having seen something inside the trunk that must've left it petrified. The lid levered up, snapping closed on its back. The sound of the raccoon's spine breaking was as sharp as the report of a .22 cartridge.

The raccoon slipped bonelessly inside. The lid closed. The trunk swayed slowly, the way a mother rocks a child in her arms. Inside, the raccoon started to scream. This had been the worst part of the dream— the way the animal had sounded very much like the squall of an infant.

A substance resembling red pancake batter burped out of the trunk. The lid opened again. The moon shone down from its icy altar, the dump wrapped in stillness once again.

14.

THE BLACKNESS SLID AWAY as Luke floated up out of the dream-pool. This long-buried memory had flooded back to him whole cloth—the sights and smells and the fear that had filled his veins that afternoon in the crawl space, a terror as bright and sharp as lemon juice squirted on a paper cut.

"Doc?" said Al, shaking him with her good hand. "You still with me?"

He was back inside his own skin now. He stood in the *Trieste* with Alice, staring at a supply crate that rested in the deepest, most shadowed point of the purification room. How long had he been checked out? It didn't feel like more than a few seconds—and maybe that was all it *had* been, each second stretching out inside his head.

Eight miles above, all over the world, people were forgetting their pasts. Trapped down here in the charmless dark, Luke couldn't escape his own.

"I'm okay," he said shakily. "My memories are so vibrant down here. I . . . I find that I'm getting a bit lost in them. Sorry."

Al said, "Good to have you back, then," and turned her attention to the crate. It didn't *look* like the Tickle Trunk, not one bit. It was plastic, and black, and ribbed. Its dimensions were roughly the same, but its lid was flat.

No, it didn't look anything like the Tickle Trunk, yet it held the *aura* of it.

It's like bullies, was Luke's strangely apt thought. *They can be hulking and potato fisted or weaselly and slender. It's that cruel quality in their eyes that identifies them as part of the same tribe.*

Which was idiotic to think. This crate had no relation to his old trunk. Luke used to chastise his own son, often far too harshly, for his childish fears: the monster in the closet; the fanged thing under his bed.

The Fig Men.

But here he was, an adult, filled with dread at the sight of a crate that projected that same air of coy menace as his old childhood nemesis.

Who, little ole me? the crate seemed to say in a cutesy-poo voice. *Menacing? Noooo. I'm just a crate, Lukey-loo. I'm a tool that stores other tools*—switching to a Popeye growl—*I yam what I ams, and that's all that I yams!*

Al stepped toward it. *No!* Luke wanted to say. But why? It was nothing but a crate. A tool that stored tools.

Al reached down and cracked the lid. A jumble of spare parts. Rooting through them, she found a plastic case. She opened it and shook out a small chip.

"Bingo."

Al closed the lid and latched it. She gave it a final considering look, the skin tightening down her throat, before turning back the way they'd come.

The chip slotted neatly into the control panel. The air quality changed—where before it'd held a steely aftertaste that built up like plaque in the back of Luke's throat, now it was . . . well, marginally better.

Al slumped against the wall.

"I don't get it," she said. "That chip just vanished. It wasn't burned out, wasn't busted. It was *gone.* Same thing would happen onboard a sub, too. Things would go missing. A guy's books or personal photos, the little tchotchkes that tethered someone to the surface. In most cases, it was petty thievery. No reason aside from boredom and opportunity."

A hollow knock emanated from the recesses of the purification room. Back where the crate sat.

Knock once for yes. Knock twice for no.

"A few times, though, things went missing and never did get found," Al went on. "Was this one guy, Fields. A machinist. Carried a photograph of his dead mother in a locket. Wore it strung around his neck. Woke up one day, it's gone. He tore that sub apart to find it. Peered in every cranny, even went through the trash. Nada. He figured someone stole it. Hooked it off his neck in the night. But sometimes things just go missing. Fall through cracks, you know?"

The knocking intensified.

Luke peered in that direction, but his view was walled off by an impenetrable expanse of gloom. The canisters glowed whitely, a clutch of huge insect eggs laid in the walls.

"Could be the system kicking over," Al said, reading his thoughts. "Lots of weird noises in a sub, too. Knocks and clunks you can't explain. Only pressure and the ocean's currents, but it can sound a little like . . . like ghosts, uh?"

"Right. Booga-booga."

Their laughter sounded both canned and forced, as if they were recording a laugh track on a soundstage.

"You ever had a man go missing, Al?"

"On a sub, you mean? That'd be the ultimate locked-door mystery, uh? I heard about something that went down on another vessel, the SS-228 *Stickleback*. A guy went missing. They turned that sub inside out, never found him. How do you vanish from a submarine, a thousand feet underwater?

"Turns out this guy got into an argument over a game of cards. Another guy, a sonar tech, hits him with a closed fist. Guy falls and hits the bulkhead all funny. Fractured skull. He dies. So the sonar tech and his buddy, a cook, chopped up the body and fed it into the garbage disposal. Those things could chew up cinder blocks. MPs dredged the disposal, found bits of the guy's spine and rib cage."

A new noise floated to their ears. A crisp, somehow silvery sound . . .

. . . the sound of a latch coming undone, maybe.

15.

LUKE SAW IT IN HIS MIND: the crate's hasp falling open just like the tongue lolling from a tired dog's mouth. The lid opening the tiniest bit.

Just a hair.

"Al . . ."

"I heard it, too."

Al had this *what the fuck?* look on her face. There wasn't a soul back there. Only the crate.

And whatever was inside the crate.

Which was nothing, Luke told himself. He'd seen inside it, hadn't he? Nothing but tools and—*and an unnaturally long hand tipped with jet-black nails*—and circuits and nothing else. Not a goddamn thing else.

Al stood and moved toward the noise, her boots going *tak* on the steel grate. She took five steps, then ten.

Tak. Tak. Tak. Tak.

Her body knit with the darkness carpeting the deeper recesses of the room—that darkness seemed to drink at her body, sucking her in.

Luke stood. "Al, why don't we—?"

But she'd already melted into the gloom.

Tak. Tak. Tak. Ta—

The silence stretched. Luke's breath came out in whistling gasps.

Al, get your dick-swinging ass back here. Let's bug the fuck out.

Tak. Tak. Ta—

An enormity of silence.

Then Al's voice wafted out of the dim:

"Jesus Christ. No. No. Jesus Chri—"

Tak . . . tak . . . taktaktaktak

Al flew out of the darkness and barreled into Luke, nearly knocking him down. Her face was set in a rictus of terror; her mouth, frozen open in fear, emitted a series of choked, hiccuping wheezes.

Luke had never seen a grown person look so petrified. He couldn't conceive what could have reduced Al—as sturdy a person as he'd ever met—to a twitching puddle of nerves.

Hu-Thump!

It came from the dark, where such sounds always germinated.

From the crate, which in his mind's eye no longer resembled a crate at all.

It was wooden now, engraved with a pattern of leering clowns.

Hyuk-hyuk-hyuk, coming to get you Lukey-loo! Hyuk-yuk, and we're going to finish it this time!

It wasn't possible. It hadn't *been* possible, all those years ago. It'd been a manifestation of his overburdened imagination. Something his own mother had planted, he'd often thought, to coldly chart the effect it would have on her younger son.

The trunk was empty. The *crate* was empty. There was no—

HuTHUMP.

Closer now. Closing the distance.

How could it get down here? Luke childishly asked himself.

The answer was equally childlike in its logic: *That's a stupid question—it got here because it's a monster. That's what monsters do.*

Luke gripped Al's shoulders. Her body rocked unstably, eyes wide and horrified.

"What did you see?" Luke hissed. "For God's sake, Al, what?"

"He's alive," Al whispered. "He's . . . he's still *alive.*" She gave vent to a series of nerveless screams. "*Still alive!*"

Luke's mind settled around the image with shocking ease: the young sailor, Eldred Henke, crawling out of the crate. His body bloated with seawater, the skin hanging off his bones like hunks of wet wool. His face torn apart by searing metal. Squelching toward Al on his water-rotted feet, leaving blots of pulpy black flesh in his wake, lisping: *You did this to me. You DID this . . .*

They were clearly seeing something very unalike—whatever horror lay inside that trunk was different for each of them—but Luke wasn't sure that mattered. Whatever it was that was *making* them see those things was no doubt capable of doing to them what it might so easily have done to Westlake. It could tear their brains apart.

"Go." Luke shoved Al toward the tube. "Go, go! We've got to move *now*."

HuTHUMP.

Al cast a dazed glance toward the noise—her face a mix of shock, disbelief, and primal fear. Luke noted the vacant cast to her eyes. She looked utterly barking mad.

Prepare the lifeboats, mates! The SS Sanity *is capsizing! We're going down!*

HUTHUMP!—this time so forceful that the metal grate shivered under their feet.

They retreated to the chute. To that gaping mouth of darkness.

What was your original face before you were born?

It was a Zen koan Luke used to recite in veterinary school. Since then it had a habit of popping into his head at times of direst emergency—like that time Zachary choked on a strip of undercooked bacon and Luke had to give him the Heimlich.

What was your original face?

He'd never been able to picture his original face, but he realized that was the point of the exercise. It created a mental distraction—a pinprick of tranquillity at the dead center of all that twisting fear, an eye of the storm within which he could operate.

We can get out of this, he told himself now. *I've saved lives before. Animal lives, okay, but a soul's a soul. I can save us both now.*

You've lost lives, too, his mother reminded him. *Lost the most important one.*

That was true, too. And he was as scared as he'd ever been—a terror more keen than he'd felt at the standing pipe or even in the crawl space. At least then he'd had the whole world to escape into.

Now, only one congested tube.

"You go first," he told Al. "Al . . . ?"

Al stared gape-jawed into the darkness behind them. A thread of saliva spooled over her bottom lip and down her chin.

HUTHUMP!

A great sinuous flex, as though the darkness itself had gulped. Luke swore he saw something pale and snakelike thrust itself forward.

"Al!" He shook her roughly. "Come on, goddamn it!"

Her eyes cleared. She nodded to say she was listening.

Luke said, "Raise your arms, okay? Keep them above your head, like a diver. That should make it easier. Pull yourself, even with that busted hand—it'll hurt like hell, but I'll set those bones again if you need it. And remember the bend, right?"

Al kept nodding. "Okay. Yeah, okay."

"Go. *Now.*"

Al ducked inside, her head and shoulders swallowed by the chute. When the soles of her boots wriggled out of sight, Luke cast a final look back.

There was a border within the room, semisolid, where light met darkness.

Eight appendages stretched over that border.

One-two-three-four-five-six-seven-eight!

Eight fingers. Just the tips.

Eight fingernails. Black, sharp.

Each finger was spread an unnatural distance from its neighbor—six inches apart, at least. An enormous hand spidering nimbly forward.

One of those fingers wiggled at him.

Hello Lukey-loo. After all this time, together again.

Luke hurled himself into the chute. He willed himself to breathe steadily; if he hyperventilated and passed out, he was certain he'd awaken to find that ghastly hand curled possessively around his ankle.

The chute closed over his head; the sea pressed down on him.

Breathe, Luke. For God's sake, just breathe.

He settled into a system: anchoring his feet against the slick metal and pushing off with his toes, inchworming through the chute. It was like doing a thousand consecutive calf-raises. His muscles screamed.

HUTHUMP!

It was at the mouth of the tube now. Five feet away. Maybe less.

It was easier to breathe with his hands over his head, opening up his lungs. He hit the bend but, knowing it was coming, was able to contort his body. His toes skidded on the metal, which was maddeningly clingy and oily at once.

What was your original face before you were born?

He willed himself to calm down. His calves were quivering; for all he knew he'd ripped the tendons clean off the bone.

Skrriiiiiiitch . . .

Nails on metal. The hand was inside the chute, scratching toward him. Tapping and feeling its way forward like a blind and hungry tarantula.

Luke stretched out, his fingers creeping, his toes muscling his aching body forward inch after painful inch. He pictured the chute elongating the same way the crawl space had years ago. An endless suffocating tunnel. The perfect kill zone.

No. It had an end, and he was reaching it. He could hear Al stumbling out someplace ahead. The air tasted a bit less polluted. It couldn't be far now.

Skriiiiiiitch . . .

On his boot now.

A fingernail scratching down the sole, gouging the rubber. Luke bit back a shriek—*don't fall through the trapdoor and into the snakepit now, sonny-boy; you fall now and it's game over, no more tokens*—and surged forward on a tide of adrenaline.

Another push, another, calf muscles twitching, sweat soaking his overalls, another push, mouth wide and gasping, fingers reaching—

The chute ended. Alice's strong hand clutched his wrist and yanked him out.

They stood in the tunnel, panting. The hatch was ten feet away. A mellow coin of light shone through its porthole. LB would be out there, waiting.

They ran for it like kids fleeing the bogeyman—which, in a way, they absolutely were. Luke hazarded one last look back. He couldn't help himself. He almost wanted to thumb his nose.

Nyah-nyah, missed me, missed me, now you've gotta kiss me.

The hand was visible at the end of the chute. *Huge*—even bigger than he remembered. Its five fingers—*no no no it has eight fingers eight like a spider*—its fingers rested on the swell of the tube, each a good five inches apart.

Luke's mind performed a few lunatic calculations. What was the distance between the access chute's mouth and the crate? A hundred feet, at least. That hand had crawled across the purification room and through the chute . . . how much farther could it reach? Perhaps that hand was attached to an arm that unspooled endlessly . . .

. . . no, it had to eventually attach to something, didn't it? A body. A host.

When Luke tried to envision that body—an image flared briefly in his skull—his mind sprinted swiftly away from its nightmarish outline.

The hand raised up ever so slightly. Rocking side to side.

Waving good-bye.

Taa-taa, Lukey-loo. We'll be seeing each other again real soon. We'll be close by. We've always been close. Bye for now. TTFN.

16.

LB YIPPED EXCITEDLY as they staggered out of the hatch. They looked to have aged half a decade since they'd stepped through it.

They were slick with the kind of adrenal perspiration that squeezes from the pores like the sweat off foreign cheese. Their overalls were stained with that unnameable oil coating the chute, the fabric ripped from their . . . escape? What had they been running from? Al's overalls were torn across her belly, a slash like a sagging mouth that revealed her abdominal muscles.

They hunched, hands on knees, gathering their breath, unable to look each other in the eye. The fear Luke had felt—the nattering, mindless fear of a child—already seemed foolish . . . mostly. Were he to stare through the porthole into the cramped, dimly lit tunnel, he knew he'd see nothing. Yet he couldn't bring himself to look.

He couldn't convince himself that what he'd seen hadn't been real, either—if not enough to hurt him physically, then at least to damage or even destroy his mind.

You're being played, Luke.

It felt that way. Stupidly, he almost believed it, too. Every angle cut off, every attempt to escape thwarted. He felt much like a rat down a hole with the terriers chewing after him and the rat-catcher somewhere above, stomping his feet to make the ground thunder. As if some calculating force was funneling him toward a dire certainty, the contours of which Luke could only dimly grasp.

Let's be serious here, brother. It's probably a classic case of the sea-sillies.

Clayton's voice.

You mustn't discount that possibility, O brother of mine.

Luke hadn't discounted it. Or that it could be the 'Gets taking hold. It could happen just this way. A person began to imagine things. That they are pursued by faceless hunters, their childhood nightmares come back to snatch them. The world warped and their brains warped right along with it.

And if two sad souls catch it at the same time? Clayton chimed in. *Well, it can certainly accelerate their mutual deterioration. They both start grasping at the same straws; they're plagued by the same phantoms. Wouldn't you agree?*

Luke glanced at Al. He didn't see any sores on her face or hands—if she was spotting already, he couldn't see it. As for Luke, he could feel a stress pimple beginning to hatch under his lip but that was about it.

LB rucked under his elbow, prodding him with her snout. She licked his palm, her head cocked at a quizzical angle.

I know this dog, Luke thought, scrupulously itemizing his surroundings. *Her name is LB. She is a chocolate Lab, a bit small for her breed. We are eight miles below the surface of the Pacific. The woman beside me is Lieutenant Alice Sykes, U.S. Navy. I am Luke Nelson, a veterinarian. I live at 34 Cherryhill Lane in Iowa City. My wife's name is Abby. My son has a chevron-shaped birthmark on his right arm.*

He shook his head, angry at himself.

My ex-wife's name is Abby. My son had *a chevron-shaped birthmark.*

"What do you think, Doc?" Al asked. "Are we going bugfuck nuts down here or what? What I saw in there"—pointing toward the purification room—"can't exist. I *know* that. But I saw it. I saw that Henke kid crawl out of that fucking crate, scuttling like a crab with his wet flesh falling off his bones . . . and he never took his gaze off me, Doc. His eyes were clear and cold and so fucking *angry*. That can't *be*, but it is. Down here it is."

Luke lifted his foot to get a look at the sole of his boot. A ragged trench was gouged through the rubber. He was only mildly shocked to see it.

"We've got to find that generator, Al."

Al nodded, content to have a plan. "We can do that."

THEY RETURNED to the main lab. Returned to the buzz behind the door marked LW—dulcet now, even harmonic. Al's gaze flitted toward West-lake's lab. Luke sensed it took a great effort for her to pry her eyes away from it.

Clayton was inside his lab. Luke saw him through the porthole and hammered his fist on the glass.

"Clay! Open up! We've got to talk!"

Clayton's hand was bandaged to the wrist now. Viscid fluid leaked through the gauze—thick and translucent, the consistency of 5 Minute Epoxy. It had gummed to the sleeve of his overalls, forming a white crust like the stuff that forms at the edges of a horse's mouth when it's been run too hard.

Clayton approached the hatch, a strange smile pasted on his face. He draped that curtain over the porthole to shield his lab from view.

"Goddamn it, Clay!" Luke hit the glass hard enough to rake the skin off his knuckles. "We need your help! You need *ours*!"

"Screw it. Leave him in there," Al said. "It's where he can do the least harm. Think of how long we've been down here, Luke. Look at how it's affecting us already. Look at what it did to Westlake, too. Your brother and Dr. Toy . . . we can't trust anyone who's been down here that long."

They headed down the tunnel that led to Westlake's quarters. Al said she was pretty sure the generator was stored in that area of the station.

"How's your hand?" Luke asked once they'd made it to Westlake's room.

"It's fucked," she said simply. "You did what you could—it feels a lot better, but it's still busted up. I'd love to pop a few heavy-duty pain pills, but they make me sleepy and I'd prefer to stay awake."

"That's a good idea," Luke said grimly. "Or if we do, we should sleep together."

Al cocked a Spockian eyebrow at him. Belatedly, Luke realized what he'd said; a flush crept up his neck.

"Pretty small beds down here," she said, with a nod at Westlake's cot.

Trapped in the tension of that moment, Luke wanted to kiss her. She wasn't one of the stereotypical corn-fed Iowa beauties he'd grown up around—but then neither was Abby, with her raven hair and Nordic cheekbones. Yet there was something deeply alluring about Alice, an aliveness, a *wildness* even; it would be like making love to a Valkyrie or something. And why not? What could it harm? He was single, lonely, and hadn't felt a woman's touch since Abby left. Alice hadn't mentioned anyone, either. They could have a friendly little romp. Make love in the foxhole, release some tension, then get back to business . . .

. . . but they wouldn't make love—they would *fuck*. Rut. Luke was certain of it. Fall upon each other like wolves, tearing and ripping and biting; there wouldn't be an ounce of tenderness or concern for each other's body or needs; it would be a brutal release, a letting go of the pressure they'd existed under for too long, no different than two swollen clouds splitting open with rain. The *Trieste* would warp the act, making it loveless and mocking—afterward they would be sweaty and bloody in places, ashamed for reasons they couldn't pinpoint, weaker, mistrustful and less unified than before.

"I'd do the honorable thing and sleep on the floor," Luke finally said. "I'm real gallant that way."

The spark that had been kindling in Al's eyes was snuffed. She gave him a strained smile and offered an awkward curtsy.

"Thank you, m'lord, for keeping me safe from predation."

Luke smiled. "Think nothing of it, milady. Your virtue must remain untrammeled until you are given away at the grand cotillion ball six months hence."

The awkwardness passed. Luke's gaze fell on the stack of Westlake's journals under the cot. Hadn't Westlake commented during that final audio file that he'd continued to update his research in those very journals?

"I'd like to leaf through Westlake's papers," Luke said. "I may find something."

Al nodded. "The genny should be just down this tunnel, through another hatch. I'll check it out while you're in here."

Al's footsteps echoed down the tunnel—she still sounded close by,
but sound had a funny way of traveling in the station. Luke did hear a
hatch hiss open, and next Al was banging around inside.

"You find it?" he called.

"Yeah," came her reply. "It'll need some work. Gimme a holler every
so often, okay? It'll keep us both alert."

"Ten-four," said Luke. He sat on the cot. His eyes itched with exhaustion; he screwed his palms into his sockets and blinked to clear the
fuzziness. LB hopped up beside him. He rummaged through Westlake's
gear and located a bag of beef jerky. Saliva squirted into his mouth. He
was ravenous. He split it with the dog; LB bolted down the tough rags of
beef and licked the salt off Luke's fingers. She tried to stuff her nose inside the bag but Luke snatched it away.

"Where are your manners, girl?"

LB hung her head and watched him indirectly, like a clumsy spy.

Luke reached for Westlake's journals. Al was still banging away at a
comforting cadence. Luke flipped through the first few journals. Scientific jargon, formulas, stuff Luke couldn't comprehend. He set them
aside.

He unzipped his duffel bag and pulled out the journal he'd found in
the storage tunnel: Psych Report. The cover was smeared with that weird
ooze.

He flipped it open. The first page and many pages thereafter were
filled with Westlake's neat and careful handwriting.

17.

Wednesday, June 18

Let me say first off, the idea of keeping a journal strikes me as foolish.
But I've been asked to keep a record of my . . . FEELINGS? As my old
mentor memorably said: "Scientists don't have feelings, they have
agendas!"

But a little about myself, since you've insisted. Cooper Westlake.
Forty-five years old. Computational biologist. A wife—my third. A
daughter, Hannah, seven years old.

On a more serious note, I'm grateful to have been selected for this
mission. Like most everyone on earth, I've lost loved ones to the Disease
(which I refuse to call by its more popular sobriquet). The Disease is
curable, I'm sure of it. My surety is shared by Drs. Nelson and Toy.

That will be all for today. Toodleoo.

Friday, June 20

I've been onboard the Hesperus three weeks now. The seasickness is
gone, but bad dreams are commonplace. Yet a mood of optimism prevails.
Having seen Dr. Eva Parks' footage of the lantern fish and the results of
Clayton's preliminary research, excitement is running high.

I have been suffering nightmares. No—a specific, recurring
nightmare. There is some background to it.

I had my daughter, Hannah, with my second wife. She was born in
Belmont, Massachusetts; I was on a grant from MIT. Our neighborhood
had wide streets, big lawns, rows of well-kept colonial homes.

When Hannah learned to walk, we reorganized our living quarters. We were fastidious in creating a safe environment.

But the basement door kept opening.

The basement held the detritus of past renters, stored in dusty boxes. The steps were shallow . . . except one step was bigger than the rest; you'd hit that big bastardly step and just about go ass over teakettle every damn time.

The basement ceiling was so low that I'd have to stoop like a crone. There was a sick, fruity odor that thankfully didn't waft up to the next floor—it smelled a little like death. As if a cat or dog had died of starvation down there, or maybe of fright.

There were spiders, too, big amber-bellied bastards—spiders and the odd skittering movement that may have been rats. I laid down traps but never caught anything. Still, every time I went down I'd hear something pattering through that warren of old boxes.

So yes, the basement door kept opening. And it attracted my daughter.

The first time it happened, my wife alertly swept Hannah into her arms and shut the door. She gave me a recriminatory look, as if I'd left it open.

The next time it happened I was alone, keeping an eye on Hannah without keeping a _direct_ eye on her—as a parent, you develop a sixth sense. When my eyes ticked up, the door was open. Hannah was perched a few feet from the basement stairs.

I shot up and gathered her in my arms. She shrieked. Most worryingly, her arms reached toward the basement—as if she'd wanted to fall. As if she believed something down there would catch her.

Afterward I found a wedge of scrap wood and pounded it under the door until the clockwork of veins at my temples thudded with blood.

The last time it happened a blizzard was raging, snow slicing so heavily that we could barely see our neighbor's porch lights. I was distracted. My grant was in jeopardy, the car needed a new muffler . . . off in my own little world. I wondered afterward if it had sensed that, and taken advantage.

IT?

How had the wedge popped loose? I'd pounded it in hard, driven by rage and fear: the wood had cracked, pressure holding it in place.

Hannah stood at the lip of the stairs. The darkness was such as I've never known.

My daughter said one word.

<u>Nanna.</u>

Nanna was her grandmother on my ex's side. A narrow-shouldered, birdlike thing. But Hannah loved her, and fairly so: the woman doted on her.

<u>Nanna.</u>

One word, spoken clear as a bell. Hannah's arms stretched toward the darkness.

I saw it then: some ineffably old thing dressed in the skin of Hannah's grandmother, the bones showing through in spots, staring up at my daughter and smiling through a mouth of rotted teeth.

Come then, honeybug. Come hug your darling Nanna.

I caught Hannah at the last instant—my index finger slipped inside her diaper, between the cleft of her buttocks. I felt the terrible weight of her body straining against the diaper clips. She would have fallen headlong . . .

That, or something may have caught her.

My eyes fled down the steps, even though every muscle and nerve ending in my body fought it.

I saw nothing. Just the steps trailing into that twitching darkness.

But I <u>felt</u> something howling up the staircase as loud and clear as if a banshee had shrieked at me.

Not a sound but a sense. Of NEED. Of HUNGER.

Something was starving in that basement. Something that had been born starving, maybe. It was never full, would never be satisfied.

I grabbed Hannah tightly. There came a harsh <u>snick!</u> like the jaws of a bear trap snapping shut. That, and perhaps a ringing note of laughter.

We moved out within a week. Shortly thereafter my wife and

I divorced. The usual boring reasons: an accumulation of petty resentments and personal weaknesses. But a sentiment existed beneath those usual ones, unique to us: for two years we'd lived atop an unknown but festering horror that could've erased us.

Whatever had invaded the basement of that colonial home in leafy Belmont had been there a long time. Eventually it would've beaten me, outsmarted or out-quicked me, and as its prize would've claimed what I loved most. It was old, <u>ageless</u> maybe, and far more cunning than I.

How can a rational man run away from a <u>basement</u>? How could he admit that he was illogically frightened of nothing? But that sense of threat never abated; it was akin to that taste you'll get at the back of your throat before a big storm sweeps through—it's imminent, it's coming, all you can do is find safety.

Which brings me back to my recurring dream.

Which is this:

I am perched at the edge of those basement steps, about to fall. There is no preamble at all—I drift into sleep and that's where the dream begins.

In this nightmare I am an adult, and I'm naked . . . all except for a diaper, the same as Hannah once wore. It should be funny, but in the nightmare it only adds to the terror: every trivial detail is precision calibrated for maximum horror.

I'm standing at the lip of the stairs with my arms windmilling for balance. I am about to fall—the nightmare seems endless and yet I am <u>always</u> just about to fall.

It is dark at the bottom of the stairs, incalculably so. Something down there is shuffling forward, about to broach that thinning light.

I'm staring down, wobbling, and see something. My waking self can't even envision what it is—some things are confined to dreams, thank Christ.

But it is coming. I feel it. Its need. Its limitless, timeless hunger.

And then I wake up.

HA! I can't believe I wrote all that. I'd be laughed out of every academy in the country if this were ever found. And look, I've dulled three pencils making a potential laughingstock of myself!

Who cares? I can't sleep anyway. Why? Well, great galloping goose-shit, I've just told you, haven't I?

No matter. This has been very cathartic. And it will all be burned tomorrow. Unreadable ashes.

Monday, June 23

Well, here we are again. I didn't end up burning anything. Never found the time or, I suppose, the inclination.

I write to you from inside the Trieste. Belly of the beast.

The journey down was surreal. We are creatures of daylight. That a world might exist below our own—a world of permanent night—is unthinkable. It is akin to asking a man to live on the moon without a spacesuit.

Thank God for Al. The woman is armor-plated. She brought us down one by one: Clayton, then myself, then Hugo. The animals and insects came last.

The Trieste is horrible. My first thought upon glimpsing it in the Challenger's spotlights was: a spider. Some hideous arachnid like the ones lurking in the basement of my Belmont home. Impervious to pressure, insensitive to light, its limbs spread across the ocean floor.

And we would be inside of it. In its twitching, repulsive guts.

The ceilings are low and ribbed—they truly did give the feel of an intestinal tract. Odd noises race overhead, the pattering of footsteps. The pressure is palpable. More than once I've run my hand over my head to assure myself the crown of my skull hasn't been driven flat.

Each of us has our own private lab. We were shown to our cots and the bathroom quarters. Our waste goes into durable plastic bags, which were vacuum sealed; our deposits would be ferried to the surface for disposal. Alice made a crack about spending fifteen years in the navy only to end up a shit carrier. We laughed, but laughter holds a strange resonance down here. The acoustics rob the joy from it, making it sound spiteful and desperate.

When Alice ascended, a pall settled over the three of us. Now that I'm down here, I can see that humans should not exist in such a place.

The first night I dreamed of a squirrel. We used to have them around the yard of my childhood home in Ledyard, Connecticut. Big fat ones. They loved the peanuts my father would leave out for the jays and cardinals. He would shoot the squirrels with a pellet gun. A narrow-minded bastard, was my father.

One afternoon I found one of them beneath the chestnut tree. It lay faceup and appeared to be breathing. But then I saw the tiny scarlet star where one of its eyes should've sat—the spot where the pellet went through and smashed its brain.

The squirrel's chest burst open and maggots spilled out. Wriggling and tumbling over its coarse dark fur. I'd never seen maggots; the closest I'd ever gotten is when I'd smashed a fly on a windowpane and spied a hundred white specks—fly eggs—streaking the glass. The maggots boiled out of the squirrel's chest cavity, squiggling in the grass; I raced down the street, wanting to put as much distance as possible between me and that horrible sight.

So yes, I dreamed of that squirrel. And of the maggots, too . . . but within their squirming lay another sound, sly and febrile—the buzz of honeybees.

Everything is normal. Such dreams are to be expected.

LUKE PAUSED. LB had been resting on his lap; she stirred, looking up at him questioningly. He couldn't hear anything down the tunnel.

"Hey, Al?" he called. "Everything okay?"

For a moment, nothing. Then her voice filtered back to him.

"S'okay. Trying to figure out this genny."

"Need a hand?"

"Funny, Doc, real funny . . . I could use two good hands, but I'm managing with the one."

Luke petted LB, giving her those long strokes down her back that every dog enjoys; she whimpered gratefully and settled her head against his stomach. Luke yawned so wide that his jaw cracked.

He picked the journal up and started to read again.

Thursday, June 26

As a child, I banged my thumb with a hammer. The thumbnail went black as a layer of blood formed between the nail plates. The entire nail peeled off. Underneath was a gummy residue of old blackened blood.

That's how my mind feels down here. A layer of blackness exists between my brain—the functioning gray matter—and my skull. It makes thinking difficult.

The three of us have kept to ourselves the past day or so. It's hard telling the days apart with no sunlight to mark the passage of time.

The first few days we'd shared meals together. Conversation was sparse but cordial. But the fondness established between us on the Hesperus dried up. We'd been having difficulty locating the ambrosia. The sensors picked up nothing at all. Clayton had been working with the smallest shred, culled from Dr. Parks' specimen and parceled out between him and Dr. Felz; it was nearly gone, either vaporized or collapsing from some organic malaise. The sea floor was empty. Had the station been built in the wrong spot? Was there any more ambrosia to be found?

Hugo in particular is far from a happy camper. He complains bitterly about the temperature (admittedly frosty), the food, and other petty inconveniences that should be expected when one is living at the bottom of the Pacific.

Hugo is agitated, too. His eyes scan the tunnels as if he's tracking something—a runaway lizard or guinea pig perhaps. I've seen him blink flinchingly, as though tiny balls of heat lightning were popping in front of his face. Yesterday I encountered him in the animal lockup, a glazed expression on his face, drool bubbling from his lips.

The sea-sillies, I believe Al called them.

As yet, the bees register no adverse effects. The dogs seem jumpy and sensitive, however. Clayton claims it's natural, but I'm not sure Clayton understands emotions at all, canine or otherwise.

As for my own mental well-being . . . I feel as one ought to when eight miles underwater, in a conglomeration of spidery metal hoses that could collapse on my next breath, combing the ocean floor for scraps of effluvia . . .

I had another nightmare last night. I suppose I should speak of it.

A man named Huey Charles killed five children in my hometown when I was a boy. He was, of all things, an ice-cream man. He drove a white truck with a rainbow on the side. The van played a jingle as it drove down our sedate streets—a tinkling song, sort of queer, like when you open the lid on a music box to see a little ballerina pirouetting inside.

Tinka-tink-teeeee-ta-tinka-tink-teeeeee . . .

Huey—he asked you to call him Uncle Huey—was a rotund, bespectacled man. The last man you'd peg for a child killer, despite the fact he was an overalls-wearing Pied Piper who drove the equivalent of a glue trap for kids. I remember his glasses. Greasy and dirty, the edges gritted with the crust that accumulates at the edges of your eyes while you've sleeping. I never ordered soft-serve from him—I was revolted by the thought that some of that eye crust might sift down from Huey's glasses onto my vanilla swirl.

He killed three boys and two girls. Although he didn't just kill them— do creatures like Uncle Huey ever just kill? What he did was beyond anything you could imagine. He was patient. Years passed between the disappearances. He had a sixth sense, I guess, about when to strike. Those like Huey usually do. He'd wait until the daylight was guttering, until that last kid scampered up to his truck . . . He'd ask if they wanted one of his special sundaes. Just step into the back, then, where it's dark . . .

If that child's parents should happen along, okay, well, Huey was only making the kid a special treat. That Huey, whatta guy! He was well liked around town, though nobody would have called him a friend or could recall spending time alone with him. He was a member of the Elks, the K of C, the Rotary Club; he'd stuff his bloated butt into a tiny car, slap a red fez on his head, and putt-putt down Main Street during the Ledyard Shriners' Parade. Yes, good ol' Uncle Huey.

Now if that child's parents <u>didn't</u> happen along, well, then I imagine a certain look must've come into Uncle Huey's eyes. And the time that child realized the danger in that look was the same moment it ceased to matter.

He took them to the woods. Lots of woods in that part of the country. Deep, dark, silent. A kid's scream could easily be mistaken for the shivering cry of a loon, or the screech of a mountain lion.

What he did to them never made the papers—only the insinuations. One article said the police found a large tool chest in Huey's house with the word <u>Toybox</u> on the lid. Plus there was the fact that the funerals were all closed-casket affairs.

One of the girls lived a few blocks away from me. Tiffany Childers. In my memory she exists as a cliche. Blond hair spilling over her shoulders in ringlets, a starspray of freckles across her cheeks.

They never found Tiffany's head. That little tidbit did leak out to the public. Loose lips at the coroner's office.

Anyway. The dream. I'm in the woods. An orange band of light limns the horizon, casting its light between the firs.

Huey's truck rests on the periphery of my sight. I can see the rainbow on the side. I walk toward it, not wanting to but helpless. The truck's making that tinkling jingle. Taa-ta-teeeee-tinka-tinka-taaa-teeeee. It's awful—not even a song. It's just a discordant collection of notes, an ugly sonic slap.

The truck's back doors are thrown open. The sun, gashing through the trees, highlights the slashes of blood on the white paint.

Things are hanging inside. Dangling down beside the soft-serve machine and next to the sleeve of sugar cones. Parts of bodies. They hang on snarled lengths of copper wire. They brush against one another in a breeze that skates across the forest floor. They make a faintly musical note, like wind chimes. They shouldn't, but they do.

I look down and see that I'm wearing a white uniform—Uncle Huey's ice-cream man uniform. I am fat, my belly swelling to the point I can't see my belt buckle. Suddenly I realize I cannot see very well, either; it's as though I'm staring through a crusty, grease-smeared window.

I become aware of the sound of my own insectile thoughts. Imagine lowering a boom microphone into a tub of night crawlers—that squishy, squirming sound. That is the noise inside my skull.

And the worst part is, I'm at home with that sound.

I awoke back in the Trieste, in the tunnels. I'd gotten up and walked out of my quarters. I've never sleepwalked before, ever.

I was caressing a pipe running down the tunnel . . . caressing it as I might the leg of my own daughter to soothe her to sleep.

I had an erection.

A raging hard-on, one better suited to a hormonal teen. Even my second wife—the most inventive hellcat I've ever shared a bed with—couldn't bring me to such nail-pounding hardness.

Morning wood. That's all it was. Morning wood.

Monday, June 31 (?)

Success! We've discovered trace elements of ambrosia. The sensors picked it up two days (???—time has surrendered most of its meaning down here) ago.

With good news, though, comes bad. Hugo has isolated himself. Surely you know this already, having watched it on the monitors. He has locked himself in the animal quarantine quarters, abandoning his lab.

He's got the sea-sillies, all right. A crippling case. Clayton and myself debated capturing him, to make sure he didn't punch a hole in the wall with the first sharp object he could lay his hands on. But he doesn't strike us as dangerous. Only terrified and mistrustful.

Not long before he locked himself up, I encountered Hugo in the main lab. He'd switched on the spotlights and was staring over the ocean floor. It is, admittedly, a soul-sapping vista. Your heart trembles just to see it.

"If you look long enough," Hugo said, "you can see it move."

Hugo's hair was unkempt, his overalls stained, and his odor quite foul.

"See what move?" I asked.

"The floor, out there," said Hugo. "It moves in waves. It stares at us with a trillion eyes."

I dropped my own eyes, speechless. It was awful to see a man go crazy right in front of your face. But I didn't blame Hugo one bit. Minds crack down here. Pressure bursts pipes, as the saying goes.

"We'll be able to leave soon," I told him. "Try to think of that. It helps me, Hugo. A simple lungful of fresh air, think of that."

Hugo stared at me. His face was a horrid, shuddering mask.

"We're not going anywhere, Cooper. We're caught now. It's got us. They've got us. We built our own trap, and now we're snared."

It. They.

"Hugo, for Christ's sake," I said, rising to quick anger. "Get a grip. Think of your family."

Hugo hissed at me—truly hissed, like a vampire staked through the heart.

"You fucking fool," he said. "Why think of things you'll never see again?"

Unnerved, I retreated into my own lab. The honeybees droned comfortingly. They buzzed sluggishly around, ferrying sugar water from the feeders to their hives.

Bees are the most mathematical creatures on earth. Their hives are marvels of geometric functionality. The drones map out their nectar-collecting routes better than a computer, calculating the shortest distance between pollinating buds.

The bees were the first—and so far the only specimens in that phylum—to develop the condition we now recognize as the Disease. The G-word. CCD, or Colony Collapse Disorder, was noted many years ago. Entire hives were obliterated. Death in the billions. Imagine it: a population the equivalent of New York or Cairo decimated in days.

How had it happened? Several possibilities were bandied about:

parasite infestations, fungus, mold, the use of antibiotics by beekeepers. Then Dr. Curtis Smails at the University of Birmingham tendered the theory that the bees were simply forgetting to do the things bees always did, the tasks grafted into their genome.

Life in a hive is perfect in the way things in nature often are. The drones collect nectar, build the combs, make honey, and defend the hive. The queens produce offspring and royal jelly. Dr. Smails noticed that the hives suffering from CCD were populated by bees that were no longer fulfilling their roles. The queens stopped giving birth or did so randomly. Drones flew miles from the hive, collecting no nectar, coming back empty-handed. They would fly into ponds and drown, sting other creatures for no reason, and die . . . They'd become fatalistic. Bees are ritualistic, and they were abandoning their rituals.

No, we realized in time—not abandoning, but <u>forgetting</u>.

Thus bees became the first bellwether of the Disease. The honeybee in the coal mine, you could say.

My specimens were healthy when we arrived, but they are now displaying the initial symptoms of CCD. Honeycombs going untended, decreasing numbers of larvae. The bees fly without purpose, bumping into the lab walls. The floor is littered with expired specimens. If this continues, they'll all be dead in a matter of days.

The footsteps overhead. Racing along the ceiling. It sounds so much like the running of children . . . of Hannah's own footsteps in our Belmont home.

It's disorienting, like so much of life down here. I don't like it.

June 32 (maybe, baby!)

There is a hole in the station.

Teeny-tiny, no bigger than a pinprick. It appeared on the wall nearest the hives. The hole is dark, nearly the color of the metal itself. I wouldn't have noticed were it not for the strange pull it emits.

It is not an unpleasant sensation. I can only liken it to a scalp massage . . . except the fingers are inside one's skull, manipulating the gray matter.

I covered the phenomenon with a long strip of duct tape. I didn't want to touch the hole. It seems unwise.

Having done so, the pull lessened.

I confess, I missed the pull.

July Something-Something (day/date immaterial)

We were able to harvest a sample of ambrosia. Clayton did it. I wasn't there. A tricky procedure, but Clayton (of course it had to be Clayton; nerves-of-steel Clayton) corralled it through the vaccu-trap. Good on him.

We got less than a thimbleful. It was split between Clayton and myself. We did not speak while he portioned it out. We haven't really spoken to one another for . . . days? A week? I couldn't tell you. Silence is our element now. Silence and darkness. I have stopped attending my psychological counseling sessions, too. I suspect Clayton has done the same. And Hugo, of course.

I have not told Clayton about the hole.

I like to look at it, I must say. The ambrosia, I mean. It's strangely entrancing.

The hole is entrancing in much the same fashion.

The hole has grown. It consumed the tape I placed over it. A slow suctioning, the tape stripping from the metal and tugged through the engorged opening . . . a sight, were you to watch from start to finish (I did not, being asleep for some of it), that would be reminiscent of an infant's toothless mouth devouring a velvet ribbon.

I've performed tests, captured on audio files knocking and howling sounds. Laughter, perhaps? There appears to be some rudimentary intellect at work . . . not the hole itself, I can't imagine that, but whatever lays in the dark space beyond.

My tests are ongoing. I perform them in secrecy. Clayton would only meddle.

We did visit Hugo recently, Clayton and I. We hadn't heard from him in some time, other than a random banging that could've been Hugo bashing his fists on the tunnels. Clayton felt that he may have been roaming around while we slept—he claims to have seen shadows stretching across the walls where the tunnels bend out of sight.

Hugo would not let us in. He is a fright. A gibbering ghoul. His mind has come unglued. He screamed at us through the porthole, refusing to unlock the hatch. He held up a piece of notebook paper that said: YOU ARE NOT WHO YOU SAY YOU ARE.

Clayton has alerted topside operations. It may be best to have someone—perhaps Al, who Hugo trusts—come and take him away. He's of no use to the mission now.

Has Hugo encountered a hole, too?

No, I don't think so. The hole is meant for me and me alone.

I took my ambrosia to the lab. The bees were very close to extinction; I'd swept up hundreds of carcasses. I introduced the lion's share of the ambrosia into the sugar-water receptacle; my hope was that the unaffected specimens would ferry it back to the hive. I trapped a few other bees—the sick, baffled ones that buzzed aimlessly into the walls—dabbed their abdomens with red ink to identify them, and fed them ambrosia-fortified sugar water with a dropper.

The footsteps. There they go again, pattering overhead as I write this.

I see the shadows on the walls, too. Clayton is not alone in that.

LUKE'S EYEBALLS ITCHED; his shoulders were tight.

Westlake's journal had developed a sinister momentum. The handwriting, which had started out neat and clinical, was starting to erode. Some of the pages were crumpled, as though Westlake had clenched his hand into a fist while writing.

Most worryingly, it . . . it seemed to be speaking directly to Luke. A voice behind the printed words whispered softly into his ear. Fingers crawled up the back of his neck—Westlake's scarified fingers racing ticklingly over his scalp . . .

. . . what an idiotic notion.

Nothing is idiotic now, he told himself. *The worst mistake you can make is to think it's idiotic.*

He could still hear Al down the tunnel, banging away. It held a rhythmic note, like the pump of a piston in a slow-running engine.

Bang . . . bang . . . bang . . .

His eyes snapped open. He'd let them slip shut, lulled by that banging, which matched the beat of his own heart. A shadow twisted across the wall where the tunnel bent. He watched the hatchway, thinking something—*fingers, four small fingers, a boy's small fingers*—might wrap around the gray metal. When that didn't happen, his eyes fell back upon the journal. The pages hooked his gaze, tugging insistently. Westlake's voice—cold and raspy with death—said: *You need to know, Lucas, because down here anything can happen. Anything at all.*

guts are unraveling out of their bellies, which makes them
onky.

pursued it in a frenzy, knocked it down and stomped on it. Its body
loded under my boot with a satisfyingly gooey pop.

There. Fucking thing. THERE YOU GO.

I couldn't find the stinger in my flesh. A terrifying thought came to
e: it had burrowed into me. There was an inflamed red bump that
itched awfully.

I dressed it with ointment and a Band-Aid from the medical kit. I
did not tell Clayton. We rarely speak. There is open hostility when we
do. I believe he is spying on me and told him as much. Clayton labeled
my accusation absurd—of course he would! Maybe it's Hugo, he said; or
maybe you're losing it, Westlake. I nearly slugged him. I feel perpetually
spied upon—eyes tiptoeing over my skin at all hours.

As such, Clayton and I pass each other like submarines in the night.
Haaaaa . . .

Before our argument, I did run into Clayton in the main lab. I
found him at the window. I, too, find myself staring, bewitched, over
that carpet of marine snow. I envision it stretching out, lunarlike and
lifeless, beyond the spotlights. The ambrosia drifts in far greater
concentrations now. We've collected a good deal.

Clayton's aspect has changed. Gaunt, wan. Lack of sunlight, of course,
but Clayton always seemed bizarrely luminous. I picture a huge insect
under his overalls—a giant tick battened onto his back. Unbeknownst to
him, this tick is sucking out his bodily juices. It's growing, gaining strength
while Clayton bows like a hunchback under its blood-bulged weight.

"I haven't been able to contact the surface for . . . a day," he said
somewhat falteringly. Neither of us are aware of time anymore. The
minutes and hours and days blend, which inspires a certain gaiety of
mind for men like us, who feel as though we've spent our adult lives in
the shadow of a constantly ticking clock.

"What's happened?"

"A storm of some sort," he said. "Under the water. It's interrupting
the signal."

18.

Science Day!

This place repulses.

There is nothing to nourish the soul. Nothing but man-m
and inert materials. Nothing is cut from nature, holding the
appeal of objects that God has touched. God's finger doesn'
down this far.

Today I wept while brushing my teeth. I wonder why I even di
bought the toothbrush months ago, on a shopping trip with Hannah.
pirouetted down the aisles, flipping silly items into the cart. A piping
adult diapers . . . she thought it was hilarious when I'd take them ou
sigh dramatically, and set them back on the shelves.

The toothbrush is old now, its bristles bent. But I bought it in a well-lit
supermarket eight miles up and however-thousand miles distant, on a day
when the sun shone brightly and I'd played foolish games with my daughter.

And now I'm here, crouched in the loveless belly of this spider-station.
Hannah is part of another world, one I have no grip on. And so I'd stared
at my toothbrush with its sad dab of minty paste and I'd cried. The
tears came effortlessly. Some days I cry without quite realizing it.

The hole is growing. Days ago, it ate my microphone.

Hungry, hungry hole.

I hear voices. They are not made by anyone onboard the station.

A bee stung me. On the arm. Who cares, right? You're a scientist who
works with bees, Westlake! Surely you've been stung before.

And surely I have. But the pain was much sharper this time. The
bee had a red-ink marking on its abdomen. I watched it fly away in
the narcotized manner that all bees possess after they've stung—

I took this in stride. Part of me was heartened. I was worried they might send a team down to round up Hugo. If so, they might snoop around my lab. I don't want that.

The ambrosia's effect on the colony has been remarkable. Both hives are thriving. The drone can be heard outside the lab now; bees festoon the bench, the walls and roof.

The question is—has the ambrosia cured the Disease, at least insofar as it manifests in honeybees? Cured it, or has it actually altered their basic cellular structure? Are they even bees anymore, as we commonly conceive them?

The bastard bee that stung me . . . the itch is worsening. A painful, maddening sensation. I have not scratched it yet. I'm terrified to. The skin has swollen so badly that the Band-Aid has torn loose. A puffy, awful anthill throbs on my arm. The hole in its center is a deep and pestilent yellow.

I will not scratch. I WILL NOT.

Update: I scratched.

Hah.

Jul?

Want to hear a story my mother told me? My mother was a Bible-basher. Bashy-bashy-bash that Bible, Ma! Ignorant dilettante scare-mongerer . . .

This story wasn't in any Bible. Don't know where she got it. Her crazy-ass stepfather? Yes, so . . .

Once there was a great exorcist. He saw demons in the waking world. They were everywhere. Perched on some poor fucker's shoulder or wrapped around a sinner's waist, its filthy hands down the man's pants, inciting him to vice.

Most of them were pests. Parasitic hellspawn who created havoc in the minds of weak men, leading them to cheat on their spouses, beat their kids, steal from their employers. But there were some very bad demons. They weren't physically big, necessarily—one of the worst was no bigger than a fruit fly. It'd perch inside the ear of a victim, dripping poison into that person's brain. The body of another was gauzy and fungoid. It wrapped around a man's head like a cocoon—it looked like a tent caterpillar nest in an oak tree.

Nobody could see them but the exorcist. He banished them. The same demons more than once, in some cases. And there was a place, my mom said, a nexus where they congregated. A deep, dark place. When the exorcist banished a demon from its host, it fled back to this spot. Sometimes the demon would remain down there a long time. It was difficult to get out, you see. The demons would swirl around, nipping and snarling, waiting for the opportunity to ascend to the human realm again.

These demons killed the exorcist. Eventually, inevitably. He didn't fling himself out a window like old Father Karras. Each encounter left scars on the exorcist—not physical, but psychic. These powerful demons hacked at the exorcist's brain, taking swipes like with a tiny razor, each fight wrecking him a little more, warping his reasoning until he couldn't fight them any longer. His body was found in an alley behind a cathedral where he'd fled seeking sanctuary, his face torn off by feral dogs.

I think of my mother's story now. That deep, dark place. If you had to hide something—if you were God, say, and could command it—if you wanted to hide the worst, most threatening things you could imagine . . . well, where better?

Answer me that. Where . . . BETTER?

Sunday Funday

The hole is bigger. I could fit my fist through, if I tried.

I confess that I want to try. Very badly, in fact.

The bees cluster around it. Buzzing, investigating. I keep waving them away. The hole is dark—much darker than the surrounding metal.

The hole shimmers like water, is black as the water, but is not water.

We'd all be dead. Wouldn't we?

Are we dead yet?

Monna-Monnaday?

It is inside me.

???

I dreamed of a boa constrictor eating a naked infant. The baby made
no sound as it was consumed, although its eyes were round and wide
with horror.

I haven't left the lab in . . . ?

Time scallops down here. Have I said that already? Days, weeks,
months, minutes, seconds. Everything is liquid and ever shifting.

It's safe in the lab. Nobody can see me. What's happened to me.

The bee sting has multiplied, despite my never getting stung again.
Instead of one inflamed anthill, dozens now festoon my flesh. Like giant,
pulsating zits. I've squeezed them, too, hoping for a gout of yellow pus and
with it, some relief. But the skin beneath each hill is hard, calcified,
and it hurts immensely just to touch them.

My arms, legs, chest, stomach, buttocks—all covered with these
inflamed hills. Fresh hills have appeared on my armpits, and recently
my big toes. So far they have not appeared on the soles of my feet
or my hands; if so, I fear I'll be immobile. The merest brush with any
obstruction brings forth blinding pain. My palms are unmarked as yet, too,
meaning I can still write.

I haven't seen anyone for some time. Every so often a staccato
knocking sound will pierce the drone of the bees, but I don't know if it's
Clayton or Hugo or something or someone else.

One knock for yes. Two for no.

I have no use of Clayton or Hugo anyway. To hell with them. I have my study.

I left the lab only once. I cleared the massing bees from the porthole window and saw the main lab was empty. I dashed out. Not a single bee fled my lab. Once out, I realized there was nothing I wanted. I wasn't hungry; I haven't wanted to eat for a long time. I needed no equipment.

My gaze fell upon the window. Darkness pressed against the glass, an insistent swirling. Shreds of ambrosia sucked over its surface like remoras.

The urge struck: find something heavy—a crowbar was the object that sprang to mind—and smash the window until it splintered and the sea rushed in.

I retreated to my lab. To my colony. It is monstrous. It has tripled, quadrupled in size. The bees carpet the walls and bench and ceiling—a humming, droning, fuzzy black-and-yellow carpet.

They do nothing but collect and build. I have provided the material: three sacks of refinery sugar, slit open with a scalpel.

The bees have abandoned their hives—they are building new structures.

A beehive is a marvel of mathematics. A home of hexagonal cells, the sides of each cell meeting at precisely 120 degrees. The hexagon is the perfect shape for storing the most honey while using the least beeswax. Every honeybee is born with the knowledge of how to build a honeycomb. They instinctively know that hexagons are the building blocks of their homes.

But these bees are building something else entirely.

Two hanging cathedrals. They descend inverted from the ceiling on opposite ends of the lab. Each is baffling to behold; the human eye can't stare at them for too long, in the same way one cannot stare into the sun. Strange and frightening edifices. One almost resembles a stalactite, with bizarre corkscrews spiraling off at unnatural angles. The other dwindles in a cochlear swirl, with sharp jutting appendages that hold the articulation of robotic limbs.

The bees build their hives night and day. Honey is produced, but not harvested. The honey—dark and thick as motor oil—drips ceaselessly from each hive, forming sticky pools on the floor.

The queens lay somewhere within. I hear them sometimes: an angry, commanding buzz that rises above the general hum.

NIGHT

The anthills covering me have worsened. Broadened, heightened, connected together on my flesh. They have a uniform look, vaguely hexagonal. Like honeycombs.

"We are just skin." My second wife said this in one of her fouler moods, when I had the bad timing to comment on her lovely figure. "Me and you and everyone, we're all just skin and fat wrapped around bones."

Yes, I'd told her, but I happen to fancy the way you're wrapped.

My own wrapper is beginning to peel. HAH!

The pain is exquisite. I am half delirious with it. The instinct arose to show Clayton my condition and seek aid. But I like it too much in my lab, with my bees . . . and my wonderful hole.

The hives stretch ceiling to floor now. The bees have begun to build into the floor grating; satellite combs are appearing at the edges of the lab bench in the manner of toadstools ringing an elm tree.

The bees are changing, too. Larger, is the most obvious difference. Some are the size of hissing cockroaches. They are aggressive toward one another—bees are communal by nature, so this is strange. They seem obsessive but in a different way: instead of building a hive for the purposes of nurturing young and manufacturing honey, the hive itself is their sole ambition: building it, growing it.

They are not aggressive. I have not been stung again. They dance lightly up my arms and legs. It tickles. Sometimes I fall asleep and awake with them covering my face, tiptoeing over my closed eyes.

The air smells of caramelized sugar. A nice smell.

NIGHT

A massacre.

The bees of one hive attacked the other. I can't imagine what provoked it. The air filled with mad buzz, the sound of a rusted band saw. They fought in the air and on the ground. It was the most vicious thing I'd ever seen.

One hive, the cochlear one, has been fading of late. Its honeycomb took on a grayish hue. Its honey was a clotted, sludgy gray. Its drones, while large, were spiritless in their fight against the drones from the other hive.

I tried to stop them—how in God's name do you stop a bee-fight? I waved my arms (my swollen, itching, bloody arms) frantically, yelling, "Stop!"

Yes, I yelled at bees. It is to laugh . . .

They didn't attack me, but they didn't stop going after one another. They danced gently on my arms as they battled, their stingers jabbing crazily.

It was over quickly. The floor was covered with the dead. The victorious bees descended upon the cochlear hive, ripping at the rotting honeycomb. They attacked the nesting queen. I never got a good look at her—her body was covered in drones, layer upon layer—but she was clearly huge. She toppled from her throne and hit the lab bench with a meaty smack. The drones stung and ripped at her—some have developed rudimentary mandibles. When they cleared off, buzzing sluggishly back to their labors, the bench was empty save a blot of very thick, red royal jelly. The color of blood.

Their industry continues unabated. They have grafted their hive to the bones of the cochlear one. It is incredibly large—I have to crawl on my belly to reach the other side of the lab (where my hole is), my head mere inches from the dripping comb and that unearthly buzz.

The new hive is profoundly disturbing to behold. It beggars mathematics. The eye revolts.

I'm sitting beside my fantastic hole now. It is larger. I could probably squeeze a volleyball through it, into . . .

?????????

The bees are entranced by the hole. They hover nearby, crawling around its circumference in a narcotic daze.

It makes such lovely noises, the hole. Those resonant knocks. And odd muttersome sounds, musically sweet, like voices from another room. If I listen closely enough, perhaps I can hear what they're saying.

Am I insane?

Does a sane man ask himself that question?

Ha! Ha! Ha! Hey!

. . .

They came out of me. They were born inside of me, fostered in me, and then they exited me.

I am the incubator.

I am the queen.

The first one birthed from my left elbow. My skin had been stirring restlessly for some time. The flesh-hills—fully connected by then, perfect hexagons spanning my body—twitched with hectic life.

The bees seemed to pause in their labors, watching me. They overrun the lab now; they bristle on the floor, huge bees, some the size of malnourished mice. When I walk, their bodies crunch underfoot. They do not protest or sting me. The remaining bees harvest the ones I've killed, picking the bodies apart with their mandibles and bearing them back inside the mother hive, which pumps out a thin drip of tarry, noxious-smelling nectar.

I tasted some of it, a child accepting a schoolyard dare. Revolting. A diseased offering from a diseased host. It killed the skin on my tongue, turned it gray and dead.

It—IT—exited my elbow with torturous languor. Its legs, tiny and black and covered in oh-so-delicate fur, slit the top of the flesh-hill. It pushed itself out slowly, its body coated in dark pus, a tumor releasing itself from the flesh.

It was not as big as its brothers and sisters, and it looked very different indeed. Its head was that of a bee, though its eyes were a bright and fiery red. Its abdomen was flesh toned—it looked like a severed fingertip—banded with angry red slashes. Its stinger was a cruel spike, dripping venom that sizzled on my skin.

They came quickly after that. From my arms and legs and neck and cheeks. From my toes and thighs and buttocks and a few very small specimens from the thin vein-strung flesh of my scrotum. I exhaled, mesmerized, as one pushed itself from my forehead—I am Zeus giving birth to Athena!—and trundled over my quivering brow to perch upon the convex of my eyeball.

When it was finished, my flesh sagged like the wattle on an old biddy's neck. I was emptied and sundered, but it was perfectly okay. I had given birth to wondrous marvels. They colonized my body, zipping around my head in a protective corona. I was their mother and father.

I was their queen. The NEW queen.

. . .

The other bees avoid me now. Their buzzing has reached a quailing, fear-struck harmonic. Good. That is good.

Not long ago I advanced on the mother hive. Drones teemed over its surface. My hands plunged through their soft buzzing bodies, sinking into the comb. It did not feel firm, as I'd expected—rather it stripped away in my hands like the flesh off a long-dead corpse. The bees did nothing to protect their hive. The new bees—MY children—battened upon them, sunk in their stingers, and tore their heads off. The old bees did nothing to defend themselves, submitting like weary soldiers at the end of a prolonged skirmish.

The comb turned dry and brittle as I ripped toward its center. My arms were coated in that revolting nectar. Here and there within the combs I'd discover some abnormal and awful sight: my hand sunk into a baseball-sized pocket of wriggling yellow larvae, the ball coming apart like cheese curds; next I tore into a vault of festering bee parts, their pulped anatomies tumbling into my upturned face and stuck to the loathsome nectar coating my arms and chest.

I knew I was nearing the queen by the sound echoing through the moldering combs: an anxious squeal. The comb was caving in around me, the entire structure collapsing in sticky, suffocating rags.

I encountered a small army of defending drones—queen protectors. They were incredibly large, rat-sized in some cases, but they were bloated and blind and seemed as resigned to their fates as the others. I knocked them to the floor and stomped them amid the stinking comb; the ones I didn't kill were dispatched by my progeny, who took great sport in pulling their limbs off and bursting their milky, sightless eyes.

I tore through a final vault of coppery comb—it ripped apart like stinking cheese—and beheld the queen.

A horror. She was immense. The size of a rump roast or a large puppy. She lay in a pool of black, viscid jelly swimming with her birth: gelatinous gray grubs that squirmed in that sticky tar, issuing crazed mewls like children hungering for their mother's teat.

She saw me and knew—I could tell, somewhere in her insect brain, that she realized—her time had come. My progeny darted, harassing her until she let out a bleating buzz, her jelly-smeared wings shuddering against her bloated frame.

Consumed with disgust, I wrapped my hands around her. The queen's body was ribbed, its texture strangely giving; my fingertips sank in without resistance. I felt the rapid thudding of her heart in my palms.

I squeezed. The queen bleated again, more shrilly. Grubs sputtered out of her backside. I squeezed until her convex eyes swam with blood—

yes, she was full of blood—and finally, with a shuddering sigh, her body ripped apart in my hands. The separate parts thrashed for a few moments before going still.

Things went very dark and quiet.

When I regained my senses my tongue felt furry, as if I'd eaten something alive.

. . . when-where-why-what-how-HEY-YO! . . .

The lab is quiet: only my progeny are left. They crawl and frolic around the hole (which is enlarging ever more), flicking their delicate wings.

I don't have nightmares anymore, doctors. Thought you'd like to know that.

I'm cured! HAH!

I've no need of nightmares now. They've invaded the waking world.

. . .

This is not about the Disease. The 'Gets. Never was. The 'Gets was simply the vehicle, the substance whose purpose was to ferry the valuable commodity—US—to the site of infection. The 'Gets was the tail we foolishly chased down the rabbit hole. There is no cure down here. There is only madness and malignant evil and death. I should say, if we're lucky, death. We've been tricked. Played. Our love and hope and desire to do good for mankind—our need to understand, to CONQUER—brought us here against our every instinct.

I am known. I mean to say, whatever lurks down here (and yes, oh yes oh yes oh yes, something is down here) KNOWS me. Knows my history and loves and fears. It has been studying me for a long time. My whole life, even. It has met me before, and vice versa. And it has arranged, through some slyboots method, to bring me down here.

I am in the basement with the beast. It is the same one, I fear, that lurked in our home back in leafy Belmont—that same beast, or somehow connected to it. The creature that tried to take Hannah (HANNAH!). The same beast whose ageless need and hunger howled up those dusty stone steps. The one I fled from like a coward.

But you can't run. It will find you. Hunt you down and find you.

It will lay a trap in the basement of the world and bait it with the sweetest fruit and it will wait. It's been waiting a long time.

It has waited long enough.

. . .

I put my fingers through. Just the tips.

Couldn't help myself. Swear to God swear to God I couldn't just could not help it—

Funny. Felt funny. Not bad-funny. Not good-funny. Not joy-buzzer funny.

Just . . . funny.

Two fingers. Pointer and middle. Same two fingers I'd stick into the bathtub to test whether the water was too hot before bathing my infant daughter. Same two fingers I'd used to fingerbang Sue Reynolds behind the utility shed in the ninth grade. Stinky Sue. Rosie Rottencrotch. Slutty Sue, the only one who'd sleep with Craterface Cooper Westlake . . .

They began to change. My fingerprints. Shift and swirl. They are the most unique feature of our bodies. Our DNA is expressed in the whorls. And I was seeing them change . . . and with it, a profound change occurring inside of me.

I cut them off. Just the tips of each finger. Scalpel. Chop, chop. It didn't hurt at all. The sound of the blade hacking through bone was only minorly unsettling. I've heard much worse by now.

The severed fingertips kept moving. Kept . . . squirming, like fat little grubs. The bees tried to spirit them away for their strange games. I shooed them off, picked the tips up with tweezers, and deposited them through the hole.

Have me, if you want. A small piece. A tribute. Won't that be enough?

The voices seemed appreciative of my gift. But they are growing louder again.

Hungrier.

Hungry hungry hole . . .

. . .

I dreamed I was drowning. Wanted to die very badly. Tried to take a breath, flood my lungs. Couldn't. I washed up on the shores of an immense black ocean. The water was thick as molasses, sucking at my bare feet. Hannah was there, singing the song I'd once sung to put her to sleep as a baby.

> Hush, little baby, don't say a word,
> Papa's gonna buy you a mockingbird.
> And if that mockingbird won't sing,
> Papa's gonna buy you a diamond ring.

Hannah's eyes were huge ovals, dead black, stretching from her eyebrows to the base of her nose. A bee's eyes. The flesh above her nose broke open and a pair of antennae pushed through like bean sprouts from a pot of dirt.

I awoke screaming . . . or laughing. So hard to tell now.

My bee-children are cruel. They grow impatient, which leads to mischief. There are a few of the old bees left. My children make terrible sport of one of the old queen-defenders. They've torn its legs and wings off. They pinch and slash it. I think they may have tried to copulate with it.

Bee rape? Is it possible? If they conceive, what will that baby look like?

The hole is much bigger now. The voices, louder. It's as if lips are pressed to the other side of that dark, glittery sheen. If I put my ear to it, I'm sure I'd hear what those lips are saying.

I want to put my head through the hole. Want to kiss those lips.

Whose lips? WHAT'S LIPS?

Is that a bad thing to want?

I won't put my head through.

I am trying very hard not to.

. . .

put it

through

. . .

Cut myself with the razor. Slashed my wrists vertically, not horizontally, the way you do when you're dead serious and not just squalling for attention, MOMMY-DADDY PAY ATTENTION TO ME OR I'LL SWALLOW A HANDFUL OF KIDDIE ASPIRIN—no I slit right down the ulnar artery, deep deep slashes, serious as a fucking heart attack, you bet your ass, the best way to let out a whoa-nelly gusher of blood.

I healed. Almost immediately, I healed.

I wept. Cut again. Wept. Wept. Jesus fucking wept.

My children buzzed about my ears, stinging me.

Bad mother! Bad mother! Don't hurt yourself, mother! Stay with us, love us, be with us forever!

Fucking things. Fucking fucking fuck fuck FUCH HUCH UG UG UUUUU

. . .

Amazing. Simply amazing. It is beauty. The purest beauty imaginable.

. . .

THE FIG MEN
   ARE DRAWING NEAR

. . .

THE FIG MEN
   ARE HERE

. . .

LUCAS. LUCAS COME HERE. LUCAS COME HOME. COME HOME LUCAS.
COME HOME SON
DADDY COME HOME

19.

LUKE HURLED THE JOURNAL. Pages riffling, it struck the wall. He shook violently, gooseflesh pebbling his scalp. LB's head popped out from underneath the cot where she'd been resting, her eyes darting restlessly.

DADDY COME HOME

Jesus. Jesus Christ.

He shouldn't have read it. He knew that belatedly, the same way he'd known he shouldn't watch a scary movie as a young boy—but Luke always had to watch, peeking through his fingers.

The final ten pages were partially glued with a rank-smelling substance; the honey produced by those bastardized bees, Luke could only guess. And the last few pages were dark with blood.

The journal's final words seemed less written than etched. Each letter had torn through several sheets of paper, their impressions carving deep into the sheets below. The letters were huge slashes, horizontal or vertical, no curves—the O's looked like crazed cubes. Westlake must've wielded his pen like a knife, slashing each stroke several times, ripping and gouging them onto the page.

DADDY COME HOME

It made no sense. Dr. Westlake had no idea who the hell Luke was. That he was a father, or Luke's tortured history with his son. Christ, they'd never met. Had Clayton mentioned him? Even if so, what would compel Westlake to write that?

THE FIG MEN ARE HERE.

This cut even closer to the bone. How would Westlake know about the Fig Men, the monsters in Zachary's closet? It made no sense. Luke thought about the words written in blood inside the *Challenger*: *THE AG MEY ARE HERE*. That's how he'd read it. But Al thought the second word was *Men*, hadn't she? Could the *A* Luke had seen actually have been the capital letter *F* and and a lowercase *I* combined? Could the blood from a letter *F* have dripped down, joining the top of that *I* to become what looked to be a sloppy, too-big *A*?

Jesus, had Westlake actually written: *THE FIG MEN ARE HERE*?

The Fig Men didn't *exist*. There was no such thing. They were something his son's fevered imagination had cooked up—something Luke himself had fixed, trapping the Fig Men in obsidian cocoons. He remembered how the act had made him feel like a minor superhero. The Human Shield.

Could the journal be a deeper manifestation of Dr. Westlake's psychosis? Rantings and ravings divorced from truth? Luke wanted to believe so. The "honey" could be something he'd mixed up in his lab, boiled sugar and some manner of toxic chemical. Physically speaking, the gunk on its pages was the only thing that separated Westlake's journal from your standard loony bin manifesto—it was full of the same delusional thinking, paper-shredding pen strokes, and yes, even blood.

Home. Come home. Luke *had been* home, safe if despondent in Iowa City. The *Trieste*, though, wasn't anybody's home. Not the home of anything human, anyway.

LB clambered onto the mattress and rested her head on Luke's lap. As he massaged her ears, Luke felt the energy coursing through her bunched muscles. Did he really believe it? The bees, the hives, the madness lurking behind the hatch to Westlake's lab? The *hole*?

Westlake had gone insane. Succumbed to the same pressures that had consumed Dr. Toy—the mental erosion Luke himself had felt from the moment he'd set foot inside the station.

Could he possibly believe the journal? Would he do that up on the surface? Presented with those pages, wouldn't he dismiss them as the ramblings of a madman?

You would, of course, he told himself. *But you aren't on the surface. You know what* is *on the surface? Westlake's corpse. Do you remember what it looked like? Put that image in your mind, Luke, and ask yourself: What's behind that hatch now?*

Luke could answer that question easily: *It doesn't matter, as long as I don't fucking open it.*

But what if someone else opened it?

I believe Westlake, Luke realized with piercing clarity. *Not all of what's written, but I believe the ambrosia drove him insane. I believe him enough to realize we're in very serious danger here.*

"Let's assess things," he said to LB, who pricked up her ears. "We've got a broken communication link. We can't contact the surface, and they can't contact us. We've got an escape vehicle with no power, and a current ring that could rip it to shreds if we try to ascend. A crazy person who's locked himself up. Another person, now deceased, who must've gone batshit, too. My brother, who'll stay here out of pure stubbornness. We've got Al, and you and me. The sane ones."

LB chuffed, seemingly in agreement. She was a wonderful companion—Luke wondered if, without her, he might've already slipped around the bend. He was getting the dog off the damn station. Lord knows she'd been through enough.

"Would you like that, girl? Early retirement?"

LB blinked and licked his cheek.

Okay, Luke thought, *what's the list?*

1. Get the hell off this station. Mission be damned.
2. Take Clayton. Drug him if necessary.
3. Get back home. Bring LB.

Three objectives. It calmed Luke to break the situation down into small goals leading to one ultimate goal: sunlight, fresh air, home.

Granted, there were obstacles. Eight miles of water and pressure. His brother's legendary stubborn streak. A sub without power . . .

And the thing or things inside the station with them. Inside, or partially inside, or struggling to gain entrance.

The thing his brother had willingly invited in. The ambrosia.

The thing whose lips Westlake could hear whispering on the other side of his beloved hole. That thing (*things?*) had wrecked Westlake. Oh, maybe it hadn't touched him directly, but it had ruined him regardless.

It must've done the same to Hugo. Even Clayton? His brother's mind was stony, but even stone eroded under constant assault. Luke's own resolve was definitely weakening; a phantom hammer tapped along the block of his brain, searching for the seam that, when struck, would crack it in half.

"Come on, LB. Let's find Al."

20.

LUKE HAD TAKEN A FEW STEPS down the tunnel when it struck him that he hadn't heard any noise for quite some time.

When last he'd consciously checked, he'd heard Al hammering away. It had possessed that steady, confident rhythm: the sound of a carpenter pounding a nail.

Now the silence was eerie. Luke wondered if Al was working on the generator's finer mechanisms. That could be quiet work. Maybe she'd even drifted off to sleep. A little power nap.

A nap. That sounded nice. Luke's eyes stung with exhaustion—except hadn't they promised each other not to fall asleep?

The storage room was shadowy. The generator sat in a fall of light slanting through the open hatch. A huge cylinder made up of several disklike batteries wired end-to-end. Which made sense: you couldn't use a gasoline genny in a closed space; everyone would die of carbon monoxide poisoning.

"Al?"

The room was dead empty. Where the hell could she have gone? Why hadn't she come back for Luke? A bolt of panic jackhammered up his spine. What if Al had slipped into one of the same dream-pools that he had fallen prey to already?

He stepped out of the room. LB's snout was aimed farther down the tunnel, where Al must have gone. Her tail pointed straight up, quivering.

"What is it, girl?"

LB's haunches tensed. She growled, then took off.

"No!"

Luke couldn't imagine losing the dog. If she disappeared in the warren of tunnels, he'd come apart.

He tore after her. Her tail vanished around a bend. Luke pursued heedlessly, not knowing what was around that corner—and in that moment not caring. He flashed around the bend, encountering nothing but stale air, then ran through an open hatchway (had Al left it open?) and hurtled headlong after the dog.

The tunnel described a wide ambit that descended so gradually that Luke wasn't sure it was happening at all, then tightened into a choking spiral; Luke was hit by a wave of nausea brought on by the disorientation—until the tunnel abruptly ended in a crawl-through chute. LB's rump was wriggling through the far end; she tumbled out, her nails skittering, and raced on.

Luke dove into the crawl-through. It was laughably wide in comparison to the access chute he'd been forced to navigate. He shifted onto his back, gripped the rungs, and swiftly hauled himself through.

Dropping out of the chute and rounding the near corner, he came to another dead stop. LB was hunched before a hatch. The hackles stood up on her shoulders.

"Easy, girl." Luke ran his hand down her back, feeling the muscles jump. "It's okay. It's nothing."

Where was Al? This was the only way she could've come. Luke inspected the hatch. It was locked from the other side. Al couldn't open it. So where—?

A face rose up in the porthole. Malevolent and familiar.

21.

DR. HUGO TOY was pallid and shrewlike, his features pinched together on the pasty canvas of his face.

But he doesn't look crazy, Luke thought. *Last time yes; this time . . . no.*

Dr. Toy looked like a man living under an incredible pressure that had warped his bones. Luke now understood how that pressure could make a man look crazy.

He held up his hands, a peaceful gesture. Dr. Toy calculatingly eyed him.

A scrap of paper slapped against the glass.

WHO ARE YOU?

The paper withdrew.

"Luke Nelson. Clayton's brother."

Dr. Toy nodded. Scribbled quickly.

DO YOU FEEL IT?

Luke nodded. "Yes. Everywhere."

Dr. Toy shivered—excitement? Anticipation?

CUT YOURSELF, he wrote.

Luke's brows knit together. "What?"

Dr. Toy slapped the paper against the glass. CUT YOURSELF CUT YOURSELF CUT YOURSELF

Luke said: "Why?"

I WANT TO SEE YOU BLEED SHOW ME YOUR BLOOD

Luke figured he might as well comply—what were a few drops of blood? He crouched over the grate. Its lattices were serrated. He raked the tip of his index finger over one. His skin opened on the third stroke, blood welling down the cut.

He showed it to Dr. Toy.

WIPE YOUR FINGER ON THE WINDOW

Luke did so. Dr. Toy leaned in, nose flattening against the glass. The blood appeared to mollify him. He wrote:

I'LL LET YOU IN BUT I'M TYING YOUR WRISTS

"I have one of the dogs," Luke said.

SHE CAN STAY OUTSIDE

Luke shook his head. "No way."

Dr. Toy bared his teeth.

OK, he wrote in thick angry letters. BUT I TIE HER UP, TOO

Dr. Toy set his shoulder to the wheel; the hatch opened inward, less than a foot. "Turn around," he said. "P-puh-put your wrists through the door."

"Listen, I'm not—"

"Shut up. Do it."

Luke turned and thrust his wrists through the gap. Dr. Toy used duct tape—it made that telltale *whoooonk* noise as he stripped it off the roll. "Tight?"

"Yeah."

"Good." He dragged Luke inside and shut the hatch.

"The dog—"

"Scruh-scruh-screw the dog."

"You said—"

"I say a lot of stuff I don't mean."

Dr. Toy led Luke to a folding chair and shoved him down. Luke could see LB's snout bobbing frantically at the bottom of the porthole.

"You lying bastard."

Dr. Toy smiled, unruffled. Glimpsed in full, he was a reedy man whose long articulate limbs seemed to be constructed from knotted wires. He was slightly walleyed, his left eyeball drifting lazily toward his nose.

The room was about twelve feet square, with a low ceiling. Symbols covered the walls—Toy had fashioned them out of duct tape. They didn't look scientific . . . more pagan. The rest of the room was scattered with papers, most of them balled up in evident frustration.

The smell was atrocious. Luke spied a heap of soiled overalls in one corner. On the surface, that heap would've attracted flies. Down here it just reeked.

"No access to the f-f-fuh-facilities, I'm afraid," Toy said, displaying a slight congenital stutter. "Does the smell bother you?"

"Doesn't it bother you?"

Toy shrugged. "I was r-ruh-raised by a nurse. She spent her days emptying bedpans and changing adult diapers. She didn't want to encounter bodily fl-fluh-fluids at home. She posted a slogan above our toilet: *If you sprinkle when you tinkle, be a sweetie, wipe the suh-seatie.* But if she ever *did* encounter tinkle, even a drop . . . She once thruh-thhh-threatened to make me clean it up with my toothbrush. And I'd have to use that same toothbrush until the bristles dulled and it was time to buy a nnn-nuh-new one."

Your mom and my mom would've gotten on like bandits, Luke thought.

"Fecal matter," Toy said. "Her term for it. Not doo-doo or poop-poo or even that old standby, *shit.* Fff-fuh-fecal . . . *matter.* Please understand—I wasn't *raised* to be a man who'd shit in a corner. But good manners have a way of buh-buh-bleeding away down here." Toy shook his head as if to dispel a troublesome thought. "What-whuh-what *are* you—I mean, what do you, do you *do?* Your job."

"I'm a veterinarian."

"So Clayton Nelson's brother is an animal sawbones. *Faaa*-scinating. Did you get your s-stuh-start fixing up his spuh-spuh-specimens? You'd have been at work all day." When Luke didn't reply, Toy said: "Chaos." He swallowed as if to center himself. "That's why I locked myself up. In case you were wondering."

That's right, Luke remembered. *That's one of Hugo the Horrible's specialties, isn't it? Chaos theory.*

"Oh, uh, it started normally enough," Toy said. "We set up shop. Three men, three labs. Instability systems was my role. Basically, uh, was it f-f-fuh-feasible? The ambrosia—did it *cure* anything, or did it simply create havoc under an illusion of cure?"

He picked up a crinkled sheet of paper and smoothed it over his knee.

"I was working with . . . theories, yes? Known thuh-theories that apply and have value on the"—pointing upward—"up there, yes? But, uh, down here, nothing b-b-behaves as it should. Theories and mathematics just dissolve. Even the most chaotic events, if you buh-buh-break them down, have a pattern and order—and if they *don't*, then at least the level of chaos can be calculated, compartmentalized and uh, uh, *understood*."

Dr. Toy grinned widely—he seemed manic, weirdly chipper. His demeanor struck Luke as that of a convict who'd been kept in solitary confinement for years, and now, finally given a chance to speak to another human being, he couldn't help prattling on. He showed Luke what he'd written. A hen-scratched theorem, incredibly complex.

"Picture a rock rolling down a mountainside. Or a bead of mercury running down the back side of a spoon. Or skeins of *fff*-fruh-frost bristling across a windowpane. The movement would seem random, yes? But it's not. If we could catalogue all the variables in the universe, we could know with utter certainty what happens next—the, uh, the . . . the next skip of that rock, the-the-the way the mercury will slip, the direction each skein will buh-branch. But we don't, so, so . . . chaos."

He stopped pacing and stared at Luke, his eyes wide as if seeing him—really *seeing him*—for the first time.

"What's on the uh-uh-other side of the hole is chaos. But not like any I've ever known. Unorderable, unnameable, untheorizable. And that's what pure evil looks like. A chaos whose v-vuh-variables are endless—so huge even the universe can't contain them. Chaos incarnate."

Luke had stopped listening by then. One word stuck in his head like a shard of polished glass.

Hole. *The* hole.

Westlake's voice, ragged and covetous, as Luke remembered it from those sound files: *I put it through . . .*

Luke shifted in his chair. Sweat trickled down his back, soaking the duct tape.

"What hole, Hugo?"

Toy's eyes narrowed. "You've seen one. Don't tell me you haven't."

"I read Westlake's journal."

"How is Cooper?" Toy asked, genuinely interested.

Luke blinked. The man clearly didn't know.

"I'm afraid he's dead, Hugo. He took one of the *Challenger*s. He was dead by the time he surfaced."

Toy's face twitched. Weird voltages raced under his skin.

Luke said, "In his journals, Westlake mentioned a hole—"

Like magic, a blade appeared in Toy's hand. A box cutter. He thumbed the mechanism. Two inches of blade slid out. Toy lunged forward, grabbed the matted hair atop Luke's head, and pressed the blade to his neck.

"You're luh-lying. You've seen a hole."

Luke's breath came in shallow heaves. "I haven't." He swallowed. The blade scraped his Adam's apple. "But since I've been down here I've felt like . . . like something has been trying to crawl inside my head."

The blade pressed harder. "Have you let it?"

Luke's pulse shivered behind his eyes and at the root of his tongue. "No."

The blade withdrew.

"This chaos . . ." Toy went on as if he hadn't threatened to slit Luke's throat mere moments ago, ". . . it's *orderly*. There's the surface chaos, you could say, like a-a-a-a tangle of leaves and twigs laid over a *ttt*-truh-trap. A camouflage of chaos with something very logical and *cunning* beneath. A guiding principle or, uh, modus operandi. The real mmm-muh-master."

Toy stood abruptly, kicking through drifts of paper to the nearest wall. Luke clenched his hands while Toy's attention was elsewhere, trying to pull his wrists apart enough to slip a hand free.

"Protective runes." He pointed at the duct-taped symbols, laughing stiffly. "I studied them as an undergraduate. Druids and, and, uh, that b-b-buh-bullshit. It's all from memory. I don't know if they have any effect at ah, at uh, at *all*."

"I don't see any holes."

Toy smiled without humor. "I wonder if that's because they don't want me."

They.

Luke said: "Westlake's journal. I read it."

"Oh, yes?" Then, almost as an afterthought but with genuine sympathy: "Westlake, my God. Poor Cooper. That poor, poor man."

"Dr. Westlake said a hole appeared on his lab wall . . . He claimed he heard sounds coming out of it. Voices."

"The voice in the sea, as your brother would claim," Toy said acidly. "Some pressure-treated harpy wailing for Cooper to stick his head out and kiss her."

Westlake's voice again: *I want to put my head through the hole. Want to kiss those lips . . .*

"A hole ate into the wall of my lab, too," Toy said. "Small at first, growing steadily b-b-bigger. I spoke to Clayton about it. Predictably, he called me a fuh-*fff*-fool. I told him to come into the goddamn lab, I'd show him. He refused. Of course, he probably had one blooming in his own lab. And Westlake too, as you say." He shook his head. "Yet none of us acted. None of us told anyone—Felz, Alice, somebody on the suh-surface. Why? Because it was so horribly *exciting.*"

A hole in Dr. Toy's lab? Luke had gotten a glimpse inside Toy's lab when they arrived on the *Trieste.* Its porthole wasn't coated in black ichor, like Westlake's, or draped like his brother's. Luke hadn't seen a hole. Of course, it could be in a blind spot. It wasn't worth challenging Toy on it. Luke worked his wrists, testing his bonds. The sweat oiled his skin. The tape was surrendering its hold in increments.

"Professionally, I'm never more alive than when I'm on the *cusp,*" Toy went on. "With surgeons, it's when they're 'in the cut,' you know? Wrist-deep inside a-a-a chest cavity. For me, or for your bruh-bruh-brother and Westlake—poor man!—it's wuh-when we're on the verge of a breakthrough. Of, yes, yes, unlocking some previously uh-uh-unknown system that our world operates under."

"And that's how you've felt down here."

"Yes! If only we can just, just, *learn* more. See how the stuff, the ambrosia, how it operates. But that's the pruh-problem—it has no stable base. It's always shifting. Worst of all, it *knows*. It understands our needs and desires. Knows how to d-*duddd*-dangle that carrot at the end of the stick. By the time we felt the noose around our necks, it was too duh-duh-damn late.

"We're in a Skinner Box," Dr. Toy said with a sick smile, the kind of expression a slipshod mortician might tease onto a corpse's face. "Operant Conditioning Chambers, to use the scientific name. Designed by B. F. Skinner, that old *sss*-suh-sadist. You put a rat in a box with an electrified grate. Two buttons on one side of the box, red and gruh-green. Push the red one, get a treat. Push the green one, get a shuh-*shh*-shock. Or vice versa. Vary the pattern however you want. Push either button and you get a tuh-treh-treat, say. Or either button earns the subject a shock. Don't you see? The *Trieste* is the box. We are the rats. And whatever's on the other suh-side of those holes are the scientists. They're watching us. Seeing how we react. We're the grand expuh-expuh . . . *experiment*."

Luke continued to work at his bindings. He clenched his hands to stretch the tape. He could slide his wrists back and forth a bit now.

"Why did you need to see my blood?"

Toy's focus was drifting. "What?"

"You made me cut myself."

Toy waved his hand impatiently. "It gets *inside* you, understand? And wuh-wuh-once it's there, you're not yourself anymore. It has ways and means to gain entry. You've heard it, yes? It has a powerful pull. Very uh, uh, *seductive*."

"I've heard it," said Luke, though he hadn't *heard* anything: just those sly fingertips worming against his skull.

"Cuh-Cooper came by not too long ago," Dr. Toy said. "He looked awful. His neck covered in sores. I couldn't let him in," he said with a touch of guilt. "I opened the h-h-hatch only enough so we could talk. He sounded as bad as he luh-looked. We talked about our children. We both have daughters. Jennifer, my own. Precious child. She's suh-sick. She's caught the Disease, as Cooper called it. She started spotting a month ago."

"I'm so sorry," said Luke.

"We were performing trial runs on the *Hesperus* when my wife called to inform me. At the time I was worried that I wouldn't be uh-able to operate in encluh-encluh . . . enclosed spaces. Claustroph-ophob-oph-oph . . ." He gave Luke a look that said: *You know what I'm trying to say.* "I was about to ask them to send someone uh-else instead. But then . . . Jennifer. So I cuh-came. I had to, for her."

"Alice has found a generator," Luke told him. "We're going to power up the *Challenger* and get out of here. Will you come?"

Toy favored him with a look of utter pity.

"Oh, you poor devil. Do you really think they're going to luh-let us go?"

Luke had stretched the tape to where he might be able to pop a wrist free. But he'd have to stand up to get the momentum needed to—

SHHHRAAAAKKK!

Hell invaded the *Trieste*.

22.

A SECTION OF THE CEILING dented down: a jaggedy fang that struck Toy with tremendous force, knocking him flat. His skull hit the floor with a hollow ringing note.

Luke jerked his arms. The tape was unraveling; he felt a ragged edge flapping against his fingertips.

Toy rolled onto his back with a groan. His nose was broken, the cartilage shoved off at a rude angle.

The children's footsteps intensified: they danced a mad tarantella now. *TRRRRRAACHIKKK!*

Another section levered down and slammed into Toy's legs at midcalf. The sound of his tibias snapping was horribly loud. He shrieked, sat up, slammed his head into the lowering shelf of ceiling and slumped back, dazed.

The folding chair's rear legs collapsed under Luke's weight, spilling him backward; his shoulder hit the ground with a sickening crunch. He struggled to his knees, sliding his bound arms down around his buttocks and under his thighs. He rolled to his back and straightened his arms, but his duct-taped hands wouldn't clear his heels.

Dr. Toy sat up again, numb with shock and clutching uselessly at his shins. Blood spritzed in thin jets, pulsing with the wild beat of his heart, slithering across the floor and soaking into the balled papers.

Luke's mind fused shut. He understood how hares caught in traps could die of fright. He couldn't yank his fucking hands over his heels. It was a physical impossibility. He was like some moron jerking at a locked door in hopes it would open. He'd literally gone stupid with fear.

The ceiling shuddered, rolling a few more inches up Toy's legs. He howled as his hands scrabbled mindlessly at his knees. It was just as

Alice had described: the ceiling of the *Trieste* ballooned and bubbled, its nature more rubbery than metallic. It groaned and shrieked but did not rupture . . . not yet. The sound of the man-made barrier fighting the pressure of water was terrifying: the trillion-dollar miracle polymer buckling by degrees, popping and splintering as it flexed. It was an arm-wrestling match, Nature versus the Works of Man, where one competitor was grinding himself to a steady advantage.

One leg at a time, nattered a voice inside Luke's head. *You can't clear both heels at once, dummy! Drop your arms, bend one leg, and try again!*

Luke straightened one leg, crooked the other, and was able to jerk his bound wrists around his dropped heel. He rolled to one knee—the posture of a man proposing marriage—with his hands under his crotch. From that position he was able to twist his wrists until his hands were free.

The ceiling shivered again as Luke crawled over to Toy. When Luke touched the man's shoulder, Toy unleashed a desperate keening scream that made Luke flinch. The metal consumed another few inches of Toy's shins, shattering bones and flattening flesh. What had Al said? Pressure equivalent to twenty-seven jumbo jets? The ceiling rolled over Toy's legs as if his overalls were filled with Styrofoam packing peanuts.

"Ub-ubb-*uuuuuub!*" he screeched, a senseless string of syllables.

The roof trundled over Toy's kneecaps in a slow, persistent advance. It was no different than watching a man gradually run over by a steamroller. Toy's bones were pulverized like shards of crockery. The veins in his wrists and neck stood out in horrid blood-bulged strings under his skin.

Luke grabbed Toy's shoulder as if it was possible to pull him away from this fate. The man's arm was tensed tight, the blood pumping it to a freakish density.

"*GlllluuuuuuhHH!*"

A rope of blood ejected from Toy's mouth, unfurling like a scarlet ribbon from a New Year's Eve party favor. His eyes rolled back to their twitching, vein-threaded whites as he shuddered in a sickening dream state.

Go! He's done for. No saving him, Luke. Get the hell out of here!

Dumbly, Luke jerked at Toy's arm even as the roof dented inward at him, its murderous weight no more than a foot from his head. He figured the pressure might sever Dr. Toy's legs; Luke pictured it the way a hot dog gets sliced off the link at a factory—a quick *snip* between two sharp blades and six inches of pink, processed meat drops into the hopper. If so, Luke could drag Toy out and maybe, with any luck, cauterize the stumps before he died of blood loss.

But the pressure was *knowing*. Toy's legs were merely crushed, leaving an inch or so of clearance to the floor. The foam popped spastically as the ceiling trundled over Toy's thighs, blood spraying in pressurized fans, then over his hips, which shattered and flattened with a percussive jolt that shook his entire frame—the sight reminded Luke of a butterflied chicken, its spine snapped with one deft downward thrust of a chef's palm.

Toy's face was greasy with shock. The gamy stink of adrenaline poured off him. The ceiling pushed drifts of paper forward; the balled-up wads accumulated at the sides of Toy's body like dust bunnies around a bedpost. The metal rolled over Toy's chest, but only enough to crack his ribs, which snapped with the sound of Black Cat firecrackers.

It's savoring it, Luke's mind yammered. *Whatever it is, this thing or things, it's taking its time now.*

Dr. Toy's eyelids sucked around their edges like the papery mouths of suckerfish. Blood burped from his ears in fits and starts, like sludgy water from a tap that hadn't been used in some time. Toy vented a volley of gluey, piglike squeals. How was he still alive?

The roof bellied down menacingly, striking Luke and knocking him aside. He stood and staggered to the hatch.

I'm sorry so sorry Hugo . . .

He spun the wheel and glanced back just as the ceiling flowed over Toy's head in an awesome wave.

Toy's skull bulged in its overtaxed wrapping of skin.

Nonononono . . .

Toy began to laugh. The sound was muffled by the frantic pop-pop of the space-age material, but Luke heard it perfectly. Horrifically, insanely, it was the laughter of a child. An infant's laugh—his son Zachary's laugh: that high, wheezing, out-of-control titter he used to make as a toddler when Luke pressed his lips to Zach's belly and blew a raspberry. A *zzzrr-rbbt!* he'd called them, that being the sound it made.

Zzzzzzrrrbbt! ZZZZZZRRRRRBT!

Toy's skull split with an ear-rending crack. The skin tore apart in a perfect horizontal seam—a tight smile splitting his scalp. Tremendous pressure forced Toy's mashed and twitching brain through the split.

Luke threw the hatch open as the metal ballooned toward him. He shoved it shut just as the ceiling flowed against it with a hissing crinkle.

The porthole glass webbed. Luke backed away and tripped over LB, who skidded backward on her rump. Luke watched the porthole with bulging eyes. He expected the glass to break and that flexible material to flow through—he pictured it stretching like taffy to project in a blunt spike, splitting his head in half as it came.

But it didn't. The glass held.

The *Trieste* shivered. The walls seemed to expand like a pair of lungs inhaling a slow, contented breath. The station settled and there came, suddenly, a persistent silence—a creeping, secretive silence that carried down every tunnel.

PART 5
THE HONEYPOT

1.

LUKE FOUND ALICE in the main lab. He'd backtracked from the horror of Dr. Toy's quarters in a daze, his entire body trembling, to find her standing in front of Westlake's hatch. The walls creaked dimly, issuing those spastic crackling noises, but the station wasn't shuddering on the verge of collapse as it had seemed to be in Toy's quarters. No, the *Trieste* felt quite solid at the moment.

It's as strong as it needs to be, was Luke's preposterous, overheated thought. *It exists—it, and everything in it—at the benevolence of something far greater and more terrible than itself.*

Luke's mind was still reeling; his hands were clamped on his skull as if to prevent his brain from ripping in half: he pictured his frontal and parietal lobes tearing apart from each other like the stitches popping along an overtaxed inseam. He couldn't stop thinking about how *calculated* Dr. Toy's death had been. There was a methodical brutality about it—there was no way it had been a mere accident.

The *Trieste* had killed Hugo Toy. It had done so in the most horrible, gloating fashion. And it had made Luke watch.

Al's face was slack. Her lips curled in a ghostly smile as if she'd heard somebody's voice and appreciated what that person was telling her.

"Oh yes, Monty," she said, "I'd *really* like to try for what's behind door number three."

Her fingers played over the keypad. She punched five digits, pressed *enter,* and got the red Fail light. Her features twisted in anger.

"No, I *am* sure. Totally one hundred percent. I want door number three." Her voice rose to a girlish squeal. "I'm feeling lucky, Monty! No Zonks!"

It dawned on Luke: Alice was dreaming—*no*, she was trapped in a dream-pool. In this particular dream, she was a contestant on that old Monty Hall game show, *Let's Make a Deal*. Luke's mother used to watch reruns of it while shoveling lukewarm porridge into her mouth, laughing spitefully when a hapless contestant risked his new color TV or tropical vacation for a shot at what lay behind door number three, only to get *zonked* with a wheelbarrow full of creamed corn, a llama, or a pair of clown shoes.

Greedy guts! she'd shout at the screen, flecks of porridge flinging from her lips. *Greedy guts got greedy so that's what greedies get!*

Al tried a different code, pressed *enter,* and got the Fail light again. Her body vibrated with rage.

"Door number three, Monty," she seethed through gritted teeth. "Show me what's behind the goddamn motherfucking door, for fuck's sake."

The drone from behind the hatch rose to an eager buzz. The porthole was smeared with that viscid substance—*honey, Luke,* he thought; *it's honey*—and behind it, in the feeble light of Westlake's lab, Luke swore he saw things zipping about.

Luke set a hand on Alice's shoulder. "Al?"

She brushed his hand away. She laughed—a flighty, quizzical titter.

"Hey, Al, come on. *Hey.*"

Luke squeezed Al's shoulder, still highly adrenalized after what had happened with Dr. Toy. Al's eyelids flickered. Her eyes were filmy, as if they'd been soaped. Her lips spat out a loop of idiot babble.

"Door three—door three—three—three . . ."

"Goddamn it, Al!"

Luke shook her roughly. Al staggered back, her spine rattling on the wall.

"The *what*—?" she squawked.

But her eyes were clearer; her expression was that of a woman roused from a bad dream. The buzz died down. Those zipping shapes zipped no more. Al regarded Luke reproachfully—the same look Abby had given Luke the night their son went missing.

"Where the hell were you?"

"Me?" Luke said. "I was right where you left me, in Westlake's room. I've been looking for you."

"Bullshit."

Luke recoiled. It was less the word itself than the icy tone Al spoke in.

"I checked Westlake's room. You weren't there."

"You couldn't have checked, Alice. You'd have seen me sitting there, reading."

Al raked her unbandaged hand down her face. "Why are you lying to me?"

Something's wrong here, Luke. Tread carefully.

"I'm not lying, Al. You were working on the generator—"

"I got it working. But I couldn't move it," she said. "It's too heavy. I needed your help. But when I went to find you . . . *poof!* You were gone."

Luke took a step back—he was worried that Al might lash out. Confused anger was kindling inside him now, too; hot coals burned at his temples.

It wants you to fight. Kill each other, maybe.

"I'm sorry, Al. I went to find you. The generator was there, but not you."

"I went looking for *you*. But you weren't . . . and then . . . and then . . ."

"Did you fall asleep, Al?" Luke raised his arms, just an innocent question. "Could that have happened? It was dark in that room and we've been up a real long time. Did you just, for a minute . . . shut your eyes?"

Al bit her lip. Her gaze kept flicking to Westlake's hatch.

"Al, Dr. Toy is dead."

Her gaze oriented on him again. "What do you mean?"

What else could I possibly mean? He's dead, Al. The station killed him.

No, Luke realized, not the station. The station didn't have the ability to kill, in the same way a pistol didn't kill a person—only its wielder did. The station was simply the instrument. The Skinner Box, overseen by whatever was administering the shocks.

"After I tried to find you, LB dashed off," said Luke. "I followed her. She led me to Hugo."

Al slapped herself, hard. Her eyelids had been sinking closed. She slapped herself again. The sound, a sharp *spak!,* made Luke wince. She jetted air between her teeth in a series of hard gusts like a weight lifter preparing for a record lift. She nodded as if to say, *Okay, I'm good now,* and then said: "Tell me what happened to Dr. Toy."

Luke gratefully let the terrible event pour out of him—sometimes the only way to disburden oneself of the poison is to share it with somebody else.

"That poor bastard," Al said, her cheeks pink from the slaps. "Jesus Christ."

Luke told Al what he'd read in Westlake's journal, too. He felt ludicrous telling her—they were the confessions of a rubber-roomed madman. And yet, listening to him, Al became very quiet. Ambrosia drifted past the huge window as Luke spoke. Shreds piled up like snow against the side of a barn. LB growled at it, a low huff that puffed the loose skin over her upper teeth.

"A hole?" was Al's first question once Luke finished.

Luke nodded. "That's what Westlake wrote. Small at first, but growing bigger. He could hear voices from it. Sounds crazy, I know."

Al's expression wasn't disbelieving. It was fearful.

"Luke, listen . . . I think . . . yeah, I might've fallen asleep. I sort of remember tightening a few wires on the generator, then sitting down to catch my breath. If I nodded off, the thing is—my dream picked up right *there.* It began in that storage room with my body in the exact same position as it was when I nodded off. And so I got up *in my dream* and walked down the tunnel to find you, thinking I was still awake. You weren't there. You're saying you were—which makes sense if I dreamed it. And then you find *me* here, trying to get in there."

She nodded at Westlake's lab. A shudder racked her frame.

"What I'm saying is," she went on, "*if* I sleepwalked to the lab, how did you miss me? I would have stumbled right past Westlake's room, right?"

Luke nodded. "You would have, yeah. And I would have seen you. Unless . . ."

"Unless you fell asleep, too. You were sleeping as I walked past."

That was the only possibility that made sense: Luke had somehow drifted off while reading Westlake's journal—slipped into a dream-pool without even knowing it. They'd both been asleep when Alice walked past Westlake's room, right past Luke, neither of them aware of it.

How else *could* it have happened? Unless the *Trieste* was reorganizing itself, arranging into new configurations like puzzle pieces, snaking in different directions to ensure they wouldn't have seen each other?

"We have to get that generator," Al said. "Get the *Challenger* powered up and get our asses out of here. And *stay awake.*"

"What about Clayton?"

"Watch him, Luke. *Hawk* him. He's been down here way too long."

2.

IT WAS A SLOG dragging the generator to the *Challenger*. An hour? Two? Four? Luke couldn't say how long. Time drew out like a blade.

The generator wasn't all that heavy, but it was cumbersome. It had handles on the sides and tiny wheels to help it roll; Luke thought they made it look like the Oscar Mayer Wienermobile, that familiar staple of small-town parades. A light sweat broke out over Luke's body before they'd even muscled it out of the storage room; it trundled across the grates like a shopping cart with a wonky wheel.

Luke was bathed in sweat by the time they reached the crawl-through chute. Working together, using the handles, Al was sure they would be able to slide it into the crawl-through like a torpedo into the firing tube. But it would require both of them to lift it, meaning the generator would fall out the other end with nobody to catch it.

"The fall could break it," said Al.

"Do we have anything to cushion it?"

A lightbulb clicked on in Al's head. "Strip," she said.

"What?"

"Your overalls," she said, unzipping her own. "I'll lay them on the other side as a crash mat."

Luke removed his overalls. His body looked sickly in the tunnel's light; the blackness of the sea, falling through a porthole above, cast a circular shadow over his heart. Al's body was muscular and milky from a life spent underwater. She had a tattoo of a propeller on each hipbone.

"Old superstition," she said, catching him looking. "Sailors used to get propellers tattooed on their ass, one on each cheek—a good luck charm against drowning. If your ship goes down, they help propel you to shore."

Preface

SOME THINGS TO THINK ABOUT

- Twenty-six of every twenty-seven people who have a bad experience with you or your firm won't tell you. The principal reason is not surprising: They expect little or no satisfaction if they do gripe. What's scary is that 91 percent of those with a bad experience won't come back.

- Even worse, the average person who has been burned tells 9 to 10 other people; 1 out of 8 grumblers will spread the bad news to 20 or more people.

That may seem like bad news, but it's actually good news for you and your firm. Why is it good news? Because people who switched their business to a competing firm gave poor service as the reason five times more often than they mentioned price or quality. That means that price isn't the problem. The problem is service, and service is not expensive to fix. This book will show you how.

More good news:

- Firms that rank in the top third on relative quality charge prices 5 to 6 percent higher than those in the bottom third and still gain market share at the expense of the low-quality firms.

- Firms with superior quality have costs about the same as the low-

iii

quality firms. This, combined with higher fees, makes them roughly *twice as profitable as firms with low quality.*

WHAT THIS MEANS TO YOU

The greatest single key to a successful professional practice can be summed up in four words: *high-quality client service.* It's the best-kept secret in the country.

If you have lost clients you shouldn't have, this book will show you how to improve your service and increase client retention. If you have clients who just didn't come back, I'll show you how to reactivate some of them and prevent losing other clients.

If you have referral sources who used to send you business but haven't referred any clients for a long time, I'll show you how to win those referral sources back. Also, you can increase referrals from existing clients: You just have to know what to do differently from what you have done in the past.

That requires you to have two personality traits that I can't provide. First is the realization that there are some things you don't know, and maybe, just maybe you could learn something new. If you already know everything, then, by definition, you can never learn anything else. Lots of professionals already know everything; they will not learn anything from this book (or from anyplace else, for that matter).

The second thing you need is a willingness to change. If you keep doing things the way you have been, then you will probably get the same results you have been, only worse. Why worse? Because your environment is changing, and you will wind up as extinct as the dinosaurs if you don't change at least a little.

The professionals who lack one or both of these traits are easily recognizable by their distinctive complaint: "That won't work here because my _____ is/are different." Their favorite excuses with which they fill in the blank are, in alphabetical order: city, clients, department, market, office, partners, practice, profession, specialty, staff.

Today, the only constant is constant change. Marketing, competition, solicitation, competitive bidding, and advertising are just the tip of the iceberg. Competition is intensifying; other professionals are aggressively pursuing clients—probably even your clients. In this competitive environment, giving excellent client service is not just a competitive weapon, it's a survival skill!

A few firms thrive in today's volatile environment, firms that grow in depressed markets, firms that far outstrip their competition, firms that have enhanced both the quality and the quantity of their services to clients, while earning appropriate—even amazing—profits and providing a satisfying work environment for the firm's personnel. I have been privileged to work with many of them and to observe others. I have discovered some worthwhile and creative common features across these superior service management performances. This book shares with you these features of superior performance.

It is said that the Chinese character that means "crisis" is actually composed of two characters, one meaning "danger" and one meaning "opportunity." The metaphor certainly holds true for the professional firm. Your knowledge and action determine whether *crises* (turning points; times of dramatic change) offer danger or opportunity for you and your firm.

This book shows what clients really want and how you can give it to them. You will learn why some clients stay with you and why some will try your competitors. In fact, using the tools in this book, you can not only keep more clients, but you can also make them so happy that they will recommend you to their friends and business contacts.

Danger

Opportunity

The Chinese symbol for crisis

This book explains how winning firms are flourishing today and fortifying for tomorrow. Specifically, I'll show you how to

- Increase the value of your services to your clients

- Earn a reputation for high quality with your clients

- Increase client loyalty

- Get more referrals from clients

- Increase profits by rendering more efficient, higher quality service

- Ensure a firmwide commitment to quality by attracting, training, and retaining personnel with the same commitment to high-quality client service that you have

- Make your marketing more effective by communicating directly to the real needs of your prospective clients

Providing high-quality service to clients is—or should be—the number one priority of all professionals. Poor quality in service is the number one cause of losing clients to competitors. Part I discusses the surprising *marketing and profitability consequences of high quality*. By finding out what your clients value in terms of quality, you can *use client-centered service to retain clients* and to encourage them to recommend you to others—turning your clients into cheerleaders.

Chapter 3 defines the five criteria clients use to evaluate your services. A critical examination of client perceptions yields practical insights into client motivations in retaining professionals.

Chapter 4 describes the unique features of service firms, and Part II shows you how to find out what your clients and referral sources *really* think of you. It also helps you to distinguish your business from your crowd of competitors' businesses and to develop and project the most attractive image to your prospective and existing clients.

Part III explains how to increase client loyalty by changing the way in which you present your services so that clients will perceive the high quality of your services.

DAVID COTTLE

Acknowledgments

Grateful acknowledgment is made to the following for permission to reprint previously published materials:

- Ballinger Publishing Company: excerpts by Jan Carlzon from *Moments of Truth*, copyright 1987 by Ballinger Publishing Company. Reprinted by permission of Ballinger Division, Harper & Row, Publishers, Inc.

- Dow Jones-Irwin: excerpts by Karl Albrecht and Ron Zemke from *Service America!*, copyright 1985 by Dow Jones-Irwin. Excerpts by Karl Albrecht from *At America's Service*, copyright 1988 by Dow Jones-Irwin.

- Harper & Row, Publishers, Inc.: excerpts from *The Practice of Management* by Peter F. Drucker, copyright 1954 by Peter F. Drucker; excerpts from *Innovation and Entrepreneurship* by Peter F. Drucker, copyright 1985 by Peter F. Drucker; excerpts from *The IBM Way* by F. G. "Buck" Rogers with Robert L. Shook, copyright 1986 by Francis Rogers and Robert Shook. Foreword copyright 1986 by Harper & Row, Publishers, Inc.; excerpts from *In Search of Excellence* by Thomas J. Peters and Robert H. Waterman, Jr., copyright 1982 by Thomas J. Peters and Robert H. Waterman, Jr.; excerpts from *The Effective Executive* by Peter F.

Drucker, copyright 1966, 1967 by Peter F. Drucker; excerpts from *Managing for Results* by Peter F. Drucker, copyright 1964 by Peter F. Drucker.

- Harvard Business Review: The following excerpts, by Theodore Levitt (except where noted): Excerpt from Chapter 1, "Marketing and the Corporate Purpose," as adapted in *The Marketing Imagination*, copyright 1983, 1986 by The Free Press. Excerpt from Chapter 5, "Marketing Intangible Products and Product Intangibles," as adapted in *The Marketing Imagination*, copyright 1983, 1986 by The Free Press. Excerpt from Chapter 6, "Relationship Management," as adapted in *The Marketing Imagination*, copyright 1983, 1986 by The Free Press. Excerpt from "Competing on the eight dimensions of quality," by David A. Garvin, *Harvard Business Review*, Nov–Dec 1987, copyright 1987 by the President and Fellow of Harvard College, all rights reserved. Excerpt from "Turnaround management every day," by John O. Whitney, *Harvard Business Review*, Sept–Oct 1987, copyright 1987 by the President and Fellow of Harvard College, all rights reserved. All excerpts reprinted by permission of the *Harvard Business Review*.

- Marketing Science Institute: Excerpts from *Strategic Management and Marketing in the Service Sector*, by Christian Grönroos, May 1983, Report 83-104, copyright 1983 by Marketing Science Institute. This monograph inspired some of the figures and concepts in the section on the Ace Widgets customer relationship and the Smith & Jones client relationship and the sections on strategic management, interactive marketing, and internal marketing. Professor Grönroos' monograph deals with all service firms and I made significant changes to reflect my views, where different, and to express my opinions of the differences between professional firms and other service organizations. Excerpts from *Communication and Control Processes in the Delivery of Service Quality*, by Valarie A. Zeithaml, Leonard L. Berry, and A. Parasuraman, June 1987, Report No. 87-100, copyright 1987 by Marketing Science Institute. Derivations and excerpts from *SERVQUAL: A Multiple-Item Scale for Measuring Customer Perceptions of Service Quality*, by A. Parasuraman, Valarie A. Zeithaml, and Leonard L. Berry, August 1986, Report No. 86-108, copyright 1986 by the Marketing Science Institute.

- Putnam Publishing Group: excerpt by Michael LeBoeuf from *How to Win Customers and Keep Them for Life*, copyright 1988 by Michael LeBoeuf.

- Van Nostrand Reinhold Company: Excerpts from *Marketing Accounting Services*, copyright 1983 by Van Nostrand Reinhold Company, and *How to Market Legal Services*, copyright 1984 by Van Nostrand Reinhold Company, both by Robert W. Denney.

D.C.

Contents

Introduction: How to Get the Most out of This Book

Take these ideas, and tailor them to your situation. Keep a pen and notebook handy as you read. When something I have written sparks an idea, stop and write it down before you forget it. To paraphrase Peter Drucker,[1] do not say, "This is a damn-fool idea!" Instead ask, "What would be needed to make this embryonic, half-baked, foolish idea into something that makes sense, that is feasible, that is an opportunity for us?" Ask yourself, "How does this apply to *my* practice, *my* clients, and *my* situation? With a change or two, will it work for us?"

Make yourself a simple "to do" list with three columns like the one in the figure.

IDEA	WHOM TO IMPLEMENT	DUE DATE

When you get an idea, jot it down. Leave the other two columns blank until you discuss the idea with your partners.

Don't just read this book through at one sitting. Use it as the framework for a series of discussions with your partners and staff. Get together and kick these ideas around. As Robert Levoy said,[2] "Something happens whenever . . . people get together in face-to-face [*inter-*

1

actions and] examine attitudes and feelings, which does not happen when you merely read a book." Once you try to define your values and to defend them to others, sparks fly, and you may be motivated to change some of them.

This book can be a creative, learning experience for you, not just a passive reading experience. And that means **action!**

This book is like a department store. If you walked into Macy's or Sears, not everything in the store would interest you. You might not need a stereo today. Similarly, not everything in this book will interest you today. You may have a one-person practice, and some of my ideas may apply better to a large practice. Or you may be an employee of a large firm with little influence in the overall scheme of things. Or a particular phenomenon I discuss may not occur in your practice or even in your profession. However, in many places in this book, there are some really valuable ideas to enhance your practice or your area of the practice. *Look for the significant ideas that will pay off big.*

A question may occur to you before you finish this book: "What happens when all the firms in my profession become client centered? What will be the advantage when all our competitors are also centered on the client?" The implied question here is, "Will we lose the competitive advantage we gained by leading the service revolution?"

The question has three answers: (1) You won't be a leader in the revolution; quite a few top-quality firms are already doing the things I'm recommending. In fact, they are the ones from whom I learned these ideas. (2) There is absolutely no risk of all, or even the majority, of your competitors becoming client centered. At most, 10 percent will be willing to make the commitment to become client centered. (3) Consider the alternative of going on as you are while your client-centered competitors continue to chew away at your best clients. And make no mistake about it, the best clients are the ones who respond to the ideas presented in this book.

Frankly, most people don't want to succeed badly enough to work to accomplish it. That's why less than 10 percent of the firms in any profession become truly outstanding.

This book is for the builders, the men and women who will make a constructive difference, whether they are the managing partners or the newest employees—whether they run the entire firm, a single department, or just their own desk. This book is for the partners and future partners who strive for excellence. Excellence is not a destination; it is a never ending journey. Or, as Tom Peters[3] said in *Thriving on Chaos*,

"Excellent firms don't believe in excellence—only in constant improvement and constant change."

This book is for the truly ambitious—those few men and women who strive for excellence and who are not afraid to pay the price for success.

NOTES

1. Peter Drucker, *The Frontiers of Management*, New York: Harper & Row, 1986, p. 261.

2. Robert P. Levoy, *The $100,000 Practice and How to Build It*, Englewood Cliffs, NJ: Prentice-Hall, 1966, p. ix.

3. Tom Peters, *Thriving on Chaos*, New York: Alfred A. Knopf, 1987, p. 4.

I

Client-Centered Service—The Key to Client Satisfaction

1
Why Quality Pays
Big Dividends

Time Magazine's cover story for the February 2, 1987 issue asked, "why is service so bad?" In the article, the author knocked

Gas stations	Automobile dealers
Automatic teller machines	Refrigerator repairers
Discount stores	Supermarkets
Airlines	Home delivery
Telephone companies	Carpet installers
Department stores	Waiters
Sales clerks	Hotels
Plumbers	Restaurants

Fortunately, professionals such as lawyers, accountants, and engineers were not singled out, although the magazine did have a few choice comments about doctors.

The *Time* article claimed, "Customers know service when they miss it, and now they want it back."

Business Week featured a special report on "The Push For Quality"

in the United States in its June 8, 1987 issue. The magazine noted that the drive to improve quality is far more substantial than the blizzard of buzzwords such as "quality circle" and "zero defects" that floated around in the late 1970s. Quality circles faded when they couldn't provide the quick fix many companies wanted. "This time around executives are being more realistic. Managing for quality means nothing less than a sweeping overhaul in corporate culture, a radical shift in management philosophy, and a permanent commitment at all levels of the organization to seek continuing improvements. . . . The core of the revolution in quality can be captured in a phrase: customer satisfaction."

THE LIFE CYCLE OF CLIENT RELATIONS

The relationship between clients and professionals goes through a life cycle. Just as human life begins long before a child's birth, the first stage in the client relations life cycle begins before clients are even seen as clients. In this stage, you must create a public image so that prospective clients ("prospects") can contact you or you can contact them. The objective of this stage, personal contacts, is achieved through traditional marketing. You must achieve a satisfactory image with prospects before you can even establish contact with them.

The objective of the second stage is to develop relationships with your contacted prospects. Given the establishment of a satisfactory relationship, when prospects develop a need for professional services or become dissatisfied with their current professionals, they will be interested in you and your firm. This is accomplished both through traditional marketing (client newsletters, brochures, etc.) and through frequent personal contacts with prospects.

The third stage is the selling phase for you and your firm (and the purchasing phase for your clients). The objective of this phase is a sale, which transforms a prospective client into an actual client. This also involves convincing satisfied prospects that you would render better service to them than would your competitors.

The fourth stage is production/consumption of the service. The objective is to "keep them coming back for more." At this stage, you retain clients through high-quality service, and you get them back into the loop at the second stage so that they will engage you again in the future.

At any stage, clients may either leave the loop or stay in it and move on to the next stage. Whether clients buy and buy again depends on your delivery of superior service.

WHY CLIENTS CHANGE PROFESSIONAL FIRMS

The reawakening of service-consciousness among consumers has important implications for professionals. It means that your clients are becoming more demanding of good service. If you don't give it to them, someone else will.

> It's a shame, but in America today when we get good service we are surprised by it. People don't expect it, they don't demand it, and they settle for a lot less than they should.
>
> *Buck Rogers*[1]

Most people resist changing professionals. If they decide to do so, they then have to find new professionals whom they trust to be more competent or consider more personable than the previous professionals. They usually have to get copies of documents such as financial statements or medical reports, or the equivalent documents in your profession. They have to answer a lot of boring questions to familiarize their new professionals with information about their background (e.g., medical, financial, or legal history). They have to confront severing their relationships with the professionals whom they previously had trusted with intimate confidences. All this is stressful and troublesome. A professional has to really turn people off to lose them as clients. And yet some professionals do. Why? and How?

In many respects, any professional–client relationship is like the doctor–patient relationship. The aforementioned *Time* article quoted a person as saying,

> We see doctors not answering questions, giving curt answers, not spending enough time with patients. Years ago a doctor was more of a family advisor. Now medicine tends to attract the person who enjoys the high-tech procedures. Almost by definition, that's not a people person.

Could any of those comments apply to your profession?

The Forum Corporation interviewed 2,374 customers of 15 business units providing such varied products and services as financial manage-ment, high-tech, life insurance, and utilities. It reported[2] that "custom-ers are five times more likely to switch vendors because of perceived service quality problems than for price concerns or product quality issues."

The evidence is clear: The reason clients change professionals is, in a word, "Service!" (or the lack thereof). What clients want—and are willing to pay for—is *high-quality service.*

QUALITY DOESN'T COST; IT PAYS

According to Buzzell and Gale, of the Strategic Planning Institute (SPI) of Cambridge, Massachusetts,[3] businesses that rank in the top third on relative perceived quality when compared to their competitors charge prices about 6 percent higher than those in the bottom third, but they have costs about the same as those of their competitors. In fact, on average, firms with quality scores in the top third of their market outearn firms in the middle third by about three-to-two, and they outearn firms in the bottom third by about two-to-one. Buzzell and Gale have been analyzing the management strategies and financial results of nearly 3,000 separate business units for periods ranging from 2 to 12 years. Their conclusion was this: "In the long run, the most important single factor affecting a business unit's performance is the quality of its products and services, relative to those of competitors."[4]

Note, however, that Buzzell and Gale are talking about relative *perceived* quality, which is not the same as the typical professional's view of quality as *conformity to professional standards.* "It demands an entirely new perspective—one that calls for viewing quality externally, from the customer's perspective, rather than internally, from a quality-assurance point of view."[5]

Nonetheless, your effort to refocus your ideas about quality is clearly worthwhile. In addition to Buzzell and Gale, studies too numerous to mention show that delivering high-quality service produces measur-able benefits in profits, cost savings, and market share.[6] Price is not *un-*important, but customers of all types are willing to pay a premium for products and services that excel in quality. Look at Mercedes, IBM, Maytag, and Häagen-Dazs.

Key Point: Quality service can enable you to command higher fees.

I agree with Karl Albrecht's[7] definition of *service excellence*, from the standpoint of competitive positioning.

> **Definition:** "*Service excellence* is a level of service quality, compared to your competitors, which is high enough in the eyes of clients for you to charge higher fees, gain an unnaturally large market share, and/or enjoy a higher profit margin than your competitors"[8] (emphasis added).[8]

Another business consultant who has skied all over the world is a big fan of one particular ski resort. At this resort, there is a box of Kleenex® at the head of each lift line. As you prepare to go on the lift, you can grab a Kleenex® to wipe your goggles, or blow your nose, or whatever, as you ride the lift. The consultant and his friends call this the "Kleenex® box resort." I have a favorite similar "Kleenex® box resort." And the resort offers other little services, such as the best-groomed slopes I've ever seen. Also, the lift tickets are about 20 percent more expensive than at competing mountains in the area, so the college students go to other mountains, and the lift lines are nonexistent. I'm willing to pay more because I get more.

Any profession will eventually see a flattening of its revenue curve because of market saturation. When this happens—and it is happening in many professions—it is only the very alert, very aware practices that will respond with "Kleenex® boxes" and stay on top of their markets. The secret to long-term client satisfaction is the client's cumulative memory of a long string of "Kleenex® box" experiences.

Thomas J. Peters and Nancy Austin, in *A Passion for Excellence,* reported that companies who find bases for quality differentiation and who produce for the higher ends of markets tend to be winners over the long haul—that is, customers will pay a tidy premium for things that solve their problems and that work and are well serviced.[9] The SPI also reports that businesses that offer superior quality and charge a premium price for it show the highest profitability.[10] In my years as a consultant, I have observed that this also holds true for professional firms.

Though your control of cost is important, you must recognize the difference between *low cost* and *competitive cost*. Your fee structure should be competitive, but few professional firms with a low-cost attitude are successful in the long run. Indeed, 65 of the 70 companies (in non-resource-extraction industries) studied and reported on in Peters's previous book, *In Search of Excellence,*[11] became and remained winners by focusing on "revenue enhancement," quality, service, courtesy, receptivity and responsiveness to customers (i.e., listening to them), and "nichemanship" (solving problems for tailored market segments). Of the remaining 5 companies studied, 4 had severe problems in the 1981–1983 recession.[12]

In a follow-up 1983 study conducted for the American Business Congress, 43 of 45 top-producing middle-sized companies became winners by delivering a product that supplied superior value to customers, rather than one that cost less. The winning middle-sized companies ($25 million to $1 billion in sales) were found to compete in terms of the value of their products and services, and they usually enjoyed premium prices.[13]

A firm needs only a very small share of a very small market to be enormously successful. I find that this also holds true for professional practices.

Examples:

- A local CPA firm in the Midwest grew from nothing to over 30 professionals within five years by serving only the health care industry.

- Many law firms have made careers of specializing in class actions or proxy fights or even drunk driving cases.

- The specialization among physicians and surgeons is well known.

- One of my client firms of architects built a very large practice designing only shopping centers.

The conclusion is obvious: You don't have to be big to be successful; you just have to be superior.

Of literally hundreds of variables tracked with long-term financial performance, one single variable is far and away the most closely associated with good financial performance over the long haul: "relative perceived product quality." This book explores perceived quality in Chapters 2 and 3.

What do winners do? To adapt the SPI findings to the professional environment, winners do the following:

1. They emphasize *real* client expectations; they focus on the client's viewpoint.

2. They research client needs; they listen to their clients in a variety of ways.

3. They use client-based measures of quality performance; they judge their own quality based on the same measures that their clients use.

4. They formulate quality control systems for all functions, not just for technical output. This means having quality control standards in client service areas, as well as in technical areas.

What about the losers? According to SPI:

1. They downgrade the client view. They view their clients' opinions as uninformed and unimportant. One reflection of this perspective is an "Ivory Tower Attitude."

2. They make high quality synonymous with conformity to their professional standards only.

3. They express quality objectives only in terms of efficiency and compliance with legal and professional requirements.

4. They formalize quality control systems for compliance with professional standards without considering additional client needs or wants.

To summarize winning versus losing strategies, **people will pay more if they get more!** This seems obvious once it's discovered. But if this is so obvious, and if the evidence keeps mounting that quality pays, why have so many professional firms refused to use client-based measurements of their performance?

Perhaps it is because professionals find it easier to measure conformity to their familiar professional standards than to venture into the subjective, "squishy" world of client needs and client perceptions. But to compete effectively, more and more professionals are going to have to react to what Buzzell and Gale call "the external half of the quality picture."

Think of the implications for your practice. Are you worried about some of your services becoming "commodities"? None of your services or products has to become a "commodity." All you have to do is find out what your clients want—and give it to them better than anyone else does. Easier said than done, and that is the mission of this book—to show you how to do it.

Some professionals act as though cost were the only variable open to them, the only factor they could control. Sometimes, they enter into a destructive cycle such as the following:

- They become consumed with keeping costs low.

- They rush to cut fees to "meet the competition."

- They hope to rely on the "experience curve" to lower their costs. They hope that by getting enough business they will be able to lower costs and make a profit.

- They quote a low-ball fee to "buy" a client and hope to make it up on volume.

This is an unstable and untenable position that cannot be maintained for long. To keep costs down, a practice eventually cuts back on the quality of the service. It may be unintentional, but the quality reduction inevitably happens.

How can this happen when no one is in favor of poor quality or poor service? Quality is a "motherhood" position. That is, everyone is in favor of high quality. Every professional wants everyone in the firm to treat clients with respect and to deliver quality service. But in the real world, it is not easy to do even one thing consistently right. So management that concentrates its efforts on cost control can end up failing at quality control through omission—that is, through lack of attention.

The old, "experience curve" way of attracting and keeping clients says to . . .

1. Cut prices in order to . . .

2. Attract more clients. A bigger practice will get the firm further down the experience curve and allow it to . . .

3. Take advantage of economies of scale, which enables it to . . .

4. Reduce costs. Eventually the firm can . . .

5. Obtain a low-cost position that helps it to . . .

6. Keep competitors away from its clients.

The PIMS (Profit Impact of Market Strategy) data base of the SPI does not dispute the desirability of achieving a low-cost position. But the PIMS pattern is the inverse of the experience curve from a cause-and-effect standpoint. The PIMS model indicates a better way for you to succeed:

1. *First,* achieve a superior relative quality edge over your competitors. If you do, you wil . . .

2. Attract more clients and be able to charge higher prices (within reason, of course). By building a bigger practice you can then . . .

3. Take advantage both of economies of scale and of experience-based cost advantages and . . .

4. Achieve higher profitability as a result of premium prices and costs equal to or lower than those of competitors.[14]

You have two alternatives for attracting new clients: (1) quickly, through sharp price cutting, which can screw up the entire market for years; or (2) deliberately and systematically, through better quality service.

The difference between these two approaches to growth is dramatic. The old "experience curve" way is to buy your way into the market with low prices, thereby jeopardizing service quality. However, without service quality you are constantly vulnerable to a higher-quality competitor. The better, "quality service" way is to start from quality and achieve low (or at least reasonable) cost as a result. Peters and Austin call the distinction "buying your way in" (via heavy discounting) versus "earning your way in" (via quality service). Only "earning your way in" is sustainable in the long run.

Furthermore, the goal of "economies of scale" is an illusory pot of gold at the end of the rainbow. Size economies are seldom achieved in the real world after a practice has reached about 15 to 30 persons (depending on the profession). Smaller, more highly focused, and more motivated firms will outperform the average larger firm every time. There are *many* small and medium-sized firms in all the professions with an average partner income that far exceeds those of the large or national firms.

PROFESSIONAL PANIC

A related problem to cost competition is that some professionals tend to get panicked by what is going on in the lowest 10 percent of the market. Indeed, there are "commodity clients"—although it would be more appropriate to call them "customers." These consumers buy on the basis of price *no matter what.* Quality means nothing to them.

Examples:

- The person who telephones a CPA on April 13 and asks, "How much would you charge to do my income taxes?"

- The person who telephones an attorney the day before his hearing and asks, "How much would it cost to get me off this drunk driving charge?"

- The patient who calls the first dentist in the Yellow Pages and says, "How much to fit me with a set of dentures?"

It's no coincidence that the example commodity customers all seem to select their professional service providers over the telephone. One firm reportedly has instructed its receptionist how to answer those inevitable "How much do you charge to—" questions: "I'm sorry but it is our policy not to accept clients who ask that question."

These commodity customers are probably a small part of the market for your services. The size of this market segment changes with local economic conditions and with competition even from nonprofessionals.

When these customers become active and start soliciting bids for professional services, it drives some partners crazy! They think the whole market is shot and the game is lost. All it takes is one significant client or prospect lost because of a fee estimate that was $100 too high. Some professionals then come to believe that price is the only variable.

Whatever the reason, some firms then panic and go after the real bottom end of the market. True, a professional practice can cover a fairly wide market. General Motors has Cadillacs and Chevrolets. But even the Chevrolet is not the bottom of the market. And GM does not compete with Rolls-Royce, either.

Questions To Think About:

- What are some examples of the "commodity customer" in your profession?

- Are these types of clients profitable? Or are they often more trouble than they are worth?

- What kind of clients do these clients refer to you? Are their referrals good clients, or are they like the commodity client?

- Would your time be better spent working on more rewarding clients?

In the past, the United States has focused on the biggest factories—in steel mills and in professional firms. But the evidence in favor of smaller firms is clear. Top quality—and higher profits—can come from smaller units. The most profitable CPA firm in a 1985 survey of practices in various cities, with average net income per partner of over $284,000, had only 21 persons total.

My own experience as a consultant to professional firms includes many firms of as few as 6 people, with similarly high incomes. Such professionals could not afford to merge with a large or national firm because they would have to take a cut in pay to reduce their income to what the partners in the large firm are receiving.

Questions to Think About:

- Look at your own marketplace. Which firms have been winners over the long haul?

- What is the perceived reputation for quality of those firms in your marketplace? (Not, "What do *you* think of them?" but, "What do their clients and referral sources think of them?")

- Have any low-end firms become long-term winners?

- Do you call any of your services "commodities"?

Look for differentiation factors and unique characteristics of your own firm. Part II of this book will show you how. True differentiation seldom comes from a single "big-bang" advantage. It does not result from doing one thing 100 percent better than your competition does; it results from doing 10 things 10 percent better than they do. That is why it is so hard to do—and so hard for your competitors to beat.

Teach and practice "quality first; cost second."

THE SERVICE QUALITY REVOLUTION

Just because clients are getting more demanding of good service and more sophisticated about recognizing it doesn't mean that all the professional firms in the country are jumping on the bandwagon. Far from it. Some lead the revolution, some follow, and some sleep through it. Karl Albrecht describes five degrees of commitment that firms display toward service quality:

1. *Going out of business.* These firms are so out of touch with their clients that they are on the way down the tubes; some know it, some don't.

2. *Dogged pursuit of mediocrity.* These firms are probably in business to stay, but service quality is not part of their thinking.

3. *Present and accounted for.* These firms know they are in the service business and have an innate respect for doing at least the basics. However, most of them enjoy only a "natural market share," which means the share of the market they are entitled to merely by virtue of showing up. Service quality doesn't play a major role in their strategic management.

4. *Making a serious effort.* These firms are on the move, and they are working hard to make service a competitive weapon. "Client-centeredness" has become a driving idea of the firm's business culture. They are innovatively reformulating and rethinking their organization's image and focus.

5. *Service as an art form.* These are the legendary firms in the professions. The mission of management is to preserve and refine the firm's image of outstanding service.[15]

As a professional, you must think about quality as more than something you do to avoid a malpractice suit, or to impress your professional colleagues, or to satisfy your desire for professional challenge. You need to think about clients' needs and preferences. Quality is more than a technical problem to be solved; it is a competitive opportunity.

NOTES

1. Buck Rogers, *The IBM Way*, New York: Harper & Row, 1986, p. 16.

2. The Forum Corporation, "Customer Focus Research Executive Briefing," April 1988. Boston, Massachusetts, p. 5.

3. Robert D. Buzzell and Bradley T. Gale, *The PIMS Principles*, New York: The Free Press, 1987, p. 109.

4. Robert D. Buzzell and Bradley T. Gale, p. 7.

5. Robert D. Buzzell and Bradley T. Gale, p. 103.

6. Valarie A. Zeithaml, Leonard L. Berry, and A. Parasuraman, *Communication and Control Processes in the Delivery of Service Quality* (Report No. 87-100), Cambridge, MA: Marketing Science Institute, June 1987, p. 1.

7. Karl Albrecht, *At America's Service*, Homewood, IL: Dow Jones-Irwin, 1988, p. 12.

8. Adapted from Karl Albrecht, p. 12.

9. Thomas J. Peters and Nancy Austin, *A Passion for Excellence*, New York: Warner Books, 1985, p. 60.

10. Robert D. Buzzell and Bradley T. Gale, pp. 112–113.

11. Thomas J. Peters and Robert H. Waterman, Jr., *In Search of Excellence: Lessons from America's Best-Run Companies*, New York: Warner Books, 1982.

12. Thomas J. Peters and Nancy Austin, p. 60.

13. Thomas J. Peters and Nancy Austin, p. 61.

14. Robert D. Buzzell and Bradley T. Gale, pp. 91–92.

15. Karl Albrecht, pp. 10–11.

2
What Is "High-Quality" Service?

What *is* "high-quality" service?

Before answering that question, notice that clients do not use the term *quality* in the same way that professionals do.

> **Example:** You may remember an occasion when you did superior professional work that your client neither recognized as such nor appreciated. You may have invested a lot of time and effort to handle an unforeseen contingency, perhaps in a very creative way. But because your client did not expect the contingency and was not aware of it, the client was irritated at the extra expense and delay rather than thankful for your superior professional skills!

So this discussion first must address, "For whom do we define *high-quality service*? Ourselves or our clients?"

THE TRADITIONAL VIEW OF QUALITY

The problem in this situation is this: To most professionals, *quality* means delivering services that conform to the technical standards of their particular profession. This traditional view of quality is primarily defensive in nature. As a result, *technical* quality controls are designed to prevent *technical* failures. It is a negative concept of quality designed to protect the public and to protect the practitioner from legal liability. That's okay as far as it goes, but it doesn't go far enough.

Clients do not buy your services; they buy what your services will *do* for them. Essentially, people will buy only two things: good feelings and/or solutions to problems. Every purchase a person makes—of anything from dinner for two to a luxury automobile to groceries—is an aspect of one or both of those two motivations. Buying *good feelings* includes paying for entertainment, amusement, personal growth, education, status, or security. *Solutions to problems* include making money, saving money, improving productivity, avoiding a loss, and so forth. Those are the only two broad motivations for buying.

Clients buy services for *their* reasons, not *yours*. When you think your clients are buying your professional services, they are actually buying their own real, personal good feelings, and solutions to their own nitty-gritty, personal problems.

In one of his television programs for Public Broadcasting Service, Tom Peters talked about "TDC"—thinly disguised contempt—which some people have for customers. He mentioned four symptoms of TDC: (1) casting aspersions on customers; (2) having contempt for customer-contact personnel; (3) writing off such things as telephone courtesy as "obvious" and as not requiring—or deserving—thoughtfulness or serious training; and (4) *technical hubris*—a belief that technical superiority is all that really counts.

The traditional view of professional quality comes perilously close to TDC for clients. For example: Another reason some professionals view quality only from its technical side is that they become fascinated with the intellectual challenge of performing the service rather than being responsive to clients. They look at clients as "interesting cases." This reduces clients to mere excuses to practice their profession.

In order to keep clients and to satisfy them so much that they become cheerleaders for you and your firm, forget about the viewpoints of professionals, and concentrate on the views of your clients. The remainder of this chapter examines quality solely from the client's viewpoint.

THE CLIENTS' VIEW OF QUALITY

Peter Drucker[1] observed that *quality* is not what you put into the service; it is what the client gets out of it and is willing to pay for. Your service is not of high quality because it is hard to do and costs a lot of money. Clients pay only for what is of use to them and gives them value. Nothing else is "quality." This client-centered view of quality is positive rather than negative. This concept of quality is aimed at pleasing clients, not just protecting them from harm.

This deserves repeating: Clients don't buy your professional services; they buy solutions to their problems. Clients buy expectations of benefits that they think you offer to them. You provide quality when you fulfill those expectations, solve those problems, and deliver those benefits.

Key Point: If you want to do a high-quality job for a client, it is crucial you know what problem the client thinks you are solving.

In other words, what are the client's expectations or desires?

THE SERVICE QUALITY EQUATION—YOUR "INVISIBLE REPORT CARD" FROM YOUR CLIENTS

The invisible report card your clients give you reflects their opinions of the quality of your service. And those quality opinions result from comparing what they expected prior to receiving the service with their actual experiences with the service. In other words, client satisfaction (the grade on your report card) equals client perceptions of what they received minus client expectations of what they thought they would receive. For those of you with a mathematical mind, this formula expresses the concept:

$$Q = P - E$$

where Q is service quality, P is client perceptions, and E is client expectations.

In other words, your grades on clients' mental report cards for the quality of your services equal client perceptions of what they received minus client expectations of what they thought they would receive. Also, as consultant David Maister points out, "Nothing in the equation has anything to do with reality!" Client perceptions and expectations are completely subjective.

When you meet clients' expectations, perception and expectation are equal and clients grade your service quality as satisfactory. When you

The Superior Service Quality Equation

What
clients get
(perception)

What
clients want
(expectation)

Figure 1

do not meet clients' expectations—if their expectations were higher than the service you actually delivered—your score is negative, and clients grade your service quality as unsatisfactory. If your service delivered exceeds clients' expectations, satisfaction is positive, and clients grade your service as superior.

Figure 1 illustrates the concept.

Tom Peters[2] described it differently:

$$CS = \frac{D}{E}$$

where CS is *c*ustomer *s*atisfaction, D is what you *d*elivered to the client, and E is client *e*xpectations. To Peters, the customer's grade on your report card is a ratio of what you delivered divided by what the client expected. It means the same thing as $Q = P - E$.

Example: If you walk into a convenience store and get a gallon of milk from the cooler, carry it to the cashier, and pay the posted price, are you satisfied? Yes: You got exactly what you expected. You might say: "The scales are balanced." Like the customer of the convenience store, clients are also "satisfied" when they get what they bargained for. When they come to you, clients fully expect competent, skilled technical service. So when they get what they expected and what they bargained for, they are "satisfied." End of transaction. Economically and emotionally, you are even. They owe you nothing; you owe them nothing.

But how would you feel if the cashier rang up your gallon of milk and then handed you a coupon good for 10 percent off on your next purchase? You would be an enthusiastic customer because you got more than you expected.

Key Point: Clients become enthusiastic only when the service you deliver exceeds their expectations, when they get something extra, something more than they bargained for.

Obviously, the more you can exceed your clients' expectations, the more satisfied they will be. Emotionally, when you give clients more than they expect, they are indebted to you; they owe you.

Example: Consultant Lisa Ford told about the time her mother had surgery. When Lisa went to visit her mother in the hospital, there was a flower arrangement from the surgeon. Lisa's mother kept exclaiming, "Can you imagine? The surgeon sent me flowers!" Lisa's mother told everyone who visited her that the surgeon had sent flowers. Even after the patient was home, every time she told someone about her surgery she added, "And the surgeon sent me flowers!"

This may have seemed like a small thing to the surgeon. In fact, compared to his fee (this surgeon happened to be a man), the cost of the flowers was insignificant. Yet think of the tremendous "good feelings" this generated with the patient. She never expected that little extra demonstration of the surgeon's concern for her well-being. When she got it, she became an enthusiastic cheerleader.

THE MISSING SIDE OF QUALITY

You may have heard an old saying in your college marketing course: "Customers don't buy quarter-inch drills; they buy quarter-inch holes."

This is just another way of illustrating that people don't buy products; they buy the benefits of those products—solutions to their problems.

You have two ways in which to get a quarter-inch hole in a piece of wood: (1) Buy a drill and drill it yourself, or (2) hire a carpenter to drill it for you. Your viewpoint as a customer will differ significantly according to the method you choose. Either way, you still get a quarter-inch hole, but you purchase a different "product" in each case.

When you choose to drill the hole yourself, you give a mental report card on the quality of the drill. The tangible product itself is the important thing. Your evaluation may be influenced by the drill's packaging or by intangibles such as its advertising or how well the instruction booklet is written, but basically the drill itself is of principal importance.

On the other hand, if you hire a carpenter, no physical product is involved. (Let's assume that your carpenter is a woman so I won't have to keep saying "he or she.") Your benefit, the hole, is provided by the carpenter, and the "product" she offers is the benefit of having a quarter-inch hole, not the tangible drill that she uses. You don't care what kind of drill the carpenter uses. She could carve the hole with a pocket knife for all you care, as long as the hole (the service outcome) is okay. But you also care about things such as, Was it easy to get hold of the carpenter? Was her answering service competent? Did she show up when she said she would? Did she leave wood shavings all over the carpet? Was she courteous?

Because service products (which I discuss at length in Chapter 4) differ from other kinds of products, the client's invisible report card for the quality of a service is not made solely on the service outcome provided; the client also evaluates the manner in which the service is provided. I call this a comparison between "internal quality" and "external quality."

What customers receive in their interactions with a service firm is clearly important to their evaluation of the quality of the service—the service outcome, or the *internal quality* of the service. Often, customers can measure it objectively. For example, when you have your TV repaired, you can tell whether the picture has been fixed. However, because services are produced in interaction with the customer, internal quality alone does not account for the client's total opinion of the quality of the services received.

The manner in which the service was delivered is also important—the service's *external quality*. Hence, we have two quality dimensions that are quite different in nature: *internal quality,* which is *what* the customer gets, or the outcome of the service, and *external quality*, which is *how* the customer gets that outcome.

> **Key Point:** In professional practice, "internal" quality is created inside the firm, and the firm's personnel are usually the only people conscious of it. "External" quality is the face the practice presents to the outside world.

→ In the case of the carpenter, you evaluate not only the quarter-inch hole (internal quality) but also the carpenter's courtesy, appearance, and promptness (external quality). Most professionals forget to consider the external quality of services in their efforts to render high-quality service. This missing side of quality may cost them key clients.

> **Key Point:** Reality is what you can perceive clearly.

Your biggest hurdle in obtaining good marks with clients is to manage not only the service outcome for clients (internal quality), but also the clients' expectations, perceptions, and value judgments (external quality). If you emphasize only internal quality, you will have only moderate client loyalty. Why? Because clients can't clearly perceive your internal quality! Clients fully expect a good technical outcome (internal quality), and they are neither surprised nor overly pleased when they get it.

> **Examples:**
> - If the patient *expects* the hospital to be clean, the hospital gets no bonus points for cleanliness; it only gets demerits if it is *not* clean. Here, cleanliness is a minimum requirement to compete in the market. If some other hospitals are dirty, then cleanliness might offer a competitive edge. If the other hospitals are clean, yours had better be clean, too.[3]
> - If clients *expect* you to prepare or file certain documents on time, you again get no particular credit for timeliness.
> - If clients *expect* their teeth to stop hurting after they visit the dentist, the dentist gets no special high marks for quality when that occurs.

Unfortunately, many professionals do not understand which service features indicate high quality to clients, what attributes each service feature must possess to meet client needs, and what levels of performance on those features and attributes are necessary in order for clients to perceive them as high quality. The gap between client expectations and partner perceptions is usually quite large.

THE KEY TO ENSURING QUALITY SERVICE

Looking again at the service quality equation, you see only two factors that determine client satisfaction: client expectations and client perceptions. Therefore, to improve your scores with clients, you can (a) lower client expectations, (b) raise client perceptions of what they have actually received, or (c) do both. This book addresses both variables.

> **Key Point:** The key to ensuring good quality service is to meet or exceed what clients expect from you. Therefore, it is important for you to determine exactly what problem the client wants you to solve and exactly what good feelings the client seeks from you.

Even new clients with prior experience with other persons in your profession may have strange ideas of the type of service you *should* render, based on their previous experiences with other professionals. And for new clients who have never worked with someone in your profession, it's even worse: Their expectations are only *predictions* they make unconsciously about what you are *likely* to do. In other words, people with no prior experience with your profession are uncertain regarding what your profession does and what results you routinely achieve. Often, clients form their opinions about various professions from television portrayals of doctors, lawyers, and so forth. They don't know exactly what to expect, and their expectations could be way out in left field.

> **Key Point:** Each client's expectations and perceptions reflect reality the way the client sees it; they may not reflect reality the way you see it. The point bears repeating: Reality (to anyone) is what that person can perceive clearly.

What's more, what you are giving your clients may not be the same as what your clients are getting. That is, what you think you are delivering and what your clients perceive they are getting may have little relationship to each other.

> **Examples:**
> - Some patients think taking "pill number 27" will cure their high blood pressure even if they keep salting everything on their plate before they taste it.
> - Some clients think merely getting their attorney to write a strongly worded letter to their adversary will prompt a generous offer of a settlement.
> - Most of the general public thinks an unqualified audit opinion guarantees that there is no fraud in the financial statements and that the company is in good financial condition.

These examples show that client expectations may have little relationship to reality as the professional sees it: Clients really buy the solutions that they expect from you.

> **Examples:**
> - You may think the landlord–client is buying a lease agreement; actually, the client may be expecting that the tenant will always pay the rent promptly and never get into financial difficulty. If the tenant should become delinquent, you may have lost a client.
> - You may think the client is buying an estate plan; actually, the client may be buying a secure retirement. If some of their mutual funds lose money, you could be facing a lawsuit.
> - You may think the client is buying your preparation of a tax return; actually the client may be buying a guarantee that the tax return won't be audited by the IRS. If the client is audited, you lose that client.

Both inexperienced and experienced clients judge service quality by weighing the difference between their expectations and their perceptions. However, for prospective clients or new clients whom you have not yet served, their expectations are only predictions that they unconsciously make about what is likely to happen when you serve them. In other words, people with little experience with you are uncertain regarding the likelihood of a favorable experience with you. Their expectations are based on what they would like you to provide, not what you will or even should provide.

Existing clients, on the other hand, have considerable experience with you. Their expectations are what they believe you should offer rather than what you will offer. Existing clients are fairly certain what to expect.

New clients with significant prior experience with other practitioners in your profession have expectations closely resembling the expectations of existing clients. This is because they have rather definite ideas of the type of service you *should* render.

To get clients to grade your services as high quality, you must learn what clients really expect from you. This means you must listen—really listen—to your clients. And you must make sure your clients have realistic expectations of what you will be able to accomplish. This requires good communication in both directions.

> **Key Point:** Clearly, it is crucial with all new clients to determine why they left their previous professional, if they had one, and what they expect of you. What, exactly, is the problem they want you to solve?

HOW TO TURN "CUSTOMERS" INTO "CHEERLEADERS"

The biggest complaint I have about some client satisfaction surveys is that they ask some version of "Are you happy with the way we serve you?" and give clients a choice of answering "yes" or "no." If 70 percent of your clients answer "yes," is that good? Or does it mean 30 percent are unhappy and about to leave? Yes-or-no answers to quality questions are almost meaningless because you don't know what a good score is.

Client satisfaction is not just a "yes" or "no" matter. Instead, there are degrees of satisfaction, and your clients give you an invisible mental "report card." On a scale of 1 to 10, your grade with some clients might be "5" or "6," while others might give you a "10." Those who give you a lower score are open to approaches from your competitors. These are the ones who, when your current service for them is completed, just might try a competitor on the next matter. Those clients who rate you a "10" are not only secure; they are probably also referring clients to you. To retain clients, you need both to raise the satisfaction level of your marginal clients and to keep it high for your supersatisfied clients.

There are several different levels or intensities of business relationships you can have with clients:

- *Customer or purchaser* is the weakest relationship. A customer has used one or two of your services but is not yet in the habit of buying from you on a regular basis. Customers don't come to you for additional work or advice, and they don't think of you as a source of help. Customers don't feel any special relationship to you or your firm. On a satisfaction scale of 1 to 10, customers might be a 5 or 6. Their loyalty is weak or nonexistent.

- *Client* is the normal type of relationship. Clients use your services and are comfortable turning to you for advice and counsel. Clients have formed the habit of buying from you. Their satisfaction might be a 7 or 8, and they are moderately loyal. In other words, clients will give you the benefit of the doubt. If you louse up one project or one contact, they are likely to give you another chance if you do a good job of making amends.

- *Cheerleader* is the highest class of business relationship. Cheerleaders not only come to you for help, they also sell for you. They tell friends and business associates about you, and they refer clients to you. Cheerleaders' satisfaction is definitely at a 9 or 10, and they are intensely loyal. These are people who, if your firm got some bad publicity in the newspaper, would defend you against detractors if the matter were mentioned at a cocktail party.

My goal is to give you some tools to help you get people to climb the ladder from *customers* to *clients* and then from *clients* to *cheerleaders.* I want you to be able to raise every client's satisfaction to a higher level.

NOTES

1. Peter Drucker, *Innovation and Entrepreneurship*, New York: Harper & Row, 1985, p. 228.
2. Tom Peters, *Thriving on Chaos*, New York: Alfred A. Knopf, 1987, p. 98.
3. Karl Albrecht and Ron Zemke, *Service America!*, Homewood, IL: Dow Jones-Irwin, 1985, p. 72.

3

The Five Grades on Your Invisible Report Card

You know that clients have both expectations or wants regarding your professional service and opinions or perceptions of how well your performance compares with those expectations. But what are these expectations? How do clients judge your performance?

The hard part of obtaining favorable judgments is making sure clients perceive all you have done for them—in other words, getting credit for what you have done. Remember: Reality to clients is what they can perceive clearly. The problem is that so much of what you do is invisible to your clients.

Look at Figure 2.[1] All your support services and internal systems are invisible to clients. Clients can't see the days of continuing education you give your staff. They can't see the quality reviews your documents or reports go through. They don't know the thousands of dollars you spend on your professional library every year.

I discuss this figure more in Chapter 4. For now, just remember that what most professionals do is almost magical to their clients, so it is very unreal to them. They can see what they *think* is the output, the tangible representation of the service, but your input is incomprehensible to most clients.

Clients judge quality in two types of service categories:[2]

1. *Regular service* includes the routine, repetitive, predictable encounters they have with you. Examples would be preparation of

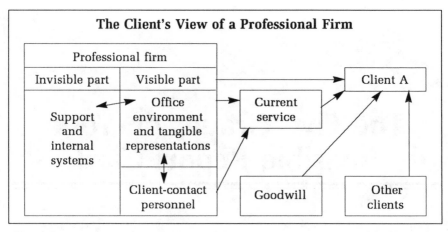

Figure 2

tax returns or financial statements for accountants; collection actions or drafting corporate minutes for lawyers; annual check-ups for doctors and dentists; and so on.

2. *Exceptional service* includes problems, emergencies, or those unusual, unpredictable—possibly unique—situations you handle as professionals. Examples might include tax controversies or loan presentations for accountants, "deathbed" estate planning for both lawyers and accountants, or medical emergencies for health-care professionals. Correction of errors—those made by you, by your client, or by other professionals—is a very important part of exceptional service.

Questions To Think About:

• What are the regular services you render to clients?

• What do clients think they are getting?

• Who performs regular services?

• What are the exceptional services you render to clients?

• What services do clients think they are getting?

• Who performs exceptional services?

• Which type of service requires more skill?

• What kinds of skills are needed for each type of service?

Clients grade you by mentally comparing their evaluations of what they receive with what they expected. These expectations and evaluations can be divided into five dimensions. What are these dimensions of quality, and in what areas of your professional service can clients measure them?

Though many professionals measure quality in terms of compliance with professional and technical standards, clients know little or nothing about such standards and care about them even less. The technical aspects of your service are of little interest to them. Occasionally they are able to perceive the service outcome—what you accomplished—but, even then, they have little clue as to how you accomplished your results.

Yet, even though they have little or no professional competence to do so, clients make decisions regarding the quality of your service every time they sign a check to pay your fees. How do they do it? If they cannot judge the internal quality of your services, what criteria do they use? Just how do they decide whether you are doing a good job?

As far as most clients are concerned, there are five dimensions of service quality:[3] (1) reliability, (2) assurance, (3) tangibles, (4) responsiveness, and (5) empathy. As I review and discuss each of these, think about how you can *demonstrate* your capabilities along these dimensions in ways that your clients can perceive clearly.

RELIABILITY

Reliability is the ability to provide the promised service dependably and accurately. It includes timeliness and the client's perception of your competence. The client judges you on how dependable you are. Reliability means performing the service correctly the first time.

Practical Tips:

- Make sure your service outcome reflects all the information the client gave you. If the client called your office after a conference and gave your secretary more information regarding his or her needs, did that information find its way into the final outcome? Or was it lost on the way?

- Start performing the service when you said you would. (This also demonstrates your *responsiveness* to clients.)

- Be sure your billing is accurate. Nothing casts doubt on your reliability more quickly than to send a client a bill with arithmetic errors or a bill that does not reflect the client's last payment to you.

- Demonstrate your research capability and your ability to solve problems. One way is to make your library visible to clients; make sure it looks neat, not disorganized.

- Ensure that your client-contact personnel and your operational support personnel are knowledgeable and skillful at what they do.

- Look for ways to demonstrate new ideas and innovative approaches to your clients.

Questions To Think About:

- What are your clients' expectations regarding accuracy? How do they judge your accuracy?

- What are your clients' expectations regarding your delivery dates? How do they judge your delivery?

- How dependable do your clients think you are? How about others in your firm?

ASSURANCE

Assurance is the client's feeling that her or his problem is in good hands. It involves the knowledge and courtesy of your personnel and their ability to convey trust and confidence. Assurance also involves credibility, which includes trustworthiness, believability, and honesty. It means having the client's best interests at heart and demonstrating care and concern. Assurance is the reason for the old saying, "People don't care how much you know until they know how much you care." Contributions to credibility:

- *Firm name and reputation*—David A. Garvin,[4] noted that reputation is the primary stuff of perceived quality. People assume that the quality of today's products is similar to the quality of yesterday's products, or the quality of a new product line is similar to the quality of a company's established products. Garvin: "In the early 1980s, Maytag introduced a new line of dishwashers. Needless to say, salespeople immediately emphasized the product's reliability—not yet proven—because of the reputation of Maytag's clothes washers and dryers."

- *Personal characteristics* of your client-contact personnel.

- *Degree of hard sell* involved in your interactions with the client—The higher the degree of hard sell, the lower the credibility you have. Fortunately, credibility is not a problem with most firms because most professions have an excellent public reputation. However, when professionals are selling, they must be very, very careful to avoid the appearance of the hard sell, which would damage their credibility, while still pursuing the sale.

Part of assurance is *security*—the freedom from danger, risk, or doubt. Security involves

- The ability to anticipate and avoid problems (Does this professional foresee all the possible problems and know how to avoid or at least minimize them?)

   Caution: Professionals who overemphasize *all* possible problems—no matter how remote—quickly get the reputation of being "deal-killers."

- Physical safety (Will I get mugged in the parking lot?)

- Financial security (Does the firm know where my stock certificates, bank statements, will, etc. are?)

- Confidentiality (Are my dealings private?)

A 1987 article on the national news wires reported a survey of patients regarding their doctors' attire. It reported that patients preferred their doctors to look the part. They didn't want to see doctors wear sneakers or casual clothes. They had more confidence in doctors with stethoscopes, neckties, and suits or white smocks. The way the doctor is dressed has an impact on the assurance the patient feels about the doctor's competence.

Part of your job is to persuade clients to follow your advice. Sometimes they just have to take you on faith because you cannot always explain some of the complex technical considerations involved in your recommendations. That's why assurance is important to your clients. Doctors call it their "bedside manner."

Particularly for nonroutine or exceptional services, clients are, almost by definition, in a state of anxiety when they approach you; certainly they are at least nervous. Your clients are often shopping as much for trust, confidence, and reassurance as for cold technical expertise.

Questions To Think About:

- How can you improve your "bedside manner"?

- How do your clients perceive their physical and financial security when dealing with you?

TANGIBLES

Tangibles include the physical evidence and artifacts of your service, your facilities and equipment, and the appearance of your personnel.

> **Examples:** Tangibles include correspondence, newsletters, brochures, and other tangible products that the client receives from you. For a law firm, tangibles would also include the neatness of contracts. For a bank, they would include the appearance of bank statements and credit cards; for accountants, the appearance of financial statements, reports, and tax returns; for engineers, the appearance of drawings and specifications.

In other words clients ask themselves, "Do these people *look* like high quality, do they have a high-quality office, and do they produce a product with a high-quality look?" I discuss tangibles further in Chapter 9.

Questions To Think About:

- Does your personal appearance speak well of you and of the firm?

- How can you improve your personal tangibles for your clients?

- What sort of appearance do your other client-contact people present?

RESPONSIVENESS

Responsiveness concerns your willingness to help clients and to provide prompt service. Responsiveness, like reliability, also involves timeliness of service. Accessibility is also part of responsiveness, and it involves approachability and how easy you are to reach. It means that

- The firm is easily accessible by telephone (lines are not busy, telephones are answered promptly, and clients are seldom put on "hold")
- Appointments are easy to get and are set at times that are convenient for clients; office hours are convenient for clients
- Waiting time in the reception area is not excessive
- Key people are not out of town whenever the client needs them
- Location of the office is convenient.

Questions To Think About:
- How long does it take a client to get an appointment with you?
- Are you as responsive as you could be to your clients?
- How can you improve your personal responsiveness?
- Are you as accessible to clients as you could be?
- How can you improve your accessibility?
- Do you return all telephone calls within 24 hours?
- How many rings does it take for your receptionist to answer your telephone?
- If your clients are placed on hold, how long do they remain on hold?
- How many call screeners do your clients go through to reach you?

Practical Tips:

- Return your clients' telephone calls promptly.

- Have no more than one "call screener." *Never* ask clients, "Who's calling?" more than once.

- Deliver your service outcome on or before the promised date and time.

- Make sure you have at least four incoming telephone lines, even if you are a one-professional office. Reason: If you are on the phone and your secretary is calling a client to confirm an appointment, two lines are already busy. Then if another person calls (a common occurrence when both you and your secretary are on the phones), three lines are tied up. If you have only three lines, it's as if your office door is locked—no one else can get through. And nothing turns off a prospect as quickly and effectively as a busy signal. It says, "Small time operator."

EMPATHY

Empathy means that you provide caring, individualized attention to clients. It goes beyond mere courtesy, although courtesy is an important part of empathy, as it is of assurance. It requires commitment to the client and involves understanding the client and knowing his or her personal needs and specific requirements. Courtesy involves politeness, respect, consideration for the client's property, and consideration of the client's time, as well as friendliness of contact personnel (including receptionists and telephone operators).

Buck Rogers,[5] the famous now-retired Vice President of Marketing for IBM observed that there's no way to tell how many clients are lost because of little human errors such as not returning a phone call, being late for an appointment, failing to say thank you, and taking clients for granted. Rogers: "As far as I'm concerned, these 'little' things can be the difference between a very successful company and a failure." Rogers notes, "If you don't return phone calls or answer your mail [promptly,] if you break appointments at the last minute . . . or have people sitting on their hands because you're late . . . , you're saying, 'Hey, [client,] you're not very important to me or my [firm].'"

Empathy is enhanced by good communication, which means keeping clients informed, in language they can understand. It also means listening to clients. It may mean you need to adjust your language for different clients—increasing the level of sophistication with a well-educated client or speaking simply and plainly with a novice. Good communication involves

- Explaining the service itself

- Explaining how much the service will cost

- Explaining the trade-offs between service and cost

- Assuring the client that a problem will be handled

Listening to and understanding the client includes

- Learning the client's specific requirements (including his or her personal eccentricities)

- Providing individualized, *unhurried* attention

- Recognizing the regular client by sight and calling her or him by name

- Possessing expertise in the client's industry

- Knowing about the client's organization

The old rule, "Never let the size of the bill be an unpleasant surprise," is an example of good communication.

Practical Tips:

- When a bill will be larger than the client expected, call or visit the client *before* drafting the bill and discuss your charges. If the client is going to have a serious problem with the size of the fee, it is better to find out before you send the bill than after. This way, if any adjustment is needed or if the client has any questions that need to be answered, you can handle them before submitting the bill, and you will normally be paid with no further delays.

- Be wary of the attitude that says, Thank-you-very-much-come-back-real-soon-here's-your-hat-there's-the-door-**next**! Don't rush.

- At the end of every client conference, ask the client these three questions: "Did you accomplish your objectives for this meeting? Is there anything else I should know? Is there anything else I can do for you?" The first question asks the client to look internally and give you an indication of your report card grade. The second question invites the client's cooperation and communication. The third question is designed to clear up any mysteries (such as "What does that mean?") or any unexpressed expectations or needs.

Questions To Think About:

- What are the client's expectations about communication?

- What is your "thank you quotient"?

- How do you treat the client's lower-ranking employees?

HOW WELL DO MOST BUSINESSES SCORE?

Parasuraman, Zeithaml, and Berry[6] did their research among customers of banks, credit card companies, repair and maintenance companies, and long-distance telephone companies. They noted, "Average expectation scores on the five dimensions vary somewhat. However, arranging these scores from highest to lowest with[in] each service category reveals virtually identical rank orders across the categories. In general, irrespective of service category, customer expectations are highest on the reliability dimension, followed in order by assurance, tangibles, and responsiveness, and lowest on the empathy dimension." Customers' expectations and perceptions are shown in Figure 3, on a scale of 1 to 100.

Parasuraman et al.'s research indicates that businesses in general seem to be doing the best job on their tangibles, which are easily visible, easiest to compare with competitors, and easiest to manage (called "hard" items). But in the "soft" items, which are the truest indicators of external quality, most businesses are doing a lousy job.

The Forum Corporation[7] interviewed more than 5,000 customers and employees (in the research mentioned in Chapter 1). They found that customers consider tangibles to be the least important element in service quality. At the same time, customers believe tangibles are the area

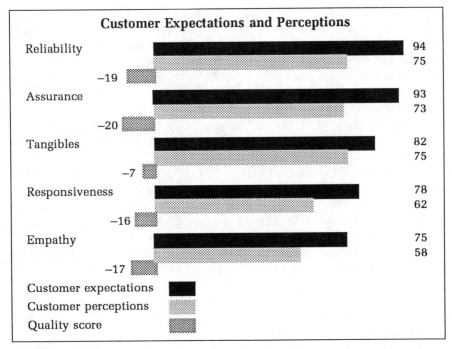

Figure 3

most competently handled by companies and report this to be the source of fewest problems. Forum's research also showed that reliability is the most important element of service quality. However, customers perceive reliability as the weakest element of company performance and the source of the greatest number of service problems.

WHY WORD-OF-MOUTH ADVERTISING IS SO POWERFUL

These five dimensions could also be ranked according to how easy they are for clients to evaluate. Because of clients' inability to evaluate your internal quality even after receiving your services, reliability ends up being the hardest dimension for clients to evaluate. In other words,

Key Point: The most important client criterion for quality service is the hardest for the client to evaluate.

Clients are never really certain of your competence. When people cannot taste, feel, see, smell, or hear your service's outcome in advance, what they are buying is only a promise of satisfaction. Because services cannot be experienced until they're consumed, *prospective* clients don't know what they are going to get. So they often rely on surrogates to assess what they are likely to get. And the surrogate frequently is another one of your clients or a referral source.

In its March 2, 1987 issue, *Medical Economics* reported that more than half of 2,600 people surveyed chose their doctors based on the advice of family or friends, while one fifth were referred by another doctor. Fewer than 1 percent based their decision on newspaper, radio, or television ads, and only 4 percent consulted the Yellow Pages.

Prospective clients take a risk when they engage you. Referral sources take a risk when they recommend you. Prospects or sources *think* they know you, but they don't *know* they know you. To a large extent, the decision to hire or recommend a professional is based on trust—the prospect's or source's trust that her or his assessment of your ability is valid.

Here's an axiom about the risk–trust relationship:

**The greater the risk to the buyer,
the greater the amount of trust the buyer must place in the seller.**[8]

To put it another way, for emphasis: the more you have to lose, the more you need to trust the person you are dealing with. In buying professional services, clients reach the highest degree of risk and thus the greatest need to trust the professionals whom they engage. The same holds true for referral sources. Your clients' reputations are on the line every time they recommend you. Because they have a great deal at risk, they need a great deal of trust and confidence in you *before* they will recommend you. Therefore, it is critical for all of your personnel to be able to earn a high degree of trust and confidence from clients and other referral sources.

That's why "executive presence" is such an important criterion in admitting partners: Because the most important characteristic of a good professional—reliability—is very difficult for the client to evaluate even after receiving your services. By default, clients make their evaluations based on other characteristics. Well, what characteristics are left?

> **Key Point:** Clients usually evaluate service quality based on characteristics they can personally experience and judge.

Clients can personally experience and judge

1. Your tangibles

2. The assurance they feel in their dealings with you

3. Your responsiveness to their needs

4. Your empathy with their feelings and needs

Clients reevaluate these dimensions each time they interact with you. Another grade goes into the client's mental "grade book" on the page with your name at the top. Every contact with a client yields another value rating for your service and another cup of water in the pool of goodwill.

Notice that only the tangibles dimension can be known by prospective clients before they become a client. To a certain extent, a client also gets a feel for assurance and empathy, but only a feel. Usually, the four dimensions other than tangibles (including reliability again) can only be known while the client is receiving the service.

Key Point: Only after clients have hired you can they know how good you are!

This means that they are already committed to you before they know how good your service will be! In fact, most clients find reliability and responsiveness impossible to evaluate; therefore, they are *never* certain of these dimensions. Obviously, this entails a great deal of perceived risk by the client.

This perceived risk is one reason why (a) it is so difficult to get clients to change professionals, (b) building trust and confidence with a prospective client is so important, and (c) word-of-mouth advertising is so powerful. Personal recommendations from existing clients to prospective clients are the only real data they can use to judge whether to give you a try.

If you look carefully at the list of criteria that clients use to judge quality and compare it with your profession's technical quality standards, you will note that the two lists probably have nothing in common!

And there are several other very disturbing things about these characteristics that clients can experience and judge:

• None of the clients' criteria can be independently peer reviewed.

- None of them shows up on internal quality reviews.

- None of them has anything to do with the internal quality of your work.

- And all of them are purely subjective feelings of the client.

This means that any work you do to improve technical standards and the public perception of the internal quality of your work could be wasted because clients perceive quality differently from the way you do.

NOTES

1. Adapted from Christian Grönroos, *Strategic Management and Marketing in the Service Sector* (Report No. 83-104), Cambridge, MA: Marketing Science Institute, May 1983, p. 49. Used by permission of the publisher.
2. A. Parasuraman, Valarie A. Zeithaml, and Leonard L. Berry, "Quality Counts in Services, Too," *Business Horizons*, May/June 1985, p. 46.
3. A. Parasuraman, Valarie A. Zeithaml, and Leonard L. Berry, *SERVQUAL: A Multiple-Item Scale for Measuring Customer Perceptions of Service Quality* (Report No. 86-108), Cambridge, MA: Marketing Science Institute, August 1986.
4. David A. Garvin, "Competing on the Eight Dimensions of Quality," *Harvard Business Review*, November/December 1987.
5. Buck Rogers, *The IBM Way*, New York: Harper & Row, 1986, p. 145.
6. A. Parasuraman, Valarie A. Zeithaml, and Leonard L. Berry, 1986, p. 23.
7. The Forum Corporation, "Customer Focus Research Executive Briefing," April 1988. Boston, Massachusetts, p. 4.
8. Charles Goldsmith, *Selling Skills for CPAs: How to Bring in New Business*, New York: McGraw-Hill, 1985, p. 10.

4

"Smith & Jones" versus "Ace Widgets"—Why Professional Firms Are Different

Many management practices for professional firms were originally developed for manufacturing and distribution companies and co-opted by service organizations. Both manufacturing and distribution companies acquire a physical product—say, widgets—as one distinct operation and sell them to customers as another distinct operation. Because of the similarity between manufacturers and distributors, I refer to both as "widget companies."

Widget companies and service companies have certain similarities. Buck Rogers,[1] the retired marketing vice president of IBM said, "IBM doesn't sell products. It sells solutions. . . . People buy products for what they can do, not for what they are. They buy products to solve problems." If a person's problem is having straight hair when the fashion is ringlets, the solution may come in the form of plastic rollers, a permanent, or a hair stylist. "It's not the product that is important to the buyer; the solution to the problem is what matters. All the buyer wants is curly hair." Buck says he sells this way: If I convince you I can make your job easier, reduce your costs, and help you give better service to your customers, I'll get your attention. I'll never try to sell you a typewriter, a copier, or a computer.

Similarly, people do not buy professional services either; they buy solutions to problems. Despite this similarity between widget companies and service firms, there are fundamental differences between

- The way companies *manufacture* widgets and the way professional practices provide services

- The way customers *purchase* widgets and the way clients purchase professional services

- The way customers *consume* widgets and the way clients consume professional services.

HOW SERVICES ARE DIFFERENT

To understand your clients, your firm, and your profession better, you need to understand the concept of *service* better. *Service* is a central factor of even the most basic tangible products such as a sack of potatoes, cold-rolled steel, or electric typewriters. All products have aspects of the tangible and the intangible.

A service is more a process than a product. This means that an activity or process is as much a part of performing a service as is the outcome or product of the service. Most of the value that a manufacturer delivers comes from the tangible product, with only a relatively small value coming from intangible processes such as interpersonal contact, service, and credit terms. Nonetheless, the manufacturer does provide *some* process with the product.

A distributor, such as a department store, a wholesaler, or a convenience store, has slightly more process relative to product than a manufacturer does because a lot of the value added by distributors is the service of getting the product from the manufacturer to the consumer. On the other hand, the service business, relative to dollar value delivered, is almost all process, and very little value is attached to the tangible product. The main difference between goods and services is the different proportion of tangibles provided, as compared to intangibles. Figure 4 illustrates this difference in degree.

The main difference between goods and services is the different proportion of tangibility as compared to intangibility. At one extreme of tangibility would be a commodity such as wheat, gold, or foreign currency. Even these so-called commodities come with differentiating factors such as speed of delivery, quantity, payment terms, and other process-oriented, intangible factors. At the other extreme would be a

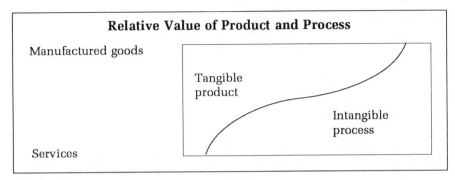

Figure 4

portrait painted on commission. The tangible value of canvas and oil would be negligible compared to the intangible value of the process by which the painting was produced. This spectrum of values attributable to product and process, to tangible and intangible, is illustrated in Figure 5.

Services differ from manufactured goods in one or more of the following characteristics: (1) intangibility, (2) human interaction, and (3) quality control difficulties.

Intangibility

The first fundamental difference: Services are intangible. Professional services usually provide some tangible evidence of the service, such as

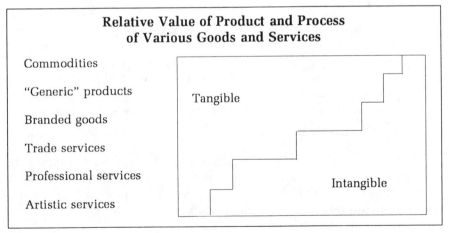

Figure 5

a document, a tax return, a written financial plan, a report, a prescription, or a blueprint. Some professionals refer to these tangible representations as "deliverables" because they are delivered to the client. Nevertheless, the service itself is intangible.

This leads to several interesting corollaries:

- Services involve no transfer of ownership. This causes interesting problems for collection on accounts receivable because services cannot be pledged as collateral, and there is nothing to repossess if the client doesn't pay you. Even if the deliverable were returned to you, it has no value because your service has already been performed.

- Because clients cannot resell your services or pass them on to a third party, the deliverables generally have no residual value. Some exceptions occur, such as a client who engaged an attorney to prepare a standard contract (such as a franchise agreement) for multiple future uses, or a client who has an architect produce a set of plans for housing development units that will be built several times.

- Services cannot be held in inventory. To the extent that your service capacity is unused, it is gone forever. If a professional has available time that is not sold, that time is forever beyond recovery.

Practical Tip:

An exception to the foregoing rule: You can perform portions of some professional services without the presence of a client. Examples include research, planning, drafting reports or documents, quality control reviews, and typing and other preparation of the deliverable. To the extent that these activities can take place at your convenience, you can use these activities to smooth work flow and avoid nonbillable time.

- Services cannot be demonstrated, and a customer or client cannot approve a sample in advance. A service person can often show illustrative deliverables or even examples of actual prior, nonconfidential deliverables prepared for other clients, but the outcome or result of the consumer's own service does not yet exist.

Human Interaction

The second fundamental difference: Services require human interaction to some degree. The service firm and the consumer must come into contact in some way to provide the service. This difference, too, leads to some interesting by-products:

- For most services, the consumer participates in creating the service. For example, a man tells the barber the kind of hairstyle he wants, or a woman tells the doctor where her body hurts.

> **Key Point:** This means that the quality of your professional work is held hostage by your client's cooperation.

- For many services, production and consumption are inseparable and simultaneous. For example, physical examination, treatment, professional consultation, dentistry, and surgery are produced at the instant they are delivered. In such cases, the consumer is in the service "factory."

- Services are usually performed in the presence of the consumer (which may be in the consumer's office, home, or elsewhere) and away from the immediate supervision of management.

> **Key Point:** Thus, production of services is observed more closely by the client than by the firm's management.

Quality Control Difficulties

The first two basic differences of intangibility and human interaction lead to a third fundamental difference: Quality control is very difficult. Here's why:

- Services are performances rather than objects, so quality cannot be engineered in at the factory and delivered intact to the customer. Quality is determined by the conduct of your personnel who actually come into contact with the clients.

- Services are difficult to standardize. In fact, you cannot set complete specifications for uniform quality because of the human element. Services are performed by different people whose performance will vary from person to person and from day to day rather than being manufactured like identical widgets.

Exception: Certain successful franchise operations in fields as varied as fast food, oil changes, and automobile tune-ups have successfully set *minimum* acceptable standards for customer service. (Chapter 17 describes how to set quality standards for your practice.)

Even for services with established technical standards, there can be wide variances among acceptable methods of performance. For example, there are many successful ways to extract a tooth, survey land, audit financial statements, and deliver babies. Even a one-person practice cannot achieve consistency because everyone's performance varies from time to time.

- In some services, consumer participation is intensive, and the consumer affects the process. In these situations, the consumer's input is critical to the quality of the service performance.

- Services cannot be recalled if you do them wrong. Sometimes, you can repeat a service, but if not, apologies and reparations are the only way to mollify the consumer.

- For most services, quality occurs during service delivery, usually in an interaction between customer and contact personnel. Therefore, service quality depends on employee performance, a resource that managers cannot control in the way that they can control tangible goods.

Key Point: Because of these differences, consumers find it more difficult to evaluate service quality than goods quality, and consumer satisfaction is largely subjective.

Whatever else happens, the customer must be satisfied, whether the supplier is a lawn care company or a professional practice. However, professional services are more difficult to evaluate objectively than other services. For example, two clients are more likely to agree on the relative effectiveness of the lawn care than on the relative worth of a partnership agreement or a medical diagnosis. In fact, you may perform a routine service almost identically for two clients, and one client may be satisfied and the other dissatisfied.

The preceding differences have important marketing ramifications that are largely beyond the scope of this book. These can be summarized as follows:

- Goods are produced first, then sold; services are sold first, then produced.

- The value of a service will vary from consumer to consumer, depending on the personal experiences, needs, and desires of each individual consumer. Consequently, value is completely subjective.

When purchasing widgets, the consumer has lots of tangible data to judge quality, such as style, color, and size. When purchasing services, clients don't have much tangible data to evaluate. In most cases, tangible data are limited to the service firm's facilities, equipment, personnel, and deliverables, if any.

FOUR KEY DIFFERENCES IN PROFESSIONAL FIRMS

Professional firms differ further from other types of service firms in four key aspects:

1. Clients of professionals are at greater risk than the purchasers of nonprofessional services or products.

Example: If you buy a consumer product or nonprofessional service such as a tennis ball, a haircut, or an oil change, you risk the money you paid and perhaps a certain amount of inconvenience or disappointment if the product or service is no good. But when you purchase professional services, such as a will, a surgical procedure, a legal defense, a financial plan, or a building design, there is a great deal more riding on the outcome of the service than just the fee. You risk not only the fees paid, but frequently also your fortune, health, or freedom: a huge risk.

---

2. Professional services are customized to respond to the individual needs of the client. Even such routine professional services as drafting a will, preparing a tax return, surveying a lot, extracting a tooth, or removing a mole are performed differently for each

client. A professional practice is a "manufacturer" of an intangible product that is unique to each client.

3. Clients usually cannot judge the internal quality of professional services. This is particularly so with professional services as compared to, say, television repair. With television repair, customers can at least judge the quality of the picture, even if they don't know whether they were overcharged; with automotive repairs, customers know whether the engine is still making funny noises. But with professional services, clients usually do not have the education or the experience to evaluate the internal quality of the service. In other words, *clients do not have a reliable way to judge your competence, even after they have received your services.*

Example: Another accountant had prepared Bob's tax returns for years and had told Bob it was too late to make a certain tax election. I did a little research as a favor to Bob and found a way for him to make the election. Because the other accountant had overlooked this, I reviewed Bob's tax returns for the previous two years, as well as his current return that the other accountant had prepared but Bob had not yet filed. I discovered a particular tax treatment had been taken that resulted in Bob paying about $1,800 too much tax for the three years. I told Bob I could amend the prior year's returns and could redo the current year's return and save him the $1,800 for a fee of about $1,000. Bob was quite pleased and readily became a client.

But Bob asked an interesting question. "Dave, I can see the money you saved me because I can compare you to my prior accountant. But how will I know next year how good you are? Next year I won't have anything to compare you to." I explained to Bob that he would seldom have any way to determine my competence. He would just have to trust and have confidence in me; that is the responsibility of being a professional—*a layperson can seldom judge a professional's work.*

---

4. Professional relationships, once established, can continue for decades, even generations. The client's decision to engage a professional is often not a decision merely to engage in a single transaction, but a commitment to a relationship of indefinite duration. This requires the professional firm to have a different

orientation and a more complex business strategy than other service businesses. The relationships between professionals and their clients only begin when the sale is made. The relationship intensifies once the buying decision has been made and the actual performance of services commences because professional engagements can continue for weeks, months, or even years.

THE "ACE WIDGETS" CUSTOMER RELATIONSHIP

Because of all these differences, customer relationships with widget companies differ from client relationships with professional firms. Customer relationships with manufacturers and retailers, especially consumer goods manufacturers and retailers, are relatively simple. The marketing function separates the production (or purchasing) of physical goods from their consumption. In effect, marketing serves as a screen between the company and the customer. The relationship between the customer and the widget company is indicated in Figure 6.[2]

Basically, the marketing mix is the way the product is provided to the customer. The company produces or purchases the widget then markets it to the customer, who then consumes it. This flow is represented by the heavy downward arrows. The customers give feedback to the company through what they buy and the price at which they buy it.

Figure 6

This flow is indicated by the lighter upward arrows. This feedback determines what the company will produce or purchase in the future and what changes to make in its widget to continue to satisfy its customers.

If you took a college marketing course, you learned about the marketing mix factors of "the four P's":

- Product (which includes its packaging)

- Price

- Place (the store where you buy it)

- Promotion (the advertising and other information available about the manufacturer's reputation).

Ordinarily, when you buy consumer goods, all you see are these four P's. As a customer, you are not aware of the manufacturer's production and administration activities because the marketing mix serves as a screen between the company and you. If the widget is good, you don't really care about the production or administration operations of the manufacturer because you don't interact with them. Your decision to buy and your opinion of the widget are determined by the marketing mix. If the company manages the marketing mix factors well, its customer relationships will be in good shape.

I refer to this relatively simple relationship as the "Ace Widgets" customer relationship. Both manufacturing and distribution companies have this "Ace Widgets" customer relationship in common. Both types of companies *acquire* the product (as one distinct operation); they then *market* the product as another distinct operation.

THE "SMITH & JONES" CLIENT RELATIONSHIP

Professionals do not have such a simple relationship with their clients. Because the production and the consumption of services are simultaneous, these two factors are mixed up with each other, as well as with marketing. Figure 7[3] illustrates the interactive and simultaneous relationship between production and consumption of services. This more complex relationship is what I call the "Smith & Jones" client relationship.

It is important to understand the terms *production* and *consumption* when applied to professional services.

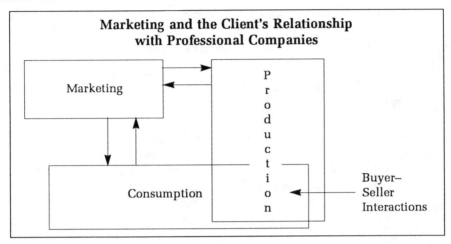

Figure 7

Service Production

When referring to physical products, *production* is the process by which the widget assumes its final form. However, as a professional, you do not deliver a ready-made service to the client because (a) your services cannot be stored in inventory, (b) your services are customized, and (c) your clients take part in the service process.

> **Key Point:** The production of your services includes all activities necessary to satisfy the client's service requirements.

> **Examples:**
> - The production of a lawyer's services starts with developing cordial relations with fellow lawyers with whom he or she might have to negotiate in the future on behalf of clients. It also includes maintaining a library and attending continuing legal education courses.
>
> - The production of an architect's services includes achieving familiarity with building codes, building inspectors, and government employees who influence zoning and building permits.
>
> - The production of a doctor's services includes developing

> relationships with specialists to whom he or she might refer patients as needed, as well as keeping up to date with the latest technical and scientific developments in the field.
>
> • The production of an accountant's services includes maintaining a library of tax, accounting, and financial publications and attending educational seminars.

Often, professionals have too narrow a view of their "product," seeing it in the way that Ace Widgets sees its widgets. They sometimes view the deliverable, or the tangible *representation* of the service, as their "product." Though the tangible representation is important as part of your overall service, it is not the service.

> **Examples:**
> • Lawyer Jane mistakenly views her service as only the drafting of a contract. She views all other activities, such as reviewing the needs of the parties to the transaction, establishing personal rapport, understanding the client's nonfinancial needs, as nonproductive.
> • Architect Jim incorrectly views his services as consisting solely of drawing blueprints and supervising construction.
> • Doctor Carolyn inappropriately sees her services as dealing with patients' diseases, not with the patients themselves.

Nothing could be further from the truth.

> **Key Point:** The view that service is only the production of a deliverable is dangerous for professionals because it defines professional services as little more than a set of deliverables. Instead, think of your services as activities that take place during production and consumption processes that are partially simultaneous, and that *always involve the client.*

In fact, a partner of one firm I consulted with captured the essence of a professional's tangible deliverables when she called them a "souvenir" of the service. In fact, that is what they are in most cases—a souvenir of the actual service.

> **Examples:**
>
> - Lawyer Jane's services are to help the parties to agree and to document the agreement clearly to make future business dealings smooth. If she has performed her service well, the actual contract will never be referred to again; it remains only a souvenir of the agreement facilitation.
>
> - Architect Jim's service is to design a building. The blueprint is primarily a souvenir to evidence the service.

Goods are products; services are performances. Also, because your client is always involved to some extent, the performance is always at least a duet of you and the client, and often a symphony involving many people in both your firm and the client's organization.

Service Consumption

Likewise, consider the consumption of your services in a similarly broad manner. Consumption begins when the client first encounters your practice and continues throughout the client's relationship with you and your firm.

> **Examples:**
>
> - A client calls your office and talks to Steven Secretary. Steven's courtesy and competence are a part of the client's experience.
>
> - Clarissa Client receives an envelope addressed to her. Inside is a letter intended for Charles Clark, another client. This mistake is part of the service of your firm.
>
> - Peter Prospect calls you, based on the recommendation of a friend. The way he is greeted and treated by your receptionist is his first "consumption" of your service.

Whether your personnel realize it or not, they are performing marketing activities throughout the time they interact with clients. This need for continuous, interactive marketing can be better illustrated by considering the client relations life cycle.

THE LIFE CYCLE OF CLIENT RELATIONS

Like interpersonal relationships, client relationships pass through different stages. These stages were described in Chapter 1. Briefly, they are as follows:

Stage 1. Contact prospective clients and make them aware of you and of your firm's availability to serve them.

Stage 2. Nurture and develop relationships with the prospective clients whom you have contacted.

Stage 3. Sell your (and your firm's) services to the prospective client.

Stage 4. Actually perform the service for the client. The objective at this stage is to retain clients through high-quality service and get them back into the loop at the second stage so that they will engage you again in the future.

At any stage, clients can either leave the loop or stay in it and move on to the next stage. This depends only on the success of your interactive marketing. During consumption, the traditional marketing functions have only a slight chance of influencing the client.

> **Key Point:** Traditional marketing can sell clients once. Only interactive marketing can get them to buy again.

THE "MOMENTS OF TRUTH"

When clients experience your services, they receive consequences of those services. Their future actions—whether they keep coming back—depend primarily on how they feel about their experiences. The more they feel rewarded by their interactions, the more likely that they will continue to return. The same applies to prospects and referral sources who visit, telephone, and so forth.

Jan Carlzon, the president of Scandinavian Airlines Systems (SAS), coined the term "moments of truth" to describe these service experiences:[4]

Last year, each of our 10 million customers came in[to] contact with approximately five SAS employees, and this contact lasted an average of 15 seconds each time. Thus, SAS is "created" 50 million times a year, 15 seconds at a time. These 50 million "moments of truth" are the moments that ultimately determine whether SAS will succeed or fail as a company. They are the moments when we must prove to our customers that SAS is their best alternative.

> **Definition:** A *moment of truth* is any event in which a person encounters some aspect of your firm and gets an impression of the quality of your service.

Notice that I said "a person," not just "a client." Lots of people interact with your firm—clients, employees, prospects, referral sources, and potential referral sources. Each interaction is such a moment of truth. Each moment of truth is an opportunity for them to experience some facet of your service and form an opinion of you.

Not all moments of truth involve contact with your personnel. Your advertisements create an impression; they are moments of truth. Driving by your office is a moment of truth. Listening to the recorded message on your telephone answering machine, getting your newsletter, receiving a fee statement—all of these are moments of truth.

> **Key Point:** Moments of truth are almost never neutral. They are either positive or negative to the client.

Like SAS customers, a firm's clients encounter and evaluate personnel, resources, and activities outside the traditional marketing activities. Figure 8 shows another way of looking at the interactions that were shown in Figure 7.

In addition to production, other processes, such as administration, also influence the client, and they are part of the client relationship as well. Figure 2 (see page 32) showed a client's view of your firm.

The figure illustrated three kinds of moments of truth that are decisive to your client relations:

1. Your office environment and other tangible representations of the service (this decisive element is discussed in Chapter 9)

2. Your client-contact personnel, including both professional and other employees who come into contact with the client (the most decisive element because these people deliver services directly to the client; their ability, client sensitivity, and service-minded-

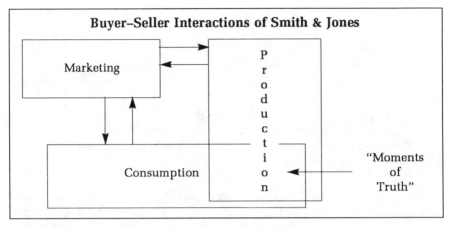

Figure 8

ness weigh heaviest in the clients' evaluation of the quality of your service)

3. The clients who take part in the service process

All of these resources affecting client relations are visible to the client.

I use the plural "clients" for the third kind rather than the singular "client" for a reason. Obviously, individual clients affect the quality of service they receive by the nature of their cooperation with your firm. Clients do not passively consume professional services, but actively participate in the service process. Therefore they have a direct influence on both the service process and its outcome.

> **Examples:**
> - If lawyer Jane's client doesn't communicate his desires to her, she cannot draw a high-quality will.
>
> - If doctor Don's patient will not take his prescribed medication, the patient may not get well.
>
> - If architect Ann's client keeps making changes to the building as it is being designed and constructed, naturally she will have to spend more time, and both fees and building costs will escalate.

Or, as the computer people say, "Garbage in, garbage out." The impact of the individual client is obvious.

What is not so obvious is the impact of other clients on the overall quality of your services. Clients who make unreasonable demands on the firm's resources can impair the service rendered to other clients.

Examples:

- The demanding client who insists you rearrange your schedule to accommodate an unscheduled appointment

- The patient in the doctor's reception room who annoys other patients

---

In addition, a fourth kind of interaction also has impact on client relations: the client's memories of past experiences with your firm, which I call "goodwill." The current service that your client perceives is the result of interaction among the three resources, tempered by this fourth aspect of client relations. I call the memory of past experiences "goodwill" because presumably these memories are good ones or the client would have taken his or her business elsewhere. However, as memories get older, they tend to evaporate. As newer experiences are added to the pool of memories, the goodwill gradually changes color to reflect the client's most recent favorable or unfavorable experiences with you.

Key Point: Every moment of truth is either favorable or unfavorable. It either increases your pool of goodwill with that client or draws from the pool, decreasing its volume.

Figure 2 also shows interactions between the firm's support services and its internal systems, which are invisible to the client.

THE SERVICE PARADE

Visualize dealing with a client in terms of a service parade, a repeatable sequence of events in which various firm personnel meet clients' expectations and needs at each point on the parade route. The parade begins at the very first point of contact between the client and your firm. That may be the instant in which the client sees an advertisement, gets a referral from a friend, sees your name on the building directory, or reads your name in the newspaper. It continues during the actual production/consumption of the service. It ends temporarily when the client considers your current service complete, and it starts again when the client decides to come back for more.

Because consumption and production are overlapping activities, the service parade is not restricted by the screen of the traditional marketing mix (the four P's of product, price, place, and promotion). Rather, client interactions emerge in the way shown in Figure 7. These could be limited, as in

- A patient for whom a doctor performs only a physical examination for an insurance policy

- A client for whom an accountant prepares an individual income tax return once a year and whose communication is solely by mail

- A home owner for whom an engineer prepares a survey for a lending institution

In such cases, the client may do little more than "watch the parade." On the other hand, the interactions could be quite broad and could involve numerous encounters, such as when an architect assists a client in a building's concept, design, finance, and construction, possibly over several years. The client might join the parade or even lead it!

But even a simple parade such as an insurance physical may involve many moments of truth, such as:

1. Receiving a list of physicians from the insurance agent

2. Telephoning the doctor's office for an appointment (When is the telephone answered? How were the receptionist's telephone manners? How convenient are the doctor's office hours?)

3. Finding the doctor's building (How's the neighborhood? How easy is the address to find?)

4. Parking (How far does the patient have to walk? Are there plenty of spaces? How secure is the lot?)

5. Entering the lobby (How's the lobby's appearance? Was it easy to read the building directory for the doctor's office location? to find the right elevator bank?)

6. Reception room (Appearance, comfort, etc.)

7. Ringing bell or otherwise notifying nurse of patient's arrival (Is

the receptionist in the reception area, or is the patient "greeted" by an empty room with a frosted glass window?)

8. Interacting with receptionist

9. Filling out patient information form

10. Interacting with receptionist to return completed form

11. Interacting with other people in waiting room (may be nonverbal)

12. Interacting with nurse (being shown to an examining room)

13. Examining room (Its appearance? temperature? Must the patient sit on an examining table, or is there a chair?)

And so on . . . .

The patient has had more than a dozen moments of truth, and he or she hasn't even met the doctor yet!

Even the most simple, routine service parade can often involve dozens of separate activities, people, and resources. These activities, people, and resources will have varying degrees of influence on the client's experience, either positively or negatively. Almost none will be neutral.

Because these interactions with clients involve so many resources and activities, the Smith & Jones client relationship is much, much broader than the Ace Widget customer relationship. Clients interact with and are influenced by a wide range of firm personnel and other resources that are part of the service process. As mentioned previously, the client is in the service factory, and the service customer evaluates the *manner* in which a service is delivered as well as the service *outcome*.

Key Point: The client relationship with a service business is broader and involves different factors than a customer relationship with the manufacturer or distributor of physical goods.

Recall that when evaluating a carpenter, the client evaluates not only the quarter-inch hole (internal quality) but also the carpenter's courtesy, appearance, and promptness (external quality).

In fact, the marketing mix of service businesses includes three factors in addition to product, price, place, and promotion. Coincidentally, these also begin with "P":

1. People with whom the client comes into contact

2. Procedures performed by your personnel when interacting with the client (moments of truth)

3. Physical evidence of the service—the deliverable, or tangible representation of the service—the "souvenir"

Key Point: The marketing function of professional practices cannot be separated from the production function.

Paraphrasing Jan Carlzon: At SAS, we used to think of ourselves as the sum total of our aircraft, our maintenance bases, our offices, and our administrative procedures. But if you ask our customers about SAS, they won't tell you about our planes or our offices. Instead, they'll talk about their experiences with the people at SAS. SAS is not a collection of material assets but the quality of the contact between an individual customer and the SAS employees who serve the customer directly (or, as we refer to them, our "front line").[5]

Yes, internal quality is necessary for client satisfaction. If SAS airplanes don't arrive on time, it doesn't make much difference how friendly the front line personnel are. So if the service outcome is unsatisfactory, your clients will not be happy regardless of how good the moments of truth. But internal quality alone is not sufficient for a good report card from clients. If the plane is on time, you will still think it was a lousy flight if you are treated indifferently by the airline personnel. If you were to ask clients to describe high-quality service, they would be more likely to mention aspects of external quality than those of internal quality. They would list things such as returning phone calls promptly, meeting deadlines, and keeping in touch.

Key Point: External quality is actually more important than internal quality to clients, so long as internal quality is adequate.

Moreover, because clients tend to perceive all professionals as equally technically competent,

---

Key Point: External quality is especially important where clients are incapable of evaluating internal quality.

Because of the greater importance of external quality, you and your firm's way of handling client contacts can compensate for *temporary* problems with internal quality, such as an unforeseen delay. But, no matter how good at client relations your frontline people are, external quality will not compensate for an overall lower internal quality. So acceptable internal quality is a prerequisite for successful external quality.

> **Key Point:** Quality assurance must happen *before* the service is performed, rather than *after*, as would be the case in manufacturing widgets. Such quality assurance is limited to training, supervision, and motivation of frontline personnel.

In summary, the Ace Widgets customer relationship is based primarily on tangible factors and internal quality and only slightly on intangibles and external quality; the Smith & Jones client relationship relies much more on intangibles and external quality. The Ace Widgets customer relationship is relatively simple; the Smith & Jones client relationship is highly complex.

So professional firms *are* different, not only from widget companies, but also from other types of service businesses. Also, knowledge about Ace Widget customer relations is insufficient to manage the Smith & Jones client relationship. Because of these numerous basic differences between widget companies and professional practices, management theories and practices that work for widget companies do not necessarily work when applied to professional firms.

NOTES

1. Buck Rogers, *The IBM Way*, New York: Harper & Row, 1986, p. 125.
2. Adapted from Christian Grönroos, *Strategic Management and Marketing in the Service Sector* (Report No. 83-104), Cambridge, MA: Marketing Science Institute, May 1983, p. 20. Used by permission of the publisher.
3. Adapted from Grönroos, p. 21. Used by permission of the publisher.
4. Jan Carlzon, *Moments of Truth*, Cambridge, MA: Ballinger Publishing Company, 1987, p. 3.
5. Carlzon, pp. 2–3.

11

What Do You Want to Be Famous For?

The simple fact of today's business life: You cannot be best at everything; you cannot be all things to all people. Most firms claim to be the "best." Obviously, only one can be truly the best, so how do you account for the sincere belief by most professionals that they are in fact *the* best?

The truth is that you can be best at *something* because there are different kinds of excellence. Similarly, several firms can legitimately claim to be the biggest, depending on whether you measure size in terms of total personnel, professional personnel, revenues, or the square footage or number of the firm's offices. Also, the defining parameters of the firms you include in your measurement affect whether your firm is biggest (e.g., the biggest in New York City may not be the biggest in New York state).

Some firms can be "best" at having prestigious clients; others may be best at challenging and innovative work; or profitability; or prompt turnaround; etc. A good professional firm can be best at any one or a few of these things and thus legitimately claim it is "best." But it cannot be best at everything.

As Zig Ziglar said in one of his speeches, "Avoid the wandering generality; go for the meaningful specific." It is not enough for you to have a reputation for some generalized, abstract "excellence." To stand above the crowd, your firm must be "famous" for specific qualities among certain target markets. What do you want to be famous for? What is your vision of excellence?

Excellence is possible in every point on the scale, from Chevrolets to Cadillacs, from McDonald's to Maxim's. But lots of people confuse excellence with high price. They think they have to build Cadillacs to be excellent. Not so. Excellent firms share a common definition of the kind of excellence they are trying to achieve. It is a question of focus.

The kind of excellence your firm pursues is more a matter of the personal taste of the partners than anything else. Do you like to work with Fortune 1000 companies, or entrepreneurs? Is your penchant wealthy retirees or younger active employed clients? Would you rather work with individuals or with companies? Which "best" you want to be will have direct impact on your marketing, recruiting, training, organization structure, and almost everything else in your firm's culture.

5

Positioning Your Firm in the Marketplace[1]

In most professions, people see firms of similar size as substantially identical. They think, "All Big Eight CPA firms are alike," or "Smith & Company is a typical small, local firm," or "All big law firms are alike." (At press time, several mergers were in progress, which may reduce the "Big Eight" to the "Big Five.")

Differentiation is the essence of competition. If everything can be differentiable, even such so-called commodities as steel, shares of stock, chickens, and money, think how much easier it is to differentiate such a unique, customized "product" as a professional service.

> **Key Point:** The advantage of market positioning is that it creates product differentiation in a profession where most people see all firms as virtually identical.

A well-defined identity in your marketplace informs clients, referral sources, and prospects about qualities of your practice that distinguish you from your competitors. This distinctive image helps you attract those clients whom you are best able to serve.

Further, because your services are intangible, proper market position can help give tangibility to your services by packaging your firm's services. This encourages clients to perceive your external quality, and it increases client satisfaction.

Positioning is a part of your corporate culture. When your personnel clearly understand your basic thrust of client service and what kind of excellence you stand for, they have a sense of purpose and direction that promotes better client-mindedness, more effective teamwork, and greater productivity.

Specific advantages you gain from appropriate positioning of your firm:

- Achieve greater growth by attracting the specific target markets you want to serve.

- Increase client satisfaction because the type of excellence you are producing is the type your clients want.

- Develop the firm's identity as separate from its principals. This creates a better goodwill factor, and it adds value to the practice should the principals decide to retire or to sell the firm.

- Respond to increased competition. Your competitors are becoming more sophisticated marketers. If you want to get your share of new business and keep your current clients happy, market positioning helps by providing them something real they can recognize.

- Attract, retain, and motivate personnel. Good positioning attracts employees who want to do the kind of work you specialize in, or who want to work with the kinds of clients you serve.

MARKET POSITION AND STRATEGIC PLANNING

Strategic planning for market positioning answers three questions: (1) How are you currently perceived in your market? (2) How do you want to be perceived? (3) What are the most cost-effective steps to shape current perceptions about your practice into the form you want them to take?

How Are You Currently Perceived?

Chapter 6 describes how to obtain this valuable information. Once you find out how you and your firm are currently perceived, you must determine the following:

- In what areas does your public perception not fit the reality of the practice as you perceive it?

- What previously unrecognized strengths did you discover?

- What previously unrecognized weaknesses must you correct?

- Are there any marketplace opportunities you were not aware of?

- Are there any threats to your existing markets or services that you should guard against?

How Do You Want to Be Perceived?

Once you know how you are perceived, you are ready to consider how you want to be perceived. An effective way of doing this is to develop a mission statement for your firm. Chapter 7 covers how to develop your mission statement. You can then use your mission statement to help develop your market position.

> **Definition**: The *market position statement* is the message you want to communicate about your practice—the distinctive image of your firm that you want in the minds of your clients, prospects, referral sources, and competitors. Your market position is based both on *facts* about your firm and on public *perceptions* of those facts.

Your image shouldn't be left to chance. By studying the ways you can differentiate your firm from others, you can gain more new business. There are several types of market position. You can differentiate your firm from others by any of the following types of market position:

- The technical skills your firm possesses, such as expertise in tax planning, structural engineering, computer systems, corporate law, etc.

- The market segment your firm serves, such as small businesses, high-income individuals, retirees, publicly owned companies, or start-up companies

- The industries your firm serves, such as providing a wide range of services, but specifically offering those services to a few special industries

- The price range of your services

- The position of your firm relative to a competitor (e.g., Avis: "We're number two, so we try harder.")

Definition: *Positioning* is a process of developing and communicating a firm's unique identity.

A brief analysis of some familiar companies may help to illustrate perceptions of market position, based on the advertising I have seen (the marketing departments of these companies might not agree, but this is the way *I* perceive these companies):

- Charles Schwab, fast execution

- Merrill Lynch, the optimist's broker, "Bullish on America"

- Dean Witter, personal relationships, "Everybody is somebody at Dean Witter"

- Apple computers, user friendly

- IBM, old reliable

- Compaq, technical leadership

- Maytag, super reliability

- Mercedes, technical superiority

- Cadillac, status and luxury

- Lincoln Town Car, as good as Cadillac, but cheaper

- Volvo, safety

The development of your mission statement and a plan for regularly obtaining client feedback (discussed in Chapter 6) will enable you to determine exactly what is most marketable about your firm. Some marketing experts call your firm's most marketable feature(s) your "unique selling proposition" or "USP."

Definition: The *USP* is the single most important characteristic that both distinguishes you from your competitors and *is valuable to your clients.*

Given your clients' current perceptions of your firm, your mission statement, and your client feedback plan, you can determine the characteristics that distinguish your firm from your competition. Whatever market position you select should meet the following objectives:

1. It should clearly differentiate your firm and its services from your competitors. The benefit premise behind the position must be clear and compelling to clients.

2. You should be able to commit to it. All partners should believe in it and support it.

3. You should be able to make it work operationally. It should require only resources and capabilities you have or can reasonably acquire.

4. It should be communicable to clients in concrete, client-centered terms.

5. It should be demonstrable to every person in the firm. You must be able to make it real and experiential for both your personnel and your clients.

How Effective Are Your Current Marketing Efforts?

Questions To Think About:
- What marketing efforts are you making now?
- What marketing have you tried in the past?
- What worked? Why?
- What didn't work? Why didn't it work?
- What is your competition doing? How well is it working?
- Who are your key competitors?
- What are public perceptions of your competition?
- What segments of the market are they not serving? Why not?
- What services are they not offering? Why not?

HOW TO DEVELOP A DISTINCTIVE
IMAGE OR "PERSONALITY"

After analyzing your position among your competitors and how you are currently perceived by your "target markets", you can decide whether you have a clearly perceived position. If you do not, or if your perceived position is not the one you want, you can change your position. That is the subject of tactical planning.

Which market segments you choose to target will influence how you choose to position your firm. Other factors include

- How your competitors position themselves
- Which practice characteristics are important to your firm's target clients
- What services you want to render
- What fees you want to charge

The market position statement should start with a single sentence that states your USP. I'll repeat the definitions:

> **Definition:** The USP is the single most important characteristic that both distinguishes you from your competitors and *is valuable to your clients.*

Note that the USP isn't just the most important characteristic, such as "high technical quality." You might have that in common with lots of your competitors. Instead, you are looking for distinctive traits that will score high in importance with your clients. Your USP should be stated in terms of benefit to your clients and not in terms of features of your firm. Chapter 8 covers ways to differentiate your practice. This chapter considers how to get your message across to your target markets.

> **Examples:**
> - "When it absolutely, positively has to be there overnight."
> - "When you care enough to send the very best."

These are not just sales slogans; they are unique benefits appealing to specific segments of each company's potential market.

Finding your USP is not easy. That's why most firms don't do it. But if you approach the task with skillful analysis and creative thinking, you can develop a USP that will make your marketing task easier.

Here are some things to think about in selecting your USP.

- Prestige—How is it defined?

- Low fees—You get what you pay for.

- Service—How do your clients measure it?

- Special expertise—How can you be sure that your clients notice and perceive it?

- Aggressive or passive—Do some market segments attract personality types who would respond differently to different degrees of assertiveness?

- Friendliness—Do some market segments have cultures or attract personality types who would respond differently to friendliness or to "professional aloofness"?

How much quality is enough? Just how high do you want to go in exceeding your clients' expectations? High quality is "playing the offense not the defense." It means actively pleasing clients with external quality, not just passively protecting them with internal quality.

Things can happen to cause you to alter your market position statement over time. Reevaluate it every year or two or whenever you make a major marketing decision.

PUTTING IT ALL TOGETHER

Tactical planning involves writing down both your goals and your strategies for achieving those goals. The end result of a good tactical plan is *effective action*. All the previous thinking is worthless without action. Strategies should include

- What will be done

- Who will do the "whats"

- When the "whats" will be done

The managing partner should monitor, report, and follow up on the chosen strategies. What gets measured, gets done.

Your Target Markets

Once you develop your market position statement, you must develop a strategic plan to take your message to the marketplace. This will require a significant commitment of time and resources.

Development of a market position statement is a pointless exercise unless you follow through by communicating your position to your marketplace. Omitting this follow-through would be like purchasing an expensive tool and letting it gather dust. Instead, apply some energy and imagination to using that tool, and create useful results.

The partners must have consistent objectives for the practice and must agree on its strengths and the image they want to communicate. The process of obtaining that agreement may require a partners' retreat.

There must be a marketing project manager with the skills and objectivity to follow the marketing program from strategic analysis through creation of the market position statement to development and implementation of the marketing plan. The project manager should possess, or have access to, significant marketing expertise.

Who are your possible target markets?

- Current clients
- Potential clients
- Current referral sources
- Potential referral sources
- Opinion leaders
- Employees
- Business media
- Professional colleagues
- Competitors

Obviously, the relative value of communicating your message to the various target markets is different for each target population. It is far more valuable to reach employees than competitors, for instance.

Questions To Think About:

- Which target markets *must* your message reach?
- Which target markets do you avidly *want* your message to reach?
- Which target markets would you *like* your message to reach?

These various target markets form their impressions of your firm from countless perceptions and interactions, many of which you may not be aware of. Because of this, you must consistently reinforce your USP with each available resource in the communication process.

Available Resources

The following resources may be used to project your firm's image:

- Personnel
- Office location and decor
- Visual identity, such as logo, stationery, business cards
- Speeches
- Seminars
- Brochures
- Advertising, such as direct mail and newsletters
- Proposals
- Articles written by your personnel
- Media-generated articles about your firm and its personnel

Charting the Course

The keys to making market positioning work for you are *focus* and *consistency*.

To communicate your positioning in a professional manner, you will need outside professional assistance. Depending on the ultimate scope of your marketing strategy and budget, you may use any of the following professional assistance:

- Marketing consultants
- Consultants to your target market segment
- Public relations firms
- Advertising agencies
- Direct mail specialists
- Graphic designers
- Interior designers
- Copywriters

However, regardless of the assistance you seek, positioning must come first. If you don't know where you are going, if you don't know the image—the USP—you wish to project, you have no way to gauge your progress, and you will find it impossible to project a consistent image to your target markets.

Questions To Think About:

- Which of the various communication resources is most cost-effective to reach your "must-reach" target markets?
- Which of the various communication resources is most cost-effective to reach your "want-to-reach" target markets?
- Which of the various communication resources is most cost-effective to reach your "like-to-reach" target markets?

Notice that you have been making important value judgments throughout this process.

1. You have created a matrix of possible resources that you could use to project your desired image.
2. You have evaluated how important it is to reach each of your target markets.
3. You have evaluated the cost-effectiveness of each possible resource against each target market.

The next step is to put it all together with a tactical plan in order to include the right mix of actions to achieve your goals.

Examples:

- Client seminars
- Articles
- Speeches
- Trade association activity
- Newsletters
- Target influential contacts
- Public relations

NOTES

1. For more information on this subject, see David A. Bradlow, "Positioning the Accounting Firm," *The CPA Journal*, December 1985, pp. 10–18.

6

What Do People *Really* Think of You?

Before you can take action to move your firm (and your firm's market position) to where you want to be, you need to know where you are now and where your clients would want you to be.

FIND OUT WHAT YOUR CLIENTS NEED AND WANT

Discover the critical determinants for quality used by your clients and target markets. In other words, what do *your* clients and targets need, want, and expect from you? What is important to them?

British Airways (BA) began a "Customer First" program and did a market research study to find out how they stacked up against their competition. The study probed what people considered most important in their flying experiences. Of all the statements made by air travelers, four factors stood out above all others as being critically important. What really surprised BA's management was that *two of the four factors* were a surprise to them. Here are the four factors. How might they apply to your practice?

1. "Care and concern." This was at the top of BA's passengers' list.

2. "Spontaneity." Passengers wanted to know that frontline people are authorized to think. When a problem comes up that isn't

covered in the procedure book, can frontline people use some discretion—can they fiddle with the system for the passenger's benefit?

3. "Problem solving." Passengers think frontline people should be skilled at comprehending the nature of the problem and solving it.

4. "Recovery." If something goes wrong, will anyone make a special effort to make it go right? Will frontline people go out of their way to make amends to the passenger? Does anyone in the company make an effort to offset the negative effects of the screwup? Does anyone even know how to offer a simple apology?

The two factors that BA was surprised about were spontaneity and recovery. Don Porter of BA said this:

We were struck by a rather chilling thought: if two of these four primary evaluation factors were things we had never consciously considered, what were the chances that our people in the service areas were paying attention to them? For the first time, we were really beginning to understand and come to terms with the real motivational factors that are embedded in our customer's nervous system.[1]

Fortunately, you can determine what is important to your clients and how well you are currently doing at the same time; that's what this chapter is about. Before you decide how to position your firm in the marketplace, find out how your various target markets already perceive you and how *they* define quality.

How do you find out what clients, prospects, and referral sources think? Ask them. There are a variety of ways to listen to your target populations; all are worthwhile. Your client—and your image—is a moving target. Clients' needs, wants, perceptions, and values change over time. To be the most effective in satisfying your clients and target clients, you need to spot those changes while, or before, they occur.

Practical Tips:

- Provide a toll-free "800" number so that your out-of-town clients can call you.

- Call three clients a week from a list of 50 good, bad, and so-

so clients. Call a new client and one recently lost. Ask why the new one chose your firm and why the lost one left.

- Regularly invite clients to visit your offices and show them around. Introduce them to everyone in your office who works on their services, especially your support people. Let both your frontline people and the clients attach faces to the voices they may usually deal with only over the telephone.

WHY BOTHER?

You can obtain many benefits by listening to your target markets:

- Determine the level of satisfaction with your firm and its services

- Identify additional services that clients want

- Identify areas where service can be improved

- Evaluate the performance of your personnel

- Increase client goodwill; especially, identify and improve relationships with clients who (a) are relatively satisfied but have not been recommending you to their contacts or (b) are dissatisfied and might have sought professional services elsewhere.

In fact, most professionals do a lot of assuming and guessing about their clients. They are like the directors of the art museum mentioned by Albrecht and Zemke.[2] The directors wanted to attract more visitors to the museum. They surveyed the people who came into the museum on a certain day to find out more about their interests. Museum employees handed out survey cards as visitors entered the museum, and the visitors dropped the cards in a box as they left. One of the key questions on the survey was, "Why did you come into the museum today?" The most frequent answer was, "Because it was raining outside." The second most frequent answer was, "To use the bathroom."

Albrecht and Zemke also relate the story of a hotel that surveyed its employees on what factors are important in a good coffee break. They asked the server who attended the coffee table, the food and beverage manager, and the manager of the hotel. All agreed that the coffee should be of high quality, well-brewed, and served in attractive china. It should be served from a polished, elegant coffee urn on a clean, attractively arranged table. But when the people attending a management workshop in a hotel were surveyed, they did not mention *any* of these factors. They wanted to get through the line quickly without having to mill around. They wanted the service area located close to rest rooms and telephones. None of the workshop participants even mentioned the quality or flavor of the coffee. Albrecht and Zemke conclude, "What we think is obvious may not even be true."[3]

David A. Garvin[4] concurs:

> The pervasiveness of these errors is difficult to determine. Anecdotal evidence suggests that many U.S. companies lack hard data and are thus more vulnerable than they need be. One survey found that 65% of executives thought that consumers could readily name—without help—a good quality brand in a big-ticket category like major home appliances. But when the question was actually posed to consumers, only 16% could name a brand for small appliances, and only 23% for large appliances.

We see the world not as *it* is, but as *we* are. In other words, our preconceived notions cause us to see what we expect to see. Similarly, many partners form opinions about their clients based on long years of experience but very little hard data. They have theories about what is important to clients, but they usually have done no real research. Otherwise, why would partners so often argue about what is important to clients? No matter how well you think you know your clients, referral sources, and targets, don't be surprised when others have a different opinion than you think they have.

Key Point—Perception Principle Number One: Others always perceive a firm differently from the way the firm perceives itself.

Key Point—Perception Principle Number Two: Others perceive a firm differently from the way the firm *thinks* it is perceived.

Key Point—Perception Principle Number Three: Different groups perceive the firm differently from one another.

This shouldn't surprise you because others sit "on the other side of the desk." In other words, there is a fundamentally different *viewpoint*:

naturally, there will be a different *perception*. The only way to discover what your target and existing clients truly think of your firm is to ask them.

As Robert Denney[5] points out, the idea of asking people how they feel about the firm and its work may be upsetting to some professionals.

- Some feel that clients are not qualified to judge their work. Agreed, at least from an internal quality viewpoint. Yet clients do judge your work every time they write a check to pay your fees. Wouldn't it be better to know what they think?

- Other professionals feel that it is degrading to ask clients and referral sources what they think. But is it better to remain ignorant or, even worse, to labor under a false assumption?

- Still others think that the survey invites previously unfelt criticism. However, the clients' critical feelings and views already exist. Would you rather discover them and have a chance to resolve them? Or would you rather not find out whether there are problems and either risk losing clients or risk not getting the referrals you could be getting?

In fact, most people are impressed that you are interested in their opinion of your firm and how well they are being served. The mere fact that you take the time to ask their opinion is a tremendous boost to public relations. Also, after listening to your referral sources and your existing and target clients, you will learn a lot about how your firm is perceived by others.

This gives you four valuable pieces of information, which I call your "SWOT"—an acronym for strengths, weaknesses, opportunities, and threats:

1. Favorable points you can strengthen and market to other clients and potential clients (strengths)

2. Unfavorable points you will want to correct (weaknesses)

3. Opportunities in the marketplace you may have overlooked

4. Potential threats in the environment you may have overlooked

Which tools you use to listen to your existing and target clients is up to you—the more, the better. The feedback program described in the next section is more expensive than the surveys discussed later in this chapter, but it yields different and richer data. Face-to-face communication is best because you can use words, voice tone, and body language simultaneously. Face-to-face communication is especially important when the conversation is difficult or ambiguous or when there are differences in background or opinion between sender and receiver.[6]

By the way, the same comments apply regarding listening to your employees.

IMPLEMENT A FEEDBACK PROGRAM

One way to listen to people is with a feedback program in which you give clients, referral sources, and targets an opportunity to sound off about your firm via personal interviews.

The feedback program is actually a quality control program for public relations. It's different from regular communications with clients and referral sources because it is done on your agenda, not the client's or source's, and because the client is not paying for your time. In effect, you reverse the normal flow between you and your clients because they are helping you with your problem instead of you helping them with theirs.

Also, a feedback program helps focus on your target market, which may not be the same as your current market. You spend a great deal of time with your clients, but that time is spent with a cross-section of all your current clients and does not specifically address the needs and wants of those types of clients you have targeted for future emphasis and growth.

The Interviewees

The program is conducted via personal interviews with those persons whose opinions you value most. Obviously, you can't conduct a personal interview with 100 people. Therefore, select those people whose opinions are most important. Robert Denney[7] suggests these two classifications of clients:

1. *Major clients.* These are your largest fee clients—the ones who, if lost, would have a significant impact. They usually include less than 5 percent of your total number of clients, though they might comprise a much larger percentage of your revenues.

2. *Key clients.* These are smaller fee clients who are important for

one of two reasons: (1) They have potential to become major clients—i.e., either their operations could grow much bigger or you could do much more work for them. Or (2) they can be important in recommending clients to you—i.e., they are or have the potential to be referral sources. Public figures, bankers, attorneys, CPAs, stockbrokers, and other actual or potential referral sources are always key clients.

To Denney's classifications, I add the following of my own:

3. *Referral sources.* Survey referral sources for the target groups you have selected. These are people who are not clients and may never become clients for a variety of reasons, but who are or can be referral sources for the types of clients on which you want to build the future of your practice.

4. *Targets.* Persons in the market segments you consider your targets—whether current clients, prospective clients, current referral sources, or prospective referral sources.

Within those four categories, try to obtain a representative cross-section of clients and referral sources to obtain opinions about:

• All partners in your firm

• Your basic or routine services

• Your exceptional or specialty services

• Different industries in which you specialize

• Different geographic locations (both yours, if you have more than one office, and your clients, if they are located in geographically diverse areas)

• Length of time the person has been a client or referral source

• Size of client's operation

• Amount of annual fees generated

The Interviewers

Who should do the interviews? Ideally, an independent researcher with good communication skills, knowledge of interviewing techniques, analytical abilities, familiarity with the professional environment, and an extensive background in marketing. Some firms hire a marketing consultant to do the reviews and interpret the results. This also prevents the interviewer (or interviewers if you use more than one) from getting bogged down in some current problem of the client so that they never get to the purpose of the survey.

If you cannot afford a professional interviewer, you will have to rely on homegrown talent. If so, the interview is best done by a partner who is not in charge of the client's account or who does not have the primary relationship with the referral source. It is easier for clients or sources to discuss things candidly with someone other than the person with whom they interact on a regular basis.

The biggest advantage of using a professional interviewer is not the technical skill of the researcher—although that is usually superior to using a partner. The biggest advantage is that the outsider will actually *do* the interviews. Many firms approach a feedback program with good intentions, but my experience is that firms who try to do it themselves usually manage to do only two or three interviews before the press of clients or other "more urgent" business stops the process. The intention is the best; it's the follow-through that is lacking.

The Setup

The best way to set up this type of interview is for the partner who normally handles the client's affairs to contact the client or source first, explain that the firm has this procedure with all its important clients and referral sources, and that Interviewer X will call soon to set up an appointment. The primary-contact partner should urge the client to be candid with the interviewer. This way, the client or source does not feel that one person is "spying" on another. Always advise interviewees in advance of the purpose of the interview. This gives them time to think and also emphasizes the importance you place on their opinion.

The interviews are best held in the interviewee's office. People are more comfortable there; it is more convenient for them; and you can better control the length of the interview by leaving when you believe you have enough information.

> **Key Point:** The sole purpose of the meeting is to get feedback regarding your firm's service to the client or that source's perceptions of your firm. Do not try to sell additional services or to get additional referrals. Ask questions. And listen.

Questions for the Client Feedback Program

There is an art to knowing what information to look for and how to ask the right questions. Preformatted questions can be dangerous, as illustrated in the following example:

> If you ask people attending a concert at intermission time how they like the music, the seats, and the refreshments, they will give you their evaluations. But if you forget to ask them how they came to the concert hall, you will probably never discover that many of them find the neighborhood threatening and often don't come to that hall because they are apprehensive about leaving their cars parked in an undesirable area.[8]

The people the concert sponsors really should be talking to are their *potential* customers: The ones who should be coming but aren't. Presumably, potential customers who find the area particularly forbidding won't come at all and thus will not be included in the interviewees because they *never* come to that neighborhood.

And don't just analyze your complaint files; only about 4 percent of clients who feel dissatisfied for any reason will ever complain. You are more interested in the majority who would never dream of complaining; they just won't come back.

David A. Garvin[9] relates this example of how Singapore International Airlines (SIA) listened to the vocal minority and ignored the silent majority. SIA has a reputation for excellent service. Nevertheless, their market share declined in the early 1980s. SIA didn't think quality problems were the cause because data on service complaints showed steady improvement during the period. Only later, after SIA surveyed customers, did they see the problem with their former measures. Service had indeed declined and was responsible for the loss of market share. Complaint counts did not register problems because the number of passengers who complained was small, and they were mostly Europeans and Americans rather than Asians, the largest percentage of SIA passengers. SIA also had failed to capture data about its competitors' service improvements.

These are the points to cover:

- What is your opinion of our firm and its services?

- What is your opinion of people in the firm with whom you have come into contact?

- Do you feel that we have responded to you promptly? Kept you informed? Followed up adequately?

- Have we helped you in other areas besides those for which you originally retained our services?

- What other existing services do you anticipate needing from us in the next five years?

- What new services would you like us to offer?

- What distinguishes us from our competitors?

- When have you felt that we let you down?

- In what areas do we need to improve?

- Have you recommended us to others?

You might also want to ask similar questions about the interviewee's former firm (if the interviewee is a client) and about the interviewee's perceptions of your competitors (particularly if the interviewee is a referral source or target).

Finally, the interviewer should ask the following two questions:

- Would you recommend us to other people if we asked you to?

- May we use you as a reference? (Obviously, if the interviewee has been negative, the interviewer would not even ask this.)

The last question is the most important one because if the interviewees agree, you can count on their honesty and sincerity. If they refuse, one of two situations exists: (1) Some people just do not want their name used as a reference, even if they are delighted with you. Accept this. (2) Most of the time a "no" answer indicates that they have not divulged some other reason for being dissatisfied. It means that they have not told you something that is very important for you to know. Tactfully dig for it. Try questions such as these:

- Is there something you hesitated to tell me that I really ought to know in order to improve our ability to serve you?

- Is there something you didn't tell me because you thought it might embarrass someone?

- Is there something you didn't tell me because you thought it might make me think less of someone?

- Is there something you didn't tell me because you thought it might reflect poorly on *[the primary-contact partner]*?

If you run a regular feedback program, you will keep your finger on the pulse of your clients and referral sources. Also, your target clients are "moving targets." Today's needs and wants will change over time, sometimes quite quickly and dramatically. The feedback program helps you anticipate and respond to changes in your market.

CASE STUDY

One of my clients, whom I will call "Brown & Davis," decided to conduct what they called "a small scale market research project" to learn how they were perceived by clients and contacts, to determine awareness of the range of services they offer, and "expectations of quality, service, and value for money." They used their public relations counsel to conduct personal interviews. The partners nominated clients and referral sources, and twenty names were selected.

Each interview took place in the respondent's office and generally lasted from 30 minutes to one hour, consisting of a brief introductory chat and then the following questions:

- What firm were you with before choosing Brown & Davis?
- What services did you use them for?
- How would you rate them on those services?

A = Excellent
B = Good
C = Average
D = Below Average
E = Poor

- How would you rate your former firm (using A, B, etc.) on:
  - Technical ability
  - Understanding of your business
  - Value for money
  - Speed of service
  - Suggesting ideas
  - Contributing to your success
  - Overall
- How many people in the old firm did you have contact with?
- Why did you decide to change?
- How did you hear of Brown & Davis?
- What had you heard about Brown & Davis?

- How did you make contact with Brown & Davis?
- What impressed you about them?
- What failed to impress you?
- How would you rate Brown & Davis (using A, B, etc.) on:
  - Technical ability
  - Understanding of your business
  - Value for money
  - Speed of service
  - Suggesting ideas
  - Contributing to your success
  - Overall
- What services do you use Brown & Davis for?
- What other services are you aware of that they offer?
- How often do you have contact with them?
- Who initiates that contact?
- Would you describe Brown & Davis as "reactive" or "proactive?"
- How large a firm do you think they are?
- Do you think they are expanding, contracting, or staying the same?
- Do you receive anything from them on a regular basis, such as a newsletter or tax planner?
- What do you think of what you receive from them?
- Would you recommend Brown & Davis to others?
- What are they good at?
- What are they bad at?
- Would you care to make any other comments?

The interviewer reported, "During the formal section, I took notes, and the respondents were generally helpful but slightly guarded. At the end of the questions, I closed my notebook and thanked the respondents for their time. Interestingly, at this point, many respondents, feeling their ordeal was over and flattered to be asked their views, continued talking and offered a number of [additional] comments. These comments proved to be the most incisive and, as a result, I concentrated on completing the formal interviews quickly in order to leave time for the 'real' interview."

SURVEY YOUR CLIENTS

Other ways to find out how you are perceived include (a) mail surveys, (b) in-office surveys, or (c) telephone surveys. Unlike interviews, these can be requested of all clients, referral sources, and targets. The cost per survey is very low. Sample size will vary, depending on the type of survey you use and the nature of your practice.

Practical Tips:

- Ask relevant questions. Ask only questions important to your practice. Some professionals go overboard once they start designing a questionnaire; they just don't know when to stop. Don't ask for personal employment history, career aspirations, place of birth, etc.

- Keep it brief. Don't ask clients to spend more than 5 minutes to respond to a mail survey.

- Set a deadline. Tell participants the deadline for all surveys.

- Survey inactive clients, too. You may find out why they are inactive so that you can prevent other active clients from becoming inactive. Also, the reminder of receiving a survey may reactivate some of them.

- Pretest all surveys. Make sure the questions are clear and can be tabulated meaningfully. One firm discovered that one question on their survey should have been phrased differently. They asked clients to rank, 1 through 6, six different qualities of the firm (scope of services, technical expertise, and so forth). Many ranked these characteristics by weight rather than in order, i.e., gave the ranking of 1, for most important, to more than one quality.

- Don't survey more than once or twice a year.

- Watch your timing. Don't try to survey around Christmas or New Year's.

Mail Surveys

This is the most popular method of gathering data from clients. Mail surveys can be anonymous, and they provide definitive, quantifiable results. For a mail survey, try to send out at least 500 questionnaires to get at least 100 responses. Don't expect more than 20 to 40 percent response. For best results, time mail surveys to arrive Tuesday, Wednesday, or Thursday.

Practical Tips:

- Send a cover letter explaining your intent.

- Motivate participation by stressing your need for client information so that you can continue providing the best service and serving their future needs.

- Emphasize your deadline. Mention your cutoff date.

- Use a real stamp on the reply envelope. To many people a postage meter stamp doesn't seem like money. If you put a real stamp on the reply envelope, people know you are serious about wanting their opinion.

- Clients should be able to answer anonymously on a mail survey.

- Check your sample size. If you haven't received your 100 responses within two weeks, send a second letter and reply form to all clients in your survey. Thank them if they have already sent in their survey. Urge those who have not responded to reply within the next week.

There are many sources for mail surveys, such as consultants or professional societies, or you may develop your own from the sample list of questions in this chapter. You can pick what you consider the most important areas in your service and design your own mail survey to be any length you choose.

Telephone Surveys

Some firms also use telephone surveys, particularly after completing a service for a client. A relatively low-salaried person can conduct up to 50 of these a day. The disadvantage is that you might not reach a lot of clients. Also, the client has no assurance of anonymity. The interviewer can preface the interview by saying that the client may request his or her survey responses to be kept confidential and that the client's name would not then be attached to the survey data, but clients might not believe it.

Practical Tips:

- Keep calls consistent. To avoid bias, one person should make all the calls and use the same script and tone of voice each time.

- Identify the caller. Your caller should give his or her name, identify your firm clearly, and state the purpose of the survey. "Hello, Ms. Smith. This is Betty Jones for the medical office of Dr. Thomas Doe. I'm calling to find out whether you have been satisfied with the services we have provided you in the past year."

- Respect the client's time. Your caller should ask, "Do you have a few minutes to answer a few questions?" If not, find out when to call back.

- Ask the questions. Once the client gives permission, the caller should read each question clearly and note the answers on a response sheet.

- Thank the client.

Exhibit 1 is an actual telephone survey form used by a large local firm (over 100 professionals).

Written In-Office Surveys

In-office surveys are only appropriate for professions in which most clients come to the professional's office for service. Examples would be doctors, podiatrists, veterinarians, dentists, and chiropractors. This type of survey would not be appropriate for attorneys, accountants, engineers, and other professionals who render service outside of their offices, because they would not get a representative sample—just the opposite, in fact, because the largest clients are served in their own offices.

Written in-office surveys only sample active clients who are in your office for appointments.

Practical Tips:

- Invite participation. Your receptionist can invite clients to complete a survey and hand them a pen and the questionnaire on a clipboard. This personal touch encourages a better response than leaving a pile of blank questionnaires on the coffee table with a sign.

Client Satisfaction Survey

Client _____   Contact Person ___ [at client] _____

Primary firm contact _____   Secondary firm contact _____

Type of engagement _____   Telephone _____

   Hello, my name is _____ and I work in the Service Quality Department at Getup & Go. FIrst, we want to thank you for having Getup & Go perform the [type of engagement] recently completed.

   The Service Quality Department was created because we feel that our future growth and success is based on client satisfaction. Your perception of our quailty of service, professionalism, and the range of services we have available is very important to us. Therefore, we're asking for your help. Do you have a couple of minutes to answer a few questions? [If "no," ask "When would be a good time for me to call you back?" _____]

	YES	NO
1. Were you pleased with the overall quality of our services?	_____	_____
2. Did our personnel perform in a competent, professional manner?	_____	_____
3. Was our fee in line with the value of the services performed?	_____	_____
4. Has Getup & Go been responsive to your needs?	_____	_____
5. Was your work done on time?	_____	_____
6. Are you satisfied with our range of services?	_____	_____
7. Are there other services you feel Getup & Go could assist you with?	_____	_____

[Solicit comments on any "no" answers to number 1–6, "yes" to number 6.]

COMMENTS:

_____

_____

_____

Exhibit 1

- Keep it short. No more than two sides of a single sheet of 8 ½-by-11-inch paper.

- When you have finished serving the client, suggest, "Don't forget to fill in a survey; we really want to know what you think."

- Anonymously collect surveys. Provide a covered box for participants to insert their surveys. Don't ask the receptionist to collect them because this might embarrass some clients who might suspect that their survey would be read immediately by the receptionist.

USE THE FEEDBACK YOU RECEIVE

For personal or telephone interviews, the interviewer(s) prepare(s) a written report on each interview, using a standard form such as Exhibit 1. After conducting 10 or so interviews, they will be able to draw tentative conclusions. After about 20 interviews, they can probably make a preliminary report summarizing their findings.

For mail, in-office, and telephone surveys, a numeric statistical summary of the results can be prepared, as well as a summary of all volunteered comments. The report should cover the following:

- What did the interviewers learn that surprised them?

- What did they hear that they did not expect to hear?

- What did they *not* hear that they expected to hear?

- What areas does your firm's public perception not fit the reality of the firm as your partners perceive it?

- What previously unrecognized strengths did the interviewers discover?

- What previously unrecognized weaknesses can you correct?

- How are your nonpartners perceived by others?

Now you be will be able to give better answers to the following questions, addressed more fully in Chapter 8:

- How do your services differ from those of your competitors?

- What characteristics distinguish your firm from your competition?

- How can you further differentiate your services?

Be sure to give the results to all of your personnel. Give them the hard numbers, not just percentages. For instance, if 97 percent of 1,000 clients surveyed were satisfied (at whatever level) and three percent were not, don't say "Three percent gave us bad marks." Instead, give the number: "Thirty-two clients said we weren't very good at returning telephone calls." "Thirty-two clients" is more real to your people than "three percent." They might just remember one or two clients whose calls they didn't return and resolve to do better next time.

Surveys and feedback programs should be an annual part of your operation. Interview each client by telephone or in the office about once a year after a particular service is completed. General mail surveys should be conducted at the same time each year so that you can watch trends. If your practice is seasonal, the best time for general surveys is at the conclusion of your busy season.

EVALUATE FRONTLINE PERSONNEL

Service quality evaluations tell you the difference between client expectations and client perceptions. Client satisfaction is measured in degrees of satisfaction, and your clients give you a mental "report card" with grades on the features of your service they consider important.

The purpose of measuring client satisfaction is to get the clients' *mental* report card in *writing*. This way, you can stop guessing about how you are doing and know where you stand.

Some firms train their frontline people to be better client handlers; some don't. If you try to recruit people who are already "nice" and don't need "smile training," and you realize you cannot objectively measure client-handling skill at the recruiting stage, then you need a way to follow up on their performance to find out where you made the right hiring choices and where you goofed.

On the other hand, if you train people to be better client handlers (and I have trained hundreds to do so), you still need a way to find out how your training is working and which people need more training.

Either way, you need to know where you made the right promotion decisions and where you goofed. This is why you need a process for evaluating your frontline performers at all levels, up to and including the partners. The purpose of such measurements is to allow you to take meaningful action based on *knowledge* rather than on opinion and guesswork.

MEASURE CLIENT SATISFACTION

To have a meaningful measurement of client satisfaction, you need to have objective questions with objective answers that provide a statistic. Such a survey provides different information from the subjective feedback program because you can actually measure and compare the performance of different people, different departments, or different offices. These measures can then be used for an objective reward system for your superior performers. You can also plot your scores on a graph and watch trends.

For this reason, avoid questions with "yes" or "no" answers like those in Exhibit 1, because it is difficult to get a statistic with which you can chart trends, or compare your progress with any particular client. If 70 percent of your clients answer "yes" to the question, "Do you think we are a good firm?" is that high satisfaction, low satisfaction, or what? For any individual client, a "yes" could mean a satisfaction level of "6" or "10." With a "6" client, your relationship is in danger; with a "10," your relationship is in good shape.

What kind of questions work best? Your survey can yield two kinds of valuable information:

1. *Quantifiable data* from questions that ask clients to rate your services objectively on a numerical or multiple-choice scale. This question format makes it easy for clients to respond. The results are also easier to tabulate.

2. *Subjective data* from open-ended questions such as, "How do you feel about our office location?" Clients have different levels of verbal skills, and open-ended questions may intimidate or confuse some clients. Such clients will probably not respond because of difficulty in putting their thoughts into words.

Both types of data are valuable, so the best approach is to use mostly quantifiable questions with some open-ended ones at the end. This way, clients who have difficulty with open-ended questions will at least have given you some good quantifiable data.

For each quantifiable answer, I recommend at least a 7-point scale ranging from "Strongly agree" = 7 to "Strongly disagree" = 1, or "Very satisfied" = 7 to "Very dissatisfied" = 1, with no verbal labels for the intermediate points of 2 though 6. The scale should accompany each statement or question. Some people use a 5-point scale; others ask clients to fill in a number from 1 to 10 or 1 to 100 beside each question.

CASE STUDY

One large Chicago firm mailed a two-page questionnaire (front and back) to 437 clients and received 88 replies within a month. Forty-one percent of the respondents reported the firm's service was "very prompt," and 53 percent found them "usually prompt." Forty percent said firm personnel were "always available," and 56 percent said they were "usually available." Seventy-three percent rated the firm's interest in their organization "sincere and more than adequate," while 19 percent found it "adequate."

Their marketing director told me that the most interesting finding concerned fees. "Of those who listed complaints, the most common response dealt with fees charged. They gave us high marks in the area of service, yet some of our clients don't understand our billing statement and, as a result, believe our fees are high."

Despite the fact that fees were by far the lowest percentage cited (seven percent) when clients answered why they had left their previous firms, the marketing director believes a better communication of the firm's fee structure can reduce unnecessary misunderstandings and enhance client relations. Because of the survey, the firm is better informed about clients' perceptions and may be better able to do something about communicating not only their fee structure, but also the benefits that clients receive from their services.

The firm also noticed a lot of low marks in one service area from clients handled by one partner. The partner did some additional training in the area to raise his scores in the future.

CLASSIFY RESPONSES

You will want to classify your responses by responsible person in your firm, by type of client, by department, and so forth, so that you can both analyze the responses to determine which past actions have been successful and identify the current areas of SWOT. Classification questions will not use the 7-point scale. For these, you can provide either blanks to fill or boxes to check "yes," "no," and "not sure." Here are some sample questions to consider.

- The firm was referred to us by:
  - Banker
  - Lawyer
  - CPA
  - *[Insert any other categories of important referral sources for your profession, such as insurance agents, stock brokers, etc.]*
  - Another client
  - Personal contact with a member of the firm
    (Name: _____)
  - Other _____ .

- Who are the two key people with whom you work in order of importance to *you*?

- The reason(s) the firm was initially engaged to assist my organization was (were):

  [List the major services you provide. This question will help you determine which services new clients come to you for. A comparison of these services with the services your clients use after they come to you may highlight SWOTs in your marketing.]

- How long have you been a client?

- What is the approximate total for fees you paid the firm in the last 12 months?

- What industry are you in?

- Would you recommend us to others?

- Have you ever recommended us to others?

- Have we ever asked you to recommend us?

- Would you give us referrals if someone asked you about *[your kind of service]*?

- If not, please tell us why you would hesitate to recommend us. *[Provide several blank lines.]*

ASK ABOUT SERVICE QUALITY

Find out how your clients evaluate the quality of your service.

How satisfied are you with us in the following areas? Please mark a check in the most appropriate column for your response.

	Very satisfied						Very dissatisfied
	7	6	5	4	3	2	1
• Overall quality of service							
• Responsiveness to your needs							
• Technical competence of firm partners							
• Technical competence of firm staff							
• Keeping you informed on relevant new legislation, business topics, etc.							
• Ability to improve your bottom line							
• Our recommendations and solutions to your business problems							

	Very satisfied						Very dissatisfied
	7	6	5	4	3	2	1
• Continuity of personnel in providing you service							
• Range of services							

	Very satisfied						Very dissatisfied
	7	6	5	4	3	2	1

- Quality of newsletters, promotional literature, brochures, etc.

- Value received for fees charged

- Timeliness of service

- Response to emergencies

Another option would be to use the following format:

Please tell us how you feel about the following statements regarding the quality of our service. Please mark a check in the most appropriate column for your response.

	Strongly agree						Strongly disagree
	7	6	5	4	3	2	1

- There are at least two people in the firm who are familiar with my situation.

- The firm seems familiar with problems related to my organization.

- The firm helps to implement any changes they suggest.

- Technical language used by the firm is explained so that it doesn't confuse me or my staff.

- The firm has made me fully aware of all the different areas in which they can assist me.

	Strongly agree						Strongly disagree
	7	6	5	4	3	2	1
• Advice given by the firm has proven helpful.							
• Adequate advice is provided regarding planning in the areas covered by the firm.							
• New changes in the law or other relevant updates are communicated to me.							
• [Documents the firm prepares] are professional in appearance.							
• Firm personnel seem technically competent.							
• Phone calls are returned within a reasonable period of time.							
• Help is always available when needed.							
• My work is handled in a timely manner.							
• My staff and I are treated in a courteous and friendly manner.							
• Services are commensurate with the fees billed.							
• My affairs are kept in strictest confidence.							
• The firm is well managed.							
• The firm's fee policy is properly communicated.							

	Strongly agree						Strongly disagree
	7	6	5	4	3	2	1

- Interference with our business routine is kept to a minimum.

- Suggestions regarding improvements in [*areas of the client's business with which you are concerned*] have been helpful,

- Adequate lead time is given to comply with requests for information.

- Instructions for filing [*documents you prepare*] are clear and understandable.

- I would be pleased to recommend the firm to others.

ASK ABOUT PERSONNEL PERFORMANCE

Find out how your clients evaluate the performance of your personnel.

Are you satisfied in the following areas with the personnel who provide service to you? Please mark a check in the most appropriate column for your response.

	Very satisfied						Very dissatisfied
	7	6	5	4	3	2	1

- Getting your work done on time

- Informing you if there will be a delay

	Very satisfied						Very dissatisfied
	7	6	5	4	3	2	1
• Taking an active interest in your business							
• Listening to your concerns							
• Understanding your business goals							
• Understanding your personal goals							
• Helping you balance your business and personal goals							
• Providing you with useful ideas in our areas of expertise							
• Handling complaints fairly							
• Being a business advisor							
• Answering technical questions so that you can understand them							
• Being accessible when needed							
• Returning telephone calls promptly							
• Acting in a professional manner							
• Maintaining a professional appearance							

ASK ABOUT YOUR FIRM'S IMAGE

Find out how your clients perceive your firm.

Please tell us how you feel about the following statements regard-

ing our firm's image. Please mark a check in the most appropriate
column for your response.

	Strongly agree						Strongly disagree
	7	6	5	4	3	2	1

- The firm is highly regarded by:
  - The business community
  - Banks
  - Its fellow professionals
  - Law firms
  - CPA firms
  - [Other types of firms you deem important to your image]
- The following firm "products" have a professional look:
  - [List the types of documents you prepare, such as contracts, tax returns, blueprints, reports, etc.]
  - Correspondence
  - Business cards
  - Brochures
  - Proposals
- The telephones are answered:
  - Promptly
  - Courteously
  - Professionally

	Strongly agree					*Strongly disagree*	
	7	6	5	4	3	2	1
• The firm's offices present a professional appearance.							
• The firm is a top quality firm.							
• The firm provides good value for fees charged.							

ASK ABOUT YOUR FIRM'S SCOPE OF SERVICES

Find out how your clients perceive the scope of your services.

> Please tell us your current needs for our services. Please mark a check in the most appropriate column for your response.

	Currently use our firm for these services	*Currently use other source*	*Do not use this service now, but intend to use in future*	*Do not use this service and do not intend to use in future*
	1	2	3	4
[List all major services you currently offer and all major services you are considering offering in the near future.]				

ASK FOR COMMENTS

Then provide a generous space for comments and ask for them.

> As a client, your opinion is valuable to us. Please make any comment you wish—complimentary or critical—on any aspect of your association with us. We will appreciate it. *[Insert several blank lines.]*

If you would like additional information on any of our services, please detach the following form and either mail it separately [*you could have the form printed separately as a postcard, with or without postage prepaid*] or bring it with you when you next visit our office.

Please provide me with information about the following services:

1. _____

2. _____

3. _____

4. _____

5. _____

Your name (optional) _____

USE THE CADILLAC, SUPERSOPHISTICATED APPROACH[10]

Client satisfaction reflects the overlap between client expectations and client perceptions. Either of two formats for the scale items can be used to measure these differences:

1. You could directly measure the difference between expectations and perceptions on each item, as follows:

	Greatly exceeds expectations					*Greatly falls short of expectations*
The appearance of XYZ Firm's physical facilities	7	6	5	4	3	2	1

The higher the ratings on statements such as this, the higher the level of service quality.

2. Or you could use pairs of matched statements on each item—separately measuring expectations and perceptions, as follows:

	Strongly agree					*Strongly disagree*
	7	6	5	4	3	2	1

*[Statement to assess **expectations:**]*

The physical facilities of [*type of profession*] firms should be visually appealing.

*[Statement to assess **perceptions:**]*

XYZ Firm's physical facilities are visually appealing.

The difference between the ratings on the *pairs* of statements measures perceived service quality. This is a very sophisticated approach, perhaps more sophisticated than you will want to use.

Parasuraman, Zeithaml, and Berry[11] recommend the second format for the following reasons:

1. Measuring expectations and perceptions separately can uncover the reasons for a particular service quality image. For example, the scale ratings can indicate whether a poor image in a particular area is a result of high expectations, poor perceptions, or both.

2. The respondents will find it easier to answer the separate questions.

3. The range of values using two questions is +6 to –6, in contrast to the narrower 6-point range possible with a single question. This provides a more sensitive measure. If you are going to measure your frontline personnel on client satisfaction and on improvements in client satisfaction, a sensitive measure is particularly valuable.

Incidentally, when surveying referral sources, you can include a set of perception statements for your competitors, to assess their positions compared to your firm. The expectation statement, however, does not need to be repeated for each competitor.

INSTRUCTIONS AND STATEMENTS TO MEASURE CLIENT EXPECTATIONS AND PERCEPTIONS

I recommend using a 7-point scale ranging from "Strongly agree = 7" to "Strongly disagree = 1," with no verbal labels for the intermediate points of 2 through 6. The scale should accompany each statement. Also, if possible, list the statements in random order in the questionnaire.

Directions to Respondents

This survey deals with your opinions of [*type of profession*] services. Please show the extent to which you think [*type of profession*] firms should have the features described by each statement. If you strongly agree that [*type of profession*] firms should have a feature, please mark a check in column 7. If you strongly disagree that [*type of profession*] firms should have a feature, please mark a check in column 1. If your feelings are not strong, please mark a check in one of the columns in the middle. There are no right or wrong answers—all we are interested in is the column number that best shows your expectations about [*type of profession*] firms.

Expectations Statements

Tangibles

1. [*Type of profession*] firms should have up-to-date equipment.

2. The physical facilities of [*type of profession*] firms should be visually appealing.

3. The employees of [*type of profession*] firms should appear well dressed and neatly groomed.

4. The appearance of the physical facilities of [*type of profession*] firms should be [*range of descriptors in keeping with the type of services provided*].

Reliability

5. When [*type of profession*] firms promise to do something by a certain time, I expect them to do so.

6. When clients have a problem, [*type of profession*] firms should be sympathetic and reassuring.

7. [*Type of profession*] firms should be dependable.

8. [*Type of profession*] firms should provide their services by the time they have promised to do so.

9. [*Type of profession*] firms should keep accurate records.

Responsiveness **(Ratings on these negatively worded statements should be reversed prior to scoring.)**

10. [*Type of profession*] firms shouldn't be expected to tell clients exactly when services will be performed. [–]

11. It is not realistic for clients to expect prompt service from employees of [*type of profession*] firms. [–]

12. The employees of [*type of profession*] firms don't always have to be willing to help clients. [–]

13. It is okay if [*type of profession*] firms are too busy to respond to client requests promptly. [–]

14. Clients should be willing to wait a little while to get appointments with [*type of profession*] firms. [–]

15. Clients should not expect to be able to contact partners in [*type of profession*] firms easily. [–]

Assurance

16. Clients should feel secure in their dealings with [*type of profession*] firms.

17. [*Type of profession*] firms should keep clients informed about matters of concern to them.

18. I expect [*type of profession*] firms to help clients learn how to keep costs down for their services.

19. Clients' dealings with [*type of profession*] firms should be very pleasant.

20. Employees of [*type of profession*] firms should be knowledgeable.

21. Employees of [*type of profession*] firms should be polite.

22. Employees of [*type of profession*] firms should get adequate support from these firms to do their jobs well.

Empathy **(Ratings on these negatively worded statements should be reversed prior to scoring.)**

23. It is okay if the employees of [*type of profession*] firms talk down to clients. [–]

24. [*Type of profession*] firms should not be expected to give clients individual attention. *[–]*

25. Employees of [*type of profession*] firms cannot be expected to give clients personal attention. *[–]*

26. It is unrealistic to expect employees to know about the needs of their clients. *[–]*

27. [*Type of profession*] firms shouldn't be expected to have office hours convenient to all their clients. *[–]*

28. It is okay if clients have to wait a long time to receive services from [*type of profession*] firms. *[–]*

Directions to Respondents

The following set of statements relates to your feelings about Smith & Jones. For each statement, please show the extent to which you think Smith & Jones has the feature described by the statement. Once again, marking a check in the 7 column means that you strongly agree that Smith & Jones has that feature, and marking a check in the 1 column means that you strongly disagree. You may indicate any of the columns in the middle that show how strong your feelings are. There are no right or wrong answers—all we are interested in is the column that best shows your perceptions of Smith & Jones.

Perceptions Statements

Tangibles

1. Smith & Jones has up-to-date equipment.

2. Smith & Jones's physical facilities are visually appealing.

3. Smith & Jones's employees appear well dressed and neatly groomed.

4. The appearance of the physical facilities of Smith & Jones is in keeping with the type of services provided.

Reliability

5. When Smith & Jones promises to do something by a certain time, it does so.

6. When you have problems, Smith & Jones personnel are sympathetic and reassuring.

7. Smith & Jones is dependable.

8. Smith & Jones provides its services by the time it promises to do so.

9. Smith & Jones keeps accurate records.

Responsiveness (Ratings on these negatively worded statements should be reversed prior to scoring.)

10. Smith & Jones does not tell clients exactly when services will be performed. [–]

11. You do not receive prompt service from Smith & Jones's employees. [–]

12. Employees of Smith & Jones are not always willing to help clients. [–]

13. Employees of Smith & Jones are too busy to respond to your requests promptly. [–]

14. You have to wait a little while to get appointments with Smith & Jones. [–]

15. You cannot contact Smith & Jones partners easily. [–]

Assurance

16. You feel secure in your dealings with Smith & Jones.

17. Smith & Jones keeps you informed about matters of concern to you.

18. Smith & Jones helps clients learn how to keep costs down for their services.

19. Your dealings with Smith & Jones are very pleasant.

20. Employees of Smith & Jones are knowledgeable.

21. Employees of Smith & Jones are polite.

22. Employees get adequate support from Smith & Jones to do their jobs well.

What Do People *Really* Think of You?

Empathy (Ratings on these negatively worded statements should be reversed prior to scoring.)

23. Employees of Smith & Jones talk down to you. *[–]*

24. Smith & Jones does not give you individual attention. *[–]*

25. Employees of Smith & Jones do not give you personal attention. *[–]*

26. Employees of Smith & Jones do not know what your needs are. *[–]*

27. Smith & Jones does not have office hours convenient to all of its clients. *[–]*

28. You have to wait a long time to receive Smith & Jones's services. *[–]*

Many professionals do not understand how clients evaluate service quality. Measure the differences between the perceptions of *your* clients and your personnel. Administer the preceding questionnaire to your frontline personnel. Then compare their scores with your clients' scores. You just might be amazed at the results.

NOTES

1. Karl Albrecht and Ron Zemke, *Service America!*, Homewood, IL: Dow Jones-Irwin, 1985, p. 34.
2. Albrecht and Zemke, p. 51.
3. Albrecht and Zemke, pp. 59–60.
4. David A. Garvin, "Competing on the Eight Dimensions of Quality," *Harvard Business Review*, Nov/Dec 1987, p. 109.
5. Robert Denney, *How to Market Legal Services*, New York: Van Nostrand Reinhold Company, 1984, pp. 45–46. Robert Denney, *Marketing Accounting Services*, New York: Van Nostrand Reinhold Company, 1983, pp. 35–36.
6. Valarie A. Zeithaml, Leonard L. Berry, and A. Parasuraman, *Communication and Control Processes in the Delivery of Service Quality* (Report No. 87-100), Cambridge, MA: Marketing Science Institute, June 1987, p. 8.
7. Denney, 1983, p. 38, and 1984, p. 48.
8. Albrecht and Zemke, p. 61.

9. David A. Garvin, 1987, p. 109.
10. Derived from A. Parasuraman, Valarie A. Zeithaml, and Leonard L. Berry, *SERVQUAL: A Multiple-Item Scale for Measuring Customer Perceptions of Service Quality.* (Report No. 86-108), Cambridge, MA: Marketing Science Institute, August 1986, pp. 7–8.
11. Parasuraman, Zeithaml, and Berry, 1986, p. 8.

7

What Business Are You In?

Chapter 5 explained why it's not enough for you to have a reputation for some generalized, abstract excellence; to be visible among the crowds of your competitors, you must have a reputation for specific qualities among certain target markets. Excellent firms focus their energies on achieving a particular *kind* of excellence in their target markets.

> Concentration is the key to economic results. No other principle of effectiveness is violated as constantly today as the basic principle of concentration. Our motto seems to be: "Let's do a little bit of everything."
>
> *Peter Drucker[1]*

As Andrew Carnegie once said, "Put all your eggs in one basket, and then watch the basket." Concentrate on a particular segment of your market, and fill the needs of your segment better than anyone else. Don't turn down other business that comes your way, but focus your efforts on a specific market that you can serve in an excellent manner. Given this, what market should you focus on?

THE SERVICE LIFE CYCLE

Every product or service offered by any business—professional or otherwise—has a life cycle. Professionals sometimes act as though all their services will be rendered the same way and at the same levels of profitability in the future as in the past. But this attitude is wishful thinking; tomorrow will not be like yesterday.

A manufacturing company with a large investment in plant may have to retool to accommodate changes in its market. Fortunately, your assets are your people, and they are much more flexible than machines. You can retrain instead of retooling.

Consider the instructive example of computer consulting. When computers first grew beyond scientific uses and were adapted to business use, software had to be individually written for each company and for each application within a company. The equipment alone cost hundreds of thousands of dollars, sometimes millions—and this was in the 1950s. Only the largest companies could afford such an investment, but these giant enterprises were able to benefit from this large investment in mechanization. Such clients would select their computer consultants based on hiring the best possible expertise, and they were willing to pay for it because the potential benefit was so great. These were cutting-edge services involving unique, first-time issues and a completely customized approach to problem solving. Faced with this situation, clients looked first for the creative talent and skill of particular individuals, and second for prior experience in their industry or understanding of the peculiar problems facing their particular industry. Such services could be billed based on value to the client rather than time spent by the firm.

In the 1960s and 1970s, as computer technology and the computer expertise of the accounting profession developed together, prices came down, and the technology of systems design became more widespread. More and more clients came to recognize that their problem had probably been faced before by other companies. By this time, clients could look less for sheer creativity and technical expertise and more for a firm that could apply its past experience to their situation. A high degree of skill and creativity was still desirable, and efficiency or cost were not unimportant, but experience was the dominant selection criterion. Many midsized companies were able to automate many of their accounting and business systems. Profitability of individual contracts for services declined as more firms entered the market and the know-how became more widely available.

In the 1980s, with the advent of the microcomputer and off-the-shelf software, computerization became affordable for even the smallest companies, and organizations have a wide variety of choices in computerizing their various operations. Most clients know their problems can be handled competently by a broad range of firms and even some storefront operations. Cost, timeliness, and superior service are paramount.

The Professional Service Life Cycle—
"Trappers," "Ranchers," and "Farmers"

The same cycle has occurred or is occurring with estate planning, auditing, inventory controls, and a myriad other CPA services. It can be expected to occur in almost every service offered by any profession. Remember when leveraged buy-outs were cutting-edge legal work? Remember when open-heart surgery was only performed a few places in the world? Remember when the New York City traffic tunnels were considered engineering miracles?

Key Point: Every product or service offered by any business— professional or otherwise—has a life cycle.

You cannot manage your practice as though your services will be required at current or expanding levels indefinitely. The client-centered firm offers new services as needed, slacks off on services where demand is declining, and changes its methods of marketing, managing, and performing existing services to respond to changes in client needs, attitudes, competition, and technology. The life cycle of most professional services evolves through three phases: trapping, ranching, and farming, as described in the following paragraphs.

Phase One—Trapping

Trappers were the first to explore the American West in search of adventure and riches. These intrepid pioneers relied on their own resources to wrest a living from an unexplored wilderness. They were alone and no one could hear a cry for help if they got into trouble. They blazed new trails for the others who eventually followed. I call pioneering firms, like the bold adventurers who preceded them, "trappers." Trappers typically identify a new service and are the first—or among the first—to offer it to the market.

Consultant Robert Beale[2] called these new services "Stars." He defined them as new services that we think will mature into a good market. When the Star catches hold, with reasonable marketing and sales effort, we can sell as much of it as we have planned, and we can price the service at a level that produces a good, reasonable profit. We can do this again and again and again.

Consultant David Maister[3] calls these "brains" or "expertise" services.

> Examples of this "brain surgeon" type of practice can be found in every profession. In management consulting in the mid-80s, examples might include work on flexible manufacturing systems, the recently introduced technique of ordered logic in market research, recapitalizations involving Eurofinancings, or competitive strategy advice to industries undergoing rapid environmental change. In the law, work on hostile takeovers (attack or defense) represents the classic illustration of expertise-based work, while in accounting such work might best be illustrated by work on helping clients understand and take advantage of new tax laws. In architecture, the design of a new corporate headquarters would fit the category of being complex, high risk, and demanding the creativity of complete customization to meet unique client needs.

These trapper services arise because some change in the environment causes clients to face a new problem for the first time. Or else the environmental change has created a new opportunity available to the clients. The risks and rewards may both be quite high, so such clients will choose professional help with the best possible expertise, almost regardless of cost.

Here are the characteristics of trapper services:

- Maister believes that clients facing this situation (which may even involve a crisis for the client) will look first for the creative talent and skill of particular individuals, and second for prior experience in their industry or understanding of the peculiar problems facing their particular industry.

- Whether or not this is true, the trapper service can initially be performed by only a few creative, innovative, highly talented individuals.

- Because they are so new, trapper services are often completely customized.

- Leverage (the ratio of lower-level staff to high-level personnel such as partners) is quite low because the service is performed at a very high level.

- Trappers are largely self-taught and may be highly research oriented.

- Because the supply of professionals who can deliver the service is so limited, formal marketing is not much of an issue and is mainly devoted to getting the word out that the firm can deliver the new service.

Trapper services represent a small portion of the total demand for professional services because such services quickly enter Phase Two—"Ranching."

Phase Two—Ranching

In the settlement of a frontier, after the trail is blazed by the trappers, the cattle ranchers come to harvest the riches of the newly opened territory. The ranchers' service is still very valuable, but it is no longer unique or rare.

Many management texts call this phase the "Cash Cow." Even though several firms in each marketplace are rendering the service, there is not much competition because the service has found a much larger market. Maister calls this phase of service "gray hair" or "experience."

Examples of this type of work in management consulting might include large mainframe information systems studies, strategic planning analyses in specialized industries, or implementation of quality circles. In architecture, design and construction work for hospitals fits the profile. . . . In law, much of the work done by corporate lawyers is characterized by clients who place a greater emphasis on prior experience than on innovative approaches to unique problems.[4]

Clients may have read of the new service in their trade press, and they realize that other companies have faced the same problem or had the same opportunity and have achieved the same benefit.

These are the characteristics of ranching services:

- The innovative technology becomes more widespread. Other firms recognize a good thing and begin to offer the service.

- The market has expanded and total demand for the service may increase dramatically, so prices and profits will not decline much.

- More individuals in the firm acquire capability to perform the service under supervision, and the benefits of leverage become available.

- The trappers who pioneered the service begin to "draw maps" and disseminate their knowledge throughout the firm via apprenticeship training.

- The lead individuals also begin to systematize their methodology by developing the first procedures checklists, which are used as a supervisory device to allow leverage of the top brainpower.

- Research may be directed toward how to duplicate the trappers' skills elsewhere in the firm.

- Rancher services are tailored but not customized, and they may not be a problem requiring solution as much as an opportunity available to exploit. In this situation, clients are looking for firms that can apply their past experience with other companies in the industry or with companies that faced similar circumstances. Maister concludes that a high degree of skill and creativity is desirable, and efficiency or cost is not *un*important, but experience is the dominant selection criterion.

- Because both supply and demand for the service have grown, the marketplace is larger, so marketing becomes a more formal attempt to communicate to prospective clients that the firm is one of the several that can offer the new service.

Ranching services represent a much-larger revenue base than trapper services, but they will eventually be surpassed by Phase Three—"Farming."

Phase Three—Farming

Eventually, the previously virgin land is settled by the largest population of all—the farmers. Now the technology is widespread and no longer innovative. Farmers not only draw maps, they survey, fence, fertilize, and irrigate the land to turn it into a standardized, even mechanized production facility. In this phase, it is general knowledge in the marketplace that clients' problems can be handled competently by a broad range of firms offering similar services.

Maister[5] calls these "process" or "efficiency" services because the emphasis is on efficiency of the standard procedures employed.

> Much work in such consulting fields as market research, production planning, and wage and salary systems fits this profile. In architecture, warehouse and factory design work is most frequently purchased mainly on efficiency criteria, and most (but not all) audit work in accounting is of the same nature. In law, most of the transaction work done for banks and insurance companies represents efficiency practices.

Characteristics of farmer services:

- Clients place emphasis on the efficiency of their professional firm, which includes both cost and turnaround time.

- Almost any firm can provide the service.

- Marketing becomes very important to distinguish the firm's service offering from other similar firms.

- Prices and profits decline.

- Services are highly standardized, and procedures are checklisted.

- Quality control systems allow the use of paraprofessional or lower-level professional personnel.

- Leverage is quite high because a small number of high-level personnel can supervise the work of many lower-level staff—and thus reduce costs.

- The rancher's apprenticeship training system has given way to formal training with practice cases and classrooms.

These three phases—trapper/rancher/farmer—actually form a spectrum along which any particular service can be located. Just as there was no particular dividing line in the settlement of the frontier, there is no dividing line between each of the three phases but a gradual evolution from one to the next. Historically, most professional services in most professions started as trapper services when they were first introduced. However, services have a life cycle in which they progress to ranching and finally end up at farming. You might almost view it as a progression from "art" to "science."

IMPLICATIONS FOR YOUR FIRM'S CULTURE

Every aspect of a firm's affairs is affected by its practice mix—the proportions of trapper, rancher, and farmer engagements it performs. These features include recruiting, compensation and economic structure, organization structure, management style, promotion policies, relative importance of long-term client goodwill, and marketing and training (both discussed in separate sections later in this chapter).

Recruiting

Trappers place high value on hard-driving, innovative, creative geniuses. An "up-or-out" promotion philosophy keeps only the best and brightest. The "eccentric genius" type is tolerated by clients because they have no alternatives.

Ranchers want organizers with good management skills. Rancher practices can accommodate a wider level of skills by supplementing individual skills with the experience base of the firm. Management of client relationships becomes important because clients have numerous alternatives. Professional personnel can be easily motivated toward client service because it is the visible route to success.

Farmers will be weighted heavily toward "job holders" rather than "career track" personnel because of the limited advancement opportunities. Client service is paramount, and the partners emphasize the firm's client-centered focus with all frontline people at whatever level. Reward systems based directly on client satisfaction are a key to keeping all personnel focused on client service.

Compensation and Economic Structure

Up-or-out dominates the *trapper* firms. Because leverage is low, trappers make their money on high billing rates or value billing. Income ratios between top-producing partners and the bottom partners are quite wide, frequently running as high as six to one.

Rancher services are usually billed based on time and expenses, rather than fixed fee or value billing.

Farmer services are priced at fixed fees, and cost sensitivity requires the use of as much junior time as possible. Because of the high leverage of many lower-level staff to each high-level person, there are few partners, and the partners must be skilled supervisors.

Organization Structure

Trappers have low leverage and relatively fewer people at the middle and bottom of the firm. *Farmers* have a broad pyramid with lots of paraprofessionals. *Ranchers* are somewhere in the middle.

Management Style

Anarchistic, "do your own thing" style is common for *trappers*. Some professions would describe the style as "collegial." *Ranchers* are more team oriented and cooperate to bring diverse firm resources to bear on client problems. *Farmers* try to do things by the book. Efficiency and standardization are the watchwords.

Promotion Policies

Trappers provide feast or famine, with high turnover for people who can't cut it. *Ranchers* promote good managers with client-handling skill. *Farmers* offer few promotions and those few are principally for employees with good people skills either in sales or in management of the largely job-oriented work force.

Value of the Firm

Trapper firms' reputations are based on individual reputations. Much work is nonrecurring. Accordingly, there is little goodwill value to the practice. *Farmers* have mostly recurring work of a routine nature that lends itself to long-term client relationships. Goodwill value is considerable. *Ranchers* are somewhere in the middle.

Summary

All the preceding aspects of the firm's corporate culture may also apply to different departments or different offices within the same firm. Each department or office may offer a different mix of services and thus may have different cultures and different practices appropriate for each of these aspects.

TWO IMPORTANT TRENDS

Two trends in the professions make it important to understand both the distinctions between each of these three phases and the professional practices that focus on one or two of these phases: (1) degree of client sophistication about a service and (2) rate of evolution of a professional service.

Client Sophistication

First, clients are more sophisticated than they were in earlier decades. Therefore, they often think (rightly or wrongly) that they can diagnose their own needs for professional services and distinguish among the types of firms whose style of practice and level of expertise and experience matches the specific benefits they seek. This is particularly so in large organizations with professional management. Smaller entrepreneurial organizations continue to rely on outside professionals' opinions, but they now demand a higher level of service commitment from their professionals.

A firm that continues to take a trapper approach to marketing, managing, and pricing a service even after the market for the service has evolved to the ranching phase will become extinct as the marketplace passes them by. Likewise, a firm that continues to try "ranching" when the farmers have already fenced the open range will be obsoleted by firms that cater to clients whose now-well-defined needs allow them to select their professionals based on efficiency.

> **Example:** Look at what has happened in the area of individual income tax preparation. An entire segment of the middle-class has evolved from needing CPAs to using an H & R Block type of tax preparer.

> **Example:** Accounting system design can now be done in some cases by retailers of microcomputers and software.

Alternatively, a firm that makes heavy use of systems and procedures to deliver a high-volume, uniform quality, "fast food" type of service is not a likely candidate to obtain cutting-edge contracts for services.

There is nothing inherently good or bad about which portion of the market spectrum a given practice serves. And there is no inherent difference in either profitability or growth at any part of the trapper–rancher–farmer spectrum. There are very profitable firms providing all three types of services. However, both the PIMS (Profit Impact of Market Strategy) data base and my observations indicate that serving the higher-quality client at any place on the spectrum results in greater profitability and growth.

Look at stock brokers. They offer a true commodity. A share of AT&T is the same whether you buy it from Charles Schwab or Merrill Lynch. Yet what they "sell" is the distinction of their execution and extra service and advice. Schwab is a classic farmer who sells execution quickly and at low cost. Schwab prides itself on efficiency. Merrill Lynch, on the other hand, is a rancher who sells research expertise and superior personal service and experience. Certain of the smaller, more specialized brokers are pure trappers. In short, even though the generic product of a share of stock is identical, the way it is offered is differentiated, and each of the three types of companies serves a different need of the marketplace.

All can be financially successful, but they position themselves in the marketplace differently.

Key Point: A firm cannot successfully render all three types of services; the cultural differences are too great.

Most firms can span up to two of the three phases in a single office or department. It is very difficult to accommodate all three because the cultural requirements are too disparate. You can extend your practice "umbrella" over trappers and ranchers or over ranchers and farmers, but not over all three. The moral is clear: Select the service segment you will target, and organize consistently around the best management practices for that service type.

Rate of Evolution

The second, and less visible, trend in all professions (indeed, in all markets of any type) is *the increasingly rapid evolution of products and services through the phases of their life cycles*. Heart and lung transplants are now almost routine. Innovative legal theories quickly become widely known and used. Architectural innovations such as atriums and glass-walled exterior elevators become commonplace design features. And on and on.

As Peter Drucker[6] pointed out, no one knew they needed an office copier before the first Xerox machine came out around 1960; "five years later no business could imagine doing without a copier." When the first jet planes started to fly, the best market research pointed out that there were not enough passengers for all the transatlantic ships. "Five years later the transatlantic jets were carrying fifty to one hundred times as many passengers each year as had ever before crossed the Atlantic."

The life cycle of professional services can also become the life cycle of the firm. All the various cultural implications must be addressed if the firm is to remain viable as it passes through its own life cycle.

MARKETING TACTICS

Briefly, *trappers* market based on individual skill and reputation; *ranchers* market based on both reputation (experience) and market positioning; and *farmers* sell a common product and have to rely on better market positioning.

Trappers

The best marketing of a trapper practice is what most of us would consider the traditional approach to marketing professional services. Because the client is seeking the best available talent for this type of service, the keys to winning clients are prominence and reputation. In effect, as David Maister says, the firm's marketing message is "Hire us because we're smart."

The most effective marketing techniques are indirect and involve such activities as

- Speeches
- Articles
- Being quoted in the media.

These establish the firm's credentials as an expert. In fact, the most effective practice development may involve creating an individual "star" practitioner by building the personal reputation of one or two individuals instead of the firm as a whole. The client's buying decision may be clinched by assuring the client that a specified, key individual will be closely involved with the work. In fact, a primary motivator for prospective clients may be the feeling of assurance that the firm's stars have the intellectual horsepower to handle this exotic, mysterious assignment.

The disadvantage of a practice dominated by trappers is that the practice is volatile, diverse, and fluid because few clients have continuing needs for such unusual services. They cannot be scheduled or predicted in advance, and they create no continuing income stream unless the firm can use them to feed a more routine type of service.

Incidentally, being first or getting in ahead of the crowd doesn't count for much. You've got to keep running just to keep up. Compaq wasn't the first in the microcomputer business by a long shot, but look at its large share of the market today and some pioneers end up face down with arrows in their backs.

Ranchers

For ranchers, the marketing task is to create an institutional reputation based on its ability to use collective knowledge derived from past performance of services. Here, practice development includes identifying, documenting, and promoting the specialized knowledge of your experienced professionals. Maister says the marketing message is "Hire us because we have been through this before. We have practice in solving this kind of problem." Promotion would involve

- Brochures describing previous engagements
- Client newsletters directed to the industry
- Special seminars on topics of interest to the industry

The focus is not on promoting individuals but on enhancing the joint credibility of the department or firm. Again, clients are concerned about assurance, and the firm's experience gives them a good feeling that their problem is in capable hands.

Rancher practices have a more clearly focused and stable clientele, and long-term relationships are more important.

Farmers

On the farming end of the spectrum, the firm demonstrates that it has established systems and procedures to handle specific types of services.

Key selling features are service, cost, reliability, speed, etc. The marketing message, again as phrased by Maister, is "Hire us because we know how to do this and can deliver it effectively." The client mix is focused on high-volume clients. These services are promoted by

- Brochures
- Competitive presentations
- Advertising, if appropriate

Assurance is in the guise of "You won't have to worry about this routine annoyance because our highly trained, experienced personnel are eager to serve your every need."

MARKETING STRUCTURE

The best marketing structure of "who does what" is also different for each type of practice.

In *trapper* practices, marketing is a personal responsibility of each partner, supplemented by public relations. Marketing consultants are used only to educate the partners on the best marketing methods and to coordinate public relations and reputation-building efforts.

As the practice area evolves to *ranching*, firms develop a more formal approach to marketing. This is the stage at which a firm will consider using marketing consultants on a regular basis or hiring a marketing director to oversee a regularized, continuing marketing effort. Marketing directors can be very effective in larger *farmer* and rancher practices. However a structured marketing approach will not be cost-effective in a trapper firm, except in the public relations function to promote the reputations of star individuals and in developing the personal marketing and selling skills of the partners.

Rancher practices are very marketing oriented at the high end of the market. Unimaginative, low-profit rancher firms are not; they mistakenly rely on the "traditional" marketing suitable for trappers, with limited success.

TRAINING

Trappers

Trapper practices must hire only top graduates who meet the quality needs of the frontier skills. Leverage is necessarily low. The organiza-

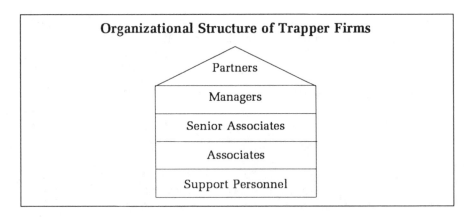

Figure 9

tion structure is shaped like a house (see Figure 9), and training is accomplished through an informal apprenticeship system. *Trapper* training is very technical, with emphasis on cutting-edge technology. A rigorous up-or-out promotion system ensures that the firm retains only the "best and brightest."

Ranchers

As the practice evolves to ranching, it can support a broader spectrum of skill levels. This is because the stars can now leverage themselves with lower-level professionals, and the individuals in the practice area can supplement their talents with the experience base of the firm. Therefore, hiring can be more broadly based and can accommodate a larger number of lateral hires. There is less need to enforce the up-or-out system because experienced individuals can be productive and marketable team members even if they are not stars. The organizational structure forms a narrow pyramid, as shown in Figure 10.

Rancher training is more formal and structured, to capture and disseminate internally the firm's experience base. Training may include case studies taken from the firm's client files.

Farmers

Farmer firms have a major role for paraprofessionals and less-skilled professionals. They use standard systems and procedures and require less-mature talent. The organizational pyramid has a broad base, as shown in Figure 11. Promotions tend to be slower, even for highly

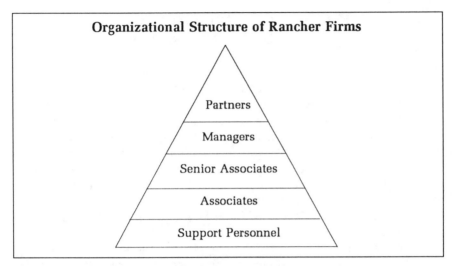

Figure 10

qualified professionals, because the practice is highly leveraged and has fewer higher-level positions.

Farmer training focuses on processes, emphasizing organization and replication of successful actions, as well as client service. Training is formal and uses classroom hours, practice manuals, forms books, and standard checklists.

Figure 11

THE CLIENT-CENTERED FIRM VERSUS
THE RESOURCE-CENTERED FIRM

Because every service has a life cycle, the client-centered firm offers new services as needed and drops old services where demand is declining. I have observed (at least) two different philosophies about strategic management: client-centered and resource-centered management.

Client-centered firms focus their planning on the needs of their market, both current clients and target groups. Some refer to this as "market-driven" management. Client-centered firms decide on which of their client needs and wants to focus so that they can direct their resources in a client-centered way. In other words, the market is "cause," and the strategic plan is "effect" and is determined by the needs of the market.

Resource-centered firms focus their planning around their existing capabilities, talents, and resources. Some refer to this as "asset-driven." These firms concentrate their planning on production and cost considerations and their existing capabilities rather than on the needs of clients. You might say their existing resources are "cause" and their strategic planning is "effect."

Examples:

- The traditional example of resource-centered thinking, as opposed to client-centered (or, in this case, "customer-centered") thinking, is the railroad industry before World War II. The railroads thought they were in the railroad business rather than the transportation business. They followed a resource-centered philosophy and addressed their current resources instead of the needs of their customers. They directed their attention *inward* rather than *outward*. Instead of asking themselves, "How can we best serve the needs of our current and potential customers?" they asked, "How can we best utilize our railroad assets?" As a result, their strategic decisions were based on the current situation, and they assumed that the current environment would continue unchanged. They ignored how to best serve the transportation needs of their customers. Because of this failure to center on customer needs rather than current resources, they missed out when market needs changed to trucking and air transportation.

- The hotel industry prior to World War II catered to the travel needs of the upper class and business traveler. As the travel capabilities of the middle class expanded with the development of long-distance highways, and as businesses located outside the city centers, a market developed for suburban lodging for families traveling in automobiles and for people doing business in suburban locations. Presumably the Marriotts, the Hiltons, and the Sheratons should have created the motel industry. But they saw themselves as in the hotel business, and "hotel" meant downtown locations. And they were not aware of (or chose to ignore) the emergence of an entire new market segment that they had the expertise to capture. In fact, the motel industry was created by a different set of players, principally Holiday Inn, who saw this entirely different market demand developing.

Key Point: Be client-centered rather than resource-centered because your client is a moving target.

The nature of your business is not determined by you but by your clients. It is defined by the wants that your clients satisfy when they buy your services. The question, "What is your business?" can only be answered by looking at your firm from the outside viewpoint of your clients and target markets. And you should get honest answers from the clients themselves rather than attempt to read their minds or, worse yet, read your own partners' minds.

It's often difficult and always challenging to decide and define exactly what business you should be in. Sometimes, your feedback program will clearly indicate how to position your firm in the client's mind. At other times, you may have to grapple with complex issues and even resolve basic disagreements in the partners' views of the firm and its market. Nonetheless, you have to do it if you want the best results from your personnel.

Who Is Your Client?

The first step toward defining your business is to ask, "Who is the client?" The current, the potential, and the target clients—Where are they? How do they buy? How can we reach them?

The plain truth: Even corporate clients are really individuals because individuals in the corporation make the buying decisions. If your market is Fortune 1000 companies, your *real* client might be the controller, the in-house counsel, the research and development director, or the purchasing agent, depending on your profession and the particular segment of the market you serve.

What Do Your Clients Buy?

The next question: "What do your clients buy?"

> The Cadillac people say that they make an automobile . . . but does the man who [buys] a new Cadillac buy transportation or does he buy primarily prestige? Does the Cadillac, in other words, compete with the Chevrolet and the Ford; or does it compete—to take an extreme example—with diamonds and mink coats?
>
> *Peter Drucker*[7]

I've heard that a friend passed the president of Rolex watches on the street and asked, "How's the watch business?" To which the Rolex president replied, "I don't know; I'm in the luxury business."

What are *your* clients really buying from you?

What Do Your Clients Value?

The most difficult questions are, "What do your clients value? What do they look for when they buy your service?" What your clients consider valuable is so complicated that it can only be answered by the clients themselves. Don't even try to guess at it; ask your clients, as described in Chapter 6.

Your clients determine what your business is. What you think you are providing is not as important as what your clients think they are buying. The future of your practice depends on what your clients consider valuable.

WHAT SHOULD YOUR BUSINESS BE?

So far, we have been addressing the present. Now it is time to ask, "What should your business be?" To answer this perfectly requires a crystal ball, and few of us have one. But you can at least consider the

- Kinds of services you like to perform
- Kinds of clients you like to work with
- Existing market potential and market trends
- Expected changes in market structure because of technology, competition, regulations, demographics, etc.
- Innovations you *know* about
- Client needs not being adequately met today

After looking at the present and the future, ask the decisive question, "Are we in the right business, or should we change our business?"

Key Point: Don't let your practice run by accident; manage it with purpose.

THE MISSION STATEMENT

One way to help focus everyone in your firm on your firm's purpose is to adopt a mission statement. The *mission statement* is like the game plan in football—it is the strategy by which you will address your environment to take maximum advantage of your strengths and opportunities and to minimize your weaknesses. The mission statement aligns the goals of your personnel so that when you say "best," you mean the same "best" as the other person you are talking to.

Every firm, regardless of size, needs a set of basic principles that underlie its activities. The culture, objectives, planning, strategy, policies, and procedures of the firm are built upon these principles. These principles should be well thought-out, internally consistent, concise, and reduced to a written statement so as to define the firm's professional self-image and concept of its practice and the values it delivers to its clients. The larger the firm, the more important that these principles be clearly written, clearly communicated, and frequently reviewed by the partners.

I call this a "mission statement." The starting point for client-centered planning is the mission statement:

Definition: A *mission statement* is a client-centered, action-oriented statement of how you provide benefits to your clients.

The mission statement should be client centered to comprehend the needs of the markets that you want to serve. The mission statement should be action oriented to focus on how your firm can serve these needs.

The mission statement guides the firm's development along lines compatible with the needs of its market. It is an organizing principle that channels the efforts of the firm's personnel toward services that have significant perceived value to your target clients.

> **Key Point:** The mission statement describes the value that you offer your clients.

Albrecht and Zemke define what they call the "service strategy" as "a distinctive formula for delivering service; such a strategy is keyed to a well-chosen benefit premise that is valuable to the customer and that establishes an effective competitive position."[8]

To paraphrase Albrecht and Zemke, outstanding firms have discovered, invented, or evolved a unifying idea about what they do. This service strategy directs the attention of the firm's personnel toward the real priorities of the clients. This guiding concept becomes the rallying cry, a kind of gospel, and the nucleus of the message to be transmitted to the client.[9]

An old story describes three people working at a construction site. All three were doing the same thing. When a passerby asked them what they were doing, the first worker replied, "I'm earning a living." The second worker said, "Cutting stone." But the third worker said, "I'm building a cathedral." Which worker would you rather have working for you? Which worker would be more helpful to fellow workers? Which worker will be able to respond flexibly and on purpose to unexpected events? These differences aren't just a matter of different personal motivations of each worker. The primary factor is the leadership provided to the workers and the communications and examples set forth by their supervisors. The mission statement helps people see the cathedrals in their everyday endeavors.

Whether you prefer the term "mission statement," "statement of philosophy," "service concept," or "service strategy," the important thing is to know (a) the market you want to serve, (b) the needs of that market, and (c) the resources you have or can reasonably acquire to serve the continuing needs of your market. This requires that the mission statement be client centered rather than resource centered.

To enable personnel to envision "the cathedral," mission statements should

- Describe what the firm does
- Represent something concrete and valuable to clients, something they are willing to pay for
- Differentiate the firm in some meaningful way from its competitors in the eyes of clients
- Be clearly understandable and easy to remember
- Imply movement and direction
- If possible, be dynamic and action oriented
- Inspire people, providing a noble vision and values to be proud of.

Here is how some firms are refining and even redefining their missions:

- The mission of some architecture firms has broadened from solely designing and supervising the construction of buildings to including feasibility studies, financing, land use, zoning, and the planning of entire towns. The benefit to the client is "one stop shopping."
- The mission of the health care professions is gradually broadening from "healing the sick" to "keeping people well." The mushrooming of health maintenance organizations (HMOs) is a response to changing needs of patients—perhaps better referred to now as "clients."
- The mission of accounting firms has radically changed in the past generation from an orientation dominated by the accounting and auditing function, which is essentially historical in nature, to a future-oriented concept of management consulting, business advice, and personal financial planning.

Some companies have two mission statements, an internal one to serve management in aligning its planning activities, and an external one that describes the company to its public. The external mission statement can even be a slogan to use in advertising, e.g.,

- "Progress is our most important product"
- "Better things for better living through chemistry"
- "Quality is Job 1"
- "Reach out and touch someone"

What makes these more than slogans is the degree to which these phrases capture something that people in the organization deeply believe in.

To develop your own mission statement or service concept, ask yourself questions such as these:

- What business are we in?
- What business do we want to be in?
- What benefits do we provide to our clients?
- Are there other means by which our clients can achieve those benefits?
- Why do clients come to us rather than other firms?
- What types of clients do we have? What types of clients do we want?
- What environment do we operate in?
- What values are important to our firm?
- What makes us different from others in our profession?

For example, the mission statement of my consulting practice is to "provide management, marketing, and personnel advice and training so that professional firms can enhance both the quality and the quantity of their services to clients while earning appropriate profits and providing a satisfying work environment for firm personnel."

Now draft a mission statement for your firm. Is it short, understandable, uplifting, believable, achievable, worthwhile? Does it set forth a significant benefit to your clients? Use this space:

_____

_____

Show your draft to your partners, your secretary, and several staff people. Ask for their comments. Now revise the statement to incorporate their comments. Again, show it to your partners, your secretary, and the staff, asking them to confirm that it now expresses a mutually agreeable mission statement. Don't be surprised if it takes several tries; drafting a mission statement sounds simple, but it isn't.

NOTES

1. Peter Drucker, *Managing for Results*, Harper & Row, New York, 1964.
2. Robert Beale, speaker at the American Institute of CPAs Private Companies Practice Section Conference, Miami, Florida, 1988.
3. David H. Maister, "The Three E's of Professional Life," *Journal of Management Consulting*, vol. 3, no. 2, 1986, p. 39.
4. David H. Maister, p. 39.
5. David H. Maister, p. 39.
6. Peter Drucker, *Innovation and Entrepreneurship*, New York: Harper & Row, 1985, p. 190.
7. Peter Drucker, *The Practice of Management*, Harper & Row, New York, 1986, p. 53.
8. K. Albrecht and R. Zemke, *Service America!*, Homewood, IL: Dow Jones-Irwin, 1985, p. 64.
9. Albrecht and Zemke, p. 39.

8

How to Stand Above the Crowd

Chapter 7 alluded to the differences between stock brokers Charles Schwab and Merrill Lynch. In their own ways, each of these two firms stands above the crowd of their competitors. Schwab sells execution quickly and at low cost. Merrill Lynch sells research and personal service. The generic product (the internal quality) may be identical, but the way it is offered (the external quality) is so highly differentiated that the two companies serve different needs of the marketplace and don't compete for the same market.

As Peters and Austin said,

> The problem is that if we label something a "commodity," we often turn it into one. We listen to bankers describing the commercial loan as a commodity, to Big 8 accounting-firm partners calling the audit a commodity. When the label is used, it usually, or often, means that one big step has been taken toward "self-fulfilling prophecy."[1]

If you call any of your services "commodities," is it any wonder the clients think so, too? If you view your services as no different from anybody else's, then that is what they will somehow turn out to be. The key to a perception of quality in your marketplace is to differentiate your firm and your services from your competitors.

Chapter 7 compared phases in the life cycle of professional services to trappers, ranchers, and farmers. The analogy is simply a thinking tool to give you multiple viewpoints of your practice. Here's yet another viewpoint: Most professions render two types of services. Consultant Don Istvan calls these "Type I" and "Type II" services.

TYPE I SERVICES

The first kind comprises services that clients have to have, though they do not necessarily *want* to have them. These "Type I" services have some of the following characteristics:

- Clients need them, but they don't necessarily want them. Frequently, clients buy these services because they are required by a third party, such as a government, insurance company, title company, etc. In effect, the third party creates the market for Type I services. The benefit to the client is negative—avoidance of hassle.

- Often, the service is past-oriented, meaning it may relate to reporting the past or cleaning up the problems of the past.

- As long as the service satisfies the third party who requires it, internal quality is not particularly important.

- Price is easily compared to other service providers, even if quality of service is not.

- Technical expertise required is usually routine.

- The services involve a low degree of customization.

- You sell these services once and perform them many times. Therefore,

  - Once you get the clients, if you do a good job at a fair fee, they will almost automatically use you the next time they need this service. You might almost think of them as an annuity.
  - Sales cost as a percentage of revenue is low after the first sale.

- The services are frequently billed based on time or on a standard fee for the type of service.

- The services are often billed below standard rates.

- These services can usually be scheduled in advance to smooth your work flow.

Examples:

- For CPAs, Type I services would be tax returns or audits
- For attorneys, routine incorporations
- For engineers, boundary surveys
- For architects, applications for zoning variances
- For doctors, insurance physicals
- For dentists, filling or extracting teeth
- For veterinarians, these would be boarding and vaccination services

---

TYPE II SERVICES

The second kind of services—Type II—are those that clients both need and want. Type II services may have the following attributes:

- The services are salable on their own merits because they address a real problem or opportunity.
- The services are often future oriented and relate to improving future profits or otherwise obtaining future benefits.
- Internal quality is important to clients even if they are not qualified to evaluate the service outcome.
- Neither price nor service quality is easily compared to other service providers.
- High-level technical expertise may be required.
- Services may be highly customized.
- Each service is performed only once, so
  - Each job must be individually sold
  - Sales cost as a percentage of revenue is high
- Services are billed based on their value to the client.

- Price is not a particularly dominant issue; the key issue is perceived benefit to the client.

- Services may be emergencies or otherwise unexpected and often cannot be scheduled in advance.

Examples:

- For CPAs, these services would include management consulting and income tax planning

- For attorneys, estate planning or contract negotiations

- For engineers and architects, designing and building new corporate headquarters

- For doctors, elective surgery or diet counseling

- For dentists, gold crowns or orthodontics

- For veterinarians, these would include oral surgery

Some consultants have said that Type I services are becoming commodities. I disagree. As Theodore Levitt[2] points out, people usually presume that these services are very price sensitive: "A fractionally lower price gets the business. That's seldom true except in the imaginary world of economics textbooks." In the real world, other considerations are also involved, even where price competition is heated. The only reason some people say that price differences are so powerful is because price is so visible and easily measured, and the other factors may be quite subtle and subjective.

Certainly price is not *un*important; it may even be highly influential. But influential does not mean omnipotent. Price is so visible and measurable that it often diverts attention from ways to successfully avoid price competition. Sometimes, price pressures are so compelling and obvious that you don't consider other possibilities. Nor are these other possibilities confined to so-called "nonprice competition" such as advertising, harder selling, or what is loosely termed "better service."

As Levitt[3] points out, "*there is no such thing as a commodity.*" All goods and services can be differentiated to some extent. It is precisely when the "generic" product is identical—like a collection action, a tax return, a teeth cleaning, boarding a pet, or a boundary survey—that the other considerations that you promise make the difference in your getting and keeping clients.

WHAT IS YOUR PRODUCT?

Chapter 2 noted that clients do not buy your services; they buy what your services will do for them. What your services furnish ultimately boils down to two things: good feelings and/or solutions to problems. You might think of "good feelings" as the external quality dimension and "solutions to problems" as the service outcome, such as making money, saving money, improving productivity, or avoiding a loss. Though most professional services are bought primarily to solve problems, good feelings can be important to clients, too.

What you sell to your clients is an agreement with each client to solve his or her problem, and you hope to make him or her feel good about it at the same time. The probability of that agreement being fulfilled lies somewhere between a hope and a commitment, depending on the nature of the service. If your client has been to five other professionals who have all said his or her problem is hopeless, your proposed service might only be a faint hope to solve the problem. On the other hand, a client with a routine service request might take your proposal as a hard commitment to achieve the desired results.

What Levitt[4] calls "the generic product" is the basic service that you and all your competitors offer.

Examples:

- For lawyers, this product is having passed the bar exam and being licensed to practice law.

- For real estate brokers, it is possessing the necessary license and having listed properties for sale.

- For stock brokers, it is having a seat on a stock exchange and the facilities to process customers' buy and sell orders.

The generic product is the entry fee to play the game. It is the "commodity" underlying the service you offer.

Remember three facts:

1. Reality is what you can perceive clearly.

2. People cannot clearly perceive the differences in your generic product.

3. People respond only to differences.

limb was the thickness of an oil tanker. Those limbs convulsed as it detached from the cliff, lowering its terrible body onto the ocean floor. Its limbs smashed down into the ghostly muck, sending up combers of marine snow that rolled in awesome white waves. . . .

"Lucas."

Luke spun. The flashlight pinned Clayton in its beam. Luke inhaled sharply. Even LB let out a low yowl of concern.

"You look pained," Clayton said.

Clay's body appeared to have shrunk—it was as if the incredible pressure of the water was gradually crushing him down. His chest seemed thicker, his legs, too: Luke had the awful image of an accordion being squeezed with inexorable force.

Clay's face bore the same hints of compression. Where before it had seemed aristocratic, with the high forehead and flinty cheeks, it now had a fleshy, porcine look. His eyes were squeezed between wadded-up skin, making it seem that he was peering through slits of fatback.

"Are you all right, Clay? You don't look well."

"Never better, brother."

His lab was open. Light spilled across the floor. That familiar dripping noise invaded Luke's ears.

Drrrrrthilllipppppp!

"Come inside," Clayton said. "You'll catch your death of cold."

Another one of their mother's pet phrases. Luke's memory raced through a few others. *Useless as tits on a bull. Snowball's chance in hell. Lord love a duck*—the phrase she'd screamed after Chester Higgs had beaten her with that hoe.

"It's not that cold."

Clayton nodded dismissively and turned back to the lab.

"Clay, wait."

Clayton wore a sweater, the kind fishermen wear. His left hand was swaddled in gauze. His left arm seemed thicker than his right. Luke figured the whole limb was encased in bandages. God knew what lay underneath.

"Dr. Toy's dead," Luke said simply. "The ceiling caved in. Crushed him."

"That's too bad," said Clayton.

"Christ, Clay. Did you hear what I just . . . ? No, of course you did. Westlake, now Toy. The ambrosia is . . . it's not what you think it is."

Clayton scoffed. "It's simply a substance, Lucas. A tool."

So goddamn sure of himself. He never learns.

"Do you have any idea what was happening just behind that door?" Luke pointed at Westlake's lab. "What still *is*, for all we know? Two men have been killed by . . . I don't know what. It's all linked. The station, the ambrosia, and . . ."

. . . whatever controls the ambrosia . . .

Clayton said, "Do you have any idea how stupid you sound? Westlake went crazy. By the sounds of it, Toy died in a structural collapse. Both of which were known threats. Men have perished underwater in such circumstances before, and will again. It's the danger of working this deep."

Luke wanted to grab Clay's arm (his unbandaged one; the prospect of gripping the other arm was wildly revolting) and drag him to Dr. Toy's destroyed quarters. He wanted to show Clayton the metal pulsing in the ruined porthole.

But he knew it would be useless. Westlake and Toy were fools. That's what Clayton would say. And to an extent he was correct, if the only measuring stick for their intellect was his own immeasurable gifts. But they had been smart men, serious men, and they had shattered, utterly. This place had done it to them.

"What if you're wrong?" Luke said. "Just this once? What if this stuff is of no benefit at all? It can't cure the 'Gets, can't cure anything. What if *you* can't control it? What . . . what if it's controlling *you*, Clay? If it knows you—your habits, your flaws? Maybe it's playing you. What if . . ."

Westlake's voice: *We're in the basement with the beast—*

". . . Clay, what if it never lets you go?"

Clayton's reply was shocking.

"I don't really care if it cures anything."

". . . wait, what?"

"I . . . don't . . . *care*," he said, enunciating each word. "People *need* to die. Of cancer and AIDS and whatever else. There's too many of us. Too many by half. It's a planetary imperative. Not enough resources to sustain the hordes. We needed a grand curative. We call the 'Gets a disease but it's not. Mother Nature has taken out her broom; she's sweeping up the trash."

Luke's skull throbbed. "Jesus, then . . . why agree to come down here, if you disagreed with the whole purpose?"

"Because I'm fascinated, Lucas. I really just want to know how it *works*."

Luke found it almost impossible to grapple with his brother's misanthropy. It wasn't that he was hateful, as their mother had been—you required a working emotional barometer in order to feel anything at either pole, be it love or hate. Clayton's barometer was zeroed out. His emotional weather patterns were unvarying. No shutter-rattling storms, no radiant sunlight. Just an endless string of gray, edgeless days.

Luke had never really known Clayton. It would have been like trying to comprehend the mindscape of a meticulously disguised alien, a creature composed of sentient goo poured into an empty shell that he'd called his brother.

"If you don't give a shit," Luke said, "then why the fuck didn't they send down someone who does?"

"Because none of those people can do what I can do."

"You *fuck*. You miserable fucking specimen of humanity."

Clayton's expression suggested he took this as a compliment. It was perfectly acceptable to be a miserable representative of a species you cared nothing for.

Drrrrrrithhlipppppp!

"What is that, Clay?" Luke said coldly. "What the *fuck* is that noise?"

Luke shoved past his brother, adrenaline tweaked as he stalked toward the open hatch. LB was stuck tight to his heels.

4.

THE LAB WAS BRIGHT and ordered, not a hair out of place. Positively *Claytonian*. Luke's gaze fell on the cooler containing the guinea pig . . .

. . . the guinea pig, and the strange shape wrapped in durable black plastic.

Ttthhwillipp!

The sound was coming from behind the Einstein poster. Ole Albert with his tongue stuck out of his mouth. A sense of unreality washed over Luke. It was so plainly obvious, wasn't it? How had he missed it?

Hell, on my last descent I brought a poster of Albert Einstein for your brother, he remembered Alice telling him.

"Oh, shit. I don't . . . how could you . . . you *Shawshanked* us," he said softly. "Oh, Clay. You sly dog, you."

"You cannot move it," Clay said, setting himself in front of Luke. "Do you understand? It's forbidden."

Who was he, Bluebeard with his locked room full of severed heads? What did that make Luke then—his cringing, servile wife?

Luke took a step toward Clayton; a challenging smile tweaked his lips. LB came forward, too, her eyes resting on Clay with bright menace.

"You can't move it." Clayton spoke carefully. "Trust me, you don't *want* to."

The buzz drifted through from the main lab, adding to the riot in Luke's head. It was as if wasps had built a nest between his ears, stinging the insides of his skull.

"I think I ought to know," Luke said, deathly soft. "I'm not a scientist, right? Why keep your secrets from me? Unless, I mean, you're working on a new dog-neutering system." A hollow laugh. "You're not working on that, Clay. Are you?"

"Get away from me."

"Shouldn't I know, brother? I came all this way."

"I never asked you to."

"Oh, I think you did." Luke's throat was dry, and the words came out in a choked rasp. "I think you've done plenty down here without even knowing it."

Next they were grappling with each other. They waltzed awkwardly around the lab bench, locked up like professional wrestlers—not yet committed to actual violence, just testing their strength. Luke's fingers sunk into the bandages on his brother's hand; his flesh had a sickening *give*, spongier than skin should ever be.

Luke was dismayed to discover that Clayton's strength overmastered his own. It was that age-old truism: no matter how old two brothers got, the older brother still had the upper hand in any physical confrontation. Clay's elbow clipped the bridge of Luke's nose. The room exploded in cold blue fire; Luke's synapses lit up like a pinball machine. He stuttered backward on his heels and fell, a shockwave juddering up his spine.

Clayton's face shaped itself into an expression that did not often grace it: concern. He stepped forward, his hand instinctively outstretched.

"Luke, I'm so—"

LB sprang. Her skull rammed into Clayton's breadbasket; the wind whoofed out of him. He tottered backward, arms held out to ward off LB's jaws. She was harrying him now, not nipping but really *biting*, aiming to do some serious damage.

"LB! Heel!" Luke shouted. "*Heel!*"

The dog paid him no mind. Clayton's hip hit the edge of the lab bench, spinning him sideways. He fell backward, arms thrown out to check his fall.

His fingertips snagged on the poster. A look of helpless panic entered his eyes.

The poster stretched—for a heart-stopping moment it appeared as if it might hold—then it ripped from its hooks and fluttered down onto Clayton's chest.

Dear Christ, Luke thought. *It's worse than I thought. More awful than I ever could have imagined.*

5.

A HOLE. Halfway up the wall.

Except it wasn't really a hole, was it? Whatever Westlake had seen, however he'd contextualized it, he'd been wrong.

Its surface was darker than the sea beyond the wall; it shimmered like the placid surface of a lake stirred by a breeze. Upon casual inspection, it may've seemed solid—it held back the water, didn't it?—but Luke knew if he were to touch it, his fingers would pass through into . . . his mind couldn't grasp what might occur next. It couldn't even form an outline.

The (not a) hole was rung by smaller ones, the same way moons ring a planet. A few were the diameter of nickels; others were quite a bit larger.

The hole—*stop calling it that, Luke. A hole is ordinary and of this world; this is something else entirely*—the hole-*thing* followed the curve of the wall: Luke could see a heating pipe running beneath it.

The hole-thing, the *rift*, glittered dully around its edges. It was growing. The smaller holes appeared to be enlarging, too, nibbling into the wall.

A new sensation: fishhooks sunk into Luke's brain, tugging insistently.

He leaned toward the hole, the pain of his nose forgotten. He felt no danger; not an imminent sense, anyway. A voice buried in his subconscious warned him not to trust that sense of calm, but . . . yes, he trusted the hole. Oh yes, he trusted it completely. More than he trusted the structural safety of the *Trieste*, in fact. He tasted blood on his tongue but this, too, was a faraway sense. The hole—

It's not a goddamn—

But it *was* a hole, wasn't it? Sure it was. What was a hole, after all, but a, a . . .

Doorway?

A split in the surface of things. An absence of matter. You could fill that absence with any old thing, couldn't you? Put a lid over it, keep everything precious hidden from sight. You could bury dangerous things in holes, too. Holes were good that way.

Holes kept secrets. Holes and standing pipes and Tickle Trunks, yes, those too. We buried bodies in holes, and the dead were the best at keeping secrets. If a hole was big enough, well, you could hide any old thing at all.

Something was coming through the hole now.

Its surface split as a wriggling tongue pushed itself out.

It's ambrosia, Luke realized, icy splinters filching into his heart. *This is how it gets inside the station. It's how Clayton's been collecting it.*

The ambrosia slipped through the hole and dropped—

Thwwwiiiilllliiipppp . . .

—into a small collection vessel Clayton had affixed to the wall, which had also been hidden by the poster.

It was the first time since Luke had been down that he'd experienced something undeniably not of this world. Everything else could be fobbed off as the product of his overheated imagination, or of Westlake's runaway psychosis. Even Dr. Toy's death could have been a structural mishap. But *this*—the hole, the ambrosia sliming out of it—stood outside all earthly logic.

"Don't look at it directly," Luke heard Clayton say.

Luke was on his knees now, crawling toward the hole. He found this distressing in a distant kind of way.

Hey, Luke, your arms and legs are moving on their own. Isn't that kind of freaky?

Some*thing* was drawing him forward, pulling him closer to the, the *doorway*. He was struck with the profound urge to touch it—reach *into* it. He imagined it would feel warm and embracing. It'd crawl lovingly up his flesh as some strong current drew him deeper, to the wrist and then the elbow and eventually the armpit.

And it would feel like home, wouldn't it? Like the summer sunshine he remembered from childhood, slanting in golden abundance from a cornflower-blue Iowa sky, hot but not uncomfortably so—*cockle-warming*, as the old men at the Hawkeye barbershop would say. Yes, it would feel just glorious.

A hand closed over his wrist. Clayton gripped his arm fiercely. Luke wanted to rip out of his brother's grasp and continue toward the door—it really was more of a door, wasn't it? He'd open the door and see what was on the other side. It would be simply wonderful, he was certain of it.

"Look at me," Clayton said. "For Christ's sake, Lucas—*look*."

It required an epic force of will for Luke to keep his eyes locked on Clayton's. When he did, the pull of the doorway lessened the tiniest bit.

"I have to put the poster back up," said Clayton, his voice solidifying. "Don't look at it. I know it's hard—it *wants* you to look."

A relentless pressure in Luke's skull was torquing his head toward the hole.

"Talk to me, Lucas. Sing a song. It helps."

Luke hunted his mind for one of the silly kids' songs he'd sung to Zach. There were dozens; their lyrics danced on the tip of his tongue. But something else inside his head, a persistent presence, had other ambitions.

Why not take a look, Lucas?

An insistent voice. The voice of the hole.

What's the harm? Little door, little door, open me up! One quick peek. You know you want to. Or touch it, why not? I bet it feels just dandy.

The urge to look was almost sexual. Luke felt the need twisting in his groin with giddy excitement. His penis throbbed with it. There was an unpleasant burn high in his sinuses, as if he'd just dived into an over-chlorinated pool. Except it was a dreamy feeling, too, vaguely childlike— the need to peer into a darkened closet, if only to assure himself nothing was inside.

But what if something *was* inside? And what if it could bite?

"The wheels on the bus go round and round," Clayton sang. "Round and round, round and round."

"The wheels on the bus go round and round," Luke joined in. "All around the town."

"The wipers on the bus go swish-swish-swish," they sang together. "Swish-swish-swish, swish-swish-swish; the wipers on the bus go swish-swish-swish, all around the town."

Clayton picked up the poster. He approached the hole, his posture that of a man walking into a gale-force wind.

"The horn on the bus goes beep-beep-beep," he sang, "beep-beep-beep, beep-beep-beep . . ."

He hung the poster upside-down, punching the paper through the hooks. Einstein's expression now appeared baleful, his tongue cocked at a lewd angle.

As soon as the hole was covered, Luke's mind cleared. The brothers retreated to the far side of the room. They sat in silence, breathing heavily.

"I know this must be a lot to take in," Clayton said finally.

"It's just like Westlake said." Luke's voice was barely above a whisper. "His journals. You knew he wasn't crazy. You knew all along."

Clayton's face, oddly compressed and sun starved, gave him the look of a man in the final stages of tuberculosis.

"He wasn't crazy, Luke. He was just weak."

6.

"WHEN DID YOU FIRST see it?" Luke said.

Clayton leaned against the lab bench. He shot a furious glance at LB.

"Keep that dog away from me, you understand?"

Luke grasped his nose and gave it a wiggle; the cartilage crackled. He tasted blood, thick and ironlike. He felt no anger, only a dull shock. But the shock was tempered by the sense, deeply buried but sincere, that the holes *did* exist—he'd known it even without seeing them, so the adjustment now was easier. He wanted to hit Clayton but there was something about his brother, expressed in his sick pallor and swaddled arm, that indicated he was suffering in a serious way. And what would anger solve? It would only rip them further apart and reduce their chances of survival—which was just what the holes wanted, he was sure of it. So Luke would stow his childish hurts and stay calm.

"Just answer the question, Clay. When did you see it?"

"I don't know," Clayton said. "It's tough keeping track of time. At first it was so small, the size of a penny. And it wasn't so much that I even *saw* it at that point. It was that I . . . I *felt* it."

Clayton clearly hadn't hung the poster to stop anyone from seeing the hole—he'd hung it to stop the hole from seeing *him*.

That his brother had continued to work mere feet from it, collecting the ambrosia as it widened and grew, sucking ceaselessly at his psyche . . . Luke understood, not for the first time, that his brother's mind was built to a different tolerance.

"How does the poster muffle that feeling?"

Clayton shrugged. "I don't know the principles behind it. I only know it works."

What if it only works because whatever's behind the hole wants *Clay to* think *it works?* Luke wondered. *Could be it's slackening its pull, letting Clayton believe his flimsy poster is worth a tinker's damn—and what if Clay's too far gone to realize he's being played in such a simplistic fashion?*

It was conceivable. The smartest people were too often the stupidest—the most blind to manipulation, believing themselves immune to it.

"How much goo have you collected?"

Clayton's face puckered with distaste at the word *goo*.

"A good deal," he said. "At first we didn't see *any* of it. Frankly, I'd begun to despair. We'd built this station already. A man had died to get it operational."

"Not that you'd care about him," Luke snapped.

"True," Clayton said without rancor. "It was his job, as this is mine. But there was the expense to consider, too, in the trillions. And for days, *weeks*, there wasn't hide or hair of the substance the *Trieste* had been built to study. But the sensors began to pick it up—scraps drifting lazily around."

"Like iron filings to a magnet, huh?"

Clayton shrugged again. "I tried bait boxes filled with colorful shapes and reflecting mirrors, but it exhibited no attraction. It was *there*, Lucas, the ambrosia was there in tantalizing, taunting abundance, but I couldn't lay my hands on it."

"And then?"

"Then it invited itself inside. Problem solved."

"In Westlake's journal, he said that you collected a sample in a . . . a vaccu-trap, he said it was."

"I lied about that." Clayton's shrug indicated this could have been one of many lies he'd told. "I didn't want him knowing about the hole."

Westlake didn't want you knowing about his, either, thought Luke.

LB padded over to sit beside Luke. Her gaze flicked anxiously to the cooler.

"It's not safe," Luke said. "The hole. Rift. Whatever. For Christ's sake, Clay—whatever's on the other side of these holes *killed* Westlake. Killed him, or drove him insane and made him kill himself. And I can feel myself slipping, too. My mind coming undone little by little. Do we know what it *is*, Clay?" Luke stared searchingly at his brother. "Could it be some kind of . . . Christ, does it lead someplace else? Not into the sea on the other side of the wall, but another place entirely?"

Clayton said, "That may be the stupidest thing you've ever said."

The rage Luke had been struggling to tamp down exploded inside his brain—as if somebody had pushed the plunger on a detonation box wired to a stick of TNT sunk into his most sensitive neuron clusters.

"You colossal fucking idiot! Clay, you're squirreled away in a lab, thinking that hanging a fucking poster over something as powerful as *that*"—jabbing his finger toward the hole—"will do a goddamn thing! And you're calling *me* stupid? You may be the smartest man on earth, but you're fucking *clueless* down here and you're too mule-headed to admit it. Well, I'm here to tell you, brother of mine, you're severely outclassed. *Severely.* You're an idiot child compared to this thing. You'd need two brains, or three, to even *begin* to understand this. And even then you'd be too much of an obnoxious, smug, know-it-all *prick* to admit that you can't comprehend it."

Clayton withstood Luke's tirade as he always did: silently, motionlessly, but with a supercilious smile, as if he were a shrink weathering the blatherings of a raving maniac.

"So you're under the suspicion that it's some kind of—what?" Clayton's hands fluttered in front of his face: *Oooh, spooky!* "A hole that takes you away to the Land of Nod? Or back in time, perhaps?"

"Jesus, Clay," Luke said. "There's a *hole* in the fucking *wall* of this station, which happens to be at the bottom of the fucking ocean!"

"Lucas, listen to yourself. Calm down. It's nothing to be afraid of— cautious, yes, but fear is a wasteful emotion."

You're insane, Clayton. You have to be, if any of this strikes you as reasonable.

The bandages had unwound around two fingers of his brother's hand. The material was sodden with dark blood and something else, something fouler . . .

Luke's breath hitched; he nearly screamed.

When Luke was a boy his neighbor Cedric Figgs had developed a goiter on his neck. The massive, throbbing lesion resembled an unpopped zit. *Never look at it*, his father instructed. *Why make him feel bad?*

But it had been almost impossible *not* to stare at Cedric Figgs' goiter. The eye was drawn naturally, as a child's eye usually is to such horrors.

Clayton's hand was far more difficult to avoid staring at. But Luke couldn't let Clayton know that he'd noticed—because if Clayton saw Luke's eyes dodging to his hand, he'd know that Luke had perceived what he'd done.

And if Clayton knew, then *it* might know, too.

7.

THE EXTINCTION KIT. The thought blitzed through Luke's fevered mind. The one Clayton used to kill that guinea pig. Was it still under the lab bench?

Luke had seen its contents. There was a vial of Telazol, an animal narcotic. Back in veterinary school, a student had gotten hooked on the stuff; the guy had been discovered in the drug lockup, limp as a cooked noodle—he'd nearly choked to death on his tongue.

But how could he prep a hypo without Clay noticing?

The next heartbeat, the lights went out.

Luke was trapped in a bubble of pure animal panic.

They snapped on again—not the regular lights, though. These were small red lights strung down the ceiling.

"Emergency backup," Clayton said.

"We lost power?"

Clayton turned to face him in the blood-red glow. "For now. It should come back. It's happened a few times."

"Is there a power grid?"

"A fuse box, yes." He favored Luke with a wintry smile. "Maybe we can reset the breaker. Why don't I go check?"

Without another word, Clayton stepped into the main lab.

This is your chance, Luke. Your only chance, maybe.

The Extinction Kit was still under the bench. A much larger medical kit sat beside it. Luke found the Telazol. His hands shook as he snapped the cap off the vial, a motion he'd done a thousand times, so often it should be automatic. But right now his thumbnail couldn't find the stupid seam.

Goddamn it, move!

He set the vial aside. He unwrapped a syringe and affixed a needle to the tip. It was a small gauge, not much thicker than an insulin needle; if it bent while he grappled with Clayton—and he anticipated a struggle—then he might not be able to inject enough to immobilize him.

Prepare two syringes, then. Split the dose.

He unwrapped another syringe and needle. His hands shook. His brother was knocking around the main lab. Harsh rattling sounds.

Convenient, isn't it? his mother said from the deepest pits of Luke's subconscious. *The lights going out. What perfect timing for you, hmmm? Almost as if it was predetermined. Planned, somehow.*

The red lights pulsed against Luke's eyes. He didn't care why the power had gone out, or how; he had thirty seconds, maybe less, to make use of it. He shook the vial and tried to sink the needle into the rubber stopper—only to have it skate off the metal cap he'd forgotten was still on.

His brother was thumbing breakers now; Luke could hear the heavy *thu-thuck!* as he reset them in turn.

Had Clay noticed yet? The bandages unraveling off his fingers, revealing . . . ?

Don't think about it now, Luke. Just work.

His thumbnail found the groove; the cap popped off. He jabbed the needle in and withdrew 3 ccs, released the excess air, and set the hypo aside.

Clayton's footsteps approached across the main lab floor.

Luke sunk the second needle through the stopper. Shit. Too much air in the hypo; if he injected it, an air bubble could travel to Clay's heart and flatline him.

Would that kill him now, though? Would it kill what he might have become?

Clayton stepped through the hatch. Luke dropped behind the bench.

"Lucas?"

Luke drew the plunger back and this time he got the telltale *suck* that told him he was drawing only fluid.

Clayton rounded the bench. "Lucas, what are you up to?"

His voice had gone cold. A grating, gravelly rasp.

Luke depressed the plunger. A stream of Telazol pissed from the needle tip.

Clayton's hand fell upon his shoulder. The ragged, gummy edge of a bandage flapped against Luke's ear. Clay's hand squeezed with terrific force.

"Are you being bad, my child?"

The voice didn't belong to Clayton anymore.

In one move—remarkably smooth, considering how scared he was—Luke jerked up the hem of Clayton's overalls and sunk the needle into his calf.

It was, Luke imagined, like being stung by a hornet: it took a second for the message to travel to Clay's brain, then back down to the sting site. Clayton roared and lashed out. His boot struck Luke's chest. The glancing blow was enough to send Luke across the floor. The grate shredded his overalls and sent glittering shards of cold down his thighs.

"Very bad, my child. Oh yes-yes-yes, very bad indeed . . ."

Clayton's eyes. Oh God, his *eyes*. They glimmered in the bloody red light. There was nothing in them—not hostility or hurt or lunatic rage. They looked like lead-colored marbles socked into the face of a stuffed animal.

Those eyes rolled from Luke's face down to the hypodermic, which jutted straight from his calf, stiff as a diving board. Clayton's mouth pursed in a wry smile.

"Clever boy."

Luke crab-walked away. Clayton pursued sluggishly, dragging his leg.

"Clever, clever, clever . . ."

Luke's back hit the wall. He spun, disoriented in the red light, and scuttled away as Clayton made a clumsy and almost playful lunge.

He moves like a child, Luke thought wildly. *A baby learning how to walk.*

Luke tripped awkwardly against the lab bench. Clayton spun like a happy drunk, a blankly joyous look on his face. His leaden eyes widened: the look of a predator whose prey had stumbled carelessly into its midst.

Clayton reached for Luke. His bandaged arm had elongated in some terrible way, his fingers stretching, each digit acquiring extra joints . . . a version of that terrible arm that had *hu-thumped* out of the Tickle Trunk.

LB charged at Clayton, snarling. With disturbing quickness, Clayton shifted his attention from Luke to the dog. He caught her deftly, almost lovingly. LB snapped and bit, her teeth tearing shallow grooves in Clayton's neck—his flesh tore all too easily, like tissue paper.

"Good dog-gie."

Luke scrambled up, hunting for the second hypo. The floor was scattered with bits of medical equipment.

Gauze, a box of Band-Aids, a scalpel . . .

Clayton's hand tightened around LB's ear flap. With one spastic movement, he tore it off. It came off the dog's head with a gristly burr, kind of like an obstinate sleeve torn off an old letterman jacket. LB issued an electric yelp of pain.

The second hypo had fallen halfway through the floor grate; the plunger was hooked precariously on the saw-toothed metal. If the grate got rattled, the hypo could fall. Luke's fingers weren't long enough to reach it if that happened.

His brother's fingers, however . . .

LB strained in Clayton's grip, her legs scrabbling desperately. Clayton's smile widened—a madcap leer that threatened to split his head in half.

Luke closed his thumb and forefinger around the hypo, pulling it carefully from the grate. He moved behind his brother—whose unearthly eyes seemed to track him from an impossible angle, telescoping like a snail's eyes—then rose up and sunk the needle into his throat.

Clayton gargled and dropped the dog. The needle protruded from his neck. His bandaged arm flailed; Luke ducked as the limb swung over his skull like the unmoored boom on a sailboat.

Clayton staggered back and hit the wall and slid down, still clawing at the needle. He sat, legs splayed, toes pointed at the ceiling. His head dipped. His posture was that of a wino passed out in an alleyway.

LB had crawled to a corner and lay there whimpering.

Luke said, "It's okay, girl."

Gingerly, he pulled her paw away from the wound. A ragged tear, the flesh ripped unevenly to leave an inch or so of ear. Blood stained her golden coat.

"I'll fix you up. You'll be good as new."

Clayton's unbandaged hand still clutched LB's ear. Luke knelt beside him, fearful that his brother's eyes would pop open. He wrenched at Clayton's fingers until he pried LB's ear free. Staring at the blood-soaked flap, Luke was rocked by a wave of despondency and loneliness as profound as he'd ever known . . .

. . . the only time that came close to it was years ago, in that playground . . .

Luke's mind heaved. Another chunk broke off the crumbling landmass of his psyche, drifting into the dark. The portion that remained could comprehend that madness—true, uncaring lunacy—was not far away. Madness had been there since he'd set foot on the station; it had been dogging him persistently, waiting for the cracks to develop so that it could slip painlessly inside. That's exactly how it would happen, too: a quick little jab like a needle administered by an expert nurse. He'd barely feel the insanity take hold.

"You stuck your hand through the hole, Clayton. Couldn't help yourself, could you?"

8.

TWENTY MINUTES LATER LB's ear was bandaged and the dog was curled up, resting. Clayton was strapped to the bench in the main lab.

Luke used a Tensor bandage to lash his brother's heels together, then tied them to the bench. He hacked another Tensor in half and tied his wrists down. He could only hope that the restraints, plus the coldcocking dose of Telazol, would keep Clayton immobile while Luke inspected his arm.

"Let's see what we're dealing with, brother of mine."

Luke found latex gloves and a pair of medical shears in the first-aid kit. He slit Clayton's sweater up to his shoulder. Bandages covered Clayton's entire arm. They were encrusted with some kind of paste that smelled faintly of honeysuckle.

Luke cut the bandages away, starting at Clayton's shoulder. The flesh was pale and sweaty. But as Luke pulled the wrappings back, things began to change.

Pencil-thin threads of black appeared. They darkened Clay's flesh like tattoos. These gradually knit into a band of solid black, roughly four inches above his elbow.

Luke touched that flesh with his finger. He had a lot of experience with frostbite, which could turn skin black, but this wasn't it. Frostbite turned flesh pulpy and pestilent. The flesh of Clayton's upper arm was firm, just terribly discolored.

"What the hell what the hell what the *hell* . . ."

He snipped and gingerly peeled the bandages away; they trailed strings of gummy translucence like strips of duct tape whose glue had softened in the sun. The flesh beyond the black layer—about two solid inches—was the chalky white of processed lard. No arm hairs, no freckles or blemishes.

"Jesus, Clay. What have you done?"

He'd cut around the elbow and a few inches down the forearm when Clay's flesh became opaque. The sight reminded Luke of bacon grease stored in a glass: a top of hardened grease that gave way to clearer fat studded with burned bits of bacon. A few more snips and he was peering *into* Clayton's arm: a gray, gelatinous sheath of flesh—was it even flesh anymore?—that displayed the blue tubes of his veins.

The shears were gummed with translucent ooze. The bandages came away much easier now, anyway. He could peel them off with his fingers.

LB poked her head around Luke's hips. "Go on," Luke warned her. "Scat." The dog tucked her tail and retreated to a corner, watching him fearfully.

When Luke uncovered Clayton's hand, black dots popped before his eyes.

He could see bones. That wasn't the worst of it. Clayton's flesh quivered like Jell-O fresh from the fridge . . . and yet it didn't seem squishy, as Jell-O would be.

A chrysalis, he thought. *I'm seeing the same process that happens inside a cocoon, when a caterpillar turns into a moth . . . or a pollywog turns into a frog. A transformation so intense that everything melts and is reborn.*

Clayton's swollen fingers ended in stubs. Strips of medical tape sloughed off each one . . . Why had Clay taped them? His finger bones appeared to overlap one another, like photographic negatives set slightly off-kilter—

Clayton's arm tensed. His hand curled into a fist.

His eyes were still closed.

Was there a ghost of a smile on his face?

His hand uncurled. Then something perfectly awful happened.

With a gluey suck, Clayton's fingers . . . *unfolded.*

9.

CLAYTON'S FINGERTIPS BENT BACK from his palms, each digit trailing a runner of ooze.

He's folded them down, Luke realized in horror. *They grew longer and longer and he got scared so he folded them over themselves and taped them down. It was the only way to convince himself it wasn't happening.*

He pictured his brother doing it. Teeth gritted, gagging back his horror, gripping each terrible finger and bending it into his palm, then taping the doubled-over digit tight.

His fingers unkinked one by one; they looked like pocketknives unfolding. Fully outstretched, each finger was monstrously long: the pinkie at least six inches, the others longer than that. They were skinny and cruel, spread on the bench like the tines of a garden rake.

The tips were wide and spoon shaped, with large nail beds. The perfect mulch in which to cultivate dark, sharp nails.

It was a hand Luke had seen before. A hand that, as an adult, he'd convinced himself couldn't possibly exist.

But here it was. Grafted onto—growing *out of*—his brother's own flesh.

He would cut the fucking thing off. Not just the hand, the whole goddamn arm. It revolted him at a subcellular level. He thought that—and his thoughts were unfocused on this item, perhaps even a wee bit delusional—well, that if he took the infected arm off, maybe he could save Clayton. Excise the cancer, save the rest. Even though his brother was a miserable shit, Luke had to salvage what he could. The dog, Alice, even his brother. Everything else he would abandon to shriek and gibber down here at the bottom of the world, alone in its misery.

As he stood debating this, still grappling with the sight of his brother's

horrible appendage, Clayton's hand clenched again. A sudden spastic movement as if it had been hit with high voltage. Luke backed out of its range,
watching pop-eyed. The wrist swiveled, those snakish fingers hooking the
edge of the bench. With a convulsive flex, they tightened. The flesh of Clayton's wrist stretched like carnival taffy. The ulna and carpal bones pulled
apart with a meaty *thok*. The fingers crawled forward, reseated their grip, and
contracted again. The realization dawned on Luke.

It's tearing itself off.

The skin of Clayton's wrist stretched and thinned, then began to rip
apart. It did so noiselessly, like fork-tender beef. There was no blood at all;
in that way it was as clean as unscrewing a hand from a mannequin. Luke
knew this sight should bother him much more than it did—but now, right
this minute, it didn't seem nearly as strange as it ought to. That his brother's
hand was pulling itself off, amputating itself from the limb it had been attached to since birth, didn't seem that unnatural at all. It wasn't really *part*
of Clayton, was it? It was infected. So in a way, Luke was happy to see it
go—sort of like watching a tumor excise itself before a surgeon was forced
to do it.

Clayton's body juddered as his mutinous hand jerked and clenched,
the last few tenacious rags of skin shearing through as it snapped forward, free now, the wrist trailing off blue ropes of nerve and veins filled
with blackened blood. The hand went limp as soon as it had detached,
the fingers relaxing. Gravity carried it off the edge of the bench; it hit the
grate with a smack. Disgusted, Luke kicked it under the bench.

A sense of numb duty drove him to bandage up Clayton's wrist
stump—there was no blood at all. Events were happening too swiftly; his
mind was struggling to process them. His one simpleminded ambition
was to drag Clayton's body to the *Challenger*, but the immensity of that
task filled him with a bone-deep exhaustion. And even if he dragged him
there, what then?

. . . *skritch, skritch, skritch* . . .

10.

THE NOISE HOOKED ITSELF to motes of dust, which drifted lazily through the air to Luke's ears.

... *skritch* ...

A playful scrape at his thighs. It was just LB, of course it was. The dog was trying to get his attention. But no—he could see LB in the corner, watching him with obvious concern.

... *skriiiitch* ...

His overalls tightened a few inches below his groin. A thrilling tension. It reminded him of his first sexual experience in eleventh grade with Becky Sue Morgentaler. Becky was a good Baptist girl—she refused to take Luke's pants off or to actually *touch* him down there. But she'd permit his hands to roam freely under her sweater while she grabbed his jeans midway down his thighs and pulled with aching pressure, drawing the denim tight over his throbbing erection.

Pulling isn't touching, she'd murmur. *Pulling isn't touching, or sucking, or anything much at all.*

... *skritch* ...

Clayton's amputated hand. It was on the floor at his feet. Its pointer finger curled in a come-hither gesture. Every time it curled, it brushed Luke's overalls.

It's just the nerves, Luke thought. *Nothing but nerve endings firing one last futile salvo. I saw a decapitated corn snake bite its own tail; I watched venom spurt from its neck stump as it bit and chewed* ...

But this was slow and deliberate. Worst of all, there was something *sexual* to the gesture, that finger flirting lovingly along his ankle.

Hey big boy ... *pulling isn't touching, right?*

Luke lunged away. His arm swung, sending bandages and vials across the floor.

The hand flapped once more—a fey, mocking wave—and went limp.

Luke bit back his disgust and reached down for Mr. Hand—that's how he suddenly thought of it; not Clayton's torn-off hand, but *Mr. Hand*—although it really resembled a huge and horrible spider.

Go ahead, Luke, Mr. Hand seemed to say. *Touch me. Grab me.*

Jaw clenched, nerves jangling, Luke vised his fingers around Mr. Hand, gripping it by the mangled remains of its wrist. He held it at the end of his arm as though it was a poisonous snake. He realized that those long, crablike fingers could easily wrap around his own wrist—hell, they could reach halfway up his forearm.

"Go ahead," he seethed. "Go ahead and try. See where it gets you."

The hand remained limp. Luke threw open the cooler lid. A sad puff of mist billowed out—with the power cut, it wasn't that cool anymore.

The small guinea pig rested in a thawing mantle of frost. The thing beneath it, the one wrapped in trash bags and duct tape, remained motionless.

Luke heaved Mr. Hand inside. It bounced off the cooler lid. Mr. Hand skidded down the side—then came alive, spidering about with nimble movements.

It finger-walked over to the frozen guinea pig and tightened into a fist.

The guinea pig . . . *compacted*. Its half-thawed flesh squished between Mr. Hand's fingers. Rags of flesh splattered the cooler's insides.

Mr. Hand unclenched again. Lay there covered in gore.

One finger twitched. Coyly beckoning.

No hard feelings, right, Luke? We can be friends. Heck, let's shake on it.

Luke slammed the cooler shut, gagging on his fear. He set a heavy box of lab equipment on the lid.

Clayton was still passed out. Luke wanted to check on Al—it was critical to keep an eye on *everything*, but he couldn't possibly be two places at once.

Luke pushed up Clayton's eyelid. His pupil was a piss hole in the snow. He'd be out awhile—and when he awoke, he'd be groggy and safely trussed up on the lab bench. Luke could risk leaving him for a few minutes, couldn't he?

"Come on, LB. Let's go see Al."

11.

LUKE SENSED IT right away. An emptiness in the storage tunnel.

His footsteps faltered as he rounded the gooseneck and made his way to the *Challenger*. He could dimly make out the generator and the cables snaking out of it.

"Al?"

He picked up the flashlight Al had left behind. He trained it down the tunnel. He walked past the genny to the far end of the tunnel. The hatch was locked. He walked back. LB padded obediently behind.

"Hey, Al?"

Was she inside the *Challenger?* Luke rapped the hatch with his knuckles. Long minutes went by. The hatch didn't open. Was the sub still there? It had to be. Alice would never . . .

He sat, knees tucked to his chest, arms wrapped around his knee-caps. He wanted to cry but was too tired. LB rested her head on his crossed arms and peered soulfully into his bloodshot eyes.

The flashlight cut out. Luke slapped it with his palm a few times, flicked the switch on and off. Nothing. Christly fuck. At least the emergency lights were still on.

"Where could she be, girl?"

LB gave a noncommittal chuff. Al couldn't have returned to the lab; Luke would have spotted her. She might have headed down one of the other tunnels, but why? They had two goals: get the sub working and get home. Neither of those goals could be met by wandering aimlessly down empty tunnels.

What if Al had fallen asleep again? She could've wandered any-place . . .

Maybe she left, Lucas.

His mother's cold voice, back once more. The bitch always came back.

She could be halfway to the surface by now, she said reasonably. *Maybe she discovered there was only enough power to take one person. Maybe she said to herself: I'll go and come back with a fully powered vessel. Or maybe, Lucas—and you have to consider this as a very strong possibility—she just left because she* could. *Because she was shit-scared. People do that, you know. Given their druthers, people do the nastiest, most weak-willed and insensitive things imaginable.*

No. Luke didn't believe that. He wouldn't let his mother—his *dead* mother, dead nearly three decades now, her bones moldering in a Celestial Sleeper casket under six feet of Iowa clay—poison his thoughts.

No more, Ma. You don't have that hold over me anymore.

The emergency lights flickered, then died. Darkness fell like a guillotine blade.

12.

THE SENSATION was not unlike being doused with a bucket of freezing water. Luke's body went stiff as the fear shot through his veins. His chest convulsed with hiccupy inhales but he couldn't let them go.

The most profound darkness he'd ever known swept over him. The absolute absence of light, fueled by a fearsome pressure. Workers in a caved-in mine shaft might have an inkling of this sensation, but how far down was the deepest mine shaft? A mile? At eight miles, the blackness was some new kind of scientific thing, a darkness nobody had experienced before . . . except this *wasn't* new, was it? It was the opposite. This darkness was ageless. And it had been waiting a very long time for Luke to inherit it.

A reddish tinge painted the backsides of his eyes; his final sight—the tunnel, the generator, LB's face—lingered in the afterglow before dissolving. The darkness pushed against his eyes and flitted against his shut lips, seeking entrance; it was so thick that he could feel its weight in his lungs. It was a different, horrible breed of darkness: brooding, *knowing*, full of all those things that as a child you were certain it must hold. But beyond that there was the sheer terror of that dark itself—its immensity, its incalculable isolation. And that's what Luke felt most keenly: his abrupt and total isolation, as if he'd opened his eyes to find himself floating in deepest space, beyond the light of a single guiding star.

He staggered sideways, striking his knee on the generator; pain needled to his crotch. He shuffled forward in halting baby steps. His fingers grazed the wall; he flinched. The metal was as clammy as the rocks in a sea cave.

The dog yelped—a short, breathless note.

"LB?"

He couldn't hear her nails clicking on the floor anymore. If it weren't for the sound of his own raspy exhales, Luke would have thought he'd gone deaf.

"Where are you, girl?"

No sound of her breathing. He'd lost the distinctive scent of her breath. She was gone. Surely he'd have heard her go? A hole couldn't have opened up in the floor and sucked her down . . .

Oh no? his mother said.

"LB? Come on, baby. I know you're there. Don't be scared."

Nothing but the overwhelming dark and a faint rustling from all sides. A hard, prolonged compression invaded Luke's chest. LB was gone. She'd been taken by the station. By its new—*no, Luke, by its very very old*—inhabitants.

It was as if a critical part of him had been stolen—the twine binding everything together. The dog had been the first creature he'd encountered on the *Trieste*. His anchor. The direness of her loss cleaved him in two. Alice was AWOL—Christ, maybe she *had* left. His brother was useless. Dr. Toy was dead. The power was out.

Luke was entirely alone.

Alone like your son was left alone in the woods alone because you lost him because you took your eyes off him at the moment it mattered most—

He heard a lush, tickling note. From where? It was so hard to tell in this darkness.

There. It must be coming from beyond the gooseneck, toward Toy's quarters.

But that hatch was locked, wasn't it? Yes. He'd checked only minutes ago.

It came again. A moist note like a mop dragged over a tile floor. Silence. It came again, closer this time.

Otto Railsback.

The name leapt out at him. Railsback, who'd welded this station together. Down here alone in the dark—this exact same dark. A wee scrap of a thing, isn't that what Alice said? He finished his job, laid his head down and died.

But he wasn't dead. *No-no-no.* He was here now, crawling toward Luke. His legs had been torn away above the hips; the knobs of his spine projected through the bloody meat. The moplike sound was made by his unraveling intestines, still wet and juicy, *whishing* across the grate.

Luke had no intention of confronting whatever was really making those sounds. He backed away, struggling to recall where the tunnel bent so he could trace his way out again.

In the dark, a man's thoughts described an unhealthy spiral. No matter what he tried to orient his mind on—the shape of his wife's face or the sound of his boy's laughter or the taste of a fall peach plucked right off the tree—every thought seemed to loop back, unerringly, to those shapes in the darkness with their guts unfurling from cracked-open bellies . . . And it was worse down here, so much worse, because that hammering Christly goddamn *pressure* never stopped welting down on him, a never-ending compression that cinched his brain in a vise, warping all rational thought . . . *Nothing is impossible down here, Luke.* This singular thought blazed across his mind. He was in a place where truly anything could happen. The edges of reality were blown out, inviting in every conceivability. That terrifying notion—*all was possible*—stripped a man's mind to its fragile bedrock.

The sounds changed. Became a *clitter-clitter-clack.*

Nails on metal. Dog nails?

LB?

No, it wasn't LB. Luke couldn't put this sense into words, but he knew. It was something else . . . though perhaps not entirely. A new kind of LB, maybe. Whatever a dog might become after the station had swallowed it and spat it back out.

Click . . . click . . . click . . .

A growl. A rippling rusty sound like a balky chainsaw revving up.

Luke turned and fled. His face slammed into a wall; his mouth filled with a bracing metallic tang—the same as when, as a boy, he'd slipped on a patch of ice and smashed his face on the frozen schoolyard slide. He spun, regained his balance, and kept running. The air in front of his face had a staticky appearance, like TV snow on a dead channel.

Click . . . click . . . click-click-click—

Luke ran headlong into another wall and reeled away, convinced that the LB-thing was close behind now, accelerating on legs bunched with muscle, its fang-studded jaws open wide.

His hands slapped the storage area hatch. He ran his palms over it until his fingers slipped around its edge. He slid through the hatchway just as something slammed against it, jarring the hatch shut and jolting him to the ground.

The hatch's hinges squealed. Luke skittered away as the metal groaned. The porthole must have broken; Luke could hear cracks threading across the thick glass.

He imagined that glass shattering—imagined whatever was on the other side *pouring* through the broken glass like hungering oil.

The shuddering stopped. But Luke could still feel his pursuer behind that hatch. His mind was unable to conjure its shape. That was surely for the best.

He needed a flashlight. He was certain he'd seen one in the communications room. Why hadn't he grabbed it then? Stupid idiot. He stood and got moving, feeling blindly along the wall. His fingers brushed the edge of another hatch. It led to the comm room, he was certain. Through this hatch and down a short tunnel, past one hatch to the next one. Yes, that was it.

The flashlight would be there. It *had* to be.

Luke swung the hatch open. He crossed the threshold timidly—he half expected the floor to be replaced with plummeting nothingness. His toe hit metal. He crept down the tunnel until he reached the second hatch. He stepped through into the comm room. His hands feathered along the wall. His fingers brushed something smooth and tubular like a sleeping boa constrictor. Luke recoiled, his breath whistling in his ears.

It's just a pipe. A harmless heating or cooling pipe.

His entire frame was tense. Soon, very soon, something would reach out of the darkness and grab him . . . or worse, enfold him in a loving caress.

His hands closed on the flashlight. When he released the clips, it slipped through his fingers and clattered to the floor.

Damn-damn-DAMN!

He groped after it, hoping to God he hadn't cracked the bulb. He found it and thumbed the switch. A circle of light appeared on the wall. Luke's heart flooded with relief. It was weak, but goddamn, blissfully, it was light.

He followed the beam out of the room and back down the tunnel. He returned to the main tunnel and trained the light on the storage hatch.

It was unmarked. The steel unbuckled, the porthole unshattered.

This station does as it likes, he thought. *It ruins itself and fixes itself. Stop questioning any of it.*

Laughter.

He swung the light behind him. Nothing. He aimed it on the storage hatch again, then in the other direction, toward the main lab. Nothing.

A prepubescent giggle shot through the dark, splintering the air.

A mocking titter.

"Daddy . . ."

Another titter. Zach's voice, unmistakably. Luke backed away from it—but that was impossible, wasn't it? It came from every angle: a cold and airless giggle that made the flesh jump down Luke's throat.

The flashlight felt pitiful in his hands, a piss-poor little toy, totally unfit for the task of pushing back the enormous dark that assaulted him . . . a darkness rebounding with his son's laughter.

He didn't *want* to see Zachary. He didn't want to confront what this place had done to him. But his arm moved nonetheless, the beam staggering over the walls and floor and cei—

Pajama bottoms. A pair of them hanging pendulant from the ceiling.

Something jutted from the leg-holes. Thick and tubular, holding the mellow glow of well-polished metal.

Tiny appendages were studded all along their length, anchoring it to the ceiling.

Legs. Dozens and dozens of little legs. A millipede's legs jutting out of his son's old pajamas.

The titter came again. Choked and somehow insectile this time.

Luke could not even begin to conceive of the organism that might make such a sound.

It's me, Daddy. Just little ole me. Ole Zach Attack. Shine your little light on me. You'll see, I promise you'll see everything!

Luke wouldn't—*couldn't*—let the light touch the thing hooked to the ceiling ten yards away, wearing his son's pajamas. If he allowed that to happen, he would go mad. It would happen instantaneously, the moment the light touched the thing's teeming face. A sharp note would sound in the dead center of his mind, a brittle snap or click, and his sanity would be burned out like a fuse going dead. A deadness would enter his eyes. He'd begin to titter along with the thing on the ceiling.

He might even be inclined to . . . to *hug* it. The two of them entwined lovingly in the dark. Yes, he could imagine that happening quite clearly.

The flashlight beam lurched, taking in the thing's chest. The pajamas were stretched under the bulbous weight of whatever lay beneath them, the way his mother's old clothes had stretched under the tortuous bulk of her fattening body. The fabric was split under the armpits and across the belly; Luke saw parts of some awful anatomy bristling and constricting through those tears.

"Daddy." The voice was cold. Commanding. "*Look at meeeee . . .*"

And dear Jesus, he *wanted* to. Even if it drove him insane. It would be an end, wouldn't it? He could give up. His obligation would end. Just switch the flashlight off and surrender. Let the things inside the station slither and hiss out of every dark hollow and claim him.

It wants to drive you mad, Luke. A final, desperate plea from his subconscious. *It'll make it all so much easier. You'll be their plaything—do you really want that, after all you've been through?*

The beam crept toward the thing's head. It hung from the ceiling, batlike, its horrible body shuddering and bucking. Its hips thrust lewdly, in furious rut.

Luke's thumb found the flashlight button. Something fought his intent—*no no no you must not do that you disobedient boy you must look must look look you fucking bastard look at me look at US*—but Luke fought back, overriding it.

He clicked the light off.

"You don't exist." His voice quavered, but only slightly. "My son is not down here. You do not have that control—not over him, or me. If you want me, I'm here." His hand curled around the flashlight. "Come get me, you fucker."

Silence. Then: a soft note like a silk scarf unwinding from around a metal pole. Next, a percussive *pop* followed by the gentlest outrush of air.

The tunnel was empty. Luke didn't have to switch the flashlight on to know that. He felt it. The presence, whatever it was, had departed for the time being.

He flicked the flashlight on and got moving. Darkness was netted in the crawl-through chute; he went through feetfirst—he wanted a chance, at least, to kick at anything that might try to slither through from the other side. He slid through and continued on to the main lab. The beam roamed up the walls to the ceiling—

What the hell was that?

Holes were eating into the ceiling now. He saw one, then two, then a third, staggered a few feet apart.

Fresh fear scuttled up from the balls of his feet on febrile spider legs; when he swallowed, his throat felt like it was lined with carpenter's glue.

The main lab was empty. Luke shone the flashlight on his brother. The stump was . . . *gooey*. Some gluey substance had already soaked through the cap of bandages; strings of ichor dangled to the bench.

"Al? LB?"

Luke's despair thickened. After all this, Luke was left with his misanthropic, one-handed brother. He'd have to carry on as planned. Lug Clay to the *Challenger* and wait. If it became clear that Al and LB were truly lost and gone, he'd have to leave. He didn't know how to pilot the damn thing, but Al said there wasn't much to it. Seal the hatch, drop the weights, rise like a cork. Maybe he would rise too fast and the bends would twist the Nelson boys into human pretzels. Luke didn't care. He didn't want to die down here. If he had to die, okay, he was nearly resigned to it now—but he wanted to die while moving toward the sun.

He leaned on the bench, summoning the remains of his physical energy. His flashlight traced idle patterns on the wall. The beam touched the window, which was now covered in a gelatinous sheet of ambrosia. The stuff shuddered in the light—a sight not unlike a thousand eyelids snapping open and closed in rapid motion.

Luke swung the flashlight away, sickened. The beam landed on Westlake's lab. The porthole was smeared with that tarlike black. The light pelted right off it.

Until a hand slapped the glass.

13.

LUKE FLINCHED, even though the glass was too thick for the slap to have made a sound. He bobbled the flashlight and when he trained it on the porthole again, the hand was still there.

His arms broke out in gooseflesh. The hand pressed to the glass, that squalid black squeezing between its fingers. Then it was gone.

A small hand.

A feminine hand.

Al's hand?

How had she gotten inside? The hatch was locked and only Westlake's combination would open it . . . unless it'd come unlocked during the power outage?

When Luke tried to push off the bench to investigate, he was dismayed to discover his ass was tightly glued to it.

Get up, for Christ's sake. Open that goddamn door.

He heaved himself up. His legs carried him forward as his mind raced through a View-Master's reel of horrifying images, both real and imagined.

Click: Westlake's scarified body in its cooling vault.

Click: The pages of Westlake's diary smeared with black gunk.

Click: Huge fire-eyed bees droning around Westlake's lab, trundling through carbuncled, ooze-dripping honeycombs.

Click: A hole in the lab wall, bees flitting in and out, the narcotic buzz of their wings melding with the whispers drifting from the hole.

Luke's fingers fell upon the wheel on Westlake's hatch. It wouldn't budge. He stuck the flashlight under his armpit and used both hands. Nothing.

Did the lock have a fail-safe in the event of a power outage? Was it wedged shut from the other side?

Luke settled his ear against the hatch. He tried to pick up a sound apart from that frenetic buzz. Al's voice, perhaps. Her screams, even.

"Al?" he whispered. "Jesus, if you're in there . . ."

The drone spiked—a warning? an invitation?—then settled again.

Luke couldn't get inside. But thankfully that meant Al couldn't be inside, either.

Unless she's locked herself in. And wedged the hatch shut.

Why in Christ's name would she . . . ?

Quit thinking about it, he chided himself. *You can't get inside. She's not in there. She has more sense than that. This place is fucking with you again—it* wants *you to open the hatch, don't you see? You've got to keep moving. Stick to the plan.*

The plan. Okay. First things first. Transport Clayton to the *Challenger*.

Luke cut the Tensors and rolled Clayton onto his side. His brother showed no sign of awakening, but Luke filled another hypo with Telazol and slipped it into his pocket just in case. After a moment's consideration, he slipped a scalpel in with it.

Luke raised Clayton's arm and ducked his head under to heft him up. Clayton was incredibly heavy, especially with Luke as exhausted as he was. He'd manage it somehow. As he was leaving the lab, Luke heard a muffled thump from Clayton's lab.

The cooler.

Oh, God. Its contents were thawing. And they wanted out.

He set Clayton down and shone the flashlight into the lab.

The cooler lid rattled ominously.

Thump. Tha-thump-thump.

The box of lab equipment Luke had set atop the cooler jumped. Before long, it would get knocked off. Then the creatures inside would be set loose in the dark.

Luke retrieved the Tensors he'd used to bind Clayton. Working quickly, he strung them under the cooler and knotted them tightly across the lid. When he was finished, it looked like a birthday present that nobody in their right fucking mind would want to open. He put the lab equipment back on top, thinking it couldn't hurt.

With his ear pressed to the cooler, he could make out noises inside: long slow scratches, not unlike nails raking the inside of a coffin.

He shut the hatch to the lab and turned his attention back to Clayton.

"Okay, brother dear. Let's get cracking."

Dragging him through the tunnels was draining, awkward work. Luke tried a modified fireman's carry, but the tunnel was too low for that. He tried carrying him the way you'd hoist a drunk, one arm hooked over his shoulder. Clay hung limp and heavy, toes scraping the floor. It was hard to carry him and keep the flashlight focused forward at the same time. Eventually Luke sat Clayton down and hooked his arms under Clay's armpits, hands clasped across his chest, and dragged him. Luke hated not being able to see where he was going—he couldn't see what, if anything, was waiting in the dark—but it was a lot quicker this way. Every few feet he stopped to sweep the flashlight behind him, ensuring that the tunnel looked as he remembered it.

He reached the crawl-through chute. Jesus. How was he going to manage this? It'd be easier to shove his brother in headfirst, humans being naturally top-heavy, but without anyone to catch him on the other side, Clay would fall bonelessly; he might smash his head open. So feet-first it would have to be.

Luke shone the flashlight down the crawl-through. Its insides glittered fitfully; the beam didn't penetrate the solid dark on the other side.

"Fuck it," he muttered. "Upsy-daisy."

He wrangled Clay's heels and calves into the chute. It was hard work to shove and shoulder Clayton's body up and in; Clay's scalp got cut open on the grate and one of his arms got hooked behind his back in a painful-looking chicken wing. Luke was breathing hard by the time Clay's knees cleared the lip of the chute. He felt like a mobster feeding a dead stoolie into a wood chipper.

Luke cranked Clay's midsection up and levered him into the chute. Luke figured he should go feetfirst, too, his heels braced on Clayton's shoulders to push him along. Progress would be tortuous, but he could do it.

He pushed Clayton down the crawl-through as far as he could using his hands, then pulled himself out, gripped the first overhead rung in both hands, swung into the chute, and settled his feet on either side of Clayton's head. Pushing with his hips and hauling with his arms, he was able to get Clayton's body sliding forward. Luke's shoulders and head were swallowed into the chute. He braced his palms and pushed against the rungs, propelling their bodies forward. The flashlight jutted from the hip pocket of his overalls, shining directly into his eyes—

Something was behind him. Coming down the dark tunnel.

He couldn't see it, not yet—but oooh, he could *smell* it.

A childhood smell. The same one that would waft up from the white Styrofoam container with the perforated lid he'd buy at the local bait shop for two bucks. He'd put that container in his backpack and sling his fishing rod over his shoulder and head down to the river. On the banks he'd open the container and see them wriggling under a layer of sawdust. Maggots. The best bait for rock bass. Luke had always found them re-volting—their fat, milky bodies so translucent you could see the weird workings of their guts through their skin. They wriggled delightedly, it seemed, when he pinched them between his thumb and fingers—just happy to be touched, even if it meant they'd shortly be skewered on a barbed hook. Their skin would dimple like a badly inflated balloon before the hook punched through their bodies—and their elated paroxysms would persist *after* they'd been skewered, these crazed squirms that would entice a fish to bite . . .

This was what filled Luke's nose: that rancid, sawdust smell of mag-gots in a bait cup.

He snatched the flashlight and twisted onto his stomach. The beam flooded out of the crawl-through and hit a sheer wall of darkness where he'd just been. The light picked up a patina of dust—dead skin cells, it could only be, seeing as there was nothing else down here that could be-come dust.

Lubbaduuuuu . . . Loooooolubbaduuuu . . .

This sound came next, sluicing out of the dark. A slick and *gooey* noise, like a ball of Vaseline-smeared yarn squished in a fist.

Luke felt it out there now—pulsating and lewd, a giant maggot. A horrific white grub in search of its wormhole; the very hole Luke and Clayton were trapped inside.

The tunnel lights flickered on for a moment.

Luke saw it, or was certain he had. Enormous. It curled around the tunnel and out of sight, thirty feet of it visible, as thick around as an industrial trash can. Its pale ringed ugliness seared his eyeballs; its huge gelatinous body convulsed along the floor in a series of giddy, peristaltic flexes. The sight filled Luke with a narcotizing terror—a slow-acting nectar that oozed into his veins.

The lights went out again. The thing continued to suck and shudder itself forward.

. . . *looolubbaaaaaduuuuu* . . .

Frantically, Luke pushed himself backward. His hands slipped uselessly on the frictionless coating inside the tube: he may as well be trying to climb a greased pole. He reached up, spine bowed, and shoved desperately at the rungs with his palms.

The flashlight picked up an oily slab of chalk-white flesh no more than a yard away from the mouth of the crawl-through . . .

Loorblovvaducthhh . . .

Luke paused, trapped in a breathless bubble of panic. That noise, which he'd mistaken for the sound of the maggot's body shucking across the floor, was something else.

It was a voice. A familiar one.

Looooordloveaducthhhhh . . .

A quivering mass of unctuous, marble-white flesh plugged the end of the crawl-through. The air turned dense; that stink rolled off the maggot in thick, drowsy waves.

The maggot's face was not his mother's—of course not; maggots didn't *have* faces—and yet, this was exactly what Luke saw. Her visage stitched onto the maggot's shuddering, enormous body. There was a porcine fleshiness, that flat-hanging sagginess his mother's face had held at her heaviest. And its eyes—two of them, socked deep into the puddled sickliness of that sallow face—were black and empty, as his mother's would get when she was angry. Its mouth was a puckered orifice like an anteater's: a long, needlelike proboscis.

Looooordloveaductthhhh . . . it sputtered, putrid bits of goo flinging from its mouth. *Looooordlovvvvaducthhhhh* . . .

OhGodOhGodOhGodOhGod—this was the only thought Luke's mind could summon, a brainless yawp of fright. He rammed his heels into his brother's shoulders, trying to get them both moving again.

The Beth-maggot squelched deeper into the tube; Luke could hear its massive body drumming against the tunnel, coiling and bucking like agitated eels in a bucket. Its mouth opened with stunning elasticity, a rubbery O big enough to consume his entire head. Its insides resembled a huge intestine, a funnel of suffocating corrugated flesh.

He grabbed another rung and pushed. His brother's body lurched as his feet dropped out of the crawl-through chute and hit the floor.

The maggot was a yard from Luke's face. It shuddered over the flashlight, which lit up its body—it looked, Luke thought with paralyzing horror, like the vein-strung insides of an eyeball. The featureless white was strung with tiny veins and capillaries. Next, the flesh split raggedly down the middle of the maggot's face. It made no sound, as its skin had the consistency of a waterlogged sponge.

It's too big to fit, Luke thought frantically. *It's ripping itself apart.*

He watched, horrified, as his mother's face tore in half. A new face was pushing through the split, though, and this one was also all-too-familiar . . .

Nononononono—

Abby. White and gory as a newborn babe. Her eyes were wet jewels; her lips stretched across the canvas of her horridly misshapen features, pursed in a lascivious come-on.

Giveuttthhakistthhh, babbeeeee . . .

Luke knew that if those lips touched him, he would go insane.

Are you sure you're not already? asked a frail voice in his head. *At least a little?*

Elbowing, squirming, he retreated down the chute in total desperation. The Abby-maggot squelched after him, hungering for a kiss. Just one little kiss, baby.

Its face split for a final time—just as Luke knew it would, in the deepest chambers of his heart. The crowning detail. Abby's face tore apart, molting in wet, waxy rags, her mouth issuing a very human scream of pain and despair, and, bristling through her sundered face like a knotted fist . . . his son. It looked nothing like Zachary—a face so wizened and repellent that it could only belong to some terribly ancient and hateful *thing* that had never tasted sunlight on its flesh, its eyes peering with a cheery and mocking avarice—and yet it so clearly *was* Zachary. It was what this place had made of him, and Luke's soul shuddered to see it.

Daaaaaddeeeee . . . it lisped through cracked, pus-weeping lips. *Heeelp meee* . . .

Luke's feet slipped from the tube. With one convulsive shove, he propelled himself out. His feet got tangled with his brother, who was slumped gracelessly on the floor. Luke tripped backward, his son's voice—*Daddeeee*—still ringing in his ears; his skull rung off the side of the tunnel and—

—he came to with a spastic jerk of his limbs. He squinted. The flashlight had rolled out of the crawl-through, pinning both him and Clayton in its beam.

The crawl-through chute was empty. He didn't need to see that to know.

The maggot was gone. The station had had its fun and, for now, was satisfied.

He picked up the flashlight, hefted Clayton, and continued on.

14.

LUKE REACHED the storage tunnel hatch and hesitated.

The station wants to keep you frightened so you'll make mistakes, Luke. Make enough of them, take long enough, and it's game over.

Clayton's eyelids twitched. Was he waking up? Luke fingered the hypodermic in his pocket. He didn't want to overdose his brother. But the last time he'd been conscious, he hadn't behaved all that nicely.

He could leave Clayton right here at the hatchway. He was a lot closer, at least . . .

Fuck half measures, Luke. Dump his ass at the Challenger, *then either wait for Al and the dog or go find them.*

Luke gripped the wheel. The lock disengaged with a *thunk*. The hatch opened half an inch. For an instant, Luke swore that hell itself was breathing through that gap.

The feeling ebbed. He opened it and shone the flashlight into the storage tunnel. Nothing moved. Nothing appeared out of place.

He dragged Clayton around the gooseneck to the *Challenger*. The generator was making odd whirrs and clicks like a computer warming up.

He rested with his hands on his knees, centering himself. He felt okay. Dog tired, but okay. Things were falling into place. He had Clayton where he needed to be. He'd find Al—this sudden surety filled him with a bright gaiety that pushed the bleakness away a fraction. He *would* find her, or she would come to him. And LB, too. The world owed him, didn't it? The world had taken, and now it would give back. That was the way things worked, wasn't it? On a long enough time line, you paid what you owed—but you also got paid *back*. And hadn't they all paid enough? Weren't they *owed*, by God? Al, the dog, his brother. That was all Luke was asking for. A helping, fortuitous upward draft. Let a single beam of light in and let him follow it up, up, up out of the dark—

Click . . . click . . .

Luke trained the flashlight in the direction of this new noise—with the station swathed in darkness, sound had become his key sense. He slid one hand into his pocket and closed it around the scalpel.

Click . . . click . . .

A head appeared around the gooseneck. Two eyes shone like balls of mercury in the flashlight's glare.

"LB?"

She *woofed*—a grating, jagged note. Her jaws widened, strings of saliva stretched between her teeth as she chewed anxiously on the air.

She's scared. Totally terrified.

Luke swung the flashlight behind him. Nothing. When he swung it back, LB had emerged a little more—half of her body was now visible. Her fur was torn away in places, each spot almost perfectly round. Luke didn't see any blood.

"Come on, girl. It's okay. It's only me."

She whined plaintively, then ducked back behind the bend. The *click-click* of her nails retreated.

"LB!"

Luke scrambled after her. He ran the way he should have run after Zach that afternoon in the park—as if the devil himself was on his heels. She yelped someplace ahead, a harrowing note that stung Luke's heart.

He reached the spot where LB had been. Drops of some viscid substance swayed from the floor grate. A smell rose to Luke's nose: dank and vinegary, with an undernote he couldn't name.

He rushed on. The flashlight lit the holes along the *Trieste*'s hull. They *bulged*. Bubbles pushed up from their surfaces, shiny with tension.

"LB!"

He gritted his teeth and dove into the crawl-through chute, sliding for a few feet, then transitioning to his back and hauling himself over the final yards. He could hear LB barking not far ahead.

He ran into the main lab. Clayton's lab hatch was open again; he could see something moving inside. Luke edged up to the hatchway and shone the flashlight inside.

LB's head poked from behind Clay's bench. She barked consumptively.

There was something *off* about that sound.

"You okay, girl?"

Luke trained the flashlight on the bench. LB rounded slowly into sight like a showgirl stepping into a spotlight. Her head, shoulders, chest—

"Oh, LB. Oh, Jesus. What happened to you?"

Something was wrong with the dog's legs. They were sticks, winnowed and black like charred wood in a campfire. They made bonelike *clicks* as she came forward, her tongue—her long, seeping, cancerous tongue—dangling queerly from her mouth.

"What did this to you, girl?"

Luke beckoned her forward. *I can fix her*, he thought, although the chances of that were laughably remote. *She'll be all right . . .*

She lurched toward him. Her front legs could not bend—the bones had been fused somehow; she tottered as if walking on pegs.

Click, click . . .

Her back legs looked even worse: they'd been compressed, the bones snapped and jellied, leaving her with the squat hind end of a much smaller dog. Her paws had been flattened into clownish disks that slapped the floor.

Click, click. Click-click.

Something projected from LB's hind end. A red string unspooled from her anus. Jesus, what *was* that? Was something *inside* of her, trying to get out?

She staggered closer. *Click-click-click.* Her head sat weirdly on her neck, off-kilter like a doll's head that had been cut off and clumsily glued back on . . .

Luke's hands trembled. He didn't want to touch her, and this fact shamed him. She needed someone to hold her, didn't she? But he was terrified—the fear shot through his arteries like battery acid.

Her mouth opened in a too-big yawn. Her teeth were fearsomely long, crowded into sharp rows in her mouth. Her tongue was needled with holes where she'd bitten it . . .

. . . and what was *that*?

He squinted. Something was skewered on LB's teeth. Black and shiny and—

Plastic. A shred of plastic.

Spilled-out pieces of a complex puzzle slotted together in Luke's mind, forming a picture of shocking, horrifying clarity.

He jerked the flashlight toward the cooler. It was open, as he knew it would be. The lid had been torn off its hinges. It was surrounded with shreds of thick plastic and rags of duct tape. The creature that had resided inside it, the thing wrapped in black plastic, was out.

Luke trained the beam back on the dog-thing. It seemed to be smiling at him now.

Oh, God, this isn't LB, he thought. *It's the other one. Mushka. Little Fly.*

15.

THE DOG—SWEET CHRIST, was it in any way a dog anymore?—staggered closer. Luke wanted to pull away but he couldn't: his limbs were frozen.

Everything was so clear now. Clayton. He'd shaved away disks of fur to attach monitoring electrodes. He'd put something up the poor dog's anus, too: a device to measure heat or nerve stimulus; the wire was still sticking out.

Clayton had done all this, then he'd . . . he'd . . .

Pushed the dog through the fucking hole. Fed it into the rift, the same way Westlake had fed that microphone through . . .

Luke could picture it: the dog whining and kicking, its legs braced against the wall as his brother shoved it rudely through. Or else he'd drugged it and fed the poor thing through while it was narcotized.

He wanted to see how the thing or things on the other side would react, Luke realized. *What they would do. The dog was an offering.*

So it had gone into the hole and come back as . . . *this*. Clayton must've known immediately that something was wrong, so he'd killed it. Cut its head off, as he'd done to the guinea pig. But it had come back, hadn't it? So he killed it again and again until it was dead enough, for long enough, that he could encase it in plastic, bind it with tape, and stuff it into the—

A feral, considering brightness entered the dog's eyes. Its facial features were stretching. Rank foulness pumped from its pores. The flashlight picked up a faint glimmer over its coat. Its mouth stretched wide. Its eyes sunk back into its sockets.

Get out of here. RUN.

The tendons mooring its jaw snapped like overtaxed elastic bands. It issued the anxious mewls of a hungry baby. Luke stood in spellbound horror, transfixed as the dog's mouth cantilevered open, wider and wider, so big it seemed capable of swallowing hearts, souls, entire worlds . . .

It growled—but how could it, with its mouth ripped into that fearsome leer?

No, that growl was coming from somewhere else—

LB charged into the lab. Luke's heart leapt. Where had she come from? She ran right past Luke, making a beeline for her old pal. The dog-thing shifted its attention nimbly, but not quite quick enough. LB hit it broadside, jaws snapping; they tumbled around the bench and out of sight.

Luke took a few steps forward, sweeping the flashlight to make sure nothing else lurked in a darkened cubby of Clayton's lab.

LB issued a muffled yelp that rose to a pain-filled shriek.

Luke stepped around the bench and saw.

"Oh, God, no . . ."

The Mushka-thing's mouth was sunk into LB's flank; its jaws were scissored around LB's left rear leg, high up where it met her body. But it wasn't merely *biting* her; it was . . . *fusing* to her, was the word Luke's fevered brainpan spat out. As he watched in a delirium of panic, the Mushka-thing's muzzle flattened and spread over LB's fur; there were a series of dreadful metallic *fnk!* sounds, one after another, which reminded Luke of an industrial sewing machine punching through tough leather. Darts of blood shot from LB's skin. She whimpered, clawing toward Luke.

Luke rushed to her. His legs went to jelly at the exquisite horror of the scene; he reached her at a crawl. He was staring right into LB's eyes—two shocked orbs that radiated animal terror of a sort he had seen too many times. Yet they were unquestionably a dog's eyes. Luke had no idea where LB had been these past hours, but she was still the creature he'd known. The station hadn't changed her; she had not surrendered her innate . . . *humanity* was of course the wrong word, but the sentiment was the same—LB was fundamentally unaltered, still a dog, a very good dog who was terrified now and that fear shone starkly in her eyes.

Luke tried to wrap his arms around LB's front legs but they were scrabbling with such mindless intensity that he quickly changed course. Instead he grabbed her head and neck in a modified front headlock and tried to pull her away from the Mushka-thing . . . away from the hole that it was so clearly backing toward.

"Come on, girl," he panted. "Hold on, hold on with me here."

The Mushka-thing's entire head was now welded to LB's flanks, stitched to her flesh by some grisly alchemy. It was already difficult to tell where LB's body stopped and the Mushka-thing's started. Its skull was flattened and fanned out, the fur bunching up between its ears like the folds of a shar-pei dog. Its eyes, which were flat and gray as oysters, slid across the loosening canvas of its face until they merged into a single jellylike eye that stared at LB with an unquenchable hunger. It issued ceaseless sucking sounds. LB's body convulsed as something was hoovered out of her from the inside, creating a fleshy indentation in her chest. She howled.

"No no no," Luke heard himself shouting. "No please no please no—"

He tightened his grip and pulled as hard as he could. LB shuddered. The bandages ripped away from her torn ear. The Mushka-thing continued to back toward the Einstein poster on its stick legs. *Clickety-click.* Luke pulled with so much force that he felt's LB's spinal cord pop as the discs dislocated. It was useless. He may as well try to pull a tree out by its roots.

You're going to kill her, he thought. *You'll snap her neck.*

His next thought: *Would that really be so bad?*

The Mushka-thing was relentless. It had waited a long time to claim its prize. Luke pictured the two dogs coming down in one of the *Challengers*. Had Al brought them? Maybe so. They would have been shivering and worried as the fathoms dropped, but they had each other. And maybe that's all the Mushka-thing wanted—for them to be together again. To explore whatever lay behind the hole as one.

Luke couldn't budge her. Functionally, they were one creature now. Physically fused together. Finally, heartbreakingly, Luke sat in front of LB. He stopped pulling her. He hugged her instead. Even as she was

being tugged remorselessly toward her fate—one Luke could not derail—
he hugged her fiercely. He kissed her nose, hot with shock. It was, he realized, the same standard of care he offered shelter strays. Every few
months he would volunteer at the local pound, putting down creatures
who were too old, too sick, too irredeemable or simply unwanted. A
dozen, fifteen at a go. It wrecked him. He would stagger out to his car
afterward, shivering, and cry. It was easier with animals who were loved;
their owners, whole families, would stand around that cherished fur-ball
as Luke ushered it out of this life and into the next. But strays were euth-
anized in a cement room where a single light bulb hung on a cord. They
may have gone their whole lives unmothered and unloved. They didn't
deserve that. No creature did. The one thing that anyone should be able
to count on receiving in their lives, *love*, had too often been withheld
from those poor souls. And so Luke would comfort them. Each animal.
He would spend a few minutes cradling them, rocking them, speaking
softly to them. Sometimes they wouldn't stop shivering, or nip his fingers. This hurt him—not the pain, but the fact that love and gentleness
was so foreign to these creatures that they didn't know how to accept it.
Then he would kill them. It was not fair, and he hated himself for being
the agent of that pure, inevitable fact. The world did not hold to any
standard of fairness that Luke could comprehend. All his life stood testa-
ment to that. Good men die in wretched agony and bad men die happily
in their beds. Creatures live and die never knowing love.

The Mushka-thing jerked. LB was wrenched backward again, yanked
out of Luke's grip. He slid forward and reseated his grip. He wasn't desperate anymore. His fingers caressed those soft spots behind the jaw that
all dogs loved to have rubbed. He rested his forehead against hers. He
felt the thud of blood pounding in her skull.

The Mushka-thing reached back with one clownish rear leg. It
snagged on the poster and tore it down.

The whispers assaulted Luke immediately. A yammering, mindless—

No, not mindless there is a mind behind all this

—riot. Those fishhooks sunk into his head again, skewering his
brain.

The hole was the width of a manhole cover, but wider on one side; it resembled a mouth twisted into a murderous sneer.

He began to cry then, clutching LB. The tears came easily. He had not cried tears of such distilled regret since his son had gone missing. LB was going limp, either spent, tired of fighting, or resigned to her fate. Luke hugged her so, so tight. He wanted LB to remember his touch. The warmth and love that radiated from his whole body, coupled with the sadness that she was being ripped away from him. He wanted her to take that one physical memory with her wherever she was going. The imprint of his hands on her. He wished it to be a reminder that she was a good creature, and loved, and that there were places on the continuum where love and kindness still existed, even if she did not share that world presently. She did not deserve this. But things happened. They happened.

LB's body came alive in his grip, bucking in what Luke hoped was a final death-spasm. Her paws beat a frantic tattoo between his legs. White foam like beaten eggs emitted from the sides of her mouth.

"Oh no," Luke said. It was all he could say, in the end. It seemed to say everything. "Oh no oh no oh *no*."

The Mushka-thing was being sucked into the hole. Once its body made it halfway through, the pressure intensified exponentially; LB was jerked forward, at the mercy of whatever monstrous force existed on the other side. Luke kept pace with her. He stroked her head as gently as he could, but his hands were shaking badly.

Please remember this, he thought. *Please remember that you are part of the goodness of it all and that, and that, oh God oh please girl oh no oh no oh—*

LB's body was steadily sucked into the hole; she could have been on a conveyor belt, such was her unstoppable ingestion. She had calmed by then, her struggles over. She peered at him with sorrowful, weeping eyes and bit down gently on his hand, as if that might anchor her to Luke. Her grip loosened by degrees, freeing Luke's hand again. She gave him a hopeful look, as if this might all be a terrible dream they would both wake from shortly. Luke held on to her forelegs, her paws, the tips of her nails. She pulled away from him reluctantly, a kindergartner leaving the arms of her father on the first day of class. Fearful, yet perhaps understanding that this was the way of the world. Separations were unavoidable. These things happened every day.

She was snatched from Luke's numb grip, the upper half of her body dragging bonelessly up the wall. She gave a puppyish, exhausted bark. Her head went through last, and it went soundlessly, leaving only the faintest ripple on the hole's surface.

16.

LUKE GRABBED THE FLASHLIGHT and stumbled from Clayton's lab, away from the horrible whispers coming from the hole.

His breath escaped in sharp whinnies. Oh, Jesus. *Jesus.* LB was gone. Worse—*eaten.* No. Eaten would be preferable. Chewed up and digested and gone, her suffering over. But she'd just been . . . *taken.* And whatever lay on the other side of that hole was worse than a million cramped dog crates or vicious dogcatchers or rolled-up newspaper whacks, worse than anything any dog on Earth had ever suffered.

And Luke was terrified that LB would suffer for a long, long time.

The main lab was quiet. Disembodied voices fluttered against his eardrums, the wing beat of moths. He shut his eyes and swayed unsteadily. He could feel it now. Madness hungering at the edges of his mind. Maybe it was for the best. He could just go gibberingly, shit-smearingly insane. Then he could wrap his arms around his chest and huddle in a corner, shivering and drooling, until whatever was going to happen, happened.

Luke swung the hatch to Clayton's lab shut. The voices dimmed. He turned and immediately sensed something moving just below the flashlight's beam. A shape bristled up the wall, seeking the light.

Mr. Hand. His old friend.

It didn't look like anything that could once have been part of his brother. Pallid and gelatinous, sharp bones running under a horrible stretching of skin. It had sprouted additional fingers, too: it had eight now, giving it an arachnid appearance.

It walked up the wall and paused. It . . . *stretched.* A showy display, each finger lifting gracefully before settling back in place.

It looks like Thing, Luke thought with giddy, unhinged hilarity. *From* The Addams Family, *that old TV show.*

"What do you want?" he croaked at it.

Mr. Hand twitched—had it heard him? One of those long crablike fingers tapped the wall as if in deep thought.

What do I want, Luke? What do I want, indeed!

Mr. Hand hopped on the wall, playful little bobs. Each time it landed, there came this *squitch* from its fingertips.

One finger pointed straight up: *Aha!*

Mr. Hand leapt off the wall and advanced on Luke. He reached into his pocket and held up the scalpel in one trembling fist. Mr. Hand shivered—*Oooh, so scaaary!*—then flopped over like a dog playing dead.

One finger curled. That beckoning gesture again.

Follow me, follow me, said the spider to the fly . . .

Mr. Hand righted itself and skittered across the lab. Luke tracked it with the flashlight. The hand danced impishly along the floor, spinning balletically. Mr. Hand feinted left, back right, then flipped onto the wall. Where the hell was it going . . . ?

The keypad to Westlake's lab. A glowing square, each numeral outlined in a faint red square. Mr. Hand sprung up and landed on the keypad.

You always were the curious cat, weren't you?

His mother's voice in his head now, bitter as aspic.

Always sticking your nose in. Same as when you were a boy, wanting to get into your brother's lab even though he told you no, no, no. You couldn't take no for an answer, could you? You wanted to drink your greedy eyes full.

Mr. Hand punched a number. Punched another.

Curious, curious boy. You want to see what's behind door number three, my son? Do you want to play the bonus round, where the scores can really change?

"No, Mom," Luke croaked. "I don't want to see. Don't show me."

Mr. Hand tapped another number, and another . . .

There are some secrets, Lucas dear, that really ought to stay secrets.

"I don't want to see," Luke said hoarsely. "Please. Don't show me."

Take your medicine, son. Bitter, yes, but it's oooh-so-good for you.

Mr. Hand pushed the red button. The keypad went dark.

A hiss as the pressure valve on Westlake's hatch let go. A sweet, corrupted smell hit Luke's nostrils . . . the scent of rotting honeycomb, just maybe.

The hatch opened. Only a crack. The metallic squeal peeled back the nerve endings over every inch of Luke's skin.

And after the squeal came the buzz.

17.

COME-COME-COME-COME-COME-SEE-COME-SEE-COME-SEE

The whispers were louder now. Almost as loud as the maddening drone that curled through the hatch. The whispers vacillated, the sing-song call of a bird.

Come-SEE! Come-SEE! Come-SEE!

The buzz fell and rose like crazed laughter at some insectoid dinner party.

Come-SEE! Come-SEE!

Luke's feet obeyed this command. He begged them to stop but they just went stupidly on. His brain was a horrified inmate inside his body—Rapunzel trapped in a garret.

The flashlight illuminated the edge of the hatch, coated in foul syrup. The whispers mingled with the buzz, unifying in a single voice.

A bee—one of Westlake's bees, Luke realized with druggy horror—struggled through the syrup, its wings beating weakly. It toppled from the hatch and fell to the floor, its crooked legs waving uselessly in the air.

Luke's foot came down on the bee. It crunched agreeably under his boot. He felt the mad buzz of its wings through the sole. He laid one hand on the hatch. His fingers sunk into the desiccated syrup, crusty as old shaving foam.

Westlake's lab was muggy, the air perfumed with that sweet reek. The only light came from a serrated ring set an indeterminate distance away: that light was coming from the hole, it could only be.

By the hole's light Luke saw the bees—thousands; *tens of thousands*—surging around him on unseen currents, as if riding zephyrs that gusted through the lab.

He could sense rather than see a structure to his left. Monolithic in scope, far larger than this room should possibly contain. The hum found its center here: sonorous, rhythmic. It wasn't a bad sound, far from it: it was natural and clean, hitting notes that softened pleasantly into his bones.

You wanted to see, said his mother. *So see, Lucas. See it all.*

His hand rose, and with it the beam of his flashlight.

"My Lord . . ."

The hive was enormous. A carbuncled mass of wax and honeycomb that rose beyond the light. The ceiling had risen against the tremendous weight of water, becoming a great domed cathedral that could scarcely contain the colony.

It was horrible and beautiful. It was not unlike a city: parts of it were rotting and sloughing off in decayed rags, while industrious drones built new spires and whorls elsewhere. Its surface was crawling with industry. The bees were huge, some the size of sewer rats. They moved with a sluggish, almost stupid lethargy.

Uncomprehendingly, Luke traversed this staggering kingdom with the flashlight. He couldn't get a true measure of its size. The ceiling was out of sight and the walls had been blown back and out. Everyday notions of scale dissolved.

His eyes caught something. A ribbed tube, off-white, projecting through the honeycomb. It hung like an executioner's noose. Heavy-bodied bees trundled over that tube, pasting it to the hive with the ichor that spurted from puckered orifices on their abdomens.

Luke could see *stuff* moving through the tube. Slowly, like sludge through a partially blocked pipe . . .

Get out of here, Luke. Before you see something that ruins you.

He almost laughed. Too late for that. Too late by far.

The beam swept the hive. Lab equipment was studded through it. He saw half of a beaker. A glass pipette . . .

. . . a trio of blunt twigs projected from the comb. They looked like hardy buds sprouting from a pot of dirt. The bees busied themselves about them, tending to each bud in the manner of patient gardeners.

The sticks twitched.

The bees took flight with an aggrieved buzzing of wings before settling again.

Fingers. Those are fingers they're fingers they're—

Luke's hand operated of its own accord now. He saw things. Dreadful things.

A dusky loaf suspended from the hive on a strip of organ-meat . . .

A glint of bone that shone a delirious sapphire-blue . . .

A pinkly grooved ball that twitched when the light touched it . . .

Other things. Some worse, none better.

You wanted to see, my son. Do you like it? Does it please you?

Finally, horribly, the light fell upon a ball crawling with bees.

It projected from the hive a few feet above Luke's head. At first Luke had no idea what he was seeing—it could have been the bottom of a wide-bellied beaker. The bees fretted lovingly over its surface. Perhaps an exhaled breath sent them off; whatever the cause, they lifted away to attend to other labors.

I'll kiss it better.

That was the stupid thought that zipped through Luke's mind while his eyes drank in this most sublime horror. Abby used to say it to Zach whenever he scraped his knee or stubbed a toe. As if something so simple as a kiss could salve all hurts.

Don't worry, Alice, I'll kiss it better. Just a kiss and it will all be okay . . .

Her neck bulged from the hive, webbed with syrup. Her face had been sliced open vertically and horizontally, the cuts intersecting at her nose; the flesh was skinned back from the center of her face in four triangular flaps, stretched out and stitched to the comb. Her scalp was split down the center, the skin peeled back in thick folds; each fold had been anchored to the hive on thin metal armatures that must have once been part of Westlake's lab equipment. Her naked skull bone was dull as chalk.

Alice's body had been teased apart and strung all through the hive. Luke understood that without actually seeing all the evidence. Every limb and vein and nerve stem woven throughout the comb, tended to by diligent drone bees. Luke could only hope that she'd been dead before any of this began. He could only—

Al's eyelids snapped open. Her eyes were so very white in the flayed redness of her face. They rolled down languidly to meet Luke's horrified gaze. She smiled, her teeth ripped out. The grin of a newborn.

Luke felt no fear at the sight. That emotion had burned out quite suddenly, like an overloaded electrical switch. He felt nothing but an ineffable hopelessness—which in its way was so much worse than fear.

The buzz grew louder—*hungrier*. The whispers drummed into Luke's skull. Bees jigged nimbly around his head, alighting on his ears and hair. They returned to Alice, too, landing daintily on her skull, their antennae dancing lightly on the raw bone. Alice threw her head back, her mouth open as if in laughter; the flaps of her scalp strained threateningly against the metal armatures.

The scalpel was back in Luke's hand. He took a step toward Alice. Sensing his intent, the bees darted at his face, their wings paper-cutting his flesh. He slapped at them and caught one solidly; it fell to the floor with a squeal and Luke stepped on it, enjoying the sound of it pulping under his boot. The hive came alive. Drones emptied out of it, their fat bodies squeezing from the comb.

Luke would kill Alice. Slash her throat open—one swift sideways swipe to let the blood out. If these putrid things killed him for that, so be it. But he'd kill her before they finished him.

Alice's eyes filled with red as they hemorrhaged blood. They became the same color as the bees' eyes. Her lips formed a single word.

"No."

Luke's hand stilled. Bees alit on his arms, friendly now, nuzzling his flesh with their furry abdomens.

Alice smiled—it was the same one he'd seen on Abby's face at the hospital after Zachary was born.

The smile of a new mother.

The bees lifted off his arms, whirring into the dark. Luke followed them with the flashlight—

He saw it then. The final horror.

A huge translucent sac hung pendulant from the underside of the hive. It was the size of a trash bag—this was Luke's first, incredibly domestic thought. The big orange ones he'd stuff with autumn leaves after Zachary had finished jumping in the piles Luke had so diligently raked.

Instead of orange, this sac was milky, strung with blooms of red and blue veins. The bees zipped around it in protective patterns, a thousand insect nursemaids. A few large bees tiptoed over its surface, which was convulsing with unnatural birth.

The sac hung in close proximity to the hole—which was far bigger than even the one in Clayton's lab. Light poured around its edges.

By that light Luke could see something moving inside the sac. Limbs strained against its membrane the way stray elbows and knees will push against the canvas of a tent. Luke could barely glimpse the fearsome outline of whatever lay inside.

The sac ruptured. Thick, veiny broth gushed out. Luke shone the flashlight up to Alice. Her face was dented, her nose and cheeks forming a horrifying concavity—the pressure of this unnatural birth was caving her skull in.

But she was laughing. High, breathless screams of laughter.

Luke backed toward the hatch. There was no saving her. No saving LB. No saving no saving no saving—

The bees formed a corona around his head, their bodies beating at his back. Something breached the sac. Luke didn't get a good look at it, which was a mercy. Only a sense of some gaunt and nightmarish limb slitting its own womb apart with mechanical ruthlessness, making a sound like a thousand knuckles cracking as it tore and gouged.

Luke's heels hit the lip of the hatch, spilling him into the main lab.

The hatch swung shut on Alice's deformed, gibbering laughter.

18.

LUKE STARED DOWN at Clayton.

He did not know how he'd gotten here. Things had gone black after he'd left Westlake's lab. The hands on the clock had melted, and next he'd found himself back here. He must have slipped into another dream-pool. All he remembered was this sense of having moved through a huge intestine. The walls flexing, pushing him through like a stubborn shred of last evening's pot roast.

He'd lost the flashlight somewhere along the way. No matter: the station now pumped out a sick radiance all its own. The holes provided it.

His brother was propped awkwardly against the generator, which had been shoved almost flush to the wall. Had Clayton tried to sabotage it? Luke would kill him if he'd done that—that certainty rested easily in his mind. Kill him just as easy as breathing.

Clayton's face glowed in the dim. He looked even more horrible, as if some nightmare creature had gunged down the tunnel and sucked the blood out of Clayton's throat. Luke pictured Clay's neck winnowing and withering until it was no thicker than a pipe cleaner. This image made Luke smile.

"You killed it. The dog." Luke's voice was flat and toneless. Very much like his mother's voice, he noted.

Clayton's eyelids cracked. "Whu?"

"The dog. Little Fly. You pushed him through."

Clayton's head lolled. "That's what it was for."

Luke kicked him. Not hard, but not softly, either. "Get up."

"No."

"They're all dead. Alice. Hugo. Westlake. The dogs. All killed, all taken. We're the only ones left."

Are you sure they're really dead, Luke? Are you sure you're really so alone?

Luke kicked his brother again, harder this time. "Get your ass *up*. We have to at least try to get out of here."

"You try, Lucas. You always were the trier."

Things nattered and clicked beyond the tunnel bend. Luke's guts turned over—the fear had been replaced with a churning nausea.

"I want to see the sun again," Luke said, disgusted at his petulance— he sounded just as he had as a boy, begging to be let into Clay's lab. "I want to talk to Abby. Just one more time. Tell her how sorry I am. How much I miss her, and miss our boy."

"Go, then."

"There's nothing down here, Clayton. Can't you see that? There never was. This was all a trick. We chased it down here. We were tricked. *You* were tricked."

Clayton hung his head. "I can't go, Lucas."

Luke didn't feel anger—it would be as senseless as being angry at a dog for digging up a yard or a mallard for flying south for the winter. Genius or not, Clayton remained a creature of stupid instinct.

"You'll die, then, you dumb bastard."

Clayton shifted. Had the cap of bandages sloughed off his wound? The position of Clayton's body shielded the stump from view.

"Please, Clay. I've never asked you for anything. Just this once."

The clicks and scratches grew more insistent. Luke knelt beside Clayton. He'd pick him up and drag him into the *Challenger* if he had to. He'd wrestle and punch and choke and bite if it came to that; the sonofabitch only had one hand, anyway, and was drugged to the gills.

Luke gripped Clayton's shoulders. His brother thrashed, suddenly furious.

"I said, I *can't*. For Christ's sake, Lucas, please don't—"

But Luke wasn't to be denied. His hands slipped lower, pinning Clayton's arm to his side—Clayton issued a kittenish moan of protest— while his other hand brushed against the stump of his wrist . . .

Luke saw it then. No shock, no horror. His mind accepted the fact dully. In a way it made total sense.

The rope, the tube, the . . .

—umbilical cord—

. . . ran out of a fresh hole in the wall, a hole that had been obscured by the generator. The cord was bright red, same color as Alice's eyes. It was attached to Clayton's stump; thick bands wrapped the flesh of his forearm like tropical creepers.

Luke's fingers had sunk into that livid, twitching rope. They'd gone in without resistance, as if into warm mud. He glanced at Clayton, terror leaping up his throat; Clayton stared back with a look of ineffable sorrow and perhaps, finally if too late, understanding.

"I'm sorry," he said simply.

Luke tried to pull his fingers free. But he couldn't; they were stuck in a warm, fleshy Chinese finger trap. He glanced at his brother, their eyes locking—

Luke felt his consciousness traveling *into* Clayton's eyes, into his body, up his brainstem, and into his brain itself. His mind entered Clayton's somehow; a hidden latch lifted, a secret trapdoor springing open. Luke's mind was swallowed into Clayton's own; a chilly metallic veneer settled over his thoughts—the way Clayton must see the world.

Next Luke was rocked by a vision of searing clarity that swept over him like a tidal wave, obliterating all consciousness.

A MEMORY. A shared one, but now Luke was seeing it from his brother's perspective instead of his own.

They were kids again. Luke was eight years old—except he wasn't Luke, not right now. He was Clayton, nestled inside Clayton's body somehow, staring across the kitchen table at . . . well, himself. Their mother sat at the head of the table. It was night, blackness painted to the windows.

"I've got a job for you, my little soldiers," she said slyly.

She put a small pot on the table. Beside it, a hacksaw and two paintbrushes.

Luke remembered this night. Oh yes, he remembered it well.

Clayton and Luke donned their boots and warm sweaters. It was so odd, watching the world through his brother's eyes—a little like being strapped into an amusement park ride that he had no control over.

"You sure this is such a hot idea, Clay?" Luke heard his young self whisper once they were alone in the backyard, out of their mother's earshot.

Luke felt the words forming in Clayton's mouth before he spat them out.

"Shut up, dummy."

They stole into their neighbor's backyard. The branches of Mr. Rosewell's crabapple tree stretched over the fence into their yard; its hard, inedible fruit always fell on their lawn. Their mother had asked—really, she'd *ordered*—Mr. Rosewell to trim its branches, or better yet hack the awful thing down. Mr. Rosewell, a retired mailman with a buzz cut who'd recently lost his wife, said to hell with that. They'd stared at each other over the fence; then their mother had spun, graceless in her bulk, and waddled back into the house.

The boys knelt at the base of the tree. Clayton spun the lid off the pot. Their mother had bought it at the local hardware store that afternoon; its label bore a picture of a wilted, cronelike tree.

Clayton notched thin cuts in the tree with the hacksaw. Luke watched his younger self cast worried glances toward Mr. Rosewell's porch, as if in expectation the old mailman would step through the screen door, shotgun in hand.

The boys spat on the paintbrushes and painted the tree with whatever foul poison lay inside that pot. Then they dashed back to their house, eyes fairly shining with their deviltry.

"The two most precious boys in the whole world," their mother said. She'd baked a "celebration pie." Lemon meringue, Clayton's favorite. Trapped inside his brother's head, Luke could feel the sugary meringue dissolving on Clayton's tongue.

The memory took a weird lurch forward. Suddenly it was daytime. Luke was staring at the crabapple tree through Clayton's eyes. Its leaves were wilting. Gravity was treating it cruelly—punishing it, shoving it hard to the earth. Clayton picked up one of its fallen apples and took a bite. It was revolting, like sucking on a busted-open battery. Luke tried to get a grip on his brother's mind, searching for something—a shred of pity for the tree, perhaps, which shouldn't have had to die so horribly. He got nothing but a chilly backwash, as if he'd touched the insides of an industrial freezer.

The memory lurched again, the scene shifting. Clayton was in his basement lab now. A key rattled in the lock. He turned to see their mother filling the door frame. She wore her housecoat—the ratty one with the bleached-out stripes that gave her body the look of a moldering circus tent. The one she wore all day and night that stunk of her crazy sweat and bones.

"Go away." Clayton's voice was preternaturally calm, but Luke could feel an intense heat cooking at his brother's temples. "Leave me alone."

Their mother smiled. The most feral, cunning expression Luke had ever seen, her head cocked coyly to one side. The look of a predator who'd boxed in its quarry. She turned, carefree, and locked the door. Then she untied the sash on her robe, her back still turned. She did something with her hips, a lewd little shimmy; Luke felt the hairs standing up on Clayton's arms. She slipped the robe off one shoulder—the salacious movement of a peep-show worker—and turned to look over that same shoulder, pinning her son in a flat and viperish stare.

When she faced him again, the robe was open a few inches. Her body was obscenely enormous, bulging in thick rolls down to the shadowy delta between her legs. A smell wafted off her: not her normal stink, the one a body develops when deprived of sunlight and clean air, when all it does is sit on a cracked chesterfield and shovel porridge between its spittle-wet lips, a smell not unlike the stink that wafts off a mildewed shower curtain—no, this was raw, throttlingly hormonal. The smell of arousal.

"Come here, boy," she said softly. "Come to your mama."

Luke felt it seeping out of Clayton's skull—a jumpy, rabbity *tick-tick-tick* that made him think of cockroaches roasting and sputtering in a hot pan. That jumpy pop and crackle washed all through Luke's piggybacking mind, too—it was fear, or the closest approximation to that emotion his brother could feel.

Their mother advanced, limping slightly. Clayton backpedaled, his hip knocking a flask off the lab bench, where it shattered on the floor.

"Tsk-tsk. Clumsy boy. You'll have to pay for that in trade."

Her body was a sheet of suffocating flab but her arms were oh-so-strong. Luke felt his brother's heart pounding as he fought back wildly, aiming a knee at her wounded hips; she only laughed and pulled him closer—his struggles were nothing compared to that of the residents at the Second Chance Ranch. The heat of her body was weirdly narcotic; Clayton went limp, exhaling into the shelf of her enormous breasts, lips sputtering as he gasped for air.

"It's okay," their mother cooed, one hand fussing with Clayton's trousers. "You like it, remember? If you didn't like it, you wouldn't get so . . . so . . ."

The scene fried out in a stinking puff of smoke. Next: Clayton was back in the lab. Alone. The pot of tree killer sat on the bench. Clayton was concentrating on it intently. Luke could feel his furious focus. Clayton opened the lid and tapped a small amount of the pale blue powder onto the bench; it looked like pulverized robin's eggs. He opened other jars and vials containing compounds Luke knew nothing about. Mixing, measuring . . .

A series of memories shuffled past like holiday photos in a slide projector:

Flash: Clayton in the bathroom, shaking powder into their mother's shampoo bottle.

Flash: Clayton in the master bedroom, stirring powder into their mother's facial cream.

Flash: Clayton in the kitchen, tipping powder into the huge pot of porridge simmering on the stove.

A final memory:

Luke staring through Clayton's eyes again, up the basement stairs at their mother, who lay on the kitchen floor, nothing but skin and bones. She'd lost hundreds of pounds, the weight sloughing off. Doctors and specialists had paraded through the house for months by then; she'd visited hospitals as far distant as Houston and Rochester, Minnesota. Her condition left the best medical minds stumped. Bethany Ronnicks continued to wither into decay, her body the equivalent of an old jack-o'-lantern left on a front stoop weeks after Halloween had passed.

"Please," she whispered. "Stop this. I know it's you, Clayton . . . a mother *knows*."

Luke felt a smile spread across Clayton's face, a sliver of teeth in the dark. He must've looked beatific, a child saint.

Upstairs, their mother wept. These raw, hacking sobs.

"You bastard . . . rotten-ass bastard."

Luke felt something trickling down from the fuming stew of Clayton's subconscious. *Pleasure.* The most incredible pleasure imaginable, beyond sexual in its intensity.

Luke had always known Clayton was a monster of sorts—he now understood that Clayton grasped this fact of his essential self with a rational, clinical objectivity. He was a monster of detachment, eternally unmoored from his fellow man.

But their mother was a monster, too, and one much worse than Clayton. She'd given Clayton a reason to let his own monster out of its box . . . and his monster was a steely, calculating, devouring one, able to kill another of its kind with relative ease.

Clayton lay at the base of those steps, drinking in the sobs of the woman who'd given him life—the woman whose life he stole by subtle degrees until she was gone, her scarecrow remains buried in a cedar casket in the Memory Gardens cemetery on Muscatine Avenue in Iowa City—and he smiled. His contentment was more sublime than anything he'd ever felt until then or had felt since.

LUKE'S FINGERS pulled out of the ambrosia rope with a gluey suction. His consciousness fled back into him as he broke contact with Clayton's mind. Luke gagged, his skin feeling too heavy on his bones—like being smothered under a sopping bear pelt.

Clayton slumped against the generator, his eyelids hanging at half-mast. *Just taking a little catnap*, as their mother called them. Luke was still reeling from the revelation—not a vision, not a dream; that had been a truthful recounting of his brother's past, a shard chipped off the granite of his memory. He'd killed their mother. It was that simple. He was smarter than her and he'd made her pay. No guilt, no consequence. Clayton was simply expressing that monstrous part of himself—perhaps the *truest* part.

And Luke was grateful to him for that. He'd surely saved them both. But, like most of the great things his brother had done, it had been to satisfy himself and nobody else.

"I could try to cut through it," Luke said softly. "Maybe we could still . . ."

The cord undulated lazily, as if it had heard Luke's plan; Luke could sense its immense power coursing through his brother's body.

"You go, Lucas," said Clayton. "Go up. Go to the people you love, if they're still there. You . . . you *try*. You keep on trying, yes?"

The cord jerked, dragging Clayton with it. Luke reached for him . . . then he stopped. This was how his brother wanted it. More importantly, it was what he'd earned. Clayton belonged to whatever lay on the other side of that hole more than he'd ever belonged to the human race. Maybe the voices had sensed this and called out to him. They'd found a way to bring him down.

Clayton smiled. He kept smiling as the cord retracted into the hole. Smiled as his stump and shoulder were swallowed into it. Smiled as his skull bent against the *Trieste*'s unyielding wall. Smiled as his spine broke with a wishbone snap, his heels beating a jittery tattoo on the floor. His head was consumed. The rest of his body followed.

Afterward all was silence. Nothing came back out of the hole. Maybe it had taken all it could possibly take.

"Will you let me leave?" Luke asked it. "I only want to see my wife again."

Nothing answered him.

Luke faced the *Challenger*'s hatch. He hadn't been back inside it since Alice had sent him through into the *Trieste*.

The wheel spun smoothly. The hatch opened with machined precision. He anchored his hands and boosted himself up into the—

19.

—INSIDE.

Light. The first sensation. Stinging brightness. His rods and cones went haywire; tears squeezed out of his eyes and sheeted down his face.

Warmth. The second, glorious sensation.

For a second, Luke imagined he was on a beach. Warm sand, sun blazing overhead. Gulls screeching as they wheeled in the postcard-pretty sky. Abby and Zach would be somewhere close by. Romping in the surf, snorkeling for starfish. He would find them and sweep them into his arms and never let them—

"How you doing, Doc? Ready to blow this Popsicle stand?"

The *Challenger* came into focus incrementally. Luke's jacket was still slung over the web chair; he'd slid it off when it'd gotten too hot during the descent and had forgotten to take it with him. An energy bar wrapper was folded and threaded through an eyelet on his chair . . .

Luke's gaze traveled upward, a rising note of confusion hammering his chest—

"Doc? Hey! Jesus, what happened?"

He ignored that impossible, treacherous voice. His eyes traversed the instrument panels, the shiny metal switches hooded with red switch guards. The buttons and gauges were all labeled—*somebody must've used one of those old DYMO label makers*, Luke had thought during the descent. *The ones that punch each letter onto a sticky black strip . . .*

"Doc?"

Alice Sykes stared down from the *Challenger*'s cockpit, looking a bit worried.

Whole. *Intact*. Smiling cautiously. Alive. *Alice . . . Sykes*.

Luke reached a trembling hand toward her—then stopped, partially due to the puzzled look on her face but mostly out of the fear that . . .

Toy's voice: *You are not who you say you are . . .*

"What's up, Doc? Look like you've seen a ghost."

The gears inside his head spun wildly, burning out in gouts of smoke. Her hand fell on his shoulder. Luke flinched from her touch.

"Doc? For the love of . . . What the hell happened to you?"

Luke said, "Are you . . . *you?*"

Alice recoiled at the rasp of his voice—or was it the capering lunacy in his eyes?

"Who else would I be?"

Was it her? Or was he dreaming? Had he dreamed that terrible hive in Westlake's lab with Alice's body strung all through it? Had she been here all along, waiting for the *Challenger* to charge up?

"You can't go inside the station," he said, his breath knocking hollowly in his lungs. "It's . . . it's death in there."

She nodded—a bit oddly, he noted, her chin dipping to touch her chest like a marionette in the hands of a clumsy puppeteer.

"You bet, Doc. We're getting out of here. Clear seas above. We're gonna bob right up like a cork. We'll be eating broiled snapper al fresco in a few hours. You just sit tight, okay?"

Luke nodded, puppyish in his desire to please her. He'd sit tight as a drum, he'd be quiet as a church mouse oh yes indeedy, everything would be just right as rain, *neato torpedo* as Zach used to say, *wowee zowee* and *neato torpedo*; Luke would do any goddamn fucking thing Alice wanted as long as she—

"Huh," she said in obvious puzzlement.

"What is it?"

She flicked a switch. A relay kicked over, shuddering the hull. The lights dimmed, then brightened again.

Alice glanced down at him. She looked different.

Her dark hair was thinner, with kinked gray threads shot through it. She smiled. Luke recoiled. Her teeth looked all wrong in her mouth, yellowed and rotten like shoepeg corn.

"Everything's fine," she said in a queer singsong. "Fine as cherry wine."

She started whistling a familiar tune. *Papa's gonna buy you a mocking-bird.*

There was an unbuckling sensation inside Luke's head, the feel of a hasp popping under extreme duress. With it came relief of a sort. His brain smoothed out, achieving a state of total unconcern. It felt good. Very good indeed.

"You're dead, Alice," he said, his voice itself dead as a dial tone.

The whistling stopped. In its place came a sucking, whispering exhale.

"You're dead, Al, and I'm very sorry. I wish . . . I wish you were here. I wish that so, so much. But you're not. This is just another game."

"A game, a game, a game . . ."

Alice's voice had changed, too. Higher, reedier. A child's voice.

". . . all the world's a game . . ."

Something slammed into the *Challenger*, rocking Luke in his seat. An alarm pealed; the emergency lights kicked on, bathing him in their blood-red glow.

"Oh my child," that voice said, "the game is only just beginning."

He looked up, unable to help himself. Alice's eyes were melting.

They puddled in her sockets as she stared down at him, smiling through her rotted mouth. The corneas liquefied to a jet-black fluid that flowed upward against gravity, over her forehead and hair, fanning out, crawling over the insides of the *Challenger*.

"It's fun, Daddy," she said in perfect mimicry of Zachary's voice. "The Fig Men have the very best games. Oh, it's just the most fun you can possibly imagine."

The blackness unraveled from her eyes, black scarves fluttering over the submarine's interior, coating the consoles and blotting out the lights. The *Challenger* rocked again, the metal squealing—*please*, Luke thought, *please rupture*—as something hammered at the hatchway, hard staccato beats like an enormous fist rapping on a door. Alice was laughing now, howling while the black fluid poured from her eye sockets and crept down the walls toward him.

The power cut out. The *Challenger* plunged into total darkness.

A voice spoke right next to Luke's ear.

"I'm so happy, Daddy. You've come home."

PART 6

THE FIG MEN

1.

LIGHT. HIGH ABOVE HIM.

Beautiful golden light.

Luke stretched toward it. He was underwater. The light came from the sun. It shone upon the surface of the water, a plate of mellow gold.

He kicked, surging toward it. His legs were strong, his strokes confident. A dark square rested atop the water. It was a floating dock. A rope trailed down from it. Thick nautical gauge, clung with algae. It hung down through the water and disappeared into the darkness below.

His eyes hugged that darkness for a moment. Things thrashed and tilted down there, a few inches past the point where the light went bad.

He looked away. Looked up.

Two shapes jutted from that dark square. Shoulders, heads. Instinctively, he knew it was Abby and Zachary. The smaller shape dipped his hand into the water. The tips of his fingers sent out delicate ripples.

Luke thought: *Don't touch the water, Zach. Don't give yourself over to it, ever.*

His body speared toward them. His lungs burned. It felt good, necessary. You had to suffer to reach those you loved. To suffer was to care.

An emotion bigger than joy, bigger than relief, bigger than hope ripped through his chest: bigger because it was all these emotions, concentrated and magnified.

He arrowed upward. He was moments—a mere heartbeat—from breaking the surface.

Their faces. He could remember their faces again. Soon he'd touch them, hug them both, never leave their sides, not for a moment. Not for anything or anyone.

His hand stretched upward, fingers straining toward the surface—

2.

—**LUKE SNAPPED AWAKE** in the dark. Inside the *Challenger*.

Calling his son's name.

How much time had gone by? He didn't care. Something had broken inside his head. He lacked the ability to properly acknowledge this fact. His mind could no longer process the scale of its own ruin.

He laughed. A cold, empty note. It dissolved into a hiccuping cough and petered out in a prolonged moan. He sat in the silence. Alone.

A voice.

"Daddy . . . Daddy . . ."

Luke stirred. Sat up straight.

"Daddy, where are you . . . ?"

The voice came from outside the *Challenger*. Inside the *Trieste*.

"I'm scared, Daddy . . ."

Luke strained toward that voice. His son was inside the station. Zachary was cold and lost. And he needed his father.

Luke crawled to the lip of the porthole. A chill crept over his flesh.

"Daddy, please . . ."

He went. Unthinkingly, he went.

The storage tunnel was lit with an alien glow. The generator still partially hid the hole that had consumed Clayton, but its surface was placid now.

"Daddy!"

Luke broke into a run. He flashed around the gooseneck and spotted Zach in the hatchway wearing his favorite PJs, the ones with the fire trucks and police cars.

"Zachary!"

His son turned and fled. A spike of ice penetrated Luke's chest. Was

Zach *scared* of him? For God's sake, he wasn't the monster here. He was desperately trying to protect *him* from the monsters. He wanted to be a good father. The Human Shield. It was all he'd ever wanted.

He followed Zach toward the main lab. The *Trieste* looked different. The walls were rusted and dull. A thick layer of dust had settled over everything.

He glanced down. Hey! LB was there, trotting at his side. His heart swelled to see her . . . until he looked a little closer.

"I thought you were dead, girl," Luke said.

LB's eyes were two plugs of midnight stuffed into her sockets. Her jowls sagged and her fur was bone-white and hoary, like ancient corn silk. She opened her jaws in a canine grin; the inside of her mouth was a cottony white, the blood all leeched away. Her teeth had rotted to nothing, gums drooping inward.

Nope, boss. I'm not dead. Wish I was some days, but what are you gonna do?

Luke smiled sadly. "You look . . . you look real old, girl."

LB chuffed. It sounded painful, her insides rattling.

Well, time works differently down here, boss. Sometimes I feel like I've lived a thousand lifetimes . . . it's funny. The pain is a constant. Sometimes it's so much that I can't stand it. I bite at myself, tear my skin off, but I can never quite die. Like I said, funny. But to hurt is to love, right?

"You bet," Luke said companionably. "That's just about the size of it."

He leaned down to pet her. LB bit him. It didn't hurt. She had no teeth. But he could tell that she wanted to hurt him—she wanted to hurt him real bad. He almost wished he could grant her that wish. He pulled his hand gently from her mouth.

"I'm sorry," he said. "I don't think I can be hurt anymore."

She chuffed again. *You can't blame a dog for trying, Doc.*

He reached the crawl-through chute. LB didn't follow him through. He caught sight of Zach on the other side. His arms projected from his pajama sleeves as if they'd been pulled, the bones broken, the flesh stretched like gruesome taffy.

Zach's hands were very big indeed. His fingers trailed down and down, these long twitchy wires that, for all their gauntness, looked incredibly strong.

His son's face broke into a smile. Not a particularly nice one, Luke had to admit. He'd certainly never taught the boy to smile that way.

Mind your manners, kiddo.

Zachary lifted one arm. His index finger curled invitingly.

My son, my son, what long fingers you have . . .

All the better to beckon you with, Father . . .

Luke followed Zach, but more reluctantly now. The ceiling lowered. He had to duck. He breathed shallowly, drawing the curious scent of the station into his lungs. He stepped over something that looked very much like a human rib cage. The ceiling abruptly rose to an apex he could no longer chart. He turned another corner, and his son was waiting no more than five feet away.

Luke took an instinctive step back.

Zach's pajamas were torn and moldering, the clothes of a disinterred corpse. His hair was gone. His scalp was bare and frighteningly wrinkled, summoning images of a living apple doll.

His fingers were enormous. Four dead snakes attached to his palms, their tips dangling to the floor. His face had stretched, too, becoming vulpine and weird. The flesh around his eyes sagged: the eyes of a sick beagle, the corneas jaundiced and incalculably ancient.

His mouth was overstuffed with teeth—they jutted outward, slicing his lips and pushing them apart.

My son, my son, what big teeth you have . . .

All the better to bite you with, Daddy . . .

Zachary thrust his chin forward, hurling bursts of laughter at him. Spittle jetted between his teeth to leave wet spots on Luke's overalls.

Luke held his arms out. "Zachary, *please.*"

His son coyly turned away. Shapes thrashed and fretted, half glimpsed, as if his face had given birth to a nest of snakes.

The tunnel plunged into darkness. When the lights came on again, Zach was gone.

3.

LUKE WALKED AIMLESSLY.

Sometimes he laughed. Other times he wept. He made no conscious distinction between the two anymore.

The tunnels split and meandered. His footsteps echoed into silence. The pressure welted down on him. The children no longer raced overhead. Perhaps they'd lost interest or had been scared away.

The tunnel bellied into an alcove. The walls collapsed inward to create a perfect pocket of dark. Luke squinted until he saw what lay inside that darkness. A leaden wash of dread spread over his groin; he felt a sudden, dreadful urge to pee.

The Tickle Trunk rested in the alcove. The clowns on its lid—Pit-Pat and Floppsy and the rest—leered and jested, their tongues flicking over teeth the color of old bone.

Hello, Lukey-loo! So wonderful to see you!

The latch sprung open. Luke took a step back, but the walls had pushed in all around him. There was nowhere to go. The lid creaked open. The air filled with tinny notes, the sort that play when you opened a music box.

Tinka-tink-teeeee-ta-tinka-tink-teeeeee . . .

A flesh-colored bowling ball spun around and around inside the trunk . . . no, not a ball. Hugo Toy's severed, split-open head. It lay awkwardly on its side, gummy strings of blood vessels and nerve endings trailing from the stump of its raggedly hacked neck. The flesh had been peeled off his face, making his eyes look very big and round indeed. The head revolved in a slow circle, much like a ballerina pirouetting inside its music box.

"I can hear the muh-music in my head." Dr. Toy smiled. Flecks of brain shone on the flayed sinew of his cheeks. "It never ends, Lucas. Nuh-nuh-never, ever . . ."

The Tickle Trunk shut. Luke could still hear those cold, jangling notes. The walls exhaled again. He left the alcove behind. In time, he rounded back into the main lab. It was empty. He glanced at Westlake's lab. Alice's face was framed in the porthole.

"Oh hello, Al."

Hiya, Doc.

Bees squirmed in and out of Alice's eyes.

"You don't look so hot."

She opened her mouth and bees poured out, coiling around her neck in a yellow-and-black noose.

I've seen better days, Doc.

He turned away. He saw something beneath the lab bench. Had it been there all along? How had he not seen it before?

He set his shoulder to the bench. Despite its size, it slid easily.

There was a door in the floor. Solid wood with a ringbolt. The sort of door you'd find in old cabins and farmhouses, leading down to the . . .

—*basement*—

. . . root cellar.

The wood was warm and faintly pulsating. The skin of a slumbering elephant.

Luke gripped the bolt and pulled. Narrow stone steps sawed down.

". . . *Daddy!* . . ."

Zach's voice quivered up out of the dark, strained and fearful.

"*The Fig Men, Daddy!*"

"They're only figments," Luke croaked. "Figments of your imagination. They can't hurt you if you don't believe in them."

Silence. Then: thick, chortling laughter. The laughter of the Fig Men? The hairs stiffened on Luke's arms. His son was down there somewhere. And he needed his father.

The steps were worn smooth, as if subject to much traffic; the stone wept beads of moisture like the rock in a cave. Luke's feet fit perfectly—the steps could have been built for him specifically. They carried him down under the lab to the bottommost place on earth. The true basement of the world.

Darkness slipped up his calves and knees in sly tendrils. It coated his chest and filmed his eyes. Somewhere above—a few feet; a million miles—the wooden door slipped softly shut.

He could see here in the dark. Not well, but enough to navigate by. Luke got the sense he was on an unsupported stairway spiraling down; if he slipped he'd fall forever, never hitting anything . . .

. . . or perhaps something would catch him eventually.

The air grew thicker. He inhaled the scent of ancient earth. He was beneath all things now. Beneath every pure element in life, beneath hope and joy and perhaps even love. None of that could touch him here.

A rock wall materialized to his left. It ran sheer beneath his fingertips, as cold and featureless as iced steel. He heard a sharp *thunk* somewhere below. It sounded a little like a door sliding open.

He followed the stairs until the rock vanished under his fingertips. He stared at the spot where it had been with dull shock.

"Hello, Lucas."

Clayton was curled into a box carved out of the rock. A perfect square cut into the sheer rock face, barely big enough to hold his body. Luke stifled the moan that rose up in his throat. His brother was naked and skinnier than any human being should possibly be. A living skeleton. His joints bulged. His head was nothing but a skull covered in latex-thin skin. He was folded into the rock-box in a cross-legged swami pose, his head bowed to fit.

"How . . . how long have you been here?" Luke whispered.

Clayton cocked his terrible fleshless head, considering his brother's question.

"I can't say exactly," he said. "How long is forever?"

Clayton's hands fussed over his caved-in stomach. His fingers, tipped with sharp black nails, sunk into his belly. The flesh ripped with sickening ease. He tore and gouged at himself. The thinnest hint of a smile painted his lips.

"Oh, Clay, really, I wish you wouldn't . . ."

Clayton's innards spilled into his lap. They were chalky and dry, like sausage links coated in flour. He rummaged through the knotted loops, selecting the finest portion and raising it to his mouth. It made the lovely *snap* of a good Coney Island hot dog when he bit into it. Fine bluish powder spurted out. Robin's egg blue: same color as the chemical inside the pot of tree killer.

Clayton chewed thoughtfully, absorbed in the act. His lips were stained dark blue, like a child who'd eaten too many grape Popsicles.

"I really shouldn't," he said shamefacedly, "but honestly, I can't help myself."

He turned away, embarrassed. Luke was filled with an ineffable despair; he reached toward his brother—then the rocks slid over him in a solid sheet, shutting Clayton back inside his tiny box. The wall was solid again: not a seam, not a mark.

He continued down until the stairway abruptly ended. Luke stumbled the way a man does when misjudging the number of steps in a darkened house, his arms outflung.

The ground was spongy. He got the sense of standing atop a pair of lungs taking the shallowest breaths.

Zachary was there. Luke saw him clearly. He looked the way Luke remembered him. His hands and fingers proportional again. Luke beheld the boy he and his wife had raised in a cheery sunlit house in Iowa. The boy who still held his plastic cups with both hands when he drank cherry Kool-Aid, which left a crimson mustache above his lip. The boy who would nestle his chin into the swell of his father's throat at bedtime—the groove so perfect, two bodies locking together in flawless synchronicity—and whisper: *I love you more than ice cream and pizza.*

It's very nice to be loved, Luke thought. *Is there anything nicer in life?*

He opened his arms. "Zachary. Please."

The space behind Zachary swelled with light. The darkness blew away; beyond that lay a new emptiness, illuminated by an aquifer of sickly light. A pair of arms filled that emptiness. Enormous, world swallowing. Flabby and wrinkled, sallow flesh draping the bones like proofing dough. Ghastly arms ending in huge, cruel hands. Thick knuckled, each finger curled into a sickle.

Familiar hands. Those of his mother.

Behind those hands lay a shape or shapes that Luke could not fathom. It spanned out and up, sheer as a cliff face, rising beyond the reach of his sight and his mind. The cliff shone in places—the dazzling but condensed light of a camera flash reflected in tinted glass. It was dark in other spots, a shade more profound than any Luke had known.

Zachary ran into those hands the way a child might chase a bouncing ball onto a busy street. Luke opened his mouth, but no sound came out. The hands enfolded his son. Zachary turned and stared at Luke through a gap in those massive fingers. His eyes emptied out, his face melting as his skin ran like candlewax.

The hands opened. They were empty.

Next the hands decayed and collapsed, flesh dripping off in gobbets until only the bones remained. Those were then absorbed into that nest of livid industry . . .

. . . but they left something behind. An ovoid ball that pulsated gently.

Next, his mother and father stepped from the trembling darkness.

4.

A CHILL SWEPT OVER HIM. His mother, corpulent and fearsome—
and a few steps behind her came his father, stooped and hangdog.

"You have come, child. After all this time."

No, it wasn't his parents. That wasn't his mother's voice. Whatever
these creatures were, they were merely draped in the flesh and figure of
his parents. The imitation was good, cunning, but imperfect in some
way—perhaps purposefully so.

The two figures who stood before him seemed to have been birthed
from the cliff of flesh that backgrounded them. Their fleshy coverings
withered and peeled. His mother and father's faces rotted away in pestilent rags. The creatures underneath were humanlike in their rudiments,
but not so in their particulars.

One was tall and shockingly thin; the other was squat and pear-
shaped. Their flesh had a boiled, piglet-pink sheen; raw sinews cabled
the visible portions of their anatomies.

Their legs were squat and elephantine, their groins sexless. Their
arms were so long and thick—engorged fire hoses—that they trailed to
the ground and curled back, networking into the roiling cliff.

Luke found his voice. "Dear God . . ."

"God is not here," the tall one said.

"Perhaps he should apologize for his absence," said the squat one.

Ancient. These things were older than anything any human being
had ever laid eyes on. Their flesh was flayed open, the raw tendons
scored with tiny cracks. Yet their skin was nearly translucent, too, as if
their bones had been smeared with a thick coating of Vaseline—it was as
though the years in their endless accumulation had sucked the pigment

from it. Their skulls showed through in places, the bone as brittle as the parchment in a dusty book.

These creatures were carved out of time itself—the hands on the clock couldn't touch them anymore, though they had certainly left their mark.

Pitiless. This was Luke's second and overriding sense. Beholding them, Luke realized for the first time in his life that there are things on earth, or beyond it, who are careless in the most quotidian terms: they lack the inclination or desire to care for anything. They are pitiless in the most simplified fashion, as they simply lack the ability to feel it.

"What are you?" Luke asked.

"Call us the Fig Men," the creatures said in unison.

Luke shook his head. "The Fig Men don't exist. The Fig Men are *figments.*"

"We go by many names," the tall Fig Man said. *"It is of no matter."*

"We exist in many guises," said the squat one.

"Is all this . . ." Luke shivered involuntarily. "Did you . . . ?"

The creatures inclined their heads at one another, teeth chattering in their seemingly lipless mouths. Was it laughter?

"Why?" was all Luke could ask.

"Fun," the tall Fig Man said in a honeyed voice.

"Fun," the squat one echoed.

"Games."

"Games," came the echo.

Torturously, the gears in Luke's head began to mesh. He was beset by the same sense that he imagined a field mouse might hold the moment before the falcon swooped down: the sense of having been singled out, tracked at great distance, studied for a purpose that he could not possibly understand—and then, when the time was ripe, he was plucked squealing from the long grass. Meat for the feast.

"Why me?" was his next, utterly selfish question.

"You?" the squat one scoffed.

"*You were not the key,*" said the tall one.

"Then who . . ."

The Fig Men's faces split in lewd rictuses.

"*Oh, child,*" they said in unison.

Luke knew. Of course he knew.

"*We observed you,*" the tall one said. "*For as long as you can remember, we have been watching you both.*"

"*Tedious,*" the squat one said.

"*Our reach is not insignificant.*" The tall one angled its head like a dog intuiting a high-pitched whistle. "*We have connections to your world. You have seen them, child.*"

It arrived with a thunderclap of understanding. The thing in the drainage pipe. The thing in the Tickle Trunk. Maybe even the thing in Westlake's basement in Belmont, Connecticut . . .

. . . the thing lurking in the park not far from Luke's house in Iowa City?

All the same thing, or parts of it. The Fig Men were their proud parents. And their children were malevolent, but not as old or repellent as these things.

The tall one said, "*We have observed many of your species, over centuries.*"

"*Eons,*" said the squat one.

"*Your brother intrigued us.*"

"*As much as any of your kind do.*"

"*The special qualities of his mind.*"

"*Mulish, but intriguing.*"

"*We chart these qualities. There is so little else to occupy us down here. There have been other minds to capture our interest.*"

"*Better ones,*" said the squat one.

"*The short-eyed Florentine,*" the tall one said.

"*Da Vinci.*"

"*And the other one. The insomniac pigeon-keeper.*"

"*Tesla.*"

"*Fine minds.*"

"*Superior to your brother,*" the squat one said.

"*Perhaps so,*" the tall one agreed. "*And of a quality suited to our purposes . . . and yet.*"

"*And yet.*"

"*You were not ready. As a species. You lacked the knowledge to find us. But now you have that knowledge,*" the tall one said mock-brightly.

"*And here you are,*" said the squat one.

Tricksters—the word raced through Luke's mind. Merciless game players. Everything that had occurred had been the work of these . . . *things.*

"Why not just leave this place if you hate it so much?"

The tall one shook its head. "*We cannot, child.*"

"*We have been shackled,*" the squat one said petulantly.

The Fig Men's eyes swiveled skyward. Heavenward. Luke could only wonder at their origins. Perhaps they were the last surviving members of an ancient tribe who'd been cast out, cast down. Shunned. They had lain down here, licking their wounds. Next, they set about baiting their trap—and when that moment arrived, their knives were sharp for the opportunity.

"Why?" Luke asked.

"*We like to toy,*" they said in perfect unity.

Toy. Never in Luke's life had the word sounded so monolithically sinister.

"*We fiddle,*" the squat one said.

"*We test,*" said the tall one.

"*We discover how things work.*"

"*How they fail.*"

"*Their pressure points.*"

"*Their tolerances.*"

"*We are curious.*"

"*Eternally curious.*"

Luke envisioned these ageless tinkerers examining bodies and minds for the sheer sport of it. Flaying brains open and plucking each synapse like the strings of a lute, teasing out every private fear and horror. Caring nothing for those they entrapped and tortured, committed solely to their games. They had done it to everyone down here. They had turned the *Trieste* into their laboratory. Their killing jar.

"I remember everything down here," Luke said. "My mother. My family. My old life. But it's too clear. The clarity is . . . *hellish.*"

The Fig Men grinned like children.

"*Oh, yes?*" said the tall one.

"*This pleases us,*" said the squat one.

Luke's brain pounded within its bowl of bone; it seemed to expand, the grey matter expanding with the mad hum of his tormented thoughts, pressing against his nasal shelf until he was ill with it. Memory as a sickness.

"*Your species is so busy forgetting,*" the squat one said.

"*But not you, child,*" said the tall one.

"*It is our special offering.*" The squat one stared at Luke placidly. "*Does it not please you?*"

Were they even evil? Luke considered the fact that these things may well exist above the terms that humankind ascribes to certain actions or behaviors. The Fig Men were elementally themselves, as surely they had always been.

But their natures must have gotten them in trouble with the higher ups. And so they had been put in a place where they could do the least harm.

"The ambrosia," he said. "Yours?"

"*Your kind requires a small enticement. You need . . .*"

The tall one looked to the squat one in search of the word.

"*Bait,*" the squat one said.

"*Yes, bait. The hounds must chase the hare down the hole.*"

"And the 'Gets?"

"*A happy convergence,*" said the squat one. "*Our powers do not extend to such a degree.*"

"*You would have come for less,*" said the tall one.

"*You are a vain species,*" the squat one sneered.

Luke knew this was true. Ambrosia appeared to cure the 'Gets, and so that was how the narrative played out—the hunt to find a solution for the incurable disease. But Clayton and others of his ilk would have pursued the lure of the ambrosia regardless of circumstance, whether it promised relief from cancer, AIDS, or old age. The unknown was a profoundly powerful intoxicant.

"Why me?" he asked again. "You had my brother already. So why?"

"*Because,*" the tall one said, "*we had nothing to offer him in return for bearing our gift.*"

"*There was nothing tying your brother to the surface.*" A look of true confusion graced the squat one's face. "*He prefers to be with . . . us.*"

"*There is no accounting,*" the tall one said.

"*But you.*" The squat one flicked a serrate black tongue over its teeth. "*Ohhh, now* you . . ."

"*You have loved, my child.*"

"*You have supped that weak nectar.*"

"*You have ties to the sunlit world. And you see, we too wish to see the sun again.*"

"*After all, we were there for its birth,*" said the squat one. "*Your brother was the key. He was a satisfactory tool. But his use has been served.*"

"*Your use has yet begun,*" the tall one told Luke.

"I just want to go home," Luke said. It was the simplest request he'd ever made, and he asked as a child would.

"*And you may,*" the tall one said laughingly. "*Of course, of course. We insist upon it. But with our gift. You will bear it.*"

Gift?

The cliff behind the Fig Men flexed and cramped. A shrill, prolonged moan filtered out of the dark. Chillingly, it sounded like a dog's moan.

"*Our gift,*" the tall one repeated.

"*You must take it,*" the squat one echoed. "*We have arranged it. You must accept our terms.*"

"What terms?"

The tall one grinned. "*Oh, come now.*"

"*It took all of our powers to accomplish it,*" the squat one said. "*It* was . . . draining, *would be your understanding of it. We had to slumber afterward.*"

"*Such sweet slumber.*"

"*Sweet, yes. And when we awoke we had company.*"

"*Such merry company.*"

The long con.

It was a term Abby had described to Luke years ago, after they had watched a movie about a pair of bunko artists plying their trade across the Midwest.

There are two types of cons, she'd told him. *Short and long. The short con is a confidence trick that can be pulled in minutes. Three-card monte's your classic short con. The other one, the long con, unfolds over days or weeks, even years. It involves preparation, props, costumes, scripted lines. The long con takes time. The con men have to gain the full trust of their rubes; it's got to be seamless, you know? A perfect facsimile of life.*

How the hell do you know all this? Luke had asked her. *Should I be watching my wallet around you?*

Your wallet? Abby sniffed. *That's pure short con. You should watch your bank account.*

These creatures had *known.* Luke saw that now. All along they had known.

They had seen the shape of the world to come and had bent it to their own devices. They had divined it all a lifetime ago, back when Clayton and Luke were only babes. They had watched the two of them their entire lives, doting over them like careful babysitters . . . no, more like pig farmers waiting with idle interest while the spring hogs were fattened for slaughter. These things had toyed with the fates of both Clayton and himself, engineering their lives to the finest calibration . . .

. . . and then, one autumn evening at a park not far from Luke's home, they'd played their finest trick of all.

"You stole my son."

The squat one tittered. "*Foolish child, you must always mind your belongings. Never let them out of sight.*"

In a conversational tone, Luke said: "Fuck you."

The squat one's face peeled back from its skull, its teeth elongating into curved rat's teeth. Its arms undulated silkily.

"Have you any idea what I could—"

The tall one hissed warningly. The squat one cringed.

"Such a harsh word, stole," the tall one said. *"We have held him. Kept him safe. And we did so knowing you would pay what you owe to reclaim that which was once yours."*

Luke closed his eyes. Ole Zach Attack. They had taken him. Ruined his family. Ripped Luke's life apart—they knew he would have to be utterly hopeless before he agreed to come to this watery hell in pursuit of his insufferable brother. Luke must have nothing left to live for. Well, they had seen to that. Zach had spent the last seven years with these things. Seven human years, the passage of which seemed immaterial in a place like this. More years than he had spent with his own parents. What would that do to his son—to anyone?

Luke opened his eyes. "What do you want?"

"To be free," they said simply.

"You don't deserve it," Luke croaked, a ghastly smile spreading across his face. "You deserve to be down here. Alone."

The Fig Men smiled back. Luke's soul shuddered. The cliff was swelling behind them—it seemed to be curling over in its upper recesses, beyond Luke's sight, a horrific wave preparing to break.

The Fig Men smiled bashfully, coquettishly. It's just little ol' us, child. What harm can we cause?

"Our gift . . ."

"I won't accept it."

The tall one said, *"Why ever not?"*

Luke set his feet. "I'll die here."

They chuckled mordantly.

"Oh my child," the squat one said, *"will you remain a stranger to yourself to the very end?"*

"You love too much," the tall one said. An expression flitted across its face that could have charitably passed for sorrow. *"Your kind does so—*

loves heedlessly, without restraint or governance. It can lead you to grand places, surely. Places we have never seen or ever will."

"But love has other uses, too," said the squat one.

The ovoid ball those monstrous hands had left behind began to throb, its exterior issuing crackling birch-bark sounds. It bulged and heaved as whatever lay within struggled to set itself free . . .

A cocoon. Of course it was. Just like the one he'd once pointed out to Zach in the backyard, the one with a lunar moth crawling out of it. This cocoon was tar-black, just like the ones that had encased the Fig Men in his son's closet . . .

The cocoon expanded, pulsing like a diseased heart. Its exterior shed in crackling layers as it stretched with an awful elasticity.

Something split through. Dark and bladelike. A broth of pulpy sludge issued forth. One appendage was joined by another. Two arms, two huge and spidery hands. Tearing and sawing the cocoon apart.

A bulbous head appeared. It was all black. It opened its mouth—out came the shocked cry of an infant.

Its eyes opened next. They pinned Luke in a gaze that was equal parts malevolent and loving.

"*Daddy,*" it said.

It slipped from its sheath. Its shape was incomprehensible. Its lunatic anatomy humped toward Luke, those two gnarled but powerful arms dragging the ruin of a body still slick with amniotic fluid.

Zachary. After all this time, Luke's son had returned to him.

He fell to his knees. The Fig Men watched impassively.

"*Our gift,*" they said. "*Will you accept it?*"

His son drew nearer. His skull was swollen and hairless; veins bulged over his scalp, pulsating weakly. Luke saw elements of others he'd known in the awful contours of that face—his brother's pursed lips, his mother's delicate ears. His son's mouth split into a smile. His teeth were tiny, his old milk teeth, each one trimmed to a sharp point.

Luke held his arms out. He wanted to touch his son again. To be Zachary's protector, his Human Shield—he'd failed his son once at that, failed Zach and Abby both, but never again. Not in a million years. He'd die first.

My son, my son. Come back to me. Let me hold you again. I'll protect you this time, I promise. I will never let you go. I WILL NEVER EVER EVER LET YOU GO—

Tendrils spooled out of Zachary's mouth, each no thicker than baby's hair. They danced toward Luke's face, licking and sampling. They needled painlessly into his flesh, twining with the twitching tendons under his skin, hooking around his skull and tightening with the fierceness of a devoted lover.

Yes, Luke thought dimly. *Together again. Together forever.*

Luke could feel it inside him now: blooming outward like an oil slick, covering everything with darkness.

Luke Nelson's final memory was this:

Zachary was five. Abby had enrolled him in peewee soccer. Zachary was the goalie. He'd let in the winning goal. They walked home afterward, Zachary in his cleats and shin pads, his white socks stained with grass.

People think it's about winning and losing, sport, Luke told him, because he could tell his son was upset. *About winning, mainly. But that's not it. It's about the trying. The not-giving-up. We're all going to lose. So it's about losing and going on, keep going on, even though you may lose again and again. You may never* win, *buddy, not at some things. So it's about working as hard as you can, every day, to find your spot on the mountain. And then it's about being okay with where you are so that you can get some enjoyment out of that, and out of the things in life that are more important than whatever place you end up on that silly old mountain, anyway.*

Zachary turned his face up to his father, the underside of his chin lit by the paling sunlight. He'd nodded stoically—a gesture well in advance of his years—and kept his silence. Perhaps he'd understood that even if his father hadn't managed to put his mind at ease, at least he'd tried. Being a father was an imperfect science, and its test subjects, that man's sons and daughters, had to accept their father's imperfections just as each father must eventually accept those same imperfections within himself.

Luke felt his face opening as the tendrils stripped his flesh back. He felt no fear or pain. His skin parted in a solid flap—a door swinging open.

Inside was the warmest, most inviting light Luke had ever known.

His son came inside. Luke invited him in with every ounce of love in his heart. Zachary's hands pushed through Luke's face, entering his skull. First one, then the other. There was so much space in there now. His house had many rooms, all splendorous.

Yes, yes, my boy my boy oh do come in . . .

Zachary's head came next. Luke stared into his son's cruelly slitted eyes. A flutter arose in his chest, a dark wingbeat . . . it went away. It all went away.

Luke was happy to let it go.

It felt so good to simply let . . . go.

I'm sorry, he thought, though to whom or for what cause he was incapable of expressing. *I'm so sorry so sorry so sorry so—*

Finally, Luke Nelson slipped silently inside himself to join his son. His passage made no sound at all.

Somewhere, a door swung shut.

5.

THE *CHALLENGER* ASCENDED.

And within it, nothing human.

The vessel's ascent was swift—the sea ripped away in deferential sheets in order to aid its climb, or perhaps to cast it out.

Far below, the *Trieste* lay in spiderlike contemplation. No light shone in its labs. Its tunnels ran empty. It waited as it had since the beginning of all things, in one guise or another. Its walls bellied against the ceaseless pressure. Perhaps the thinnest stream of water would needle in, and moments later the strange and horrible edifice would be flattened . . . but some places are resistant to both time and pressure. Their occupants—their *true* occupants—are similarly impervious to such things.

Perhaps the *Trieste*'s many-splendored halls would entertain life again. A select group of good-hearted souls entrusted with the salvation of the human race. Students of rationality and science who had heard the breathless stories of those who'd gone before and smartly dismissed them. The *Trieste*'s prior occupants had been weak-minded, superstitious fools.

And so they would come down in ones and twos, arriving with their hopes and goals and adamantine minds—minds they believed to be unbreakable.

And who knows? They might bring a dog or two with them.

The power would be restored. The lights would flicker down the tunnels and over the wide window in the main lab. And whatever existed there would retreat into the darkness, its natural element, until the time came to call itself once more into the light.

* * *

NIGHTTIME NOW. The *Hesperus* sat in isolated abandonment. Pinprick fires danced from the points of its blackened architecture.

A single figure awaited. Its body was a canvas of scars. It stared through clumsy slits it had made in its own face, its eyes peering through bulbs of scar tissue with feverish avidity. When the sea began to roil, it gibbered with excitement: the unconcealed glee of a dog at the return of its long-lost master.

The *Challenger* surfaced. The heavens flinched.

The hatch swung open.

Moonlight fell upon its darkest cargo.

What shambled forth was unspeakable.

ACKNOWLEDGMENTS

MILLE GRAZIE to the people responsible for getting this book into your hands—my wonderful agent, Kirby Kim; my fantastic horror-guru editor, Ed Schlesinger; and Stephanie DeLuca and the whole publicity team at Gallery.

Beyond that, thanks to my fiancée, Colleen, for putting up with my slovenly habits and somewhat brooding demeanor on the days when the writing got dark. And to my eighteen-month-old son, Nick, for sleeping pretty well while I wrote the last few chapters of this book, giving me a much-needed energy boost (even if that run of restful sleeps didn't persist).

Also, thanks to my folks for being nothing like Bethany and Lonnie, the two appalling parental units featured in this book. I've heard it said that an emotionally-scarring childhood is great fodder for fiction, but I'm thankful that I don't have to draw inspiration from the poisoned waters of that particular well.

Get email updates on

NICK CUTTER,

exclusive offers,

and other great book recommendations

from Simon & Schuster.
